WID.

For my wife, family, friends and colleagues

Chapter One

2006

To Pat Monaghan, the scene looked not so very different from that day many years before when he'd first approached the building. Even at this early hour taxis were emptying optimistic clients onto the pavement in front of the Europa Casino, and now a stretch limo whispered to a halt at the main entrance. He watched as a uniformed doorman leapt from the shadows and with all the care of a duck shepherding her brood, escorted his charge from the car to the Casino, as if the precious occupant, left un-aided, would lose his way during the five-yard journey.

When he'd worked there many years before, the building had housed the Ventura Club. He grimaced; that name would forever be synonymous with all that was odious.

To this day he was sure that someone connected with that club had been responsible for...

He shook his head and refocused his eyes in the opposite direction, as if those actions alone could rid him of the haunting memories.

The traffic here was unregulated by lights so he was poised, waiting for a gap in the flow of vehicles, when someone grabbed his arm.

'Is it yerself, Pat Monaghan?'

Pat wheeled round to see a face that was undoubtedly familiar, but to which he couldn't immediately attach a name.

'I recognised the walk, actually you haven't changed much,' added the man. There was just a trace of a Scottish accent.

'Is it Ian, Ian Lowe?' Pat asked, as the man's face, though somewhat older, at last triggered his recall system.

'The very same.'

'Jesus, it's great to see you. What you been doing all these years, how many is it now... twenty-...?'

'Don't think about it, it's scary!' Lowe rolled his eyes. 'What've I been doing? It's a long story. Actually I've just been to a conference on the new Gaming Act. You still in the business?'

'Funny you should ask that, I've been out of it for some time but I'm going into the Europa here to see Ralph Draper about a possible opening in the PR Department,' answered Pat.

'Aha, sounds interesting. I saw Ralph at the conference... we're now competitors, of course.' Lowe laughed. 'So what've you been up to?'

'Oh well, I went back to Ireland for a while. After that, worked with various hotel groups, recently a bit of corporate entertainment,' said Pat, 'saw the advert for Europa, phoned Ralph and he told me to come in for a chat.'

'Sound's good... and a Mrs Monaghan?'

'No, afraid not, couldn't decide which one to marry,' replied Pat.

'And you?'

'Wife and two girls,' said Lowe proudly. 'You wouldn't know the wife, Vera, she wasn't around during the Ventura period.'

'She was lucky...' The memory of that time threatened to dampen Pat's mood again. 'No, after that... to get away from it all, I went back to Ireland for a spell. But it's difficult to get over such a thing.'

'Well, that whole situation was traumatic for many of us,' said Lowe. 'You know, earlier I thought Elena and I had something going, I liked her a lot.'

'Yes, me too, but...' Pat sighed.

Lowe nodded understanding and looking up at the former Ventura building. 'Well, the hoo-ha surrounding that investigation brought it all down on Trist and his bunch in the end, if nothing else.'

Pat nodded slowly. 'So who survives in the business from those days?'

'Oh, not too many. Ralph, as you know... Colin Bland's working with me again and Roland, remember him, he was a chef at Ventura? He's group F&B Director...'

'Yes… Roland,' Pat recalled, 'He was a union rep with Elena, and your other old flame… Carmen wasn't it?'

'Oh, Carmen, what a case she turned out to be! I thought she was a bit moody then but…' Lowe shook his head with disgust.

'Why, what d'you mean?'

'Roland found out what I didn't know, that she was one of that pimp Ahmed's girls and he had her hooked on cocaine. Apparently, when she first went out with me she was trying, unsuccessfully, to break the habit. Later, the bastard took her to Spain to do tricks for him, but dumped her when she completely lost it. She's apparently in and out of jail and drug centres, a real mess. He's got a lot to answer for, that bastard Ahmed. His name came up more than once during the enquiries. But of course the arsehole was well gone as soon as he smelt trouble.'

'Yes, that slimy bastard did a lot of damage,' said Pat thoughtfully. He fished a card from his top pocket. 'Anyway, look I've got to go, here's my number, we must have a drink sometime. And, just to prove there's no Scottish blood in the Monaghans, I'll get the first round.'

'Wow! I should've been sitting tae receive that news!' countered Lowe with a laugh.

Pat crossed, walked up to the casino building with an eerie feeling, but this diminished once he had entered. The changes made to the internal structure removed all sense of being in the old Ventura. A recognisable Draper, with less hair but more body, came to reception to welcome him and take him through a rather less complicated registration procedure than Pat remembered from his day.

The interior had several levels, each one themed to look like part of a town square from a different European country. Draper led him past several card tables on which monitors displayed a progressively accumulating prize. Electronic displays also blinked on roulette tables to indicate what numbers had recently come up while in another corner even more extravagant signage advertised the attraction of playing The Honey Pot slots or battling with The Galactic Crusader for a share of the treasure. Even in mid afternoon both tables and slots were fairly busy. They stopped at the cocktail bar in The Piazza.

'What d'you think, bit of a change eh?' asked Draper.

'It felt the same until I got inside, but this is much, much, bigger and of course brighter - dazzling, in fact!' Pat continued to look around.

'Yes we haven't done much with the outside, we're still waiting to see what we can get away with, in the way of advertising, with the new law. But the difference internally is that we've removed most of the back-of-house to the lower basements to enable us to expand the public areas and make it all open-plan. But really,' said Draper dryly, 'the biggest difference from those days is you don't have to be constantly looking over your shoulder for the knife in your back.'

Inevitably, in the preamble, before discussing the real subject of Pat's visit, one tragic event of the past threatened to dominate the conversation. But eventually both men seemed to recognise the futility of trawling through material that had been gone over so many times and returned to the matter in hand.

Having arranged to meet in a few days to sign a contract, Draper, before hurrying off to another meeting, suggested Pat tour through the building at his leisure. His secretary Wilma would facilitate entry into staff areas and find appropriate people to answer any questions Pat might have.

As Pat moved around he found it hard to believe that this was the place where he'd worked all those years before. The structural changes were so radical. But just occasionally, he passed a small recognisable corner of the building and memories of those earlier days would nudge their way through to his consciousness.

On one such section, prospective croupiers were being interviewed. Pat was of a mind to pass on quickly but was strangely and hypnotically drawn to the proceedings. *Yes*, he thought, *they look as I must have looked, full of nervous expectation. Is it really that long ago since I sat here hoping to start as a croupier?*

1974

'Good afternoon, I'm Marta Woods, Personnel Manager for The Ventura. I think by now you should have completed the application forms. My assistants are distributing another paper that should remain face down until you're told to turn it over. This is a small test that will help us decide if you are suitable for training as a croupier. But before that, our Assistant Casino

Manager, Mr Gordon Mayfield, will talk to you about the job you've applied for, and the course you must pass to qualify for that job.' She gestured to the gentleman behind, who nodded acknowledgement.

Pat was struggling with the complexities of the application form. The job of setting out his employment record honestly without disqualifying himself as a candidate was proving difficult. While thinking how best to present his history, he found himself examining his examiners. The razor-sharp creases on Mayfield's trousers, his spotlessly laundered white shirt, club tie and brilliantly polished shoes gave the impression that he spent considerable time preparing for his work-day. Even his greying hair, trimmed unfashionably to what Pat's mother would call 'a respectable length', seemed to blend in with the overall colour scheme. Marta Woods, on the other hand, looked as if she'd overslept and only just made it to work on time. Her tousled black hair, lack of make-up and ill-fitting clothes draped over a somewhat overweight frame suggested to him either a shortage of time or a lack of interest. Her demeanour supported the latter explanation.

Three assistants, not showing a great deal more enthusiasm, distributed the tests to the applicants who now numbered— Monaghan turned to make a quick estimate.

Jesus! He thought. *Now I'll find it even more difficult to concentrate!* When he'd arrived, in his nervousness he'd kept his head down, trying to focus on the instructions he was being given. He'd been conscious of others arriving, but they had been mostly seated behind him. Only now, after this quick reconnaissance, did he realise the beauties that had assembled around him. There were a handful of male applicants, but the great majority were stunningly attractive young women. With this fresh incentive, he attacked the application form once more, just as Mayfield coughed a warning that he was about to speak.

'Good afternoon and welcome to the Ventura Club. I have special responsibility for Training and Development.' Marta Woods rolled her eyes. A quick aside to her assistants had them stifling an outburst of laughter. Mayfield didn't seem to notice, and continued.

'In common with all casinos in the U.K. The Ventura Club's marketing policy is largely influenced by the strictures of the Gaming Act of

1968. Under this legislation, no direct advertising or promotion of casinos is permitted. Each establishment therefore develops an individual identity to secure a position in the market. Some create the elegance of a French-style salon or the exclusiveness of the traditional businessman's club. Others rely on the seductiveness of the female form. In London, our competitors such as Playboy benefit from their International brand image; Ladbrokes and Corals, the main street presence of their bookmaker divisions.

'At Ventura, we have the attractiveness of our female staff, who are called Chicas. But success depends on the friendliness and efficiency of all our employees. It's therefore essential to select only those applicants who can measure up to all our requirements and the tests you've been given will help us to do that. A croupier needs a high level of intelligence, pleasing personality, smart appearance at all times, a willingness to work and an ability to do that work under extreme pressure.'

While still toiling with the application form Pat suddenly became aware he was being addressed.

'Excuse me Mr…?'

'Oh, er sorry, I'm Monaghan… Sir.'

'Well, Mr Monaghan, from the information I've given, do you think you'll qualify for our course and get through it successfully?'

'Well… I… I… er… think I'll be happy just to get through the application form.'

When the laughter subsided, Mayfield gave a humourless response - to the effect that Miss Woods would explain the form more fully - then picked up the threads of his speech.

Mayfield finished his address and took his leave, but not before reminding Marta of the strict criteria to apply in the final selection. The Personnel Manager and her three assistants all nodded acknowledgement, but when he had gone they broke into a stream of derision.

'Okay, quiet now. Let's get on.' Marta, worried that the applicants would overhear, whispered, 'Listen, make sure the Irishman's test results are good. Know what I mean?'

'You said we should only do that with the best looking girls,' said Tracy, the most recent addition to Marta's team.

'I know, I'm making an exception. I need a laugh and if it's at that prick Mayfield's expense, so much the better.'

Tracy giggled, took another pre-prepared test paper from her folder and moved off to collect Monaghan's application.

Marta sighed and pulled up a chair. The whole process was tiresome. On one side, she had top management informing her that her position depended on the continuous supply of beautiful girls, and on the other Mayfield, her immediate superior in the recruitment of gaming staff, insisting that everyone pass his infernal tests before being considered for employment. Neither side recognised that the two positions had become incompatible. Company policy was to employ beautiful girls to work as Chicas; they were also to be intelligent and sophisticated. With the numbers involved it was always going to be difficult to meet this criteria, but the rapid growth of the business and high staff turnover made it impossible. Girls became disenchanted with the work, got married, pregnant, sometimes both. Others lost some of their physical assets and had to be 'released'. Marta, under pressure to fill vacancies, suggested they relax entry qualifications. Mayfield in his dogmatic and pedantic way couldn't see this and in fact had introduced tests that created even more difficulties. Fortunately, as he himself did not scrutinise the test papers, Marta's department had been able to effect a policy shift by stealth.

He was so out of touch, there were times when she wondered why the company employed him. But sadly, she had to recognise that for them he had his uses. Having a mind like a programmed robot, he was Ventura's public face. Visits from the Press, local authorities, the Police, the Gaming Board, MPs, social reformers or any other busybodies who cared to pry into the casino's affairs were invariably met by Gordon. His garrulity tired the most persistent muckraker. Nosy newsmakers suggesting untoward 'goings on' were met with a Mayfield look of incredulity and a Ventura Manual of Operational Procedures.

Her assistants were now returning to the desk with the applicants' results.

'So let's see, we have sixteen girls to go through. Oh, and five actually passed the tests. Three guys including my Irishman Mr Monaghan. He should do okay - as long as we don't give him any more application forms.'

Chapter Two

Of the games at Ventura, roulette was by far the most popular with gamblers and Pat, having been selected to enter the school, was now being taught to deal that game. He still couldn't believe he'd survived the interview two weeks earlier, especially after his remark to Mayfield about the application form. It had simply been a touch of black humour, as Pat had already convinced himself that he would not be chosen. Happy though he was to have been proven wrong, it was a little early to celebrate; the demands of the three-month training course lay before him, with frequent assessments to get through before he became a paid employee.

In keeping with the Spanish theme of the Ventura – meaning happiness or good fortune – the female serving staff and croupiers were called Chicas and each floor had a Spanish name. At street level, the reception of the Casino led on to a grand open-plan stairway to the first floor Casino Primero, the second floor Casino Playa and the third floor Casino Terrazo. The Primero and Playa operated the total permited hours from 1pm through to four o'clock the next morning, while the Terraza, not being open to the public until evening, was used by day as the training school.

Following the interviews, twenty-eight girls and only six males had been chosen. Pat was more than happy with that ratio - but not so happy with Mayfield's comment in his welcoming address, that demands on all students would increase as the course progressed. Already they had been given multiplication tables to learn and the instructor now introduced them to the first manual exercise.

'These round tokens, called chips, are the currency of casinos. This one is called a cash or value-chip.' She held up a chip, pointing to the pound sterling sign. 'Gamblers may buy them either at the cash desk or directly from the croupier at the table, each table having stock, or as we call it, a chip float. On American Roulette, in order to distinguish their bets from those of the other gamblers, players may purchase chips called colour or non-value chips.' She now held up an example of a colour chip. 'On every roulette table there are eight sets of two hundred chips, each set of a different colour. Now, there are basic skills a croupier must have: chipping - which is picking up chips at speed and stacking them in denomination and colour - and cutting – this is counting chips, again at speed.'

The instructor proceeded to give a demonstration of these skills, drawing an appreciative murmur from the new trainees, who then tried the first of the drills themselves. This exercise, devised to increase manual dexterity, produced in Pat, even after several attempts, something bordering on paralysis. The format was a speed trial or race, where the trainees would compete with each other to be first to pick up a quantity of chips, usually eighty, and arrange them in four stacks of twenty. On the signal 'Go', Pat would set off at what seemed to him a terrifying pace. 'Eighty!' A chorus of cries from the close finishing contestants usually ended the event while he slumped to the table with chips still clutched in his trembling hands. To salvage something of his pride in front of so many attractive girls, he was forced to rely on his old defence mechanism: humour. As his grandfather used to say, 'that way you can have them laughing with you, rather than at you'.

Though not terribly impressed with the results of the Irishman's efforts, Mayfield seemed pleased with the effort itself, which he witnessed during one of his brief visits. Having taken note of Pat's high entry-test results, he saw no reason why the instructors should not be able to capitalise on this and insisted Marta check on their methods. She was now worried that her little display of militancy was about to backfire. In giving Monaghan a mark that his work wouldn't live up to, she ran the risk of having to pass through someone obviously ill-suited to the job. Criticisms were often levelled at the quality of girls coming through, but their beauty and sex-appeal invariably won them sympathy and mistakes were often attributed to nervousness at being in front of the public for the first time. Male staff had always been more critically appraised.

Marta's survival depended on her being able to orchestrate the entire proceedings. She had achieved this by instigating the policy that older girls be given training and admin positions by way of promotion when they had served a number of years as croupiers on the gaming floor. It was a convenient way of kicking a favoured girl upstairs whose appearance was no longer as fresh as it had once been. In this way Marta had built a team of loyal acolytes who were well aware that, but for her intervention, they would have faced dismissal.

Now she called the training instructors around her. 'Make sure you give every attention to Monaghan. Dick-head Mayfield has got his eye on him now. I need him to genuinely pass through. Understand?'

They nodded in agreement but looked far from confident.

As the course progressed, the training team saw only a marginal improvement in Monaghan's dexterity, although it was now apparent that he wasn't the slowest in the class. That dubious distinction fell on Penny Irwin. However, her survival on the course had little to do with her hands and a great deal to do with the rest of her anatomy.

From the moment she had arrived for interview, Penny's future at Ventura had been assured. Marta Woods could just see the casino's gamblers drooling over her big blue, innocent eyes, flawless complexion, shapely figure and golden blonde mane. She would not only win the punters' money, but also capture their hearts, make herself a fortune in the process and possibly marry one. Not for a while, Marta hoped, because then she'd have to look for a replacement.

Penny and Monaghan, as with all pre-selected pupils, knew nothing of their guaranteed passage through the system. Not only because it was an undeclared policy, but also because that knowledge would destroy the incentive to improve, making graduation even more questionable. So to them, each phase in their training seemed like an insurmountable obstacle to eventual employment.

Struggling with the interminable speed trials and stumbling through the mathematical complexities of the game, they became comrades in adversity.

Pat's natural talent for humour was a useful tool. His self-depreciating banter often neutralised the most determined critics. It was also having a therapeutic affect on Penny, who'd previously been almost paralysed with fear when dealing on the roulette table. Now in the more relaxed atmosphere Pat had created, she was also making slow progress.

As they exited the school at the end of their fifth week, Pat was still hoping to extend their relationship outside of the training centre.

'Still doing that train journey to and from Tadley each day?' he asked as he saw her look at her watch. She nodded. 'Going out this weekend?'

'I don't suppose so,' she replied rather sadly.

'Really? Your friends, or boyfriend, not going to tempt you out?'

She took a little while to answer and he was surprised by her reply. 'The friends I had have moved from there and I broke up with my boyfriend,' she sighed. 'Another reason for not going out locally. He won't accept it's over, gets drunk and pesters me. My father even threatened him with the police if he didn't leave me alone.'

'That's a bloody nuisance and boring to be stuck indoors. Why not catch a later train and at least come for a drink? Clear our heads after all those calculations.' He nudged her with his elbow.

She began to shake her head, then paused. 'Yes, why not? I'll phone my mother, tell them I'll be later.'

Being early Friday evening, the pub was busy, but they'd found a corner and he'd managed to put the smile back on her face with anecdotes of his early life in Ireland, including a determined struggle to convince his mother of his unsuitability for the priesthood.

Pat, in turn, was enjoying the envious attention from surrounding males that his beautiful companion provoked. He thought about the reaction he'd get from friends and regulars if he took her to his local pub; they'd choke on their Guinness, he imagined.

'Surely your parents don't expect you to travel back and forward when you start night work at Ventura?'

Penny looked uncomfortable. 'They… they, er, don't know about Ventura. They think I'm on a secretarial course. They wouldn't approve, they're so old-fashioned they worry and are suspicious about everything.'

'Oh I see.' Pat wasn't sure what to say. 'A lot of parents worry like that. You're a young girl and there're strange people about.'

'They don't come much stranger than my father. You know, he hasn't spoken to me since I reached puberty, at least not seriously, only in a general way, like an acquaintance. And Mother, she's so square, and wants me to be the same.' Penny shut her eyes and shook her head. Then, suddenly remembering her time schedule, she looked at her watch.

'You've got time for another drink,' Pat said quickly, anticipating her concern. He rose to go to the bar and winked cheekily. 'You could of course call back home and say you're going to stay over with a friend.'

It was a throwaway line, but for the first time she was prompted to view him differently; not just as her joking colleague from the training school. Although not unattractive, his globular eyes, dimpled chin and slight Chaplin-ish gait tended to enhance his image as a comedian rather than potential boyfriend material. Penny prayed he would not now make a sexual advance that she would be obliged to reject. She was not unused to the attention of men but, coming from a small community and having studied at an all-girls school, she still often found their behaviour intimidating. The recent problems with her ex-boyfriend apart, the reactions she had invariably encountered from other men when refusing their advances, such as flip comments, verbal hostility and even aggression, disturbed her. The last thing she needed in the already nerve-racking atmosphere of the training school was to convert a friend to an antagonist.

'Pat, I'm sorry but after this drink I really have to go,' she said quickly when he returned.

'Ah, so you don't want to take up my offer?' he said, as he put down the drinks.

'Well… er… it's very… but I have to get home.'

'Dat's okay, I know it's short notice. We'll set it up for next weekend.'

'Oh, er… Pat, really I don't…'

'Relax, me love,' he laughed. 'I'm just having a joke.'

He had blown it, he should have played it in a different way, given her more time. No, it wouldn't have mattered - she was never going to fall for his old malarkey; it was always a long shot. He smiled to conceal his disappointment.

Chapter Three

Pat and Penny graduated from the training school to debut on the same gaming tables that they had been training on by day. Of the three gaming zones open at night, the Terraza Casino was often busiest in terms of head-count and volume of gambling chips. However, because of the low maximum bets permitted on its tables, most customers were small-stake players.

The arrival of a new batch of trainees was an occasion Norman Waites seemed to await with trepidation. Commonly referred to as 'Norman-brown - trousers' by the staff, due to his agitated state when anything appeared to be going wrong, he held, or some said clung to, the position of pit boss. Pat and his trainee colleagues had learned that a 'pit' was a number of gaming tables grouped together and cordoned off to form an area where only gaming personnel could enter, the customers being on the outside perimeter. Rather in the manner, joked one trainer, of a wagon train encirclement under attack by Red Indians. Waites appeared to be increasingly under attack, not only from the surrounding customers, but also from his superiors, and staff under his supervision. Recently, the tables that constituted his pit had suffered a run of poor results. Now, to further endanger his position, another group of trainees had arrived with all the accompanying problems.

A trembling Monaghan arrived a few minutes late on the floor to be met by John Nidditch, senior manager of that department.

'Who are you, and why are you late?' scowled the manager.

'Er… I'm sorry, it… it's my first night. I'm to report to Mr Waites, I…
I'm Monaghan.'

'I'm glad you've to report to Mr. Waites, he'll be so pleased,' sneered
Nidditch, 'That's him fidgeting in the pit.'

Waites viewed Monaghan's approach with a look of horror.

'I can't believe it, they've sent me one with no hands!' shouted Waites.

'Oh, sorry Sir.' Pat pulled up his sleeves. 'The shirt's a bit long and I've
no arm bands.'

Waites looked somewhat relieved - until he saw Pat's hands.

'Perhaps they were better covered up,' he muttered, viewing the short,
stubby, most un-croupier-like hands.

He assigned Pat to chip on one of the roulette tables. Although Pat
had practised this constantly in the training school, no great improvement
was evident. The Inspector at the table was soon urging him to move faster
as chips accumulated and the Chica was complaining of the shortage of
stacked chips for payments. Even those that he'd managed to pick up were
in uneven amounts. The Inspector called for Norman, who scurried to the
trouble spot.

'Take this lumpy off here, before we have to dig him out,' the Inspector
appealed to the Pit Boss.

'Oh! for fuck sake!' muttered Norman, seeing the game at a standstill. 'I
knew it! They've sent me another spastic!'

Monaghan, substituted and sent to the rest-room for a break, trudged
off dispiritedly, hoping his nervousness would subside. He paused to look
at the surrounding activities. Although still early evening, the place was
crowded. The Terraza, their training school by day, was unrecognisable by
night. In the pit where he had been working, stood six american roulette tables and six blackjack all being played. Undoubtedly the busiest was Penny's
table. Surprisingly, she was actually being allowed to deal as croupier and
Pat could see she was extremely nervous. However, her Inspector seemed
more patient than Pat's had been.

As he passed her table, the ball dropped into the slot. Penny lifted the
marker, called 'the Dolly', which is used to indicate the winning number,
and announced in a trembling voice, 'Twenty-six, black high and even.'

She hovered over the chip-covered table, but before Pat had moved on, all hell broke loose. She'd marked the wrong number, and cleared away winning bets before the Inspector at the end of the table could intervene. As Pat had learned from his instructor, there was one thing a table inspector dreaded - the wrong number being indicated and cleared on a table stacked high with chips. But perhaps one thing inspectors dreaded even more was the arrival on the scene of Norman-brown-trousers.

'Oh, for Christ's sake, what's happened here?' screeched Waites.

The Inspector was already unraveling the mess without further upsetting either the customers or Penny, but the Pit Boss's excited arrival undid the Inspector's quiet intervention. By loudly advertising her mistake and apparent doubt as to what chips had been placed on the actual winning number, he alerted opportunists from the surrounding tables to join those players with a genuine claim. Now fearing the clamour would attract his boss Nidditch, Waites was authorising payment to all claimants irrespective of their validity. Pat could see the Inspector was furious and Penny was in tears.

Some players were accusing Waites of being responsible for her distress. He indignantly fended off these allegations and called for another Chica to substitute Penny, sending her to the rest-room to compose herself.

Pat lingered by the staff exit to offer Penny some consolation. But as she arrived sniffling at the door, her exit was blocked by a small dark man in a white suit who offered her a silk handkerchief.

'What is wrong, my pretty? Tell Ahmed. Don't cry. You want for me to cry too?' He mimed distress, while urging her to take the handkerchief, which she did. This seemed to please him for he laughed and shouted something to one of his friends nearby. Pat noted he was quite young, obviously Arab, with dark curly hair and hooded eyes. Having performed his gallantry, he walked off with one foot splayed in a curious limping but swaggering movement.

The rest of the night passed without major incident. Both Penny and Monaghan spent most of the time chipping, and being diverted from any table with a large volume of chips, while Waites ran a gamut of emotional changes from nervous apprehension, through dread and despairing resignation and finally relief when the night was over.

It was 4.30 am when they finished, but for some the night was still young.

Pat had heard that many casino people, when they came off duty, went drinking, dancing or breakfasted in one of the many night-clubs. He persuaded Penny to go for breakfast and waited for her outside the staff entrance. As he was standing there, Ian Lowe, the inspector who had been on Penny's table when she cleared the wrong number, came out.

'Who're you waitin' for Paddy?

'Waites's taking me for a wee drink,' laughed Pat. 'No, I'm waiting for Penny.'

'Now you're jokin'? Don't tell me your givin' her one?' Lowe's Glaswegian accent sounded harsh but his features were almost angelic. Even in the darkness his blue eyes were a striking feature, as was his golden hair.

'No. I'm just her father confessor.'

'Well, she'll have plenty tae confess after workin' here for a wee while, I can assure you, father.' Lowe's smile faded abruptly. 'Here's someone who'll see tae that,' he gestured at the limping figure who had just climbed out of a car at the corner.

'Yes, he was talking to Penny earlier. Who is he?'

'That's Ahmed Hammoud. Chief Pimp, troublemaker, and second most powerful man at Ventura.' Lowe grimaced.

'You mean he works for us?'

'More like us who work for him, or so it seems at times!' snarled the Scot as he walked away.

'Hello, my pretty!' Ahmed called as Penny joined Pat at the staff entrance. 'I can have my handkerchief back or you take it, to put under your pillow?'

'Oh, sorry. I was going to wash it,' she smiled as the little Arab scuttled towards her before taking her hand to kiss it.

'No. Why to wash it? I will keep it for souvenir with your sweet tears. No really, you keep it to remind you of your friend Ahmed.'

'Oh, thank you,' said Penny, a little embarrassed.

'Please, you come for breakfast?' He pointed to the waiting Rolls Royce.

'Well, that's very nice, but I promised to go with my friend Pat.'

'Pat? Who is Pat, a girlfriend?' exclaimed Ahmed well aware that she was referring to Monaghan.

'I'm Pat. Patrick Monaghan at your service,' voiced Monaghan, holding out his hand. Ahmed's handshake was like a wet bar-mat.

'You can come too. We're going for breakfast, are we not Penny?' Ahmed smiled, directing them to the Rolls.

Apart from the driver, two other men were sitting in the car. Ahmed introduced them to Penny and Monaghan, adding that they were cousins of Prince Talal, who they would meet at his hotel for breakfast.

Prince Talal, it turned out, was the young heir to a throne of one of the Gulf States. His dark good looks were accentuated by the whiteness of his suit, white silk shirt and gold jewellery he wore on his hands and around his neck in an ostentatious display of wealth.

Pat, who'd never been overawed by the trappings of wealth, felt completely relaxed in this unusual company. Hearing of his hosts' love of horses and horse racing, he was soon in full flow, regaling them with tales of his misspent youth and misspent salary, backing arthritic horses.

'The horse I backed was so far behind, the Police put the jockey on their missing person's list!'

The Arabs, used to deference and mock sincerity, found Pat refreshing and amusing. The group gradually expanded, causing pauses in the conversation for the ritual greetings. Before long, Pat was holding court with a large audience, his comic humour finding appreciative ears.

Although entertained by Pat, the Prince was even more interested in Penny. And she, accustomed to the crude advances of local males, was enchanted by the attentions of the Arab prince, if somewhat worried at what she thought might happen if she accepted any more drinks. After a little while she made suitable excuse to leave without offending him and whispered her intention to Pat. Ahmed insisted on taking them home, and called his man to bring the car.

They dropped Pat off first. Ahmed then took hold of Penny's hand and leaned over to whisper in her ear. She froze, afraid of what was coming next.

'Well, my lovely, he likes you very much. If you are a good girl, I think you will do very well.'

'I don't know what you mean.' Penny looked confused.

'No, perhaps not,' Ahmed laughed. 'You are a woman. You will come to know.'

The car drew up outside her flat and she stepped out, momentarily blinded by the morning sunshine.

'See you soon, my lovely,' Ahmed called, as the Rolls slipped away.

Chapter Four

To Mayfield, the weekly management meeting should have been an opportunity for a brainstorming session. But this view differed from those of the two top company executives and others who were obliged to attend. To Morgan Trist, the Company Chairman, they were convened solely to pass instructions to underlings via his MD. Dan Pellzer used this opportunity to push out Trist's orders in the guise of his own, or vice versa. To Frank Bollard, the Casino Manager, these sessions were a weekly nightmare. Of the three casino floor managers, only Ralph Draper, who covered the night operation of the Primero and Playa Casinos, thought of them as chance to clarify policy; his counterpart Jim Ellis, covering those floors by day, and Nidditch on the Terraza, looked upon them as a waste of their time.

Trist never attended, Pellzer only occasionally. This gave Bollard the unenviable task of presiding over the charade. A customary pre-meeting meeting between Pellzer and Bollard decided the agenda for discussion and, where possible, also the outcome.

The meetings usually took place on Friday afternoons on the Terraza's punto-banco table. Having this weekly forum around a gambling table might have been considered symbolic, but it was in fact the only place where so many senior staff could be accommodated at one time, there being no conference room. Bollard believed Trist's aversion to open discussion on policy was the reason for this.

Once Mayfield had distributed the agenda that Bollard had prepared with Pellzer's help, the Casino Manager opened the meeting. As usual it wasn't long before the discussion deviated from the listed subject. Nidditch, the Terraza's manager, was first to break protocol.

'Instead of covering this stuff, what about discussing how these latest recruits ever got through the school?' He addressed the group, but his eyes focused on Mayfield. Bollard was about to intervene but was beaten to it by his assistant.

'This item isn't on the agenda, but your question has been noted.' Mayfield wrote as he spoke.

'Yes. John's right.' Ralph Draper directed his comment to Bollard. 'This is too important a subject to be left until the meeting's almost over.'

Bollard, with a look of resignation, indicated to Mayfield to respond.

'In actual game conditions, when first exposed to the public, trainees react differently. It's then that inspectors, pit bosses and managers must give the necessary support. In some cases, I feel this isn't being done.'

Mayfield's reply brought a chorus of derision. Bollard, expecting this, called for order. As the noise diminished he gave the floor to Draper, who he knew would at least give a reasoned response.

'Yes, nerves play a part in the early days, but they've been on the floor for weeks. The problem's not so much the training or on-floor support but the quality of those selected. Standards are down because appearance is becoming the only criterion.'

'You're dead right!' cut in Waites. 'Look at that girl Penny who's on our floor, I'll bet she never passed any maths test!'

Marta Woods seethed. 'How would you know, Brown-trousers? You're too...'

'Please! Marta, all of you. Let's not start this again!' Bollard shouted as others looked set to join the slanging match. 'Of course a part of our marketing strategy is the attractiveness of our Chicas. We must continue to recruit girls who fit the image while remembering that inefficiency affects our production levels.' Bollard's words echoed Pellzer's frequent rant that win percentage was below budget. 'Perhaps we can review recruitment criteria for subsequent intakes. But Gordon, perhaps you should spend more time on the floor to assist with on-going training and support.'

An audible groan came from the managers, but Mayfield nodded agreement and entered a note in the minutes.

Marta Woods was concerned by the prospect of a review of recruitment procedures but chose this moment to make another proposal. 'With Gordon on the floor to give support, Chica Penny might prove to be good for the Primero afternoon shift. Morgan thought she would be an asset there.' The latter part was a coded message to Bollard, a Trist suggestion being tantamount to an order.

Draper expected Ellis to object, although it would be purely ritualistic. But Ellis sat impassively, so he felt compelled to speak. 'So, on efficiency and production levels - how will an inexperienced girl, on games with the heaviest gamblers in London, aid win percentages?'

'Gentlemen, we don't have time to discuss this, there is other business to attend to!' Bollard chose to avoid Draper's question. 'Gordon, the assessments.'

Mayfield shuffled his papers. 'As suggested in our previous meeting, on the last Friday of each month managers should submit an assessment of all Chicas working in their department, so that when considering promotion and salary review we will have a more accurate indicator...'

'An accurate indicator of who's fucking who!' Harry Rye's audible whisper to Marta Woods triggered a round of salacious banter. Mayfield looked bemused, Bollard unsurprised, and although his assistant resolutely stuck to the task of describing how assessments should be done, he hurried him along.

'Finally, there's a proposal that the vacant position of pit boss, on nights on Primero's VIP level, be filled by Ian Lowe.' Bollard scanned the group but there was no dissenting voice for once.

'Back on the subject of trainees, who the hell allowed that mad Irishman Monaghan to get through the school?' asked Nidditch.

'He showed up well in our tests,' protested Mayfield, while Marta suddenly found something engrossing in her handbag.

'He can't continue, he'll give Waites a heart attack... Aha!' Nidditch leaned back in his chair. 'Come to think of it, maybe he should continue...'

'Very funny.' Waites responded to Nidditch's taunt. 'But you're right, he has to go. His only saving grace is, he's good with the clients.'

'Then he should be in public relations, that's where people with no brains who're good with customers work,' Draper quipped.

'Now, now, Ralph, let's take this seriously,' intervened Bollard. 'Someone mentioned that this Monaghan was a likeable chap. We're actually looking for somebody for the PR department. Perhaps he should be tried there?'

Ellis woke from his reverie. 'Then he'll have to go back into training to learn to shake hands and pocket tips.'

'Well, he's Irish, these things don't come easy,' Rye sneered. Fearing another session of jokes on nationalistic stereotypes, Bollard instructed Mayfield to close the minutes.

The assembled mangers quickly vacated the room. Apart from Mayfield, only Draper dallied.

'Yes Ralph, something else?' Bollard asked in a tired voice

'Yes, about Lowe's promotion, I need him downstairs immediately.' Draper's request received a nod of assent from Bollard. The floor manager continued as they walked. 'What we were talking about earlier - standards are slipping drastically.'

'You mean the standard of the meetings? The seriousness of the discussions?' Bollard stopped to face Draper.

'You want seriousness and professionalism? Well it has to come from the top. From your bosses. If they want only dumb beauties to grace their parties upstairs, that's okay. But don't expect that to inspire professionalism on the floor or serious discussion at meetings.' Draper didn't wait for Bollard's response. He stormed off through the staff exit without looking back.

For Bollard the most disturbing aspect of Draper's outburst was the truth behind it. Of the managers at Ventura he was undoubtedly the one who took his responsibilities most seriously and for whom Bollard had most respect. Ironically, because of this, he was invariably the one with whom he was most in conflict.

*

Feeling hungry, Draper decided on an early dinner. He called Colin Bland, his assistant manager on the floor above, to step down and relieve him on the Primero, which was Ventura's VIP level. Though Lowe, his new Pit Boss, seemed to be coping admirably, he didn't want to leave him without immediate assistance on this his first night.

Draper decided to eat in the restaurant on the Playa level, where Bland had come from. As a senior manager he could well have chosen to dine in Primero's VIP restaurant. But apart from having a temporary change of scenery, Draper also reckoned that, in Bland's absence, he could keep an eye on activity on that floor while he ate.

The irritation he'd felt earlier with Bollard had all but gone. He was well aware of the difficulties the man faced on a day to day basis. Yet there in the restaurant sat another source of irritation in the ample shape of Marta Woods, who was already dining. He joined her but lost no time in pleasantries.

'You've really laid one on the casino department this time. This Chica Penny's undoubtedly beautiful but she won't handle the action and, from what I hear, her nerves are shot to pieces already.'

'Sorry, but this time it wasn't my decision, and Ellis doesn't seem to mind, so why should you? Anyway, the word came from the new boss.' Marta chewed while she spoke.

'New boss? What new boss?'

'Sorry.' Marta, took another bite of the special club hamburger with Ventura sauce, which was now easing its way down her chin. 'Mister Ahmed.'

'Oh Christ! What's Gimp the Pimp up to now?' the manager grimaced.

Marta wiped the sauce off and made a sign to indicate her lips were sealed, then proceeded to reveal all.

'He's Morgan Trist's PR advisor, so we have to keep him sweet.' She opened her hands in a gesture of resignation.

'And of course the little bastard asked for Penny to be on Primero, so he can work on her for one of his rich Arab mates.' Ralph filled in the rest of the story. 'Doesn't it make you sick?' He watched as Marta now worked her way through a plate of pancakes and cream. Obviously not, he thought, nothing could.

Although not having eaten since breakfast, he was no longer hungry. Draper left Marta to her pancakes and went on a tour of the upper floor to see what kind of action they were getting at this fairly early hour.

Since Primero, the new area for VIPs, had been inaugurated more of the bigger players had moved downstairs, causing a reduction in the average spend per head on the two floors above. Nevertheless, on the Terraza level, he still recognised some fairly good players and many regulars who, although not playing in large amounts at any one time, could be relied upon to risk a few thousand pounds three or four times per week.

Further down the room Nidditch stood by the cash desk with a familiar customer, no doubt discussing credit. The body language told Draper that the Terraza floor manager was denying the player's request to sign another cheque to buy gaming chips. He could also predict that his colleague would eventually permit the transaction, the refusal being less than emphatic. The client had probably reached the limit set on his file. Each manager had discretion to exceed the limit: this was undoubtedly preparation for an eventual refusal.

Although Draper now managed the prestigious VIP Primero and the Playa casino at night, he had no seniority over Nidditch on the Terraza. Prior to the opening of the Primero they had both had equal responsibility for one floor and Nidditch had served longer with the company. He might therefore have pressed a claim to be considered as candidate to take over the two lower floors, but his natural propensity to do as little as possible - unless there was an appreciable financial gain – made him more than willing to let Bollard pass the burden to Draper. Bland, a pit boss, had later been promoted to assist Draper. Nidditch now seemed to be regretting his inaction.

However, whether senior or not, as shift manager Draper was entitled to request information on any customer and would have asked his management colleague for an update, but Nidditch had hurriedly moved off to attend some other problem. Draper therefore asked the cashier how much Al Shadari had taken and was surprised to learn he'd signed cheques for twenty thousand pounds - much more than he'd ever known this player to play in one day. Draper requested the player's file - it showed a limit of eight thousand pounds per visit and no new limit had been requested, although on the last few visits the player had greatly exceeded his limit. Nidditch had authorised some of this, but the majority had been authorised by the day shift manager, Jim Ellis.

Draper would have liked to ask for an explanation but Nidditch had not returned. This was nevertheless something he had to investigate.

When Draper returned, the VIP level was buzzing. Bland waited while Ian Lowe totted up the hourly result.

'We're about even, on a drop of a hundred and fifty grand.' The Pit Boss handed him the clipboard.

'Not wonderful, but we were losing and we've come back in the last twenty minutes.,' Bland added, handing Draper the notes.

Draper studied the figures. 'I see there's been a bit of activity.'

'Just about everything. You definitely know when to go for a meal-break,' grinned Bland. Lowe nodded. 'As you see,' Bland continued, 'the Shamoud brothers are in for fifteen grand, five cash, ten in cheques on Toni's account; Hassam lost three grand cash, took eight grand credit but he's in front at the moment. Aginpola won eighteen grand then went for dinner, he'll be back. But the real show-stealer was Zebeghedesh. He asked for ten grand, but on his card he'd taken twice his limit on the day shift, so I refused him. What a performance! Called me for everything, put a curse on my house, family... said he'd go to Ellis and Trist. What aggro—' He would have continued, but Draper interrupted.

'Actually, this is the second player I've heard about today who's taken credit way above their limit.'

Lowe frowned. 'Come tae think of it,' he said, 'you know, Ralph, you told me tae study all the files of players who've got cheque-cashing facilities?' Draper nodded. 'Well, I found at least half a dozen punters who've taken way over their limit on the day shift durin' the last few days. Oh, sorry !' Lowe saw the congregation of staff that he should allocate to tables and moved off with his break-list.

At 3.45 am, Draper advised his pit boss to call last three spins on roulette and last shoe on the card games. The night had been uneventful save for a few small incidents. One inspector had reported a feeble attempt at petty fraud, but no action was taken against the client, a frustrated loser; and at the cash desk Lowe, much to Draper's amusement, had spent considerable time attempting to explain to a Chinese customer why travellers' cheques could not be signed in pictographic symbols. But in the end the house advantage had triumphed over secret formulas, special systems, lucky numbers, Chinese charms and Arab curses - the estimated win for Primero's seven tables had risen to just over fifty thousand pounds.

'Looks like in the end we've got a result,' Lowe commented as he finished his calculation.

But Draper hadn't heard him. He'd gone to the cash desk to study the cheque-cashing records again.

Chapter Five

As he approached the staff entrance, he found Ahmed standing on the edge of the pavement. 'Ah, good evening, Mr Ahmed. What you doing here, lost your way?' joked Pat.

'Hello dare, my friend,' responded the Arab in a mock Irish accent, before reverting to his normal guttural tone. 'I am as a chauffeur, waiting to take a young lady to a night of magic.'

At that moment Penny Irwin, resplendent in evening dress, came out from the club and seemed slightly embarrassed to see Pat. Ahmed made a theatrical bow and signalled to the driver of a Bentley, parked nearby.

'Penny... er... don't you think this is a wee bit unwise?' Pat stumbled over his words, a little unsure of what to say.

'It's alright, Pat, it's an official function, Jim Ellis knows about it,' whispered Penny before boarding the waiting car. She waved as the car moved off into the stream of early evening traffic

In the locker room a series of unanswered questions and nagging doubts seemed to slow his movement until a voice from behind broke his reverie.

'I also dragged my feet at the thought of workin' wi Waites.'

'Oh, hello Ian.' Pat moved to allow Lowe to pass to his locker. 'Yes, I'd better get a move on or I won't be his favourite anymore.'

There were, as yet, few people at Ventura Pat felt he knew well enough to talk about work problems, but Lowe was one of them.

'Eh, Ian, I've got a number of things worrying me and I don't know who to ask about them. D'ya think we could talk sometime… when it's convenient for you?'

Lowe looked a little puzzled. 'Well… er… yes. But I'm not sure when. It may have tae wait till the end of the night.' Pat nodded approval, gave a thumbs-up sign and continued on his way down.

It seemed an unlikely spot for gaming staff to socialize but The White Lion's special licence, to cater for the market workers at Covent Garden, had made it one of the few places, other than the more expensive nightclubs, where in the early hours of the morning, after casinos closed, one could get an alcoholic drink. Lowe had suggested earlier that Pat join him and some others there for an after-work pint.

Pat arrived before Lowe but inside there were several people he knew, including some Chicas. Looking around at the mix of clientele, he imagined that the recent adoption of their favourite pub by off-duty, stylishly dressed and higher spending casino people might well irritate the generally rough and scruffy traders. One of Pat's colleagues agreed that it seemed to be the case at the start, but on subsequent visits, when the casino entourage included Chicas, Playboy Bunnies and other female staff, the traders' objections seemed to fade away.

It was more than one hour before Lowe appeared, surprisingly accompanied by Primero night-manager Draper. They ran a gauntlet of greetings, drink offers, drink requests, jokes, queries and, in Lowe's case, invitations from several females before they reached Pat.

'Hi Pat, I know I said some guys were coming down here but I didn't expect so many on a Tuesday,' said Ian, pointing to a quieter corner. 'You know Ralph, don't you?' He gestured to Draper, who was coming up behind him.

'Ah well, I know of course who he is, but we haven't actually talked.' Pat extended his hand to the manager. 'I didn't know the top guys came down here as well.'

'Depends, Pat, what you mean by "top guy". We don't expect to see Trist or Pellzer here,' said Draper smiling, 'but I think it would be a poor casino floor manager who thought his authority would diminish after a few pints with the people he works with.'

Nonetheless, the presence of Draper inhibited Pat from touching on the subjects he'd thought to discuss with Lowe. Instead, they made general conversation. Pat's observations of customer behaviour amused both his senior colleagues, while some opinions on operational matters surprisingly concurred with theirs.

'Pat, you said you had some specific worries or questions for me?' asked Lowe as Draper broke of from their conversation to go to the toilet.

'Ah yes... er... well...' He thought for a moment and decided on at least one thing he could ask about. 'It was Waites, he said at the last management meeting they'd discussed taking me off the tables. I wondered if he was just saying that or...'

'Ah you know Waites, he's liable tae say anything,' laughed the Scot.

'Yes but he did say at that same meeting they decided about transferring Penny, and they did.'

Lowe looked thoughtful but didn't reply. Pat decided he too needed to relieve himself and moved off to the gents.

'What was it Waites said to you, about the meeting?' asked Draper, when Pat rejoined them at the bar.

'Ah well, he said... ' Pat tried to recall his exact words. '"Looks like, after our management meeting today, I won't have to put up with you for much longer".'

Draper looked at Lowe and both shook their heads disapprovingly.

'Well you see, I know I'm not doin' terribly well, but... er... nobody has said anything officially. I wondered if he—'

Draper held up his hand to stop Pat. 'This isn't the way a professional should behave, but of course he's not a professional. It's true some discussion was made of the latest batch of trainees but he has no right to disclose that, and certainly no right to put his own warped interpretation to you. Since he has, I'll tell you that there was a suggestion that as there is a vacancy in the public relations department, you might be better suited to that type of work.'

'Jesus! That'd be—'

'Please! Let me emphasise - it was a suggestion, no decision was taken.'

'Okay, yes I understand. But do you think it's a possibility?' Pat began to feel excited by the prospect.

'I don't know, I can pursue it if you're interested, as I suspect you are?' Draper offered.

'I definitely am. Although I can't say I know what the whole job is about, I do think it's something I could handle... with the proper training, that is,' Pat was quick to add, in case he sounded smug.

'Aha, don't get us started on that,' Lowe interjected with a laugh, 'proper training of public relations staff, or any staff for that matter, is a sore point!'

'Yes, quite. Start on that subject and I'll never get home,' Draper downed the last of his pint. 'Look, lads, I've got to go before she locks the door. See you later, oh and I'll see what I can find out about the PR job.'

He was off before Pat could swallow the mouthful of beer and say thanks.

'He seems like a good guy, very much interested in what he does,' said Pat.

'Yeah one of the best in there, unlike others I could mention. I'm glad I got the opportunity to start as pit boss under him and not one of the others,' said Lowe, signalling to the barman to put up another two pints.

'Ah you mean Nidditch and the other Primero manager on day shift, whatsisname?'

'Ellis, Jim Ellis.' Lowe made a face.

'Ah yes, you know Penny, the girl from my training course, she was asking about him, because she's just been transferred there.' Pat considered if he should touch on the subject troubling him.

'Yeah, who hasn't noticed Penny, beautiful girl. But I think your place as Father Confessor's been taken up by Gimp the Pimp, Ahmed. He got her moved to Primero.' Lowe grimaced as he thought about it.

'I'm... er... I really don't understand a lot of things... how a client could influence things like that and—'

'That's the least of it, according to Draper,' Lowe cut in, raising his eyebrows. 'He's always moanin' about the things that go on in there and I'm just beginnin' tae find out what he's talking about.'

'You know, one of the things I was gonna ask you about, but I don't want to start trouble for her...' Pat paused, unsure how to put it. 'It's Penny. As you say, this Ahmed seems to have an interest in her. Anyway, tonight he drove her off to some function with his Arab friends. She says it was official, with permission from Jim Ellis. I don't know but I'm a bit afraid for her, she's a bit... naïve.'

Lowe looked thoughtful. 'From what I hear of Ellis, it's entirely possible he gave the okay. Strickly speaking it's against company policy but... it seems rules are different for different people.'

'So could she be in trouble, I mean, what could I advise her?'

Lowe was about to say something then hesitated. 'Okay, don't say anything for now, let me find out a bit more.'

Pat would have continued but suspected Lowe was now concentrating on something more pleasant - like the young redhead who was smiling across at him. After a few moments, the Scot excused himself and sidled off to talk to her. Pat, also in need of diversion, crossed to the other side of the pub where more Ventura people had congregated.

After speaking with Ellis and Nidditch, his fellow managers, Draper had been trying for several days to get from Bollard a satisfactory clarification of company policy on players' cheque-cashing limits. Both colleagues, in answer to his question on why they were giving excessive credit, had disingenuously responded that they were simply applying the discretion managers had always had on the sanctioning of cheques.

But Draper's resilience paid off when Bollard finally confirmed that the matter was on the agenda of the weekly meeting that afternoon.

'The first item on the agenda is personnel and much of this was covered last week, including the monthly assessments.' Bollard tried to avoid a repeat of the tone of the last meeting. 'Let's see if we can work our way through these items quickly. First, a personnel matter connected with marketing. Patrick Monaghan the new trainee will, as suggested last week, move to public relations.'

'Thank Christ!' exulted Waites.

'Since he came on the tables his hands haven't stopped shaking. He should be perfect for PR since shaking hands is all they ever do,' Nidditch added sardonically.

'Maybe Waites won't have to change his underpants so often now,' intoned Lukas, another pit boss. This provoked gales of laughter.

'Please, Gentlemen!' Bollard sighed and waited. 'This time, in answer to criticism that PR people have no real direction, I'd like Gordon, perhaps in cooperation with you, Ralph, to put together an introductory course for Monaghan, which should be backed up by all of you.'

Gordon Mayfield nodded approval as he wrote the minutes. Draper appeared a little surprised at being designated this task but raised no objection.

'Now, a general comment on marketing,' Bollard cleared his throat and looked uneasy. 'As you all know, we're facing increasing competition. Frequently, competitors try to poach our best clients.' He paused and looked round the table. For once there was no dissenting voice or flip comment. 'So, our watchword must be flexibility. The top management believe that everyone must be flexible with clients. At the moment some managers are a little too rigid and that may be costing us money.'

Draper's assistant, Colin Bland, who rarely spoke at meetings, reacted sharply. 'What exactly do you mean? Rigid in what way?'

'Well… er… in interpretation of rules… and… the management of the cheque-cashing facility.' Bollard fiddled with his pen.

'Ah yes,' said Draper, sitting up in his seat. 'I was wondering when we would get to this question.'

'It's important, it's one of the factors in the recent growth of income on the afternoon shift and on the Terraza,' Bollard quickly countered.

'When was there a change in policy on credit?' demanded Draper.

'Credit, as such, is not allowed under the Gaming Act,' Mayfield interceded, to remind them.

'Thank you, Professor!' said Draper sarcastically. 'I'm well aware credit isn't allowed, that "clients can only sign personal cheques", that "cheques must be presented to the bank within two banking days". Before you quote chapter and verse of the Gaming Act, okay?' Satisfied he'd silenced

Mayfield, he continued. 'It would seem from studying the files that we're permitting certain players to sign cheques for amounts way above the limit we set. Those limits were to be governed by the amount requested originally by the player and the replies from the bank when we ask for references—'

Ellis interrupted 'Yes, but managers always had discretion to—'

'Discretion within reason, but not two or three times the limit or more!' Draper cut in angrily. 'Our policy has always been that if the player wants to radically increase his facility, we re-apply to his bank, asking if he's good for the figure. It might be said that if we permit a client to sign for amounts which we've no idea he can cover, then this is credit. Which, as Mayfield was so eager to point out, is illegal!'

'He has a point there,' said Mayfield thoughtfully, and was about to develop his view until Bollard threw him a warning glance.

'You're splitting hairs. This is not a contravention of the Act,' said Bollard testily. 'The fact is, some managers, because of their relationship with the customers, have learned who's a risk and who isn't, and have accordingly applied a flexible policy. This is earning the company a great deal of money.'

'When was the policy changed on credit?' demanded Draper.

'Well, as a matter of fact, if you think back to the er...' Bollard riffled through his folder of previous minutes. 'Ah... yes, the meeting before last when Dan Pellzer advocated a more flexible approach...'

'Bollocks!' shouted Draper, 'that was a general comment! There was no specific instruction to change what up until now has been a strict company policy. Who gave you the order to implement this policy?' Draper turned angrily to Ellis and Nidditch.

'Well, as Frank said, Pellzer - and I suppose Trist - wanted us to be more flexible. We took it to mean with credit as that's the only thing that has any real effect on income.' Ellis's languid delivery seemed to indicate the lack of importance he attached to the discussion.

'What's your problem, Ralph?' Nidditch seemed puzzled. 'If it makes money...?'

Draper drew a deep breath and shook his head, he could see he was getting nowhere. 'So what level of credit is acceptable? Are there no rules? And what if we get stuck with a lot of unpaid cheques? Who takes responsibility?'

'Well each manager knows his players. If you're not sure about someone who normally plays on day shift, confer with Jim. Of course we can later re-reference, but the watchword is flexibility,' Bollard responded. Draper could see from the quizzical look on Mayfield's face and the concern on others' that only Ellis and Nidditch were comfortable with the situation.

'I know even you don't believe this bollocks. It comes from up-stairs!' Draper then sank into frustrated silence.

The meeting seemed to disintegrate as first Ellis then Bollard him-self were called away to attend to urgent matters. When Bollard returned Mayfield, as instructed, had concluded discussion on most points on the agenda. Nidditch was standing, poised to leave.

'To return to the subject of cheque-cashing…' ventured Bland.

'I think we've sufficiently covered this subject and in any case we've run out of time,' grunted Bollard. He closed his folder and put the top on his pen to indicate the close of the meeting.

'Whether you like it or not, Frank, this subject will come back to haunt you!' rasped Draper as he left the table.

Chapter Six

The official confirmation of his transfer to the Public Relations department was conveyed to Pat by Mayfield the day following the management meeting. Unofficially, he'd already been given the welcome news by Draper who, in his candid way, was also quick to point out that, in effect, there was no such department, merely an extension of the reception staff's duties to include some additional service to clients.

He was hopeful, he told Pat, that a more professional approach would now be taken.

Mayfield initiated Pat's induction programme by introducing him to his new colleagues. Ollie Keane had recently taken the position of reception manager by default, following the departure of both the previous manager and his assistant. The rest of the staff consisted of several reception Chicas and six car jockeys, not all of them present due to their work schedule.

Having completed these introductory formalities, the assistant casino manager informed them that Pat Monaghan would 'start an intensive familiarisation course on company marketing policy and Gaming Act compliance, to enable him to take up the position almost immediately'.

Sara, a recent recruit to reception, naively mentioned that staff on reception and public relations should all benefit from this as they were frequently asked by customers why certain procedures were necessary and were often at a loss to explain. Disturbed to hear of this, Mayfield promptly included Ollie Keane and several others in the session with the new arrival.

'Trust that silly cow to get us roped into a marathon session with this fuckin' robot!' Ollie grunted as he and Pat waited for Mayfield to begin.

'It has been brought to my attention,' intoned Mayfield as the assembled staff glared at the unfortunate Chica, 'that some of you are not fully conversant with the Gaming Act of 1968.'

As Ollie had feared, Mayfield didn't just explain the points relevant to those departments, but launched into a history of gaming legislation and the events leading up to the changes in 1968. He now explained the Acts of Parliament and the special provisions and amendments. The audience grew restless. Somebody audibly yawned, another stifled a laugh; but Mayfield continued, seemingly unaware of the unrest.

'We now come to Schedule five, part one. This concerns the issue and revocation of certificates of approval…'

'Excuse me, Sir… er… Gordon,' Pat interrupted, 'this is fascinating stuff but some here have to be on duty soon, I believe. Do you mind if we cover the bits which affect them directly, and I'll cover the rest later?'

Mayfield looked irritated but, to the relief of all, shuffled his papers, discarding a number of pages before resuming.

'I take Patrick's point, although it's important to cover all aspects of the Legislation – the general philosophy being that casinos will cater only for unsolicited demand. They may not stimulate demand by advertising or offering attractions such as live entertainment. All casinos must be private clubs and a person may only gamble if granted a membership, first having signed an "intent to game" and allowed forty-eight hours to pass to ensure they've given careful thought to their decision. Of course, bona-fide guests may enter and gamble if a member signs them in but may only remain on the premises as long as the member remains. Are these points clear?' Mayfield waited for indications that they had understood.

'They're clear, but try explaining to foreign visitors who're only in London for the day. They think were having them on. It's such a stupid law,' said Cara, a short blonde Chica who had worked on reception for some time. Everyone endorsed her opinion.

'The job of the PRdepartment is to explain to the public that the perceived inconveniences of the Act are in fact there to protect their interests,' replied Mayfield haughtily.

'What a prick this guy is!' Ollie whispered to Pat, while another colleague challenged the last statement.

'How do you explain to a multi-millionaire Saudi Prince that he needs forty-eight hours to really think if he can afford to gamble?'

Before Mayfield could respond, Monaghan had entered the discussion.

'Shouldn't we just say – it's law, we unfortunately can't change it, and have to abide by it? Instead of trying to defend something that's difficult?'

'Well yes, you could,' Mayfield conceded. 'Any other questions on what we've covered so far?'

'If in law we mustn't stimulate demand, why does this company employ only good-looking girls,' asked Elena, a receptionist who, with her shapely figure, flowing dark hair and big brown eyes, examplified that policy. 'They dress us in low-neck, mini-flamenca-dresses. Isn't this to stimulate?'

'Trust her, stuck-up cow,' muttered Ollie under his breath.

Mayfield gave Elena an indulgent smile. 'Our uniforms give us a distinctive flavour from our competitors. Some time ago, to anticipate possible objections from the Gaming Board, we modified the uniforms of the croupier Chicas,' he said dismissively, returning to his lecture. 'The Gaming Board has been formed to act as an Inspectorate which advises licensing authorities on the suitability of companies or individuals to hold licences. They also—'

'Sorry to interrupt, but if the uniforms are solely to give a distinctive flavour, why must girls retain their youthful looks to retain their jobs?' pressed the articulate Elena.

Mayfield didn't like being interrupted but was unfazed by the girl's persistence. 'This meeting has been convened to discuss the licensing regulation and its relevance to your particular department. If we are to press on and complete this discussion, as Mr Monaghan suggested, then we must unfortunately set aside other policy discussions for a later date. Suffice to say the Board is satisfied that our policies do not contravene regulations. Now, concerning the questions which clients often ask…'

'Er, excuse me...' With a look of frustration, Mayfield gave way to Monaghan. 'About the question of the female staff's relationship with customers, what's the regulation there?'

Mayfield looked puzzled. 'There is only one relationship: that of company employee providing a service to the customer and the Act does not—'

'I think what Pat's referring to is the service some girls give to punters outside work-hours!' called out Ollie, happy to relieve his boredom and add a bit of spice to the meeting.

'I don't know if you have specific complaints about any girl?' Mayfield answered. 'The Act does not specifically cover this point, but a strict company policy prohibits any kind of exterior relationship between our female employees and male members.'

'The males' members, excuse the expression, is exactly what they're entertaining outside,' announced Ollie, provoking a cacophony of sniggering, catcalls and protests.

Mayfield, seeing a pattern emerge he'd seen in many a management meeting, sought to bring this one to a close.

'Ladies, Gentleman - please! I close, but remind you, if you have information regarding any staff breaking regulations and thereby endangering the future of this company, you are duty bound to bring it to your superior's attention. Thank you and good afternoon!'

'Sometimes I wonder how that dick-head functions. Can he really be that stupid?' Ollie asked as Mayfield left the room.

Pat had no reply. On the subject of girls being encouraged by some managers to go out with members, he'd learnt precisely nothing. Mayfield was obviously not the person to answer his questions.

Pat was delighted to have been offered a place in the P.R. Department, especially as his future as a croupier had been by no means assured. He'd managed to avoid criticism from customers and supervisory staff through his humour, much of it self-depreciatory. His good nature and willingness to learn had even slightly tempered the opinion of Waites and the malevolent Nidditch. However, their tolerance was unlikely to have lasted.

But he was already finding out that Draper's description of the Public Relations Department, as an assortment of people with varied but ill-defined tasks, was essentially true. Principally they were employed to glad-hand customers and attend to their needs as best they could. Public Relations people normally formed part of the marketing department and were governed by the overall marketing strategy. According to Ollie Keane, Ventura's sales concept had been clearly defined by Chairman Trist himself, at a meeting some years before, as being 'Boobs and Betting'. It did not seem to have seen much refinement since.

Policy, Lowe was quick to point out, was made on an ad hoc basis, occasionally directed by decisions taken at the management meetings, more often by decree from Trist via Pellzer. Part of the reason for this, it was said, could be put down to the prohibition of advertising under the Gaming Act. This meant the promotion of the business could only be done indirectly. The organisation of charity events, attended by photogenic Chicas, was one way of creating newsworthy stories to project the company name. Selling merchandise that prominently featured the company logo was another promotional tool which fell just inside the boundaries of the law.

Curiously, the organisation of many of these duties fell to the Personnel Department and whichever ex-Chica Marta Woods had available. Most other events were simple internal promotions to create customer loyalty.

Short as his time at Ventura had been, Pat had already come to realise that nothing would give a quicker result than increasing the number of visits of the existing members, in particular the heavy gamblers. The problem was how to achieve this? His departmental colleagues would roll out the old mantra - keep the customer satisfied.

This replaced one question with another - what would satisfy them? The obvious answer was a win on the tables – but then Pat's job was irrelevant. If an occasional win brought them in more often, then surely continuous losses would ensure their eventual abstinence. Yet this did not appear to be the case.

These questions intrigued Pat and he took every opportunity to explore the complexities with his colleagues. Their opinions didn't always throw light on the subject but it threw light on their opinions. His knowledge of the staff might become more complete than his knowledge of the customers.

Some of those questions he intended to put to Draper in the first of their sessions.

'Hi, Pat, I thought we'd talk up here where it's quieter,' Draper said, as Pat joined him on the punto table on the Terraza level. 'On this very table, all the momentous decisions that affect the company are avoided, or taken and then ignored.'

Pat smiled. In a way he found Draper's irreverence and dissatisfaction with things encouraging, as he felt he could more easily express his concerns, give opinions and expect a forthright response rather than company dogma.

'Anyway, so far you've met Ollie Keane, the reception Chicas and the rest. You've had Gordon's input with regard to the Gaming Act, and spent a few days acclimatising yourself.' Draper looked at his notes. 'What do you think so far?'

Pat considered how to answer. 'Well, as you said earlier, our responsibilities are a bit... er... undefined.' Draper gave a nod of recognition. 'It's a start to know the Gaming Law, then of course we should know more about the customers. But... er... I think we should also know a bit more about the company and its policies – because as I see it, we have to sell the company and answer clients' questions, but I know virtually nothing about the company. Know what I mean?'

'I know exactly what you mean Pat.' Draper leant back in his chair and sighed. Okay, let me try. The company, or rather its senior executive, is Canadian. But to meet with U.K. licensing requirements, a British company had to be formed. Morgan Trist started as a nightclub proprietor where this loosely Spanish concept of Ventura, Chicas and the like first started. He brought Harry Rye, who I believe was his bar manager, to run the catering. Pellzer, our Managing Director, was, I'm told, installed as a condition of the company who financed the casino project. Being an accountant, he's certainly more money-conscious than Trist. The basic concept isn't so far away from our famous competitors Playboy, being that we also rely greatly on the beauty of our female staff and have been lucky to come on the scene in time to exploit the rich Arab's appetite for girls and gambling.'

'So the description of Ventura as "Boobs and Betting", where the P.R. department just supply a handshake and hello, pretty much sums up our job?'

'Ah yes, our Chairman's famous and subtle description.' Draper grimaced and shook his head. 'There's as much to the job as you want to put into it. Or, like Ollie and others I could mention, you can take a cynical view and reduce your input to a minimum. My personal opinion is that gambling is a basic human instinct. If not provided for legally, it'll be offered illegally by unscrupulous people. Our job is to provide a safe and regulated environment where people can enjoy themselves. The regulations as provided by the Gaming Act are irksome and undoubtedly excessive - but they are law and we must comply in order to retain our licence. That doesn't mean you can't do anything; it does mean we should have clear, consistent and ethical policies.'

Pat could see from Draper's impassioned response that this subject had arisen before. On the question of ethical policy he was of a mind to re-open the matter of Penny's recruitment by Ahmed but, fearing it might cause trouble for her, he concentrated on his own immediate task.

'So, what do you see as my main duties?'

'Your first tasks are basically what you're doing – accumulating information about the Law; Company structure; the facilities we offer – what games, what minimums and maximums; food and beverage facilities, menu and prices. But then most of all, you have to "know our customers". Something I feel we haven't done efficiently, choosing to concentrate only on a few obvious favourites. What you must know is - who they are, what they do, where they're from, what they like, what they don't like – everything that you can possibly know. However, the full contents of any files you keep should be available only to senior managers. Identification of new players is an important part of your job and pit bosses and managers will call on you for that information, not only for public relations reasons but also for security. Public relations is an important part of all our jobs but you, with a roving commission and no table duties, have more flexibility and time to entertain and, if need be, help resolve disputes and explain misunderstandings.'

Pat continued for some time with Draper on how he might best obtain some of the information the manager had highlighted. When they did eventually break off to prepare for the coming evening, he felt, in spite of some still unanswered questions, a lot more focused and enthusiastic about the task ahead.

Chapter Seven

The noise, not unusual for a dice table, nevertheless attracted the attention of Draper's assistant Gordon Bland, on night duty on the Playa level. He glanced across at what is more commonly known as the craps-game. The ladderman perched on the pulpit-like structure above the table wasn't displaying any distress signals, so Bland concluded that the din was due to the players' high spirits - not unwelcome, as it normally encouraged more play. The decibels gradually increased until another explosion of cheers some time later. This time the ladderman was signalling. Bland, by now at the other end of the gaming floor, went to the nearest internal telephone and called the phone by the craps table.

'What's the problem?'

'We need a ten grand fill, were taking a bit of a hammering.' The ladderman could just be heard above the noise.

Bland instructed the cashier to prepare the additional stock of chips requested, but before it could be signed for and withdrawn, another call came from the Dice table.

'You'd better make that twenty grand. This silly cow's gonna shoot all night.'

Bland arrived at the table with the chips. An extremely attractive girl in a low cut dress was still throwing. He handed the boxman the metal racks holding the chips and climbed up alongside the ladderman as another winner was called. The girl shrieked with delight and clapped her hands over her cheeks in wide-eyed disbelief at her good fortune.

The grooves round the table rim were filled with chips as other players cashed in on the girl's run of luck. The boxman pressed three spring-loaded chip containers that released fifteen stacks of twenty chips in three rows of five. He counted one stack and measured it against the rest, calling out the total before signing the fill slip. He deposited one copy in the drop box, and returned the other to Bland.

'Roll the dice!' he commanded.

Bland watched from behind the dealer's position. The girl threw eight and continued to throw numbers for some time. This was costing the casino a considerable amount of money as several players on the table were taking 'place' bets on all the numbers. The girl hadn't thrown a seven in all the time she had held the dice.

Though she continued to enchant the players and a considerable crowd of spectators, she no longer held the same charms for the table staff, especially since her exploits had attracted the floor manager. He in turn had called the dice manager, Chris Russell, back from his meal break.

'Coming out, same shooter!' said the stickman with a seriousness not evident earlier.

'No roll!' shouted the boxman as the girl rolled short.

'Hey, don't forget the arm action now.' The young man with her picked up the dice to show her.

'Bring in those dice!' Chris Russell ordered.

The stickman pulled the dice towards the boxman and threw the three spare dice on the table while the boxman inspected the surrendered dice.

'Why you do this? Because we win, eh?' shouted the girl's companion, a view echoed by the other players. 'I want the same dice. Give to her the same dice!' he demanded.

The boxman, having found nothing untoward, threw the dice down and nodded to the dealer on the stick to return them to her.

'Coming out, same shooter seven eleven!' the stickman continued. 'Five, the point's five!' he announced.

'I hope Plod's got some of this,' said the Dice Manager.

Bland turned to pick up the internal phone. He dialled the security-room. 'Are you by any chance catching the dice game on camera? Good, Chris will come and have a look.'

'Seven out! Lines away. Backs to pay!' The call two throws later heralded the end of the girl's run and precipitated a storm of abuse from the players.

'You see what they done?' fumed one of the regulars. 'They switched the dice!'

'Yeah, the girl was doing okay until you messed with the dice!' shouted another in disgust.

The girl's companion was also protesting loudly, while collecting their chips.

'That's it! I don't play with a casino that cannot play fair,' he announced. 'Come, my love, we cash in!'

The girl looked bewildered but dutifully followed him to the cash desk.

Chris moved off the ladder to be met by a phalanx of protesters. Bland made his way quickly towards the phone on the other side of the room, out of earshot of the irate customers, and called the cash desk.

'Hello, it's Colin. There's a young dark-haired guy, possibly Greek, about to cash in. He's with a good-looking bird poured into a green dress. Take a note of what they're cashing in and any comments they make. Try to get him to take a cheque. I'm on the bleeper.'

Bland could see the commotion around the table had died down although Chris was still trying to get free from one of the regulars. He dialled the table and the boxman answered.

'Colin here, what's the damage?'

'We're about twenty-five grand down. We were winning eight grand before she took the dice.' The boxman sounded dispirited. 'Hold on, Chris's here.'

His superior came on the line. 'I'm going up to see if they've got anything on tape. See if you can delay them, and any of the others who're cashing out.' He sounded worried.

Bland dialled the cash desk again, 'What's the score with the Bubble at the desk?'

'Looks like twelve thousand four hundred, plus the smash the lady has.' The second cashier spoke quietly. From where Bland stood, he could see the cashier was watching his colleague count the player's chips.

'We wouldn't be too worried if Keith takes all night to cash him in,' suggested Bland.

'Oh, right. I'll tell him,' the cashier mumbled.

Russell had a quick look at the dice before going to the security-room, but didn't expect to find anything.

'You think there was something wrong with the roll?' the boxman asked, concerned by his manager's demeanour. 'I've already checked the dice. They seem kosher.'

'Yeah, of course. They are now,' Chris grunted laconically as he left to go upstairs.

The dice manager requested entry and stepped into the flickering gloom of Ventura's camera control centre.

'Sorry to wake you all,' Chris said dryly, provoking retaliatory comments from the three seated operatives. One of them, to his dismay, was Sid Walker, the Chief of Security.

'I'd like to see what recordings you've got of the dice game.'

'Yeah we'd a feeling somethin' iffy was going on,' Walker said with a hint of satisfaction.

Chris smiled to himself, the possibility of them seeing anything suspicious was slight, even if they'd been watching. The C.C.T.V. system had only recently been installed. The camera trained on reception had proved to be an asset in visitor identification but the obtrusive cameras placed on each gaming floor on a trial basis had yet to convince casino professionals that they would offer much more to the security of the casino. Then there was the problem of the surveillance team. All of them, like Walker himself, had been ex-policemen. None of them had much knowledge of the games nor the inclination to learn.

Russell instructed the operator to wind and rewind until he found the parts he thought might give him what he wanted. He ignored the inane comments and questions from Walker and his staff and studied the grainy black and white images closely, trying to piece together the sequence of events. He stifled the urge to curse out loud as some of what he suspected became evident, if not conclusive. Hoping to avoid a blundering investigation by the man the staff called 'Sid the Super Sleuth', he left the room quickly.

Walker called after him. 'Here, what's going on?'

'Don't worry, I've got to check something, I'll let you know!' Chris shouted.

The floor manager picked up the phone in response to his bleeper.

'Hello Colin, it's Chris. Is the Bubble still in the building?'

'He's on his way to the door now. Have you seen something?' asked Bland urgently.

'It's not terribly clear but I think he switched the dice twice. But can we stop him? What if we can't find them on him, where do we stand?' Russell asked with frustration.

Bland paused to think, then after a few seconds: 'In the fucking shit, I should think. Fucking bastards!' And slammed down the phone.

The close of the dice table at the end of the night was normally done at great speed. The dice crew seemed to have a disproportionate amount of ladies' men and drinkers within its ranks, but tonight the all-night boozer and birds would wait until after the post mortem. The entire team stood round the table.

'You all know we've been turned over,' Bland glared at them.

'Well, we don't exactly *know* that,' countered the boxman.

'Oh yes, now we fuckin' do!' Chris called out. 'Do you want the full picture?' He nodded to Bland.

'The Bubble's name's Andreas Scolarius and the bird, Sandra Prescott. The third member was Dennis Prescott, her brother. We now know they pulled the same stroke in Manchester last week!'

'We've looked at the tape. Not the clearest picture you'll ever see, but some things are obvious.' Bland let Chris Russell carry on.

'He pretended to show her how to throw the dice and you...' he stabbed his finger at them '... let him pick up the fucking dice. That's when he probably switched. You didn't check the dice after he touched them. Did you?' He stared at the boxman. 'Why? I'll tell you why! Because you were too fucking busy ogling her tits. When he touched them the second time we checked, but then it was too fucking late. He'd switched them back!'

'If you... er... I mean, if you suspected them, couldn't the security have stopped them on the way out?' a dealer ventured.

'Yeah, we would've looked good then, wouldn't we?' Bland's sarcasm silenced him. 'Pull 'em up at the door, and without proof search them, to find nothing. Because he would've already passed them to her brother, who we didn't even know was with them then. He would've screamed for a lawyer and we would've been in the shit!' His tone conveyed the impotent rage he felt.

The senior members of the crew needed no further convincing that the scam had taken place. The action had been smooth. But they knew if procedures had been followed it would have failed. Russell knew that even the most apathetic gaming personnel felt personally violated when a cheat pulled a stroke on them. There was no need to press the point further. However, Bland and he were duty bound to give an official warning to those who had failed to carry out procedures.

'The worst about this now is that Super Sleuth Walker and his wonder team, who didn't see a fuckin' thing, will make a report upstairs and we'll all be dragged into an investigation!' Chris seethed as he contemplated the probable outcome.

The internal post mortem over, everyone skulked off to await reaction from other quarters.

The personnel officer fumbled with a bunch of keys, opened the door quickly and stretched across her desk to grab the ringing phone.

'Marta Woods! Oh, hello Morg,' she answered the baritone drawl of the Chairman.

'Yes, well okay. I'll see what I can do.' She frowned and replaced the receiver.

It was unusual these days to have Trist ask her to invite a girl to one of his parties. Up until six months before she had been providing party lists and selecting girls to invite, but there was now a regular group who almost always attended. Harry Rye provided any new waitress Chicas, and since Ahmed had become close to the Chairman, new croupier Chicas were likely to be organised by him. She preferred to leave it to them.

Jim Ellis was in the Primero restaurant entertaining several Arab customers when she got there. They were laughing over some joke, evidently about his consuming interest, horses, as Marta approached. When the laughter subsided she diplomatically intervened.

'Yes, love of my life? What can I do for you?' The day manager put an arm around her ample waist and gave a playful squeeze.

Marta smiled tolerantly. She knew he did it with all the women. She also knew that by doing it to everyone this legitimised it as a bit of fun. But the 'squeeze test' could be more searching, last longer or be a prelude to further fun, if Ellis had an interest in the girl. Although she found his lean frame and chiselled features fairly attractive, Marta didn't want to be one of 'Jim's Chicas'. Nevertheless, her pride took a slight blow when he released her immediately.

'Trist is having one of his "happenings" upstairs on Friday and would like you to let a couple of the girls off early, including Penny,' Marta said quietly.

'That's all very well, but if Talal's here? He's got a thing about her at the moment.' Ellis was obviously irritated by the request. 'If she goes early he's bound to ask me why. I could lose him off the table. Does Trist want to lose money to have her at his party?' he asked rhetorically, knowing Marta wouldn't answer.

'How serious is the relationship?' Marta asked.

'For us, it's at the best stage. He hasn't succeeded in getting into her knickers yet. His old man's been in London recently so he's behaving himself. But he's got the hots for her, and when father's gone, he'll be workin' at it – as will Ahmed of course.'

'Of course,' added Marta, frowning.

'When he finally gives her one, we can only hope she's a good screw to keep his interest alive,' the manager smiled.

'If it's okay with you, I'll speak to Penny about the party, see if she wants to go, then we'll think about the Talal problem?' asked Marta.

'Go ahead. She'll go, I'm sure - she's got stars in her eyes that one.' Ellis turned back to his Arab customers.

Penny was on the roulette table. Marta watched as she posed coquettishly while waiting for the ball to drop in the winning number. Several custom-ers vied for her attention. *She's on stage*, Marta thought, *I'll bet never before in her short sheltered life has she had such attention.* Rather than wait, Marta asked the Pit Boss to inform Penny to call in to her office on her next break.

'You wanted to see me?' Penny, popped her head round the office door.

'Yes, Penny. Come in, sit down. How are you?' Marta put down her pen.

'I'm fine, thanks,' Penny said nervously, wondering why she'd been sent for.

'Morgan Trist, our Chairman, is having a party for some friends upstairs in a couple of days and would like a few Chicas to attend. He asked if you would like to go?' Marta tried to sound casual.

'Really! Why did he invite me? Does he even know me?' Penny breathed, her eyes widening with surprise.

'Of course, he knows every girl in here. Remember, he visited the train-ing school. He's very impressed with you, thinks you're just the image we're looking for in a Chica,' Marta assured her.

'Really? That's great. When is it, what do I wear? What do I do? I don't even—'

Marta cut her off.

'It's Friday evening. Wear the Chica uniform. Be yourself, mingle and enjoy the party, that's all.'

Marta could have gone into more detail about the purpose of Trist's parties and what was expected of Chicas, but the girl would have to learn for herself. She'd have to choose, as others had done before, whether she wanted to be one of Morg's girls or not. If she did, she'd get certain priv-ileges and make a bit more money. If she didn't, she'd take her chances with the other girls who'd refused. She wouldn't be sacked, but could find promotions blocked, get no scheduling preferences and might even be transferred to another shift. Her position was protected at the moment by Talal's interest. Marta was curious to know just how interested Penny was in the young Arab prince.

'Seems you have a friend in Prince Talal,' Marta probed.

'Oh, he's very nice. So handsome. I really like him, but I know I can't go out with him.' She sounded disappointed. 'Except when it's official, like the concert Ahmed arranged.'

'You went officially? Who gave permission?' Marta was curious.

'Jim Ellis, my Floor Manager. That's okay, isn't it?' Penny looked worried.

'If it was okay'd by Jim then I suppose it's okay. Did you talk to anyone else about it?'

'Well, apart from Ahmed who organised it, only Pat Monaghan. He wasn't so happy, but I think he's maybe a little bit jealous. Or maybe he's just worried about me. You know, we're friends from the training school. Anyway, I had a really nice evening, the Prince was a perfect gentleman, had his driver take me straight home after the party.'

'Better not mention Friday's party to Talal. He might get jealous.'

'Oh no. Do you really think so?' Penny giggled.

Maybe I shouldn't have said that, thought Marta as the girl closed the door behind her. *She likes the idea of 'her Prince' being jealous. Ellis was right, she's got stars in her eyes.*

Chapter Eight

Ahmed lurched through the door of the Primero and made his way to the VIP gaming area. Even from the far end of the room, he was instantly recognisable by his walk. There were plenty of theories and rumours about how he had acquired the limp: an affliction from birth, a disease in his infancy, the result of a beating by the police after being caught stealing, and even a story that he had been maimed by his impoverished mother to assist her begging on the streets of Port Said. The truth was, no one knew. No one had ever openly asked him and he had never volunteered the information. The mere sight of him hobbling towards the gaming tables was, for some managers and supervisors, the darkest part of the day. No one actually liked him. Some thought him amusing, to a few he was useful, most merely tolerated him. Ironically for someone who addressed almost everyone as 'my friend', he had no actual friends, only contacts, customers, suppliers and agents.

His profession could be said to be marketing and public relations. He sourced potential customers among oil-rich Arabs, researched their needs and endeavoured to provide products and services that would satisfy them. His research invariably pointed to a demand for alcohol, drugs, sex and gambling. As most of his customers came from Muslim countries with strict moral and religious laws, the supply of these things had to be done in virtual secrecy. This factor worked greatly to his advantage as it encouraged customer loyalty in those who had already partaken of his services. The Ventura could have been created for Ahmed. It provided almost everything he needed for the promotion of his business, including privacy. His special 'friend' Morgan Trist valued his work.

The Chairman, himself an appreciative user of mind-altering substances and member of the sexual liberation movement, was well aware of the marketing value of offering incentives of this type. Unfortunately, by necessity, he had to adhere to troublesome legislation prohibiting the provision of these services lest the casino licence be jeopardised. Ahmed, under no such constraints, could act as marketing manager by proxy.

This tacit agreement permitted him full use of the club as a reception and showroom. New clients could be won, while established ones were nurtured in a gambling environment fully staffed by desirable young ladies. The apartments upstairs could be used for small parties, but if more exotic tastes were to be catered for, Ahmed would arrange for a suite at a nearby hotel. If even more discretion was necessary there were always 'safe' houses available. On occasion, when clients were particularly important to Ventura, Trist would participate and even house the party at one of his own private establishments. Whether or not Trist participated, Ahmed could always call on the assistance of Harry Rye to provide raw materials if his own sources were unavailable.

The Chicas who worked at reception or on the catering side could normally be invited. Ahmed tried to steer his clients clear of unwilling girls. Nevertheless, from time to time, an important client would take a fancy to a girl who was unco-operative and this was an irritation and embarrassment. If this happened too often, Ahmed would have Rye remove the girl, at the least from the VIP floor. Naturally, gamblers often became attracted to croupier girls and this could present a problem. The day-manager Ellis would assist with anything that would increase his popularity with the punters. At night on the Terraza, Nidditch could be relied on not to stand in the way of approaches to the girls and though some individual pit bosses on those floors discouraged Chicas from fraternising with clients, they were without any real authority.

His main problem was Draper and his managers on Primero VIP Salon and the Playa at night, who continuously obstructed his promotional activity by their adherence to rigid procedures. Ahmed complained frequently to Trist. But angered as he was by this, the Chairman could not remove a manager for failing to assist in the procurement of girls; other reasons had to be found. Through Pellzer, he had warned Bollard of the high-roller's complaints of the poor service and rudeness of night staff in the VIP Salon. He was ordered to give warning to those managers concerned.

Although as yet unable to rid himself of Draper, Ahmed would stealthily campaign to have a favourite girl moved to day operations as he had done with Penny. But many clients wished to play at night on the high-stake VIP tables where they could most display their wealth, so he could not have all the most desirable girls removed from that shift.

Lowe watched the 'little pimp', as Draper called him, shuffle up to the tables.

'Hello my friends! How's it gon, Lowesy, whit's new?' Ahmed's almost perfect Glaswegian accent provoked an attack of the giggles from the Chicas working on the nearby roulette tables, even a reluctant smile from the young Scotsman. A talent for humorous mimicry was only one of the weapons Ahmed could call on to disarm critics. It was said his days spent begging, or peddling whatever he could to British Commonwealth and American servicemen in the Suez ports, had honed survival skills on which he could now capitalise.

But Lowe's smile faded quickly as he watched Ahmed move between tables, offering salutations to those players he considered important. The pattern was usually the same and had been described to Lowe by another Arab-speaking customer. At each game, he greeted the Chica in English with exaggerated courtesy, while in Arabic he muttered a salacious remark about her, for the amusement of the Middle Eastern clients grouped around the table.

Lowe, looking on with distaste as Ahmed performed his ritual, at that moment was joined by Bland.

'Okay, feeding time. Everything going well down here?'

'Everythin' was going well until this cunt came on the scene,' Lowe grunted. 'He's already winding up Al Khazari, saying that he's losing because Rita's dealing too fast.'

'Of course, because he doesn't want her on this table. She's not one of his girls.' Bland watched for a moment. 'Anything else?'

Lowe brought him up to date on the general situation on the floor, then went off for a welcome break.

'Manager please!' the balding Arab on the roulette cried out. 'Change this girl, she is very disrespectful. Many times I ask her to give me time when I place my bets.'

'Don't worry, Mr Al Khazari, another girl will be down shortly.' Bland glanced at the Inspector and Chica, who looked frustrated, and muttered, 'Relax, keep your cool.'

'He was losing, but was good as gold until that slimy bastard Ahmed came,' the Inspector simmered.

'I know, but keep it cool. Don't give them any ammunition,' Bland advised quietly.

The policy on changing croupiers had been discussed and decided, in favour of a system of rotation. Table staff would normally work a maximum of one hour on the table, followed by a twenty-minute break. It was agreed that croupiers shouldn't be changed either on the whim of players or managers. A sensible policy, as any attempt to staff the tables based on the superstitions of players would inevitably end in chaos. No two players would agree, as fortunes varied from coup to coup. Managers would be put in the unenviable position of discerning who had the greater right to decide, a situation guaranteed to cause conflict. It was also recognised that some gaming executives were plagued with the curse of superstition and, believing croupiers to be unlucky, would change them in the mistaken belief that this would improve results - a policy likewise guaranteed to upset gamblers. Senior pit staff did on occasion switch dealers but not because of a player's result. The girls were young and dealing with volatile gamblers could be stressful, even without the problems of broken romances and menstrual cycles.

Bland's immediate problem was solved as staff coming off their rest period streamed on to floor to be allocated their positions. He took the opportunity to send Laura, an experienced Chica, to the table Al Khazari was playing. Certain girls had learned to use their sexuality to charm and disarm troublesome customers; she was one of them. Used to total obedience from women at home, some Arab players seemed to find the experience of being scolded by beautiful girls for minor breaches of house rules a turn-on. It depended on how it was done and of course by whom. Laura was more than equal to the task.

The punto banco game seemed to attract an eclectic mix of players, but tonight it had surpassed its usual quota. Bland was amused when he considered the respective backgrounds of those seated round the oval table. There was young Prince Al Jahalled, dressed in a black velvet suit and white silk shirt open almost to the waist. The gold medallion round his neck was probably worth more than the entire chip bank on the table.

Next to him Mr Banks-Forbes, a retired headmaster of one of England's most famous public schools, fidgeted and fretted. He would soon be expounding his own theory of probability, that after three bancos it would be a punto - an assertion not only un-scholarly but which flew in the face of his own nightly experiences.

Mrs Azzi was of unknown origin, certainly Middle Eastern, with a French passport. Possibly Lebanese, definitely not Muslim. Not for her the chador, more the Chanel. Her collection of diamond rings was limited only by the number of fingers and the length of them. In spite of her undoubted wealth, she was known to cheat for paltry amounts when luck ran against her.

The shoe was now being passed to Li Kim, a restaurateur originally from Kowloon. He came every night accompanied by two young Chinese girls. Each girl's demeanour seemed to match one of only two moods that Kim had ever displayed. They were therefore christened Glee and Glum by the gaming staff. During his more gleeful moments, when the chips were accumulating in front of him, he would cordially and noisily invite the entire floor staff to free lobster at his restaurant in Soho.

'Flee lobsiter!' had by now become a catch-phrase at Ventura, used in all situations where it was felt some reward was due. 'No flee lobsiter' meant the contrary. Lobster was at this moment not on offer because Kim was losing. One man who was winning, Mr Bin Assaid, a Gulf Arab only recently arrived in London, was being assiduously courted by Ahmed.

'This gentleman is my very good friend. Please see he is given the very best of treatment!' Ahmed commanded Bland and his staff across the green baize, before moving to talk to another client by the cash-desk.

The statement was of course made for effect, to impress his new client. Accustomed as the floor manager was to this kind of behaviour, it nevertheless annoyed him. He'd already recognised a valued customer, without intervention by the detested Ahmed.

Li Kim relinquished the deal and Bin Assaid bet three thousand pounds in chips on Banco and stretched to take the shoe. As he prepared to draw the cards, Bland moved across to the blackjack in answer to signal from that table's inspector. He was halfway across the floor when a dispute erupted on the table he'd just left.

'No, no! What is this?' Bin Assaid stood up in protest. The Inspector moved quickly to explain and reassure him that everything was in order and the player appeared to accept the explanation. Bland resumed his short trip to the blackjack table, but noted the ominous return of Ahmed to the side of the player.

A few moments later there was another explosion of sound.

'No! This was wrong!' Bin Assaid roared. Bland turned to see him grab his chips, before the croupier could remove them as a losing bet. 'That card should not be in the game!'

Bland moved across rapidly and held up his hand to indicate to the table staff that they should leave the matter to him.

'Mr Bin Assiad, please let me explain. In the rules, any card dealt in error but un-revealed must be played as the next card, in the next coup. It's unfortunate that you lost, but you could equally have won.' Bland spoke calmly and diplomatically as he could.

The player still grasped the chips but showed signs of softening on the point, particularly as his fellow player Mrs Azzi seemed to be nodding in affirmation that this was in fact the rule.

'You should explain this before!' protested Ahmed. 'This is the management's fault, you don't clarify rules,' he added, to the obvious satisfaction of Bin Assaid.

Lowe, returning to the floor after his meal-break, could see Bland was enraged by this interference. 'Sorry, the bet was a losing bet, you must return the chips!' he said, more firmly than he intended.

Ahmed responded in Arabic and after a brief pause the player threw the chips across the table in anger. 'You think I need this small money? You think I should be insulted by people like you, for small money? You will see what I will do!' he shouted as he stomped off towards the exit.

'Now you lose players and make trouble for yourself,' smirked Ahmed with undisguised satisfaction, hobbling off in pursuit of his new client.

Lowe contemplated kicking his legs from under him and was sure Bland was having similar thoughts; instead they stood, silently fuming.

Mrs Azzi broke the silence. 'Some people are bad losers.'

Chapter Nine

'Well if it isn't me darlin' Penny!' Pat exclaimed as she exited the lift. He stepped back and signalled the others to continue down without him. 'I haven't seen you for ages.'

'No, now I'm on days and you nights.' She inclined her head in a sympathetic gesture and patted his lapel. 'We must arrange something, when you have a night off.'

'But I can't wait for you outside with a limo,' he smiled mischievously.

'Oh Pat! I told you that was an official thing!' She gave him a playful punch.

'Just joking. How was it anyway, a good night?'

'Lovely. Mansur was so very nice…'

'Mansur?'

'Prince Mansur Talal, you met him with me and Ahmed, remember?'

'Yes, of course. I didn't recognise the name, I only know him as Prince Talal. Anyway, when's your next big night?'

'Pat, I think you're envious,' she said in a soft scolding voice. 'Actually, you will be, when you hear this. I've just been invited to the Chairman's party tomorrow night. Apparently, from time to time he invites some staff to celebrate. What d'you think of that?'

'Jesus, so what chance you'll come down the pub with poor Pat, you're already a big star!'

'Silly, I'm looking forward to our night just as much. So don't forget!' She gave him another playful punch.

'Right, I'd better get to work, earn some money!' He made his way downstairs, pausing to return her goodbye wave.

In keeping with guidelines, given by Draper and Mayfield, Pat checked at reception what members had entered that day. The reception procedures, although complying with the legal requirements, were imperfect from an operational standpoint because no one logged those who had since left. For this he had to rely on the verbal reports from the staff who were going off-duty; again not always accurate.

Draper also advised that when coming on duty he should quickly tour the entire premises, take note of important members present, and solicit from shift managers or pit bosses information on recent disputes, complaints or possible future points of conflict.

He'd started on the Terraza, moved down through the Playa and now approached Lowe on Primero. 'Evening. I can see it's a bit quiet down here.'

'Hello Pat. Yes, a slow start, nobody here of great importance. Talal played on dayshift but left when Penny went off-duty. Meeting her outside, I suppose.'

'Ah, I hope not. That's against the code, she'd be in trouble.' Even as he said it, he thought of her use of the Prince's first name.

'While Talal's doin' money I'm sure nobody upstairs gives a fuck about codes for Chicas. They're happy for Ahmed tae set Penny up for him, I'm sure Ellis would even help.' Ian's face contorted with distaste. 'It's like procedures for credit and other laws; they're forgotten when it suits them.'

'B'Jesus! Everything's so complicated at Ventura.' Pat shook his head and wondered again what he'd taken on. 'Actually, I was just talking to Penny, she says she's been invited to Trist's reception on Friday night.'

'Reception! That's a polite term. I'm told it's what he calls "a happening". A party for his mates and his favourite Chicas, those willing tae come across. If she disnae respond it'll be her last invite.'

Pat wondered if Lowe was being cynical. It must have shown on his face.

'If you don't believe me,' said Lowe, 'ask some of the birds who've re-fused, like Sally or your girl on reception, Elena. They're unpopular and knocked back on promotion because they wouldn't perform for Trist or his cronies.'

'But who's in on this? I know Draper isn't. And Bollard and Mayfield, they don't seem the type to approve of soliciting girls?'

The Pit Boss sighed deeply and looked around. The gaming tables were relatively quiet. He pointed to a coffee table nearby. 'Take a seat. Here, where I can see the tables.' He signalled the waitress Chica and ordered two coffees. 'I think Ralph told you a bit about the set-up and the history here, but not all. Draper, Brand, myself and some of the other guys on nights in Primero and Playa are always fighting against this kind of thing. Ralph's always complaining to Bollard, who's a good guy, but was a surprise choice for Casino Manager at the time and knows he won't be in the job long if he upsets Trist or his lackeys. Mayfield lives in his own world, nobody's sure if he really doesn't know what's happening, or just blanks it out.'

'Jesus, is nothing what it seems in Ventura? People saying one thing while doing another. Even my job's unclear. I'm still being told gamblers come for two reasons - they've got the gambling bug or they like the Chicas. If that's the case, what difference does it make what I do?'

'It's a complicated question, Pat. Obviously some are hooked on gam-bling and are attracted by the girls. Arab punters, for sure, don't see these things in their own countries.' The Pit Boss paused to ponder the question again. 'But not all. Many go home for long periods when they don't gamble at all. A lot also play in other clubs that don't have Chicas or Bunny girls. Ralph told me an Arab professor he knows said one of the reasons they gamble and spend so much is tae win status. Being unsophisticated and uneducated, they have an inferiority complex when they come to Western countries. He says they think that the more money they're seen spendin' or losin', without caring, the more respect they'll get.'

'So, the more they think you respect them, the more comfortable they'll be and the more often they'll come?' Monaghan probed.

'Except if they're too comfortable they might come more often but not feel the need tae spend so much.' Ian laughed at the irony. 'Of course there are some that play a lot on tables tae impress certain girls they want tae screw. Talal perhaps, who's doin' bundles on Penny's table recently.'

Pat shook his head but didn't respond to the latter part of Lowe's observation. He rose and looked about the floor, 'I'd better get around, smile and shake a few hands before people think I'm not making a difference.'

'Okay, but listen, sorry if I've made it sound bad, but it's best to be truthful…'

'Sssh!' Pat put his finger across his lips. 'Don't talk about being truthful, Ian, if somebody hears you, you'll be in trouble!' .

Trist was in an affable mood. The income reports couldn't be better. He opened another folder containing press clippings from the most recent editions of national and local newspapers, and magazines. The coverage was positive.

His secretary announced the arrival of Ahmed. The little Arab shuffled in. 'My friend, Morgan, sorry to disturb you, but I think I should keep you informed about everything.'

'Hey! I was wondering when you'd come around, I was beginning to think I'd lost you to Playboy,' Trist grinned and poured himself his first drink of the day.

'No, I am happy here with my friend, but I have some disturbing news,' the small man frowned theatrically.

'Hey, I was having a good day. You gonna spoil it?'

'I'm sorry. But this matter is about the loss of a good customer because of bad management. I have talked of this before, but now it becomes serious!' Ahmed emphasised the word 'serious' with an upturned finger.

Trist sat at his desk and listened with more attention.

'Mohamed Bin Assaid is new player to London and this club. He is very rich man, very fine customer for Ventura. Last night he have dispute on punto banco. This manager Bland did not explain the rules and when the gentleman made a mistake, he shamed him in front of everybody. I try to talk with him, but maybe he will not come back. It's what I talk of before. They have no flexibility, the managers who work at night.' Ahmed threw up his arms in despair.

'Fuck! Who'd you say the manager was - Bland?' Trist took note on his desk pad. 'Okay, I'll investigate. Listen, I'm having a party tonight. Why not bring this punter? Maybe we can get him laid to cheer him up?'

'I see if he will come, but please, do something about these managers and their ways,' Ahmed warned as he limped from the room.

Trist banged his empty glass on the table and reached for the phone. 'Dan, I'm having reports again about those goddam managers on night duty!' Trist roared down the line when Pellzer answered. 'This time Bland. He came in heavy with some raghead called Bin Ass or something on punto. Look into this and get back to me!'

Pellzer conveyed the message with the same urgency to Bollard, having first asked security in the camera room to send him anything they had on the incident. He knew Frank's first act would be to look for a way to limit the damage to himself.

For Sid Walker a double request from top management for film-footage meant only one thing - something 'iffy' had happened on that table. Bollard's requests for recordings were normally prompted by a floor manager or security department report. Like the recent dice table incident. Bollard had asked to see the tape only after his security team reported that the dice manager had viewed something suspicious. As far as Walker knew, this matter had been taken no further. *If I had my way*, he thought, *I'd have all these arrogant floor managers on the carpet.*

But in this instance Walker had a problem. Although they'd had a camera focused on the punto table, the crew had been changing tapes at that moment. They'd caught only the end sequence when Bin Assaid left the table apparently looking angry, but they'd paid little attention; clients often stormed off in disgust after having lost.

What a pain! On the one occasion when Pellzer had asked him for a report, he didn't have the facts, nor a recording of the dispute. He couldn't go to Pellzer empty handed. He'd have to see what he could glean from Bollard.

*

'Sidney, that was uncharacteristically quick. I only asked for the report a few minutes ago.' Bollard looked up as the securityman entered. Although, in Walker's opinion, he wasn't quite as arrogant as some of his managers, Bollard still liked to get a dig in about the security department.

'No, I don't have it yet. The lads are looking through the tape to prepare the report,' he lied. 'I came about the dice scam. How's that proceeding?'

'Oh yes, that.' Bollard sounded defensive. 'Seems there was a bit of a fuck up. We'll take the matter up at the next management meeting.'

'And now another fuck up on punto!' Sid now felt more confident.

'No, this is altogether different. This was a dispute which may or may not have been handled diplomatically. Bland, who was in charge, insists we were technically correct. Let's see what the tape and the reports tell us.'

'But you already have reports on the incident?' Walker asked.

'Only a brief pit report.' Bollard pointed to the sheet on his desk, 'I've requested a fuller explanation.'

'Yes, this is the one I've seen,' Walker lied and, picking up the paper nonchalantly, swiftly scanned the details. 'Yes, not much here.' He threw it down and sauntered to the door. 'Anyway, don't forget to give us full details of the dice thing, to prevent future fuck-ups.'

Walker went straight to Pellzer's office.

'Sid, what's happening with this tape?' Pellzer demanded as Walker entered.

'Sorry, we didn't pay full attention to this dispute because we're still following up on the more serious matter of cheating on the dice table,' answered Walker in a grave tone. 'Damaging as these disputes are, I believe cheating on tables could have worse repercussions. Our licence could even be affected.'

'Goddam it! What's this about?' asked a startled Pellzer.

'Well, we know we were cheated, but at this stage we can't be sure if there was staff complicity or not. But we'll get to the bottom of it.'

He proceeded to brief Pellzer on the incident, embellishing parts that couldn't be verified by recordings. He left the office smiling, confident he'd deflected criticism away from his department to the people who truly deserved censure - the smug gaming managers. They'd learn they couldn't mess with an old pro.

Pellzer now found himself having to give Trist a report not only on the punto banco dispute but the dice fiasco which, as Walker said, could have more serious consequences.

He was surprised by the Chairman's reaction. He'd expected a stream of profanities at the incompetence or dishonesty of the dice crew; instead Trist smiled.

'Dan, I think we've got the answer to one staff problem.' Pellzer was puzzled. 'We're continuously being screwed by some managers who think they're a goddam law unto themselves, always ready to quote the Gaming Act when asked to be flexible. This Bland's fucked off one of the best players and will say he was applying the rules. But he can't say that about the dice scam,' Trist said triumphantly. 'He was in charge that night! Call Bollard. Tell him I want this manager's ass!'

Chapter Ten

Penny left the gaming floor and took the staff lift to the Chicas' changing room. It was early evening and only a few girls were there. One of them was Katerina, a Chica who, it was said, had entered for the Miss Great Britain contest. She was certainly beautiful, but Penny felt a little intimidated by her aggressive character; her language was worse than some of the guys' in the pub.

At that moment, while applying mascara, she was complaining about a customer. 'Did you see that wanker at my station with the turban? He's buying the cheapest wine on the list, hardly gave a tip all day and had the fuckin' cheek to chat me up.'

The other two girls nearby laughed.

'Hello darling, going to Morg's do?' Katerina addressed Penny patronisingly.

'Er… yes. You going?' Penny asked tentatively.

'Sure. Me, Lisa and Mia. Wouldn't miss one, would we? It's not just for sitting on, is it?' She shook her bottom and her two friends laughed. Penny smiled self-consciously.

'Is it right? We go like this? In our uniforms?' Penny was conscious that Katerina was eyeing her up.

'Yeh. You're probably overdressed, but don't worry, they'll put that right.'

Penny smiled again, but wasn't sure if the girl was serious or having a joke at her expense. They were about to leave and although she didn't feel any particular affinity with them, she hurried, not wanting to go into the party on her own.

As the lift doors opened, music drifted down the passageway from the penthouse suite. People crowded round the entrance, including Harry Rye, who was supervising the delivery of a large package. Trist, dressed in turquoise shirt, white hipster jeans and a large gold buckled belt, greeted them boisterously

'Hey, here's the rest of my girls!' He extended his arms. In one hand he held a drink and in the other a large cigar. Katerina, Mia and Lisa chorused 'Hi Morg' and wriggled up close to the Chairman. Penny held back shyly.

'Right. Hold it there!' Rye pulled a photographer across to get a shot of 'Morg with his Chicas'. Trist called to Penny to join them. After a couple of flashes of the camera the girls broke away but Trist took Penny's arm.

'Penny, where ya'going? First time you've joined us for one of these little get-togethers, not so?'

'Yes Mr Trist, I've...'

'Hey, none of this Mr Trist, It's Morg. We're all colleagues at this club, we just do different jobs. Didn't they teach you our credo in the school?'

'Oh yes. I'm sorry Mr... er... Morg, I really like the Ventura policies and I'm very happy here.'

'And we're happy such a beautiful and intelligent girl is with us,' he said quietly in her ear. 'Harry, a drink for this young lady. Something special!' he shouted and winked.

Rye scurried off and Trist's attention turned to another newcomer. Penny was momentarily left alone. She took stock of those around her. There were several Chicas mingling with the guests, not all of them in uniform.

Then she recognised someone. Could it be? Could it really be Steven Bates, the star of The Protectors? It was, and Katerina of all people was talking so charmingly to him. No swearing or gesticulating now. Penny almost laughed as she heard her say that she was 'saving up to go back to her studies'.

'There ya go. A Ventura cocktail for our new star!' Morg snatched the long drink from the tray Rye carried and took Penny gently by the arm to lead her across the room through the noisy crowd.

'Penny, I want you to meet some of my friends.'

'*Oh my God,*' she thought, as he led her to a group of people. Two of them were so familiar they needed no introduction. She'd seen them on Top Of The Pops often and owned their latest LP.

'Hey, you guys, meet one of our top Chicas. This is Penny. Penny, Dave and Rick of Aces High.'

Penny could hardly contain her excitement. She'd never been this close to such famous people and they seemed so nice, not at all flashy or boastful. Dave, the lead singer, suggested they might write a song for her and joked that if her surname was Lane it had already been done.

The tinkle of a spoon on glass brought a momentary lowering of noise level. Rye stood by a linen-covered easel and offered the floor to a tall handsome gentleman with greying hair. Penny stared in disbelief. It was actually Tony Salinas, the film star. His familiar drawl filled the room.

'Listen, you guys! Today - although he's been trying to hide it - is Morg's birthday, so a few of us got together to give him a little present. This work has been done by one of the most famous artists of our time! Morg, come up here and pull this cord.'

The crowd cheered and clapped as Morgan moved his way from the back of the room. He grasped the movie star and whispered in his ear.

'Morg says at his age he hasn't got the strength to pull his own cord!' Salinas laughed, as did the assembled audience. 'Maybe one of his Chicas should pull it for him.' This brought further laughter and a few catcalls. 'Penny... Penny come up here and do this!' The star held out his hand to her.

She was momentarily stunned. Almost feverish with excitement, she looked for somewhere to put her still half-full glass but, deciding she needed the drink, gulped it down. Now at the side of the famous film star, she tugged the cord and the sheet fell to an explosion of cheers and camera flashes.

The painting was Impressionist, of Morgan with two Chicas on either side. The applause subsided and Morgan once again called for a cocktail for Penny.

'Penny, have you met Tony Salinas yet?' he asked.

'Hey, Morg, I've never seen anyone so beautiful. Not even in Hollywood!' the actor beamed.

Penny, laughing shyly, wondered what her school friends would think if they could see her now with film and pop stars. Rye came with another drink, as someone produced a guitar for Dave of Aces High. Before she knew it, she was being drafted in with two other Chicas as backing group while he sang. They improvised a dance piece and Penny, normally reticent about public display, found a new confidence. The routine eventually dissolved in a fit of giggles as they got the steps all wrong. Dave called for drinks for his dance troupe. Penny didn't usually drink much, but these tasted so good and she was having such fun.

Harry Rye and two Chicas now wheeled in a giant cake with candles, which Morg tried to blow out without success.

'Hey, I need help here, girls!'

Penny rushed enthusiastically to help, as did several other girls.

'Honey, you enjoying yourself?' Trist slid his arm round Penny's waist.

'Oh yesss!'

'You must have a big piece of my cake. This is a special recipe, isn't it, Harry?' Trist winked at Rye.

'This is *really* special cake. One piece of this, another cocktail and you'll be flying!' Harry confided, giving her a large slice and another drink.

'I'm already flying!' she giggled.

At that point Ahmed entered, to a chorus of greetings, with Pellzer and an Arab whom he immediately introduced to Trist. During a brief exchange between the men, none of which Penny understood, she interrupted to greet Ahmed effusively. Ahmed broke off to kiss her hand with his usual flamboyance.

'I am sorry my sweet. We are rude talking of business in front of a beautiful lady. How are you, my dear? Having a good time I see.'

'Ahmed, I'm having a great time. Dance with me!' she demanded exuberantly, swaying from side to side.

'I'm afraid I have no skill for dancing,' he said a little coldly. She didn't notice his annoyance as Tony Salinas swept her off to do a twist.

Ahmed, seeing Trist was well into the party mood, postponed talk of business and grabbed a passing Chica. 'Hello, my darling. Please, meet my friend Mr Bin Assaid!'

Penny was drifting weightlessly and sounds were passing into the distance. She was just aware Morg and Tony were with her. Her legs wobbled a little, but it was a warm, carefree feeling. Morg was being so nice, so affection-ate. She could feel him gently massaging her back as he held her. Tony was whispering something she couldn't quite understand. Now the music seemed to be fading . She was being helped upstairs. Someone in a room who had no clothes on swore; was it Katerina? Then it was quiet again. She was now lying on a bed and giggled a little. It felt good. It felt good all over. The stroking started, shivery feelings inside her stomach. She felt her legs being lifted. There was a strange sensation, a quivering and now a weight on her body. She somehow felt pinned down, her body was jolted. Something was happening, something uncomfortable. She was being lifted again, felt pain inside her and then she was choking on something. She tried to strug-gle, to cry out, to scream- stop!- but had no power. Panic gripped her, the pain intensified before dizziness washed over her.

Chapter Eleven

The toilet was only several feet from the bed but she didn't manage to get there. She clasped her mouth quickly but couldn't stop the vomit blasting through her lips and fingers and gushing out of her nostrils. The attempt to resist the evacuation seemed to cause even more violent retching, which almost burst her eardrums and had her eyes bulging from their sockets. The extreme nausea and throbbing headache gave her an immediate crisis on which to focus and diverted her, temporarily at least, from the awful truth of what had happened. She knelt for some time with her head over the toilet bowl, her hands gripping the rim. Then, trembling, she hauled herself back to the bed and, overcome with weakness, fell asleep.

Marta Woods took the call; it was Rye.

'Listen, see if you can do something about that croupier Chica, Penny. She got pissed, she's in a bit of a state. We put her in apartment ten to sleep it off.'

I should've guessed, thought Marta, as she made her way to the apartment, *if anyone was going to be silly, it would be her.*

The smell when she opened the door almost knocked her back. A stream of vomit trailed from the bed to the toilet and Penny Irwin lay sprawled across the mattress. There was no way she was going anywhere for a few hours. Marta scribbled a message, telling her to ring when she woke, and left her where she lay.

Three hours later, Marta took another look in the apartment. She found the girl crouched on the floor by the bed, weeping uncontrollably.

'Penny, listen. What's wrong?'

Penny didn't respond. Marta grabbed a pillow to prop her up against the bedside table.

'Is there someone I can call to help you?

Penny's only response was a shaking of her head. Marta draped a blanket over her naked shoulders. She was now silent but still clutched to her face a sheet saturated with tears and vomit. Marta tried to prise it from her grip.

'Did something happen at the party?'

This question seemed to provoke a return to convulsive sobbing.

Marta sat on the edge of the bed. It was clear this was no ordinary case of a girl feeling sorry for herself after too many drinks. This was something else. Deep down, Marta already knew what had happened. She would've preferred not to know but here she was, the supposed Personnel Officer with an employee in crisis. What was she to do? Though she subconsciously knew the truth, she also knew what her bosses would expect of her - to resolve this with the minimum of noise or fuss and ensure no embarrassment or scandal would endanger the good name of the club and the licence.

Although dreading what his response would be, she left the girl momentarily to go to the apartment next door to phone Rye. She tried to sound calm when he answered.

'Harry, I'm having a serious problem here. What happened to this girl?'

'Whaddaya mean, what happened? I told ya, the stupid girl got smashed, whored around, now she's sick and sorry!' Rye rasped with his customary delivery.

'She's not just sorry. I can't get through to her. She's hysterical!' Marta's voice rose angrily.

'Seems she's not the only one!' Rye replied coldly. 'You'd better get this cleaned up. You're personnel manager. If you can't handle a personnel problem, Morg's not gonna be happy.'

Marta wanted to scream out that it was their mess, but knew where that would lead.

'Well thanks for your help,' she replied sarcastically. 'Bastards!' she shouted as she slammed down the phone.

Righ, calm down, think, she told herself. *First go back next door to see if the bloody girl is pulling herself together.*

Penny had stopped crying, but still held the sheet to her mouth and was staring, as if in a trance. Marta dared not disturb her for fear of provoking another hysterical outburst. Who could help in this situation? she wondered. As far as she knew, the girl had no special friends in the club and no family in London. The only one who seemed to have any rapport with her was Patrick Monaghan. But would Penny Irwin want to discuss her problem with a man or even want to see a man at this moment? Marta could think of no other solution or way to off-load the problem.

She returned next door. Fortunately, Monaghan was in the building. She bleeped him and waited.

A few moments later he responded. 'Hi, Patrick, it's Marta. I'm in apartment nine upstairs, I have a problem you might be able to help me with. Can you come up?

She checked there was no change with Penny, then went out to await Monaghan. When he arrived she held her fingers to her lips and ushered him in to the neighbouring apartment.

'Pat, it's Penny Irwin. She's next door in a bad state. She won't talk to me about it, but I know she got drunk at a party here in the club and had a scene with some guy. Hold on. Let me finish.' Marta stood in front of him. 'She's hysterical and our bosses are worried about her, also the reputation of the club. If she was to make some allegation which she couldn't prove because she was drunk, she'd be shamed, would gain nothing and... well, you know?. Somebody has to calm her down, make her see reason. I don't know of anyone else who's close to her. Should really be a girl, I don't think she's ready to speak to a man. Do you know of anyone? Someone she might trust who can be relied upon not to start a scandal?'

Pat wasn't listening. His only thought was to go to his distressed friend. Marta, now exhausted of ideas, allowed him to brush past her.

Penny was sobbing quietly, her face swollen and streaming with tears. Her hair matted with congealed vomit. The smell in the apartment told of the physical torment she'd gone through.

'Mother o' Jesus! Who the fuck's responsible for this? Penny, Penny, it's alright,' he said quietly and knelt beside her. She immediately grabbed the sheet to her face and began wailing. He wanted to hold her, to comfort her like a baby, but was worried it might be the wrong thing to do. She was naked under the sheet she held to her face; the blanket that Marta Woods had draped round her shoulders had slipped to the floor. He delicately replaced it, covering as much of her as he could without actually touching her. He turned as the door creaked;

'How is she?' Marta Woods peeked round the corner.

'Well, what do you think?' he snapped. 'Okay, okay leave it with me. I'll sort it out. I'll call when we're ready or if we need anything.'

Given the sensitivity of the situation, Marta was uneasy about leaving it entirely in his hands; nevertheless she didn't want to hang around in the corridor.

'Okay, I'll be on my bleeper.'

With a feeling of unease she left the room.

Pat sat down on the floor. 'Penny, you're with a friend now, everything will be alright,' he repeated several times quietly. Although she didn't respond, the weeping subsided a little.

He propped himself against the wall beside her and waited. Every so often, her body would convulse with a sob and he'd repeat some quiet, comforting words, venturing to pat her ever so gently on the shoulder and upper arm.

Hours, or what seemed like hours, went by. At one point she fell asleep, but woke with a shudder some minutes later. He continued his therapy, unsure if it was achieving anything but not knowing of any alternative.

She had been silent for some time. The light had faded. It was evening and Pat was beginning to wonder if he should've called a doctor. Suddenly she stirred.

'Oh Pat, I…I don't know what to do!' she said in a faint tearful voice. He tentatively put his arm round her and cradled her head on his shoulder.

'If you want to talk, I'm listening. If not, it's okay. But I think you should get yourself cleaned up, then we get out of here, get you home.'

There was a long silence, punctuated by several racking sobs then she lifted her head.

'I don't know… where am I?' she asked.

'You're in one of Ventura's apartments. Marta Woods brought you here. You were… er… sick.'

The tears welled up in her eyes once again.

'Please Penny, let's get you cleaned up. Where's your clothes?' he insisted, gently dabbing her tear-stained cheeks. 'Your clothes aren't here. Are they down in your locker?'

She looked blank.

'Come on, sit here in the chair.' He helped her up, steadied her and went to the phone.

Woods wasn't answering her bleeper. Frustrated and irritated, Pat thought hard about who might help. The only person he could think of was Elena on reception. An intelligent girl, she could probably find a discreet way to get Penny's clothes and help him get her home. He looked at his watch, it was just about the time she'd be going on shift. He dialled the Chica-room, praying this was not her night-off.

'Hi, this is Pat Monaghan, I'm at apartment ten. Can you check if Chica Elena is in? If she's not, please call me here. If she is, ask her to call me. Thank you.' He moved back to Penny, who was sitting with her head cupped in her hands. 'Penny, you should try to get a shower,' he urged, but she didn't stir.

The phone rang. It was Elena.

'Elena, please get someone to cover for you and come to apartment ten. I've a problem you could help me with.' He spoke quietly, not wishing to alarm Penny.

Elena seemed puzzled by the request, but agreed. A few moments later the lift doors opened and she appeared in the corridor where Pat was now waiting.

'Thanks, Elena. I have Chica Penny in this room. She's in a bad way. She went to one of Trist's parties last night, got drunk and something happened to her. She's been here all day crying, sick and she's got no clothes. I need someone to get her clothes and help me get her home.'

He realised this brief explanation prompted a dozen questions and the receptionist looked as if she was about to ask them all. Instead, she shook her head in disgust, brushed past Pat into the room where Penny was still sitting in a semi-trance. Elena paused for a few moments, looking at the forlorn figure, then turned to leave the apartment.

'Wait with her. I'll be back as soon as I can!' she ordered Pat in a voice which barely concealed her anger, but then added more softly, 'Don't worry, we'll sort it out.'

Elena arranged for cover on reception. As girls often had problems with periods and other temporary ailments which left them not looking their best, there were always Chicas who could substitute. In any case, she had a feeling there were people in the company who'd be only too happy for her to assist in the departure of Penny from the premises.

In spite of periodic bouts of pilfering, not all girls secured their lockers. Elena hoped Penny was one of them. She wasn't. This meant getting a spare from the personnel department or breaking it open, and both options might necessitate lengthy explanations. She hurried to the personnel office where she found Marta Woods.

'Excuse me, Penny Irwin has asked me to get the spare key to her locker,' she said in a matter-of-fact tone.

Marta Woods looked surprised. 'Wait here a moment,' she said before going to the adjoining office. She picked up the phone.

'What's going on, Pat? I've got Elena Spencer here looking for the key to Penny's locker.'

'Yes, she's helping me. I couldn't find you and I needed someone to get her clothes and things,' Monaghan replied quietly, conscious that anything could trigger Penny's distress.

For Woods, the prospect of Elena Spencer being involved rang alarm bells. The uppity bitch, with her university education and strident views, had ruffled a few feathers among senior managers. She was already thought of as unofficial union delegate because of her readiness to speak out on workers' rights.

'You think it wise to use this girl? She may cause an even bigger problem.'

'Well, do you want to help shower and dress this girl? I can't,' he retorted sharply.

Marta didn't relish the task at all, and much as she feared Elena's participation, the fact was, she was already involved. She returned to the outer office where Elena waited impatiently and reluctantly withdrew the key from her store.

'This is the key to Penny's locker. Before you go, I must tell you that I know about this incident last night and I'm making a full investigation. I don't want you talking about it to anyone, understand?' She held the key, waiting for Elena's agreement. Elena doubted if a full investigation would ever be made, but it wasn't the time to start a discussion. She gave a cursory nod and snatched the key.

Pat was sitting quietly talking to Penny, with only minimum response, when Elena returned to the apartment.

'Pat, this may take some time,' she said, putting the clothes on the bed. 'I'll call you when we're ready to go or if I have a problem.'

He agreed and went downstairs for a welcome drink.

More than an hour later his pager rang. He answered the call. Elena talked hurriedly in hushed tones.

'Hello, Pat, it's me. Penny's in the toilet, but we're just about ready to go. I think it's best we go alone. I'm taking her to my flat. She shouldn't be left alone. I'll call you tomorrow.'

Pat went back to his drink, content in the knowledge that he'd chosen the right person for the job.

Chapter Twelve

Pellzer's demand for a full investigation into the dice incident was obviously provoked by Walker. No doubt fraud had taken place but Bollard had hoped to prepare a balanced report. But to ingratiate himself with his superiors and show the gaming department in a bad light, the Security Chief had put his own slant on events. Normally Trist would by now also be bawling down the phone but in this instance Frank was fortunate because the Chairman rarely surfaced the day after a party. So, having some time to limit the damage, he called a meeting of his managers and pit bosses to establish that the information contained in the report was accurate and complete. He could then decide what measures to introduce to prevent a repercussion, and what disciplinary action to take with staff who had failed in their duties.

All agreed that on the evidence known, the table had been defrauded, but that collusion by members of the crew was unlikely, although certain individuals had been negligent.

Opinions and attitudes were fairly predictable. Nidditch felt some dealers should be sacked for incompetence, Draper felt the individual crew members directly involved should be fined and warned, while Ellis was ambivalent and eager to conclude the meeting. The pit bosses more or less took their lead from their respective managers. Mayfield covered the legal implications, which in effect coincided with Draper's view. In the end it was decided that those who had failed in their duties would be given a written warning and have their bonuses cancelled.

The managers were dispersing when Bollard remembered the punto incident.

'Oh… Ralph, Gordon, Ian, can you wait?' he called out. The three came back to the table. 'This dispute on punto with Bin Assaid, I've read the report. But is there anything else I should know?'

'The first thing to know is that there wouldn't be a problem if that arsehole Ahmed hadn't stirred things up!' Bland blasted off angrily.

'I'll second that,' announced Lowe.

'Forget the politics, I'm talking about the technical aspects of the dispute itself.'

'Frank, please!' Draper gripped the chair-back. 'The fact is, the player drew a card by mistake, it was not revealed, so following procedures, the card was used on the next hand. This is correct. Annoyed as this player may have been, he'd probably have accepted the decision had he not been wound up by that bastard. How much are we going to take from this asshole?'

Bollard could see no fault in the procedure and had no answer to Draper's question.

He sighed. 'Well, I have to satisfy those above that we handled the matter diplomatically.'

'Well haven't they got anything on tape?' asked Bland.

Bollard's body language said it all.

'Why am I not surprised?' Draper said with deep irony. 'The Plods insisted we install this camera system. It's ugly, noisy, but do they get anything from it, and would they even know if they did?'

'Well the theory is that it's a deterrent,' said Bollard. 'But, as you know, they can't tape continuously and you can't always see clearly what's happening. Anyway, without sound recording to know what's being said, which is the important factor in this incident…'

Bollard picked up his papers again.

'With a sound recording of that little bastard we could get him arrested for all sorts of things.' Draper clenched his fist.

Bollard held out the folder, 'I have the dossier on the dice incident and I think you'll both find—'

'Yeah, yeah I know all about that!' cut in Trist. 'The important fact for me is that this guy Bland was the manager in charge!'

'Yes that's correct but—'

'Who was in charge during the punto banco bust up?' Trist interrupted, looking to Pellzer to confirm what he already knew.

Bollard was keen to explain. 'Well there we must—'

'Who was the manager?' shouted Trist

'Well yes, it was Bland, but—'

'Yeah, Bland! One night we get ripped off, the next night because of his inflexibility we lose one of the best clients on punto, both on his watch. I want rid of the guy, *now!*'

From the moment Pellzer had summonsed him to the meeting with the Chairman, Bollard knew it was going to be a difficult, but took comfort from the fact that he was armed with facts. Still, he'd seen Trist like this before and knew that facts were of no interest to him. He looked to Pellzer, but he seemed to be in agreement with the Chairman.

Usually, when confronted by Trist in this mood, Bollard would accept his decision reluctantly and provoke no further argument. But this was different. He was being ordered to dismiss a manager not only for the mistake of others but also for applying the company's own rules. Apart from the unfairness of it, and the unlikelihood of the company winning should it go to industrial tribunal, it could also provoke staff unrest.

'What about the staff who were at fault on the dice?' he asked in frustration.

'Sack 'em all!' replied Trist emphatically, rising from his chair in a gesture that Bollard recognised: the meeting was at an end.

Bollard rose slowly. He wondered if he should leave the reports but knew Trist wouldn't read them. He might even destroy them and some he hadn't yet copied.

Pellzer was already on his way out. Bollard caught up with him in the corridor and thrust the report in front of him. 'Dan, I take it you've read this?'

Pellzer brushed it aside. 'Of course.'

'And you're still in agreement with Morgan's decision?'

'I believe, as he does, that it's an opportunity to weed out a person who's a negative influence.' Pellzer walked on, causing Bollard to scurry after him.

'That may be the case, but unfortunately there are other factors to consider. We can't fire someone without legal grounds. A manager is accountable for the actions of staff, but an industrial tribunal won't see it as fair that he be sacked for their mistakes or for correctly applying company procedure.'

Bollard sensed Pellzer had some doubts. He pressed on with further argument. 'If we sack him it'll go to tribunal. We'll be forced to name punters, meaning possible legal complications, and a report to the Gaming Board. Another thing - I don't think managers will accept this decision. We could have a revolt on our hands.'

Pellzer raised his hands to call a halt to Frank's entreaties. 'Okay. You've made your point. Let me consider where we are and what we can do, I have to talk to Morg about some other matter later.'

'But, Dan, please review all the reports and the recommendations before talking to Morgan. You'll get a full picture of the issues.'

As he made his way to his office, Bollard felt a little bit better, but not much. He wasn't sure if Pellzer fully understood the implications, nor was he confident that even if he did, he could convince Trist.

Elena wasn't sure how she'd managed to get Penny to shower and dress. A mixture of cajoling, comforting, lying and reassuring, and this had to be intensified to coax her out of the building. Pat had arranged for the door to be clear of inquisitive staff for the few seconds it took to exit the club and climb into the waiting taxi. The plan was almost ruined by a chance encounter in the street with Ian Lowe, who was arriving for work. His cheerful greeting causing Penny to falter and begin another bout of weeping. Elena bundled her into the taxi, leaving the bewildered Pit Boss on the pavement.

So far Penny had uttered only a few words; mostly self-pitying, self-recriminating and doom-laden; they did not bring Elena any closer to the truth of what had happened. But she was in no doubt that the girl had been the victim of exploitation. Elena patted Penny's shoulders but didn't press her for information. It was obvious she now wanted to erase the experience from her mind and deny to herself it had ever happened.

Elena knew what would be said - that she'd willingly participated, actively encouraged a physical liaison or, in layman's terms, 'put it about'. She'd been drunk. Her recollection of the events would be questioned. Witnesses to collaborate her story would be difficult to find.

Elena's anger increased the more she thought about the girl's predicament. Part of this anger was directed at herself. She had allowed herself to be seduced by the excitement of it all, the gambling and glitz, the rich and famous customers, the attractive salary. She had no problem with the basic concept of using good-looking people to sell products and services. It was done to market just about everything from soap powder to cars. But she'd felt for some time there was something corrupt at the heart of the Ventura, otherwise how could people like Harry Rye survive and prosper. She'd heard so many stories of girls being pressed to go out with clients, or entertain friends of the Chairman. Then there were girls sacked for losing their looks at the ripe old age of twenty-four, while promotion and bonuses were given to others in favour. She herself had remained at the lowest grade although she was academically more qualified than most girls there and, by Ventura standards, a veteran. No doubt because of her refusal to attend parties upstairs.

Part of Elena's anger was the realisation that in the light of what had happened to Penny, she could no longer delude herself. Very soon she'd have to decide: resign from a job she basically enjoyed and was well paid for, or accept that she had abandoned the principles she once held so dear.

He was sitting in the casino restaurant drinking coffee. At least that's what it looked like, though actually he was on his second large whisky, served obligingly in a cup by a friendly Chica, to enable him to keep up appearances. His mind was in turmoil. What exactly had happened to Penny? Who was responsible and what should he do about it? The party had been at the Chairman's suite, but she'd ended up in that apartment. Who else knew about what had happened?

The one who definitely knew something was Marta Woods, since she had called Pat in the first place. From his brief conversations with her during the height of the crisis, he could tell she wanted the matter dealt with quickly but quietly. For a personnel officer she had shown scant sympathy for a troubled employee. Was this because she considered Penny's trouble self-inflicted, or because it would be bad for the club?

How to find the answers to these questions? Should he even look for them? The key to all of this was Penny herself and what she wanted. He decided to keep quiet until she recovered and only do something if she so wished.

He jumped as a hand slapped on his shoulder

'Hiya Pat, whit's new!' Ian Lowe sat down next to him. 'Your coffee looks a wee bit weak!'

'Oh, hi, Ian, how are you?'

'Fine, I'm having a bite early, I've not eaten all day.' The Pit Boss grabbed the menu with eagerness. 'You look as if you need that beverage.'

Pat grunted agreement.

'A strange thing happened when I was coming to work. I saw Penny making for a taxi with that reception Chica, Elena. When I shouted to her, she got really upset. The other Chica gave me a look and pushed her into the taxi. D'you know what that's all about?'

Pat shrugged. 'Er… no. Females, maybe her period or…' Lowe looked sceptical

and Pat decided he couldn't continue with the deception. As the waitress approached to serve Lowe, he excused himself guiltily.

Pellzer was reviewing the decision to dismiss Bland. The man had to go, but perhaps this wasn't the way . Like Trist, Pellzer had been increasingly concerned by reports that Ventura's premium customers were being lured by competitors. They'd agreed the key was flexibility. All casinos had to comply with a ludicrously restrictive Gaming Act, but why make it more rigid than it already was by enforcing internal procedures to the letter? Foreign customers, who made up the majority of premium players these days, didn't understand this obsession with rules. If people like Draper and

Bland refused to loosen up, they had to be eliminated but with subtlety, to avoid legal complications. As a person with little finesse, Trist was always likely to be influenced by people like Ahmed into taking rash decisions.

'On what legal grounds can a manager be dismissed?' was the question Pellzer now put to Harry Silverman, the company lawyer.

'Well, apart from offences such as stealing or other unacceptable behaviour, there's - *persistent refusal to carry out recognised duties*. It's a rather vague concept that involves a process of issuing warnings prior to dismissal.' As he spoke, the lawyer consulted notes.

'That's lengthy and complicated, there's got to be another way.' Pellzer threw down his pen and rose from his desk.

'Tribunals are likely to consider any other approach as unfair dismissal. Of course you could offer the full amount of compensation but I wouldn't advise this,' said Silverman.

'So are you telling me a manager can just go his own way as far as policy's concerned?' Pellzer now paced up and down the room.

'Well no. But the manager would have to be seen to have made a *repudiatory breach of contract*. In effect, refuse to carry out contractual duties. Go on-strike.'

This gave Pellzer another thought. What would make managers such as Bland and perhaps Draper go on strike? He couldn't tamper with their conditions of employment. It would have to be something which injured their pride or principles without infringing their legal rights. He considered the meetings he'd attended with Draper and Bland and what things provoked them to protest. Most recently, the question of credit -but this was best avoided as it had a legal aspect that might interest the Gaming Board. He remembered they were protective of the staff under their command and resented decisions being taken on operational matters without their participation.

So, provocation could be... a decision taken without their participation or approval which affected their staff; but which the company were legally entitled to do. But what? Bollard, he mused, probably knew better than anyone what that would be. But would he cooperate? He seemed to suffer from that fading British custom of fairplay. *Nevertheless*, thought Pellzer, *if he doesn't help find a solution to please Trist, he knows he'll have one imposed upon him.*

Bollard parked his portly figure in the office chair and waited as his boss read a document.

'Frank.' Pellzer spoke quietly, almost conspiratorially. 'I've given thought to this problem of Bland. I agree it's the wrong tactic.' Bollard looked relieved. 'Unfortunately, I've tried to persuade Morg, but he won't budge,' Pellzer lied. As Frank's head dropped in disappointment, Pellzer's voice sharpened. 'You shouldn't be too worried about a guy whose inflexibility could have an effect on your own future.'

'I'm not worried about him. I'm worried about sacking him without proper justification.' Bollard was shaken by the reference to his own future. 'Apart from legal implications, I'm sure Draper and others won't accept it.'

'Because he's one of their own you mean?'

'Well there's that, but in the present mood the unfair dismissal of any staff might cause unrest. I've already heard that one of the dice staff has approached the General Worker's Union about recognition, something I'm told has been happening in other casinos.'

'One of those involved in the scam?'

Frank answered in the negative.

Already tossing an idea around in his head, this latest intriguing news gave Pellzer more reason to float it. 'Then we should close the dice table. That would give justification for serving redundancy notices to the crew on that table.'

'The staff wouldn't agree with that.' Frank waved his hand dismissively.

'We don't ask them, we just do it!' countered Pellzer emphatically.

Bollard saw he was serious and became worried. 'Managers wouldn't accept such a decision,' he blustered.

'What do you mean they wouldn't accept it? Who wouldn't? And what would they do?' Pellzer laughed.

Bollard wasn't sure. Certainly Draper and Bland would be absolutely opposed, and furious if the decision was taken without consultation. 'I don't know, they might resign or… I don't know,' he finished lamely, confused even by the thought of it.

Pellzer was more than satisfied with this answer. He sat back. 'I think Morgan would accept that you close the dice table rather than sack Bland, because it's a decisive action. It sends a clear message to people like him. In any case, the table result doesn't impact much on profits, no high rollers play that game.'

He stood up and excused himself to go to the toilet, allowing Bollard a few minutes to consider the options.

Bollard's mind was in turmoil. He didn't want to sack Bland but this suggestion wasn't much better; it would also lead to conflict. They could claim the table was being removed for economic reasons and possibly in a legal sense justify redundancies, but who would believe that? *They'll reckon it's because we think the staff are bent, but can't prove it. Is that why Pellzer wants it closed,* Bollard wondered, *does he think that?*

He didn't want to sack a manager unfairly, now he had to make twelve people redundant, some of whom didn't deserve to be out of a job. However, if he didn't do it, they'd probably still be out - and he with them.

He hadn't heard Pellzer return. 'What do you think, Frank, will I talk to Morg about this proposal?'

Frank sighed and gave a non-committal shrug.

Rye was just leaving as Pellzer entered the Chairman's office. Trist was shaking his head and looked frustrated.

'Don't worry, Morg,' said Rye, 'I'll make sure that stupid broad keeps schtum.'

'Somethin' wrong?' Pellzer asked when Rye had gone.

'Nah, it's nothin', a stupid Chica who got laid at the party causin' a scene. Rye got Marta to sort it out and she made a big fuckin' deal of it.'

Pellzer wondered if it was the moment to talk about the dice table. He decided that while Trist was preoccupied with something else, he might be even more willing to let Pellzer handle this situation.

'I'm afraid I've another bit of disturbing news.' Trist listened. 'It seems some of the dice crew, perhaps some involved in the scam, have been campaigning to start a union here.' Pellzer paused for effect, then continued before a tirade drowned out his suggestion. 'As it doesn't create much profit anyway, my plan is to close the dice on economic grounds, make the crew redundant. We can do it legally, and it sends a message to those who fuck with us. It might force Draper and Bland into something stupid like resigning or striking. That'd kill two or more birds with one stone, so I suggest we wait with the dismissal of Bland. What'dya think?'

'Do it, Dan, I want rid of all those assholes!' Trist snarled.

Dan Pellzer lost no time in contacting Bollard to give him the good news.

His headache wasn't as bad as it might have been after consuming almost an entire bottle of whisky before going to bed. Pat had known the alcohol wouldn't offer any solutions, but it offered a temporary suspension of reality. However, he was now obliged to return to that reality.

His immediate task was to find out how Penny was, and how Elena was coping with the responsibility he'd dumped on her. Fortified by coffee and aspirins, he eased himself into the chair by the phone.

'Hello, Pat, where are you, at work?' Elena asked when he greeted her.

'No, at home suffering from an excess of the amber nectar.' His pitiful tone wasn't contrived. 'How's Penny?'

'Well, she's still here, very quiet. I've told her she's free to talk about what happened, but only if she wants. So far, she's saying nothing, except that she won't go back to Ventura. I don't think she knows what she wants. I'm trying to get her to stay here for a few days but I'm not sure she will. I'm scared to leave her on her own. I've taken my two days off to be with her.'

'Should I talk to her?

'It might be worth a try, Pat. I'll fetch her.'

After a few moments he heard Penny's tremulous voice. 'Hello, Pat.'

'Hello m'darlin, how are you?' Pat, tried to sound upbeat and cheerful.

There was a long pause. He feared he'd triggered off another crisis but then she spoke again.

'Thank you, I'll be alright... thank you for helping me... and for Elena, I mean... well, thanks.'

'That's alright, that's what friends are for,' he said, sensing she found it difficult to talk. 'Let me talk to Elena again – you go back and rest.'

Elena returned to the phone.

'I see what you mean, she's obviously still in shock. I appreciate what you're doing, if you need help I'm at work later and any other time I'm at this number…' He read it out, then asked, 'Has Woods or anyone from Ventura called to ask how she is?'

'No way. That bitch will only be concerned about keeping her job. She's covering for someone, probably on instructions from that bastard Trist!' Elena rasped with a venom that took him aback.

'Well, even if that's true, what can we do about it?' he asked.

'Nothing, I suppose, if Penny won't talk about it.'

Pat agreed. There wasn't much more to say. After thanking her again for her kindness, he rang off, agreeing to call the following day.

An hour later he was entering the Ventura. As he passed the front door he saw one of the car-jockeys sweep round the corner in Talal's Bentley. Pat was curious to know if the Arab prince had played any part in the incident. After checking at the PR office for any messages, he made his way to the VIP level.

In the early part of the afternoon the gaming tables on this floor were rarely busy and today was no exception. Only three players, two of them recognisable as medium level players, and another unknown to him, were at the gaming tables. Talal was sitting alone in the restaurant.

'Ah, good afternoon, Prince Talal, how are you today?' Pat greeted him cheerily.

'Pat, I am good, how are you?' The smiling Arab gestured that he should join him.

'Please sit with us, Jim has gone for one minute to ask about something.'

Pat made small-talk while looking for a way to bring up the subject of Penny but the opportunity seemed to have passed as Ellis approached. To complicate matters, Ahmed was now entering the restaurant.

After a cursory greeting to Pat, Ellis addressed Talal. 'She's still sick, I don't know exactly what's wrong with her.'

'Hello, my friends. Is this a Board meeting?' Ahmed gestured with open palms.

'I am asking about Penny. Jim said she is sick.' Talal looked concerned. 'We must send her good wishes for a quick recovery.'

'Allow me to arrange that for you?' offered Ahmed immediately.

Talal agreed, then took up the subject of credit with Ellis, who invited him to look at the account. They both rose to go to the cash desk, leaving Ahmed and Pat at the table.

'I spoke to Penny this morning,' Pat opened when the other two had gone.

'You did? How she is?' Ahmed's tone suggested that he knew something.

'She's not good, in fact she may not come back. I should've told Jim and the Prince when they were asking about her,' he said, hoping to glean from Ahmed what he knew.

The little Arab paused for thought. 'You know, I hear something about the party. I'm not sure who is to blame but she is young girl who did not know to drink or anything. These things happen. We should not talk too much, to spoil her name. Please, let me find out more. But we should not make a big scandal or she will not come back. Such a pity, a nice girl.' He sounded almost genuine in his concern.

Pat had learnt something. By his reaction to Penny's absence, Talal had not been the offender nor had he been at the party. Ahmed had heard something, from his many contacts among the Chicas, maybe even Trist himself. But he hadn't deceived Pat. His concern about keeping the incident quiet was probably for fear that Talal's interest in her would diminish. However, he was right about one thing: at this stage no good would come from idle gossip.

Before moving off to perform their respective duties in public relations, Ahmed and Pat agreed they'd make further but discreet. inquiries.

The Prince was playing roulette but Ellis wrinkled his nose as they approached. 'Your friend's not playing with the same enthusiasm without the lovely Penny being around,' he whispered to Ahmed.

The Arab nodded sullenly.

*

Later that evening, a worried Elena called to tell Pat that, in spite of pleading for her to stay, Penny had left. Since then, Elena had called her flat several times but there was no reply. Neither she nor Pat knew what that meant. Had Penny changed her mind and gone to her parents' house? Was she simply not answering the phone? Or had something else happened? They agreed to try again in the morning and if there was no reply, they would decide on what action to take.

Chapter Thirteen

Bollard had reluctantly agreed to eliminate the dice but wanted to put off the onerous task. He knew Pellzer and Trist would expect him to take it out immediately without giving warning. Traditionally, personnel dismissed from a casino were given no prior notice. To do so was considered a security risk as dealers handled a great deal of money and the temptation to compensate themselves for what they might consider an unjust dismissal might prove too great. In this case the entire crew would be made redundant, so the possibility of collusion to arrange a 'going away present' was higher. Nevertheless, Bollard felt uncomfortable about sacking a senior manager such as Chris Russell without notice. In his opinion Chris had always done a good job and would be unlikely to do anything dishonest. He also felt great unease at taking an arbitrary decision without consulting managers but to do that would be against Pellzer's express wishes.

Bollard therefore requested a meeting with Pellzer and Sid Walker to go over procedure for the closure of the game. This included notifying the employees concerned of the decision, making the statutory redundancy payment, supervising the removal of their personal effects from the locker-room and their exit from the premises. Walker, with uncharacteristic ebullience, confirmed his part in ensuring the dismissed crew would be despatched as quickly as possible.

The Security Chief's dislike of casino personnel was well advertised and was in part a retaliatory response to the scorn directed at himself and his team by many in that department, who viewed the retired policemen as un-knowledgeable Plods. As Draper had so adeptly put it, the root problem was: they hadn't come out of retirement to work at Ventura, they were simply spending part of that retirement at the club. Walker himself passed a substantial part of his time having meals – his figure being a testament to this – and a fair proportion of the remainder investigating suspected clandestine liaisons between male gaming staff and the Chicas. Prohibition of romantic relationships between table staff was common practice in casinos, as they were said to create conditions whereby a couple might collude to defraud the company. The rule was universally ignored by gaming personnel and thought unenforceable by most managers, who preferred staff to be open about relationships so that if necessary, they could be scheduled on different tables. Walker's rigid support for this controversial rule and his constant prying into the social life of employees caused intense resentment.

Knowing this, Bollard wasn't surprised by Walker's attitude, but still found the man's enthusiasm for the task of dismissing staff distasteful.

As Walker made to leave, Bollard tackled Pellzer once again. 'It would be a shame to lose an experienced manager like Russell,' he said, 'especially as he's strong on other games. I suggest we retain him for another department—'

'Excuse me interrupting.' Walker turned back. 'That suggestion's surprising in the circumstances. He was Manager when the scam on the dice took place, and withheld information from me concerning this fraud.'

'You're right, Sid. He has to go.'

Pellzer left no room for argument from Bollard, who inwardly cursed Walker, and himself for not choosing a more opportune moment to make his plea for the manager. He thought ruefully of the appropriateness of the quotation 'the die is cast' and disconsolately made his way back to his office. He hoped not to meet anyone on the way but inevitably ran into Draper and Pat Monaghan on the stairway.

Bollard smiled and attempted to pass quickly, but Draper addressed him directly.

'Frank, what happened to Chica Penny at our esteemed leader's party?' Draper also directed the question to Monaghan.

Bollard, with no idea what he was talking about, waited for the PR man to comment. Monaghan shuffled uneasily as other admin staff passed. Bollard, now curious, ushered both men to his office.

Pat had hoped to avoid discussing the incident but now considered it might be better to say what he knew and limit more speculative accounts. He described the events as he had seen them.

'How long do we close our eyes to the things that go on upstairs?' said Draper with disgust.

'This is a matter for the personnel department to deal with,' Bollard said unconvincingly.

'Come on, Frank!' Draper threw up his arms. 'You know they're Trist's dirty tricks brigade. They're not going to look into what happened to this girl.'

'First, we have to find out what Penny's side of the story is, and what she wants!' Bollard replied, with more conviction.

'For the moment that's difficult,' intervened Pat. 'She left Elena's place and she's not answering her phone. We don't know where she is!'

'That's disturbing. You think in her mental state she'd do something foolish?' asked Bollard.

'I don't know.' Pat ran his fingers through his hair.

Draper looked about to launch into one of his rants, but his pager diverted his attention. After a brief conversation using Bollard's phone, he returned to excuse himself.

'I have to go. We're opening and there's a small problem on the floor. Let me know what you hear about Penny,' he added as he left the office.

Bollard, rose from his chair, and Monaghan took his leave. 'Keep trying to reach her, Pat. I'll make my own investigations. Let's see what we can do.'

When the Irishman had gone, Bollard sat dejectedly at his desk. Things were going from bad to worse. The anger that Draper showed today would be multiplied tomorrow when the managers found the dice game had gone and the entire crew sacked - all without consultation. The next day he'd really be under attack.

Attack. The word brought his thoughts back to the unfortunate Penny. He had to find out what had happened.

Although never having participated in Trist's social events, he was aware of the organisational structure and the likely guest list.

Marta Woods was his first stop but, as he suspected, she wanted only for the whole matter to go away. 'I regret being involved at all, and certainly regret involving Monaghan because he brought in that bolshy cow Elena who's certain to cause problems.'

Predictably, Harry Rye had no sympathy for the girl. 'She knew what the score was. She was looking for the big time and got a big dick, after getting herself high. Now she's feeling sorry for herself. She'll make a bit of noise now, but when someone tells her her fortune, she'll clam up.'

Bollard hovered by the service area of the Playa restaurant, scrutinising a document. After a few minutes a small, busty blonde Chica appeared with a cocktail tray.

'Hi Frank!' The chirpy girl wasn't on Trist's party list but was friendly with many who were. She was also an incorrigible gossip, a fact Bollard had taken advantage of before.

'Hi, Joanna, recovered from Morg's party of the other night?'

'You're joking, they don't invite me!' She sounded a little petulant. 'Anyway I'm not sure I want to be, after what happened to that Chica from gaming.' She lowered her tone and looked round to see if anyone was listening.

'Some say she brought it on herself.' Bollard also spoke in hushed tone.

'I've heard she went upstairs with you-know-who and Tony Salinas, but didn't know where she was, what with the drink and "stuff" she'd been given,' Joanna whispered, and then, as if realising she was being dangerously indiscreet, added, 'I don't know really, it's only what I've heard, you know?'

Frank chatted for several minutes more to divert her attention from the subject of the party. After a few light-hearted jests which provoked her customary fit of giggles, he looked at his watch in horror, excused himself and raced off to some fictitious appointment. He now had a pretty clear picture of what had happened. Clear it may have been, pretty it wasn't. He groaned. Today, party to information about a possible rape by his employer. Tomorrow, party to... no – *perpetrator of* further injustices on behalf of his employer. Where would it end? He had a sudden irrational fear that something horrendous would happen if he stayed a moment longer in the building. He grabbed his coat and briefcase and hurried out of Ventura.

Monaghan took the call from the switchboard – it was Elena. 'Pat, I got a hold of her at last. She's okay, still traumatised, but said she'd wanted to be alone. Maybe best you leave her for now, but don't worry I'll keep in touch with her, and you.'

A relieved Pat thanked her once again for all she had done.

Later that night, as Pat entertained some guests in the Playa restaurant, Ahmed ambled to his table.

'Please excuse me gentlemen,' he said, drawing Pat to one side, 'I come only to ask my friend Pat for news. You hear something about our poor friend Penny?'

'Ah yes, she's at her own apartment now. She's… er… okay, though still upset and doesn't really want to talk to anyone. And your enquiries?'

'Yes, people say she have much to drink and some pop artists were there. You know what they are like with drugs. I fear something happened with them. I wait for more information.'

Ahmed looked relieved that Penny had been found. He again excused himself for interrupting and shuffled off to greet effusively another of his many 'friends'.

Chapter Fourteen

Draper was unusual among Ventura casino people. While his colleagues had consuming outside interests - Ellis's obsession with horses, Nidditch's religious attachment to golf, Lowe's fanatical support for his football team - for Draper 'the job' was his passion. He loved the immediacy of it all, like a theatre with a constant flow of bit-part players: the rich Sheikh, the second-hand car dealer, the aristocrat, the sportsman, the actress and the small shopkeeper. Each with their own peculiarities. Their moods changing with the turn of a card, or spin of a wheel.

Then there were the statistics: the total number of visitors, their cash drop, the win, the percentage win over drop, the drop per customer, win per customer. It had the excitement of the stock market floor with the glamour of showbiz. He'd become as much a casino addict as the most inveterate gambler.

From his first days as a croupier, his sharp intellect, ability with figures and drive had guaranteed him rapid promotion. In spite of his obvious enjoyment of the position and the financial rewards, many of his personal friends questioned his judgement in remaining in a business that still had a moral question mark hanging over it. He argued that it was a legal and highly regulated leisure activity; an industry that created jobs, contributed considerably to the treasury and fulfilled efficiently and professionally a public demand which might otherwise be filled by unscrupulous people.

Now, not for the first time, his faith was to be tested by events at the Ventura.

*

To a person accustomed to working nights, midday is early morning and a few night-caps taken when he finished at 4.30am pushed reveille well into pm. Several coffees and cigarettes were therefore needed before Draper could trust himself with a razor and he'd just begun to lather his face when Bland's call bought him to a state of full consciousness.

'Ralph, I've had a call from Chris Russell, asking what's happening with the dice.'

'What d'you mean?'

'Chris is on nights, but was called by Bollard to come in before the day-shift starts to discuss something important concerning the dice. I phoned to find out what was happening and eventually got Ellis, who said they'd removed the table before he got there, but he didn't yet know why.'

'This is fucking unbelievable! Bollard didn't say a thing about this yesterday.' Draper took a deep breath. 'I'll phone him and get back to you when I've found out what the fuck's going on.'

He dialled through to the switchboard, then waited for some time before the operator came back with the message that she wasn't able to get Bollard, nor was Ellis answering his bleep. Draper paused for thought, then decided he'd better get in there and find out for himself what it was all about.

'What the fuck's happening, Frank?' Russell asked before he had got through the doorway of Bollard's office.

'Ah yes, I'm sorry it wasn't supposed to... er... happen this way. I wanted to speak to you earlier in the morning before they... er... removed the table, but I couldn't get you...'

'Removed the table? Why?' Russell looked incredulous.

'Well, it's been decided by the company, given the recent problems and the results in relation to other tables, that dice isn't really viable. So they... er... we... decided to close it.'

Russell stared at him for some time. 'That's a load of shit! I don't get it! And what about the crew?'

'I'm afraid, as we don't have anything else at this moment, they have to be given redundancy.' Bollard swallowed hard. 'They'll be—'

'This is a fucking stitch-up! You know it is! And me, am I redundant?'

Bollard closed his eyes and dropped his head. 'Chris, I'm sorry, there's nothing I can do. I'm afraid I have to carry out the company's decision and serve you also with redundancy notice, it's not—'

'You've sold us down the river, you know my crew's not bent! I... I don't believe this!' Russell paced up and down the room. 'So this notice you're giving us, how long—'

'No, no... I'm sorry Chris,' Bollard intervened, 'when I say notice... I mean they'll be paid notice from today, and finish today as is the custom in casinos.'

Russell looked long and hard at Bollard then turned towards the door. 'Bastards!' We'll see about this!'

Draper called first at the casino office where Ellis had only just returned, having been upstairs with Bollard.

'Hi, Jim, what's going on?'

'Ah, to be truthful, I don't know. I spoke to Bollard, but he's givin' me bullshit about the dice table not being economic. All the staff are in a right fuckin' state, nobody knows what'll happen next. Some are talkin' about walking out.'

Draper shuffled nervously. 'This came from above, Bollard couldn't take a decision like this by himself. What's Pellzer saying?'

'Neither he nor Trist are in today. If you can believe the secretaries.'

Pellzer and Trist had indeed chosen not to come in today, though not for the same reasons as Bollard would have liked to be absent - embarrassment and the avoidance of confrontation. Irreverence, thought Bollard, was the word most appropriate to sum up their attitude. But it was already apparent they'd miscalculated. By not involving in their plans managers who normally supported their policies, they'd even alienated people such as Ellis and Nidditch by giving them the choice - lose credibility with staff by defending a plainly indefensible policy, or join the growing number of protestors.

Having already had heated exchanges with Russell and Ellis, Bollard now awaited Draper, who had called from downstairs and was on his way up. But instead of the expected rant, Draper entered, smiled ironically and stretched out his hands in a gesture that said: 'You have the floor.'

Frank felt no antagonism towards Draper; in fact, he respected the man's professionalism and integrity. This made it all the more difficult to deliver the agreed storyline. Nevertheless, he began in a calm and matter-of- fact tone.

'Ralph, after analysis and comparison with other games, and taking into consideration recent security problems, we decided to close the game and possibly use the floor space for a more productive game in the future. It's as simple as that.'

Staring at Bollard, Draper shook his head and after some time began to speak almost as calmly as Bollard had done. 'You and I know this is complete bullshit. Results on that table have not deteriorated and there's no ongoing security problem. A casino, as you yourself have said many times, must have a diversity of choice to attract a broad base of clientele and some tables contribute more than others. In any case, a policy change on games should be discussed with all managers and alternative employment would be offered before redundancies.'

'Ralph, look—' Bollard tried to interrupt, but Draper held up his hand to silence him.

'No Frank, this is something else, it comes from the top, from Trist. Stop bullshitting and tell me what it's really about.'

'It's as I said, of course Trist and Pellzer contributed in the decision.' Bollard was frustrated by the need to maintain the discredited line.

'And why sack Chris?

'We couldn't offer him anything else,' Bollard muttered.

Draper finally gave way to anger. 'You're fucking mad! How do you expect to get away with this? You've sold us, and yourself, down the river for those assholes upstairs!'

Bollard made some pretence of sorting files on his desk. 'Ralph, I think you'd better go before you say something you'll regret.'

He didn't lift his head again until after the door had slammed.

Ellis was standing by a closed blackjack table, looking furious. 'I can't even get the fuckin' tables opened! What a fuck-up! Some of 'em are about to walk out. They're in the staff room, refusing to come down. I didn't know what to do - sack 'em, or join 'em!'

'We've got to do something about this. We're being made to look like pricks. We're supposed to be managers, but haven't a clue what's going on!' fumed Draper.

'Yeah, I've told Pellzer's secretary I need to talk to him whatever he's doing. There's no use talking to Bollard. He's as much use as a poof in a brothel!'

'You're right, he's too shit-scared of Trist to do anything,' said Draper, adding, 'I'm off to see Chris, I'm told he's at the Coach, let me know if you get a meeting with the big two.'

'Right, tell Chris to have a few on me. I'll be round after the shift, if there is one.'

The pub, unusually for this time of the evening, was already filling up, mostly with redundant dice crew, sympathetic colleagues and those simply curious to know what had happened and why. Draper joined Bland, Russell and some of the sacked dealers in a corner of the bar.

'Thank God you're here!' Russell stood to greet him. 'They think it's my fault. Tell them!'

Not surprisingly, no one accepted the Company's reasons for the dismissals. Draper had little to say that made the decision any more understandable and could only assure them that they had taken no part in the decision. As for the rumour that suspected collusion in the coup involving the Greek had been the real reason, he could only add that Bollard and all operational managers had met and agreed that, though there had been negligence, there had been no illegal involvement of staff.

'Maybe Walker and his Gestapo persuaded the bosses there was somethin' going on?' said George, one of the sacked crew.

Draper couldn't completely discount this possibility. 'They had no material to back up such an accusation.'

'We should all refuse to work until the boys are reinstated,' Bland suggested, his anger fuelled by several drinks. This found favour with quite a few present.

'No, I wouldn't advise that,' Draper replied. 'it seems some day-shift staff are already on strike, but being unofficial it puts them in a bad legal position.'

'We can't let them get away with it!' protested one of the inspectors. His view was supported by a sizeable group.

'You're right. But we should get legal advice before taking action,' responded Draper.

'I've a contact at the General Workers' Union!' one of the dice crew offered.

'Good. Arrange a meeting. I'll also talk with a guy who deals with Employment Law. Meanwhile...' Draper frowned '... we should work normally, but drum up support for action when it's time.'

There was a reluctant acceptance of this tactic, even if it wasn't as decisive as the sacked dealers would have liked.

Draper eventually made his way back to Ventura. As he approached he encountered Elena, with three other Chicas who should've been working that afternoon.

'Hello, Ralph, joining us on the picket line?' she called out aggressively.

'Elena, I'm in complete sympathy but you're making a tactical error—'

'You're not with us then!' she interrupted.

'Look, I know the sackings were a barbarity but—'

'This is just the latest,' she cut in again, 'girls have been treated like dirt for years. Just the other day Penny was raped. Nobody's safe in that place, we've got to do something now!'

The other girls chorused her sentiments and began to give further examples of injustices.

'Yes you're right. It's just that it has to be done without giving them a legal advantage.'

'I'm going to the press with the story of that place. We'll see how Trist likes that!' declared Elena defiantly.

Draper could see no purpose in carrying on the exchange with the girls in this mood and continued on his way.

The evening shift was less than an hour from its normal scheduled start, but it was already obvious they'd have difficulty opening. Employees arriving for work were meeting pickets at the staff entrance. Some had passed the line and entered the building, but were showing little inclination to work. Others were hearing of the sackings for the first time. Rumours were born every minute, adding to those that had been circulating all afternoon. In addition, Sid Walker's heavy-handed exchanges with gaming staff had tipped the balance in favour of strike action, even amongst moderate employees. It was clear that Pellzer had misjudged the mood and the effect the dismissals would have. Instead of provoking certain managers into rash protest, it was arousing the hitherto suppressed grievances of the Chicas and male inspectors.

Ellis had tried unsuccessfully to contact Pellzer to inform him of the damage this was doing to business. There were embarrassing exchanges with customers at reception when the absence of any agreed statement on why the tables were closed led to conflicting messages being given. They were in the midst of industrial action with no plan for dealing with it.

Ellis had at first thought that enough personnel would work to permit him to operate some gaming tables and as the restaurants and bars continued in service, he had decided to open. But as more staff joined the protest he was left with the task of apologising to customers for the lack of gaming facilities. He and his team faced almost continuous enquiries and complaints without being able to answer any of them adequately.

Bollard was cocooned in his office and had given instructions to his secretary not to permit anyone to enter. Surprised that he was still there, Draper ignored the secretary, opened the door and found Bollard on the phone, sounding distraught.

'Yes, but Dan, the press have now got hold of the story and are asking some very embarrassing questions, even about parties upstairs. We must do something!' Bollard glared at Draper and the secretary behind him. Finally agreeing something, he put down the phone. 'Didn't I say…!' His remonstration was overridden by the secretary's apology and Draper's acceptance of blame for the intrusion.

'Okay, Barbara. Leave this to me.' Bollard waved her away dismissively.

'I'm sorry we don't have time for etiquette. We have a crisis down there!' Draper pulled up a chair.

'I'm well aware of the situation, thank you!' Bollard replied.

'It's a pity you weren't aware of the dangers of this lunacy before you let it get this far!' Draper returned quickly.

Frank Bollard paused. His anger dissipated into something approaching distress.

'You know I can't control what they do upstairs,' he answered dejectedly.

It was Draper's turn to pause. The stark truth of Bollard's statement had removed all need for further attack. He felt a pang of sympathy for the man while remembering the purpose of his visit. 'Okay, but what do we do now? What does Pellzer have to say?' Draper's tone was less antagonistic.

Bollard massaged his brow. 'He doesn't know either, but now the press have got hold of the story he and Trist will have to come up with something.'

'But why was it done? And don't tell me for economic reasons.'

'They have their own logic. I tried...' Frank stopped, then changed tack. 'Let's talk about the immediate problems.'

Draper would have liked to probe further but did need immediate decisions. They agreed that further damage to the club's position could only result by staying open when no gaming tables were operating.

At that moment they were interrupted by the secretary.

'Yes?' Bollard reacted sharply.

She winced. 'It's a gentleman from the General Workers' Union on the telephone, insisting he speak to the manager.'

'Tell him the Managing Director's not in the club,' Bollard rasped.

Nidditch and Ellis now squeezed passed the secretary and joined them in the office.

'We've got the press downstairs now.' Nidditch shook his head.

'Yes and I hear someone's got in touch with the General Workers' Union,' added Ellis. 'God save us!'

Bollard rubbed the back of his neck. 'We close tonight, to get all these people off our back until I can have a meeting with Trist and Pellzer to see what's to be done.'

'So what's this all about?' Nidditch started on Bollard.

'Sorry, I'd like to assist with this inquest,' said Draper, 'but I'd better go and close before further problems evolve.' He left them talking. On the way out he stopped at the secretary's desk.

'Barbara, what was the name of the person who called from the Union?' He copied the name from her notepad.

Monaghan was only just hearing of the day's events from the reception Chicas. Although sympathetic with the staff, he also knew, from personal experience, that a wildcat action could be counter-productive. His bleeper alerted him to a call. It was Draper, summoning him to the casino office on the Playa level.

'Hi Pat. You no doubt know about the so-called "redundancies" and the walk-out…?' Draper asked when he entered.

'Yes, but don't understand any of it.' Pat sat down.

'Join the club. Only those above know why.' Draper shook his head. 'Anyway, we have to close tonight. We give instructions to reception not to let anyone else in, apologise to clients, say it's a temporary situation. Those already here are another problem. We'll have to tell them that due to an industrial dispute the games won't operate tonight. Give them time to finish whatever meals or drinks they've already ordered, let them leave at their leisure. We must try not to get involved, or let staff get involved in discussions with customers about the dispute. There's already a reporter here. Absolutely nothing's to be said to her, or anyone from the Press!'

'Jesus, the press got on to this quickly!' Pat was surprised.

'Yes, your friend Elena from reception, I'd say, including leaks about goings-on upstairs.'

'What's that got to do with this dice thing?'

'Strictly speaking, nothing. But a lot of grievances will come out. I can't really blame them. This lot upstairs deserve everything that comes their way, but scandals like that could lose us our licence, then we'll all be out of a job!'

106

Pat was again troubled. The thought that Elena might have told the Press about Penny's experience worried him. Though he felt something should be done, he was mindful of the distress it could cause Penny if she'd not been in agreement. Draper's comment was also relevant. Everyone's job would go if Ventura had to close.

He made his way through the restaurant and down the main stairway. As he descended, he could hear several members complaining to reception staff about the disruption. Ollie, looking a little harassed, seemed relieved to see Monaghan.

'Ah, Pat,' Ollie grinned mischievously, 'this lady would like to speak to you.'

'Yes, can I help you?' Pat greeted the smartly dressed, attractive young lady.

She smiled and handed him her business card. 'Janet Litchman, Daily Mail.'

Monaghan shot Ollie an accusing glance but he was already enmeshed with another group of foreign members protesting the closure.

'I understand you're having problems today?' the journalist asked.

Pat chose to misunderstand. 'Oh these language problems we have from time to time. With so many foreign guests…' He shrugged nonchalantly.

'I'm referring to the industrial action by the staff,' she smiled disarmingly.

Pat maintained his casual tone. 'Oh yes, that. Well, we have a little dispute going on, but I'm sure it'll be settled soon.'

'It's been said that a lot of it's to do with girls being treated as toys, to be discarded when the bosses or rich customers think they're no longer attractive enough, and that some girls have actually been abused?' the journalist announced loudly, obviously hoping for a reaction from the Chicas on reception. Mia looked up immediately but Pat shot her a warning look.

'You know, I don't think… Miss… er… that any of us know enough about the dispute to help you. Perhaps you could call tomorrow. The manager might be able to help you,' said Pat, easing her as delicately as he could towards the door.

'Isn't the manager here now?' she asked, resisting his obvious intention.

'No, I'm afraid he's not,' replied Pat.

'Who's the manager in charge of the operation here?' she persisted.

Monaghan was about to flatly refuse and ask her to leave, but paused. 'The man you should speak to is Mayfield, Gordon Mayfield,' he announced with conviction, hoping she wouldn't see the other staff snigger. She asked him to spell it, wrote it down and left.

Chapter Fifteen

The advice from Ralph Draper's ex-colleague, an expert on employment legislation and industrial disputes, was much as he himself had suspected.

The Company's position was that Dice staff had been made redundant and to prove this wasn't a legitimate action those workers would have to take the case to Industrial Tribunal. The staff who had removed their labour in protest were on dangerous territory. The company could sack them on the grounds that it was an illegal action unsupported by union representation or even a majority of the workforce. Even an eventual successful appeal by the dismissed dice crew would not, in a legal sense, legitimise their action. So as Draper had warned, the unofficial strike was a precarious strategy whose success depended on Trist and Pellzer's fear of adverse publicity, and consequential loss of competiveness and revenue.

Draper was also curious to know why the General Workers' Union had shown interest. His friend verified that the person who had left his name at Bollard's office was a senior official, and suggested Draper call him.

The switchboard at the Union offices put him through and a gruff voice announced: 'George Mitford!'

'Hello, Ralph Draper at the Ventura Club. I was given your name by Dr Stewart Underwood at London University.'

'Oh yeah, well hello, Mr Draper, what can I do for you?'

'First let me say I'm a member of the management team at Ventura, but I'm not calling in any official capacity.'

'Well I'm sorry, I only negotiate with an official management rep or discuss the situation with a workers' rep. Your position's unclear. If you're with the workforce on this, I suggest you talk to their rep. I told him before they'd only get fairness on the floor when they were backed by official union representation.'

Draper tried to conceal his surprise at this news and wondered if he could draw more details from the union man.

'Well, does he agree with that now?' said Draper calculatingly.

'Well… yeah, of course, now he's on the street!' countered the union man immediately.

'Okay, maybe you're right. I'll contact the rep, thank you,' said Draper. Mitford grunted an acknowledgement and hung up. Draper could now see a possible motive for the dismissals, other than security fears. He'd assumed Mitford had called only after receiving a request for help from sacked employees or someone such as Elena. As Mitford had now confirmed, one of those who had been made redundant had been in discussion with the Union for some time. If this had reached the ears of Pellzer or Trist, it could be just the sort of threat to make them act as they had.

Was the buzzing inside her head, or an exterior irritation? It continued. It was the phone. She'd leave it, they'd go away.

It continued. She grabbed it aggressively, but the effort of getting there took its toll, and instead of conveying extreme irritation, her meek 'Ye-es' elicited an apology from Monaghan.

'Sorry, Elena, are you okay?'

'Oh, hi. Well, apart from my aching head, churning stomach and mouth like a sewer, I'm fine.'

'You ill, or is it just a hangover?'

'No, this is not *just* a hangover, it's a monster hangover, courtesy of the former dice crew of Ventura,' she groaned.

'That's what I called about,' he said. A grunt confirmed she was still awake. 'We had a visit from a journalist last night, claiming she'd heard about girls being abused at Ventura.'

'We've been abused for years.'

'She meant a specific case, and Draper said you'd threatened to go to the Press.'

After a long pause, which almost prompted Pat to check if she was still there, Elena summoned up a resolute tone. 'You're not suggesting we let these bastards get away with all this?'

'No, but if a scandal lost Ventura its licence, would you be happy with that? And Penny – d'you think this is what she wants?'

'Oh, I just hate the fact that we accept everything that happens without doing anything!' she cried out.

'Yes, I understand, but…!' He was about to use an alternative approach, but she cut him off.

'Please, just leave me alone. I can't take all this!' she groaned and slammed down the phone.

No such emotion was likely to be evident during the conversation between Janet Litchman and Mayfield. The journalist had taken Monaghan's advice and contacted him to ask for an interview, a request to which Mayfield had readily agreed.

Mayfield, seldom privy to sensitive material and seemingly oblivious to Trist's seedier activities, could be relied upon to refute any suggestion of irregularities. On this occasion he'd also been briefed by Bollard on the company's new policy which had brought about the dispute.

Miss Litchman wasted no time on pleasantries. 'What provoked the staff to take strike action?' She noted that, almost in a role reversal, Mayfield was taking notes.

'No official strike has been called,' Mayfield replied without giving any sense of evading the question.

'You do admit that, official or not, the workforce removed their labour yesterday?'

'Certain employees, by no means all, did not work. Ventura management, fearing this minor disruption might negatively affect the high level of service we give to clients, decided to temporarily close until this misunderstanding was cleared up.'

'What grievances provoked this action?'

'At this stage, I can only assume a mixture of sympathy and misunderstanding.'

'Sympathy and misunderstanding of what?'

'Sympathy with colleagues who unfortunately had been made redundant, and misunderstanding of the economic necessity surrounding the company's decision.'

'It's been said this is just one of a long list of injustices. That girls are treated as sex objects and discarded if the company thinks they've lost their looks, and some are obliged to go to parties organised by management, and recently one girl was sexually abused at one such event…'

Mayfield seemed genuinely astonished. 'I'm not sure who makes such outrageous allegations, but we would certainly be delighted to confront them in a court of law. Unfortunately people become emotional in industrial disputes, imaginations run wild. We have a transparent policy of employing attractive and intelligent females, and also males. Certainly, people have been dismissed after numerous warnings about their failure to maintain the high level of personal hygiene and professionalism we demand. A Chica's contract states that she may be required to attend promotional activities. For which she is paid, I might add. We'll be pleased to give you a list of activities, including charity events, in which Chicas have taken part. As to other scurrilous allegations,' said Mayfield indignantly, 'never have I heard of any girl being abused, and an exhaustive investigation would have been launched had we heard of such an outrage.'

Litchman returned to the matter of industrial action. 'How will this matter be resolved, are you in negotiations with the General Workers' Union, who I believe represent the staff?'

'This is incorrect. The GWU do *not* represent the staff, that would require an application for union representation, co-operation of the company and an acceptance by ballot by the majority of the staff. None of this has taken place.'

'Anyway, if there's a prolonged dispute your business will suffer greatly. Not so, Mr Mayfield?'

'Any prolonged disruption is bad for business. But I'm sure everything will be resolved quickly.' At this point Mayfield excused himself to go to an internal telephone point.

He returned shortly, close behind him a busty young lady carrying several box-files.

'Ah, thank you, Sally.' Mayfield took them from her. 'Sally graduated from croupier Chica to assistant training officer. She's brought our "Tablets of Stone".' He smiled at his own metaphor. 'Our procedural manuals, job descriptions and terms of employment.'

'How interesting,' Litchman said unconvincingly, but her interest focused not on the files but on the girl. 'Maybe I could have a few words with Sally?'

Mayfield displayed a brief flash of irritation but turned to address the employee. 'Sally, would you be prepared to answer a few questions for Miss Litchman from the Daily Mail?'

'Yeah, alright, fire away,' said the girl.

'When you were a Chica, were you ever pressurised by management into going to parties or other activities outside work?' Litchman asked.

'Bleedin Hell! Chance'd be a fine thing!' Sally laughed.

'Were other girls?'

'I don't know any birds I'd have to force to get paid for going to a party,' she sniggered.

'Do you think girls are fairly treated here?'

'Well, it beats workin' in bleedin' Woolworths!'

'There's been a suggestion that a girl was sexually abused here in the club,' Litchman pressed. She could see Mayfield wanted to intervene.

'I don't know about that. The only abuse they get is on the tables sometimes when a punter's bleedin' numbers don't come up.' She laughed again. Litchman thanked her and on a nod from Mayfield, the girl left.

Mayfield pulled a face. 'Sorry, she's good technically but not the most articulate.' He now turned to the material which he seemed eager to show Litchman. 'You can see here what I was referring to earlier—'

'Thank you, Mr Mayfield, but I'm afraid I have to get back to my desk now,' she interrupted. 'But I will follow up on these points, make sure I get to the truth,' she added pointedly as she moved to door.

*

Soon after the journalist had gone, Mayfield received a message that Bollard was waiting for him in his office. Pellzer was already sitting at the small oval coffee table, the morning papers spread in front of him. Bollard was looking through the Guardian. They both muttered a greeting as Mayfield entered.

'More or less on the same theme, nothing more than the others.' Bollard's words received a nod of confirmation from Pellzer.

Pellzer straightened himself and looked at Mayfield. 'Gordon, about the journalist? What'd she ask and what did you tell her?'

Mayfield took out his notebook like a policeman in the witness box. 'At approximately 9.00 hours I received—'

'Yes, in brief Gordon, what did she ask you?' Bollard cut in quickly.

'Well, she asked about the strike and what were the grievances that provoked it,' Mayfield answered, looking at his notes.

'Yes, what else?' Pellzer pressed.

'She said, there had been a suggestion that female staff had been exploited in some way.'

'Okay Gordon, read me out exactly what she asked, I'm sure you've got it there,' Bollard cut in before Pellzer could fire another question.

When Mayfield had read out his notes Pellzer nodded in affirmation that he could now see the Bollard's earlier points. As both sat silently thinking, Mayfield continued.

'Naturally, I refuted such an outrageous allegation and referred her to our code—'

'Yes, Gordon, I'm sure you handled it in your usual way!' Bollard interrupted. 'She make any further reference to the mistreatment of Chicas?'

Mayfield covered her questioning of Sally, and Sally's rather crude replies. He was now talking of the perception journalists have of casinos and how this might be changed by periodic press-days. He'd already thought about the contents of the press-package and was giving a description when Pellzer cut in.

'Hey! Give us a break!'

Mayfield looked startled by this response to his professional advice.

Bollard stood up. 'Er… Gordon… we're a little pressurised this morning,' he said. Perhaps we'll continue this at another time. Dan and I have some things to discuss. I'll get back to you.'

Still looking puzzled, Mayfield accepted this and left.

'Can you believe that dickhead?' Pellzer asked rhetorically. 'Does he ever know what's goin' on?'

'Fortunately for us, no!' said Bollard emphatically.

Pellzer, though irritated, recognised the truth of this, and nodded. 'As you say Frank, the papers are taking great delight in this strike by Chicas and the exploitation issue. As yet, nobody's written about sexual abuse, but this hack's got me worried, even if there's no truth to it.' He began collecting the newspapers.

'Dan, the problem is, there may be truth in it,' Bollard said, making direct eye contact. Pellzer hadn't wanted to hear this. He decided not to discuss it further and walked to the door.

'The danger is, if this strike goes on and gets more heated, more will come out and I'll be getting a call from the Police, Gaming Board or both,' Bollard persisted nervously.

'Yeah okay, I hear you! Keep cool, don't talk to anybody else till I speak to Morg!' Pellzer grabbed the door-handle forcibly and left.

She wanted to find relief from the percussion instruments being played inside her head, but it was some time before anything like a coherent thought found its way through the drumbeat. When it did, it added only to the sum total of her misery. What had she told that journalist? She couldn't fully remember. In her desire to expose Trist and his circle and show just how unscrupulous and corrupt they were, she might have gone too far. Would it lead, as Pat suggested, to the club being closed and everyone losing their job? She knew she'd mentioned rape. She hadn't given Penny's name, but might have given more information than was necessary. The Press always had ways to ferret out more than you wanted to say. If it came out, how would poor Penny cope with all the publicity? *Oh God*, Elena thought, *why did I open my big mouth?*

She decided her only course of action was to see Penny and somehow prepare her. She dialled and after a few moments Penny answered.

'Oh, hello Elena. It's so nice to hear you, I was about to call you.' Penny's voice sounded stronger and more positive.

'Oh, anything in particular?' Elena was relieved by the cheerier tone.

'Oh, I just needed to talk to someone about… things, you know?' This time she sounded a little more subdued.

'Will I come over?

'Oh could you? Yes please,' Penny replied happily.

Elena replaced the phone and went off to shower and dress, her head still pounding dully.

From his office Trist looked to the comparative tranquillity of the park. The green expanse he could see through the trees reminded him of home. He wished he was back there.

'This whole thing's been a fuck-up from start to finish! I shouldn't have let you talk me into this!' he ranted at Pellzer standing behind him.

The reaction, though predictable, was nevertheless exasperating for Pellzer. The plan wasn't failing because *he* had miscalculated. The closure of the dice had indeed provoked a stronger reaction from the staff than predicted, but their action, unofficial as it was, would have been unlikely to succeed. The end result could still have been the removal of a militant unionist cell and possibly Bland and Draper. What had tipped the balance was the unexploded bomb - the incident with the girl. How was he to know this would surface? And that people would have enough information about it to make it an issue.

'Morg, let's stick to the immediate problem of this girl. What can she tell them?'

'Nothing. She was out of her mind, she can't say anything.' He turned from the window.

'Can anyone prove anything'?' Pellzer asked.

'No, no… I don't think so.'

'You don't think so, but you don't know? Great!' Pellzer groaned inwardly.

'What is this, a fuckin' interrogation? I was out of it myself! All the people at that party were… in any case, who's gonna say something? You know what they're there for, at those parties!'

'Look Morg, it's not just what they prove, it's the effect these stories have. We can't afford a problem with the authorities. We've got to kill this story before it goes any further,' Pellzer insisted.

'So kill it. How you gonna do that?' Trist threw up his arms in a gesture that said *it's your baby,* an attitude guaranteed to infuriate Pellzer.

'No Morg, *we* are gonna do it, because if this gets out, we'll both lose, but you more than me!'

Trist usually dominated exchanges with Pellzer but though he wouldn't admit it, he'd begun to feel vulnerable over this business with the Chica. 'Okay. So how you gonna get us out of this mess?' he said with a shrug of resignation. Pellzer let it pass. At least now he was listening.

By the time he left Trist's suite, they'd agreed someone would meet with representatives of the workers to consider alternative positions for redundant workers, but only in a climate of co-operation. Which meant that all negative comments to the press or anyone else cease immediately.

Pellzer had already contacted the lawyers to look into the legal aspects, but it was necessary to buy time by offering talks although he had no intention of allowing Ventura to become unionised.

The improvement in Penny's mental state was evident in the way that she now took the role of hostess; making coffee, offering biscuits. Small tasks, but things that a week before had been beyond her. Elena wondered how fragile the recovery might be and waited, silently, as Penny arranged with exaggerated precision the cups and plates on the table then, smiling, sat down. Her smile seemed to slip but was then just as quickly restored.

A little embarrassed by a prolonged silence Elena spoke first. 'I see you've got some beautiful flowers.'

'Yes they're from Prince Talal.'

Elena wasn't sure how to respond. She'd obviously derived satisfaction from the gift, having taken time to arrange the flowers around the room, an exercise that would've been impossible only days before. But what were the intentions of this rich man? They were unlikely to be honourable, Elena thought. But not wishing to destroy Penny's new-found confidence with negative comments, she uttered a detached, 'nice' and steered the conversation in another direction.

'You said you wanted to talk about… things?'

'Yes.' Penny stared into her coffee, obviously searching for words. 'I want to thank you for helping me, I know I've been a problem and—'

'No, you haven't been any problem to me,' Elena interrupted immediately.

Penny smiled. 'I've reached the stage… where… I don't know what to do.' She had a quiver in her voice. Elena feared she might collapse in tears again, but after a short pause she continued: 'I… I don't know what to do about what happened to me.' She forced the words out rapidly, as if fearing she wouldn't be able to complete the sentence. Now having said it, she sighed with relief. 'I'm not sure of all the facts. I know he… they… took advantage of me. I want to get back at him, them, but I don't want to go to the Police. They'll make it look like I agreed, or it was my own fault and I'll have to face the shame.' Now she was crying, not uncontrollably, as before, and less it seemed through despair, more through anger and frustration. Elena found this less disturbing, even slightly encouraging.

'Penny, I have to tell you something,' Elena said when she thought Penny had composed herself again. 'They sacked the the dice crew for no reason and quite a lot of the girls went on strike. It was just the last straw. Anyway, a lot of girls, including me, have been telling the newspapers how they treat Chicas at Ventura. They've written about it in the papers. Look.' She took a copy from her bag and gave it to Penny. 'Anyway, I talked to this journalist and told her about the things that go on at Trist's parties. I said a girl had been assaulted – sexually. No, I didn't mention your name or give any details, I promise!' she asserted vigorously, seeing the look of shock on her friend's face.

'We have to tell them about what goes on at Ventura or it will happen all the time. I'll never say anything about you personally without your permission, and no one else knows enough about it, except Pat, but he'd never say anything. But maybe even just the threat that we'll talk can make Trist think twice about treating people like animals.'

Both girls filled a few reflective minutes just sipping coffee.

'You know, Prince Talal was very nice when I was with him, a perfect gentleman. Such a difference. And I've heard such criticisms of Arab men, but he was so... so charming. You think he knows what happened to me?' Penny asked suddenly.

'I... doubt it,' answered Elena. In fact she was unsure, but certain that this was what Penny wanted to hear.

'Ahmed said Talal heard I was ill and he's hoping I come back soon. That's why he asked Ahmed to send these flowers.'

'Ahmed called here?' Elena asked with concern.

'Yes, after I spoke to him on the phone.'

Elena was again unsure how to continue. She felt inclined to warn Penny of Ahmed, tell her he would most definitely know of her experience, and if he hadn't told Talal, it would only be because he didn't want to spoil his matchmaking plans. When Talal did find out, he'd probably drop her or simply use her to sate his lust. But for fear of destroying what little improvement she'd seen in her friend's condition, Elena watered it all down.

'You know, I wouldn't put too much trust in Ahmed. He's a tricky guy who always pursues his own interests.'

'Yes, I've heard that from Pat and others, but I've always found him okay,' Penny smiled.

'You're not thinking about returning to Ventura, are you?' asked Elena, recalling her apparent pleasure at the suggestion that Talal was hoping she would come back soon.

'No, I don't think... I could.'

It was a refutation of sorts. But Elena expected an absolute rejection, even revulsion at such a suggestion. She left shortly afterwards, confused and unsure how she should have responded. Was Penny recovering, or was she *in denial*, as the shrinks called it? And had Elena somehow failed her by not telling her what she really thought?

Chapter Sixteen

'Frank, I've spoken to Morg, he agrees that publicity of the kind we're getting, whether true or not, is bad for the club - and these union people are just the types to exploit it,' said Pellzer as the Casino Manager entered the office.

Bollard had been only too happy to leave his own office where he'd been under siege with visits from Ellis, Rye and Sid Walker; calls from the Union, journalists, Draper and Marta Woods. None of them did he want to talk to, having as yet no answers to their questions.

'So, change of strategy.' The MD spoke in conspiratorial tones. 'We talk to the GWU to buy time, pretend we'll consider union representation, but only in a climate of co-operation, which means everybody back to work and no negative press.'

Bollard was relieved that Pellzer had persuaded Trist to change tack but wasn't sure about the plan.

'Wouldn't it just be easier and safer to reinstate the Dice crew? Why make concessions to GWU? They don't represent the staff, but maybe this way we're giving them a road in.'

'Frank you've seen the papers. Although the redundancies provoked the dispute, the big news is the Chicas' strike, their grievances, the exploitation angle, sex-parties and the story about this girl, not so?' Bollard nodded an affirmative and Pellzer continued: 'We've got to make it look like a normal industrial dispute where tempers got frayed and wild accusations flew around. By danglin' the carrot of recognition in front of the GWU, they'll assist us to convince everyone that this was the case.'

'Yes, but they're going to ask for reinstatement of the dice crew. Without that they'll get no support,' Frank insisted.

'Well, we may concede that point, but only after assurances that all malicious rumours are scotched,' Pellzer said decisively.

To Bollard it was ridiculous to have provoked all this trouble only to have to backtrack. But not wishing to antagonise Pellzer, he resisted any temptation to say so and contented himself with the fact that for now, his conflict with managers and staff would be over or at least lessened. He agreed to inform the managers, make contact with GWU, set up a meeting and bring in representatives of the staff in dispute.

The next morning, Ellis was surprised to see Nidditch so early in the day, particularly as he had been working the night before.

'Jesus, you've got eyes like piss-holes in the snow. You'd better have a coffee.'

'Yeah, I hope this is important. Pellzer called an hour ago, asked me to come in. I take it everybody's here? What's it all about?'

'I'm not sure, but Pellzer told me to keep this meeting to myself. So far, there's only you and me,' said Ellis, passing Nidditch a plastic cup of black coffee.

Nidditch propped himself against the desk and drank the liquid while Ellis had a look at the report from the previous night.

'So we managed to get open again. Not exactly a great start. Any problems?'

'It was quiet. I suppose the punters didn't know we'd re-opened. There was a lot of chat from the staff but eventually things settled,' said Nidditch. He threw the empty cup in the waste-basket and they made their way up.

At Pellzer's office the secretary nodded for them to go straight through. Trist, who had newspapers spread over Pellzer's large desk, raised his head to greet them when they entered.

'Hi, you guys, come in, take a seat! First of all Dan and I want to thank you for your support during a difficult time. We also want to apologise for not consulting you before taking action on the dice. Though we handled it wrong, we were right about the need for action - a militant faction on the dice crew have been talking to the GWU for months. We also believe some managers, though aware of it, failed to pass this information upstairs at the outset. Maybe they've got sympathy with that cause. Not yourselves, of course, of that we're sure,' Trist added hastily. 'Anyway, we believed their militancy led to a drop in standards and security. Proof being the recent scam. Unfortunately, we took the wrong advice on how to deal with it. We've now had to reassess the situation.' Trist signalled for Pellzer to take over from him.

'What Morg's sayin' is, the future of this club was under threat. Even before this blew up there were certain things givin' us concern. You guys build a relationship with our customers by understandin' their needs and operatin' a flexible policy. Unfortunately not all managers do the same and we're losin' players to competitors. It seems, I'm sure our reports are true, some of those managers and pit bosses are supportin' militancy, to undermine us further. We're lookin' to you guys to give a lead...' Pellzer brandished a paper '... and you should share the benefits if you help us maintain flexibility and rid us of this union threat. We've put together a package I think you'll like. We'll include other managers and pit bosses, as and when we have confidence that they're workin' as you are. You should help with that assessment.'

Pellzer handed them a paper and he and Trist waited while they read the offer.

'I'm impressed,' said Ellis. Nidditch nodded agreement.

'Naturally, for the time being, this has to be between the four of us here in this room, no one else. Agreed?'

'Including Frank Bollard and Mayfield?' asked Nidditch.

'For the moment, yes. That's why the bonus is a separate agreement, not shown in the budget.'

Pellzer, watched to see how they would react. Neither manager seemed concerned or surprised that their immediate bosses were playing no part in this agreement.

'Okay, but what's the situation with the GWU? I hear we're giving them an in?' Ellis looked at Pellzer then Trist.

'No, that's not the case.' Pellzer shot a sideways glance at Trist as it was still a touchy subject between them. 'Because of the disruption and unprecedented amount of negative press, all bad for business, we offered a carrot to GWU. So, we'll have a coolin' off period, minimum of three months. Durin' which, both sides do everythin' to repair the damage to our reputation. Then we ballot all employees on the question of union recognition. Within this deal we offer alternative employment to the dice crew—'

'That's the official picture,' interrupted Trist, 'but they won't get the majority to win recognition. Their support is only in the gaming department. Bit by bit we'll weed out people who're trying to bring this place down. During these months you guys have to help us remove the threat, and as you see, we'll be appreciative.'

Pellzer preferred to present the proposal as an accord between like-minded professionals rather than just a bribe, but Trist's crude assessment had the merit of leaving no room for ambiguity. To his relief, the two managers showed no inclination to qualify their earlier agreement.

On Pellzer's instruction Bollard called a management meeting to clarify the company line, at least the one for public consumption. He made sure he was last to appear, to avoid embarrassing preambles. However, Mayfield had contrived to cause him some embarrassment. Having been told of Chris Russell's return, he had reinstated him to the forum and entered him on the list of attendees as *former dice manager*.

Those present displayed a mixture of hostility and cynicism as Bollard prepared to open the meeting. At that moment Monaghan appeared announcing a breathless 'Sorry I'm late. I was downstairs, thought it was being held on the dice table!'

The explosion of laughter left Bollard with no option but to put on a false smile and call for order again. 'If I may proceed, without further interruption…' He took up his notes. 'I've called this meeting to bring everyone up-to-date with developments and—'

'Ah, a radical change in policy, letting managers know what's going on!' Draper's sarcastic remark provoked similar outbursts.

'Please! If you continue to interrupt, this meeting will go on for-ever!' Bollard called out. 'After some consideration the… er… Board, has decided to re-employ those made redundant when the dice table closed.

We're therefore happy to see Chris back with us today.' He ignored the ironic murmurings. 'The decision of course sparked a series of protests, not all of them directly connected. But they highlighted a number of concerns and this now affords us an opportunity to address them.'

Bollard disregarded the intermittent comments and the general mood of cynicism.

'To... er... show good faith, the company has decided to permit a debate on union representation. It's of course our opinion that employees will not be best served by an industrial organisation with no knowledge of our business. That message we must get across during the months before a ballot takes place. I hope, in this, we can count on all of you.'

He paused, and in doing so, provoked a torrent of questions. Some began discussions with each other across the table.

'Please, colleagues!' Bollard attempted to gain control once again and pointed to Russell, who was signalling he wanted to speak.

'We still haven't heard why the dice was closed. Don't tell me it was an economic decision. Why was it done, and what guarantee do we have of keeping our jobs now?'

'Well, the table wasn't as profitable as other games. It was also felt that discipline had deteriorated, an example was the coup that—'

'No, no, I'm sorry, Frank, this is bollocks!' Draper slammed the table.

'You're interrupting again before I've answered the question!' Bollard countered testily.

'You want us to convince the staff they don't need a union. If that's true, the company must first win our confidence. You won't do that, by feeding us crap,' Draper asserted, with audible support from others. Bollard could think of no response and allowed him to continue. 'If better results was the aim, it should've first been discussed with gaming managers. A company that doesn't discuss strategy with its managers really does have a problem. Maybe the real reason for the closure was that some on dice had already made contact with the GWU. Undoubtedly this back-down is because of adverse press about "other matters". The only way to clear up this mess, is proper management participation in policy making, less interference from "above" on operational questions and a recognition of employee's rights.'

Bollard could find little to disagree with in Draper's words but to say so would have been one of his last acts at Ventura. Instead he gave the floor to Nidditch.

'We could go on about what was done and what should've been done, but the fact is, we've got the threat of the union and the bad press that their supporters have created. What do we do about it? Do you want a militant union running the show?' Although Nidditch addressed the meeting, his comments were obviously directed at Draper.

'The scandal and support for the union is the fault of Trist and his—!' The warning hand of Draper on Bland's sleeve curtailed his outburst.

'To reiterate,' Bollard broke in, 'we must now demonstrate to staff that they don't need a union because conditions will improve without its input. Above all, we must work with members and public to renew our good name.'

The absence of a dissenting voice didn't delude him; they'd probably realised the futility of voicing opinions in an assembly with no power. He waited for Mayfield to finish minuting what he hoped would be the closing statement, but could see Monaghan was indicating a wish to speak.

'Sorry, a couple of practical questions. What do I tell customers who ask about the dice? I can't say we closed because another table could win more money, and what do we say to journalists who ask about… er… parties and incidents with Chicas?'

Monaghan had blown on the embers of an almost extinguished subject. Bollard could see the interest on the faces of the others as they waited for his answer.

'The journalists… I think it's better to direct them to Gordon. As for the dice, I think you can say that there's an ongoing dispute that we hope will soon be resolved.' Frank's reply to the dice question provoked the expected derision. He paid no heed and signalled an end to the meeting, announcing in a slightly ironic tone, 'Thank you, gentlemen, oh and of course, the lady.'

The belated acknowledgement diverted Marta Woods from the task that had engrossed her during the entire meeting; the manicure of her nails. In a desultory manner she addressed Bollard.

'Oh, before we go, has there been a decision on where the reinstated people will work, if they'll be paid for time lost, and will their work conditions be the same? Also, will we deduct from those who were striking and put notes on their files?'

'Oh oh, more of those nasty difficult questions again!' Draper mocked as he pulled out his chair to leave.

'Always ingredients guaranteed tae spoil any meeting!' added Lowe.

Bollard sighed and let the jibes pass without comment.

'Shall I minute Marta's questions?' asked Mayfield in a detached tone.

'Yessss Gordon!' hissed Bollard, annoyed by Mayfield's uncanny ability to be the unconscious straight-man for the assembled comedians. 'The answers to those questions will be given in due course. For the moment dice personnel will be re-assigned to other tables. Jim, if I may ask you to organise this?'

'Oh t'anks very much.' replied Ellis sardonically.

Frank had misinterpreted his unusually benign participation as a wish to co-operate.

Chapter Seventeen

Penny Irwin needed affirmation of her worth. She'd already decided it wouldn't be at her parent's home. Even at her lowest ebb she hadn't thought of going back there. But the place where she had truly begun to feel happy and valued was now the scene of her degradation. Ironically, it was also where she had met the only two people she could now truly call her friends. What was she to do, start again? Find a new job? New friends? The prospect terrified her. She continued to brood over her predicament without coming any nearer to a conclusion. To take her mind off her troubles she decided to watch television and picked up a newspaper to check what was on. A headline caught her attention: *Card Carrying Chicas?* Penny scanned the article.

'The Ventura Club has conceded that all employees, including their famous Chicas, will have the right to decide whether or not they are to be represented by a Union. This comes after industrial action by the curvaceous croupiers in support of sacked colleagues and allegations that the top management had failed to protect employees' rights. Both the Ventura management, and George Mitford of the GWU, who seek to represent the workforce, said that the time had come for open discussion rather than malicious rumour. Their statement perhaps alludes to the stories which have been leaked to the Press of management sex parties and the cover-up of an assault on a Chica.'

Oh my God! she thought. *What if it all comes out?* She sat staring at the paper not knowing what to think or feel, then remembered: Elena had told her about this story.

It seemed likely, as Elena had hoped, that the threat of exposure had forced them into concessions that perhaps would make life a little safer for other girls. Penny's thoughts once again returned to that night. The events leading up to those few horrific moments may have been blurred, but the reality of what had happened was not - Trist and his famous friend had raped her. This she could now admit. Tears welled up in her eyes, she began to shake; but once where there had been only despair, now a bitter anger dominated her emotions.

A sudden shock jolted her upright. It was the phone ringing. She decided not to answer. The ringing persisted until she finally lifted the receiver.

'Yes, Penny here.'

'Ah, my sweet. It is Ahmed here. How are you?'

'Oh yes, hello. I'm… er… a little better, thank you,' she replied shakily.

'My very good friend Mansur is asking about you every day. He worries that you have not yet come back and also you promised to take tea with him.'

She hesitated, not knowing what to say. 'Well… yes… I'm not completely better yet. But please thank him for the flowers, they were very beautiful,' she responded a little more confidently.

'Why not come to take tea, then you can thank him yourself?'

'Well, that would be very nice, but…' She searched for an excuse. 'You know we're not really allowed to go out with customers.'

'My sweet one, Prince Talal is Ventura's most important customer. Believe me, no one makes trouble for you if you are with him, not even Morgan Trist.'

Hearing the name Trist sent a shock-wave through her system but one message registered: *No one makes trouble for you if you are with him, not even Morgan Trist.* She found herself agreeing to meet Talal at the Ritz the following day.

Ahmed felt pleased. He had arranged the meeting and Talal would be more than grateful. Now he had another mission to perform for the Prince and this one could be more lucrative.

'Agh, do I see a mirage!' shouted the Arab in mock horror as he entered the Playa casino and saw the dice table about to be re-opened. He continued the cabaret for the audience, which consisted of Ellis, Russell, a cashier and three dice dealers, by making a Christian sign of the cross and proclaiming loudly that he'd witnessed a miracle. He then hobbled off towards the restaurant.

When Ellis had opened the table he joined him. 'What are you doing here so early in the day, Ahmed?'

'I come for the Grand Re-opening of the Dice!' he announced, laughing. 'No, I wait for Morg, he is delayed. I will speak about this credit problem with Prince Talal.'

'What problem is this?'

'You know, he does not like that you send his cheques to his bank for payment immediately after each time he plays.'

'Ahmed, this is the law. It's not our policy, we're forced to do it.'

'Yes, okay, the law. But it creates a big problem for him. We must find other way. If he stops to play - what?' He left his question hanging. Ellis nodded sympathetically but didn't answer. 'He will play more if he don't have to pay from his bank each day. Everybody can make something more,' Ahmed whispered conspiratorially.

The Pit Boss was signalling for Ellis's assistance. As he moved off he said quietly, 'Listen, if we can find something that will work...' His gesture implied he'd agree.

Ahmed looked at his watch and took the lift to the upper floor.

'Ah, Ahmed. Sorry, I know I said one-thirty, but I got tied up!' Trist waved him in.

'So she now untied you, that's good.'

'Hey, how do you know these old jokes? Do we export them to the Middle East when we're finished with them?'

'Of course. You send everything you finish with to us poor Arabs, not true?'

Trist laughed.

'Now, to talk about one thing you finish with, maybe. This girl Penny...' Ahmed said slowly, watching Trist for a reaction.

'Who the fuck's Penny? Do I know her?'

'She is the Chica who, some people say, had a problem at your party,' Ahmed answered, aware that Trist knew exactly who she was.

'I don't give a fuck what some loopy dame says. You know what they're like.'

'Yes, but she or her friends maybe can cause trouble. Anyway, I want to say - Talal has interest for her and I think, she for him. If she come back to Ventura it's good. He will be happy, play all time on her table. She will get some jewels and things. He will get... anyway, she will forget about everything.' This presentation he made in a disinterested tone while leafing through a magazine.

'I don't care if the stupid broad comes back or not, as long as she doesn't cause trouble!' Trist said, trying to sound unconcerned.

Ahmed smiled, put down the magazine and moved closer to Trist, taking a more serious tone. 'My good friend Morg, I come on more important business.'

Trist was preparing a cigar so Ahmed waited until he had cut, lit and drawn on the large Havana before continuing.

'Some of the bigger players have a problem with this credit system.'

'Hell, not again. I told our guys to loosen up on the limits!'

'No, not limits. It is problem of sending cheques to the bank after each day.'

'Oh yeah. That *is* a bummer. But Pellzer and Bollard tell me it's somethin' the law's very strong on.'

'Yes, yes, I hear about the law. The problem is, the players don't care about this law. They don't like many cheques going from their account every day. One thing is, the bank manager knows too much and most use their business account. It can cause problems. You know many are Muslims. These things should be done in a more secret way.'

'Look, I understand, but what can we do? Every casino's in the same boat in England. The law's shit, but that's the way it is.'

'The biggest problem is Prince Talal. He loses the biggest money, but I worry other casino will make something special for him. He wants to pay from foreign account when he owes big amount, not every day. It could be good for you also to take money outside, no?' Ahmed whispered, to show how discreet he could be.

'Jesus! How do you expect me to fix that?' Trist exclaimed, but the idea intrigued him.

'Jesus, I think, will not help a Muslim Prince, but maybe you find a way?' said Ahmed smiling.

'I don't promise anything. I'll think it over. No promises, eh!'

'Okay, that's all what I ask. Now, I leave her to tie you again.'

He could see Ellis was engaged in pacifying a regular who was evidently disputing a decision on roulette, so Draper joined Tony Roberts, the day-shift pit boss, who was completing his hourly report.

'How's it been Tony? Making money?'

'Hi, Ralph. Yeah, it's been a good day. Seems to be picking up after our little vacation.' He handed Draper the clipboard to have a look.

'Aha, it *is* good. Who's been doing the money? Our friend Costas, I suppose, judging by his face, and Taher, no doubt?' .

'Yeah, and earlier that Nigerian chief Abowo… whatever his name is.' Roberts looked happy to see Lowe arriving to relieve him. Ellis finally extricated himself from the protesting player and joined them.

'What's all that about?' Draper asked.

'The usual. When he's losing he complains about everything. We called no-spin and before the dealer could stop the ball it landed in his number. Of course he wanted paid. We had to humour him. You hear about the dice?'

'Just found out. What a joke this place is! Those idiots don't know from one minute to the next what they're doing. Maybe the threat of the union's what they need!'

'We'll all be in the fuckin' shit if those commie bastards get in!' Ellis exploded. The fierceness of the attack surprised Draper, but he let it pass. The day manager gave a brief report on the current situation – who had signed cheques, winners and losers – but seemed anxious to get away. Draper knew the information, in more detailed form, would be transferred between the pit bosses; the rest he'd find in the cash desk, so he didn't detain him - certainly not to exchange views on unions, though Ellis's extreme reaction had intrigued him.

In terms of time served at Ventura, Ellis was senior to Draper although he held the same title. His was no fast-track promotion. At a time when public relations was becoming all important, he'd worked his way through the field, largely by capitalising on an easygoing manner with customers. Like the recently promoted Monaghan, they'd found his prankish wit and bonhomie went down well with the largely foreign clientele. For him the task of looking after punters took precedence over all else. Keep the players happy; keep them coming; keep them at the tables. Those were the three rules he gave to his staff.

Unfortunately, in the strict legislative environment of the UK, the gamblers' desires couldn't always be catered for. All managers found the restrictions tiresome, none more so than Ellis. But even on the subject of gaming law, Ellis's pet hate, Draper hadn't heard such vitriol as that directed at the union.

'Well, Jim seems to have made up his mind about the union,' Draper commented when Lowe brought him the hourly result sheet.

'Yeah, seems he's been putting the wind up the day shift staff,' Lowe grimaced. 'A couple of them told me they've been told if they support a union they'll be back on nights and can forget about days off and holiday requests.'

'Really? The fact that he feels able to make those threats is a good argument for representation,' said Draper thoughtfully, before moving to the cash desk to look at cheque-cashing records of the players present. He noted that Ellis had permitted two players to considerably surpass their limit. One of them, Costas, who'd been in the dispute when Draper arrived, was still playing, had several stacks of chips and hopefully wouldn't ask for more. Draper returned to address his Pit Boss.

'Ian, I'll be upstairs in the Playa, bleep me if there's any problem. I'm going to make sure nobody's removed the dice table while I wasn't looking.'

'Six… six easy, big red, no field… hard six down… come bet goes six,… still looking for an eight, shooter…'

Nice to hear the stickman on dice again, thought Draper. The table was crowded. It seemed the publicity over the last few days had provoked interest in the game.

'Looking less of an economic liability tonight, eh F emerged from the crowd around the table. Then, lowering ̶most a whisper: 'You know this about the dice crew having p̶r̶e̶v̶i̶o̶u̶s̶ tact with the GWU? It seems it was Ray Potts and his mate Pettigrew. They're now presenting the union's case for recognition.'

'My God! Petty and Potty! You mean the removal of the dice and all this furore was to get rid of those "demagogues" before they started a revolution? Two less articulate and less charismatic people you couldn't find! Their advocacy would have killed the idea stone dead without all this hassle!'

'Yeh, you're right. They're killing it now, by talkin' a load of bollocks!'

Chapter Eighteen

He said he'd bring the car at two-thirty but Penny wasn't sure she'd be ready. Having tried several dresses she was now pulling on her white knee-length boots for the third time. Doubts were creeping in. Why was she going? Would she be able to talk? What would she say about her absence from Ventura? What would she answer if he asked her when she would return? Was a mini-skirt appropriate for the Ritz? Did she have too much make-up on? Did she really want to go?

The doorbell startled her.

She looked out of the window; Ahmed's car was there. Oh, she wished she hadn't agreed to this! She sat looking at herself in the dressing-table mirror, thinking how she could get out of it.

The doorbell rang insistently.

Finally she went to answer it, to make her excuses and call it off.

'Ah my sweet, you look so so beautiful. He is a Prince, but today you will make him feel like a King!' Ahmed announced, before she could say a word. He now bowed with an ostentatious sweep of his arm. 'Your servant waits with your car!'

Penny was embarrassed and amused by this display on her doorstep, but her fear was dissipating. She found herself asking for a few more minutes to pick up her handbag.

The journey by limousine to the Ritz Hotel gave Ahmed an opportunity to tell Penny something of the history, pedigree and financial status of the Prince, his direct descendency from his country's Royal Family, his properties in the South of France, Marbella in Spain and of course in London. The stable of thoroughbred horses, six Rolls Royces and a private jet were added as further verification, should it be needed, of his wealth.

Penny had never been in the Ritz before. She felt a little self-conscious as Ahmed escorted her past the top-hatted doorman into reception. From there a few more steps to the lounge where she could already see the dazzling smile of the Prince, who was leaving his chair to come towards her.

'I bring to you an English *wardah*, Miss Penny !' Ahmed, with another of his theatrical bows, presented her to the Prince, who viewed him with a look of amused tolerance.

Talal greeted her with a kiss on the hand. 'Welcome, Penny. I am so very happy you could come.'

After a short exchange in Arabic between the two men, Ahmed bid her farewell with another flourish and the Prince guided her gently to his table, already being fussed over by a waiter and maitre'd. The lounge was busy but Penny could see the staff were paying particular attention to Talal's table, which also seemed to have been positioned in a way to give it more space than other tables in the room.

'Will Madam be taking tea or some other refreshment?' the waiter asked with exaggerated deference.

'Oh… er… yes, thank you.'

'Earl Grey will be good for Madam?' the waiter asked while his senior hovered nearby.

'Penny, I am so very happy to see you again,' said Talal with obvious enthusiasm, before taking a more serious tone. 'How is your health?'

'Better, thank you. I'm also very happy to see you. It was so kind to send those beautiful flowers, I'm really much better now,' she said convincingly. Indeed, for the first time since her terrible experience, she was beginning to feel better about herself.

'I have missed you from Ventura. It is not the same place without you. You will return, I hope, now you are well?'

Penny wasn't sure how to respond. The arrival of the tea permitted a temporary postponement of the need to answer this question.

The maitre'd joined the waiter again to assist with the extremely difficult operation of arranging crockery, pouring tea and positioning the teapot. The cake-stand with its petit-fours required a special effort. Penny was amused by the level of attention, but the Prince appeared oblivious to it. He smiled and offered her cake, but ominously did not speak, as if still waiting for her answer.

'What Ahmed said… what does it mean - English warda, or something? she asked, still avoiding the subject.

'English Rose. Wardah means rose. But will you return, my sweet rose?'

'I am feeling much better but I've been… wondering if I want to return to Ventura,' she said haltingly.

'But why?'

'Because they don't treat the girls very nicely there,' she replied, again not knowing exactly what to say.

'Who is it that treats you badly? Not Jim?' he asked, showing genuine concern.

'No, not him. No one on the floor. Other people…' She couldn't bring herself to say Trist's name, not knowing what it might lead to if she did.

'But who are these people who upset you? They cannot be so important,' he pressed her. She didn't want to answer. 'Okay, so you don't like to work there…' he said, accepting her position, but she interrupted him.

'Actually I love the work and customers - like yourself, of course,' she added quickly, smiling shyly. 'It's just the behaviour of some people I don't like.'

'Well, I don't understand, but if you do not return I will also not return. If you do, I will make sure nobody treats you badly. I have some influence, you know.'

She wanted to tell him about Trist and what had happened to her, but was ashamed and afraid he might think her behaviour had encouraged the attack.

'I'll think about coming back if you would like me to, but please Mansur, don't tell anybody for the moment,' she pleaded.

'I will be very happy if you return, but will not do or say anything until you give me the command,' he smiled, then added, 'Please, take some tea and cake. Are you hungry, should we have lunch?'

'No, no thank you, I am happy with tea, unless you would like…'

He laughed and made a joke about being on a diet. For many Arabs who came to Ventura this might have been taken as a serious statement, but the Prince, slim and athletic, was in fact one of the most handsome men Penny had ever seen. On top of that his charm and undoubted intelligence set him apart.

He now talked with boyish enthusiasm about his horses, their individual characters and their changeable moods, explaining how they should be treated to ensure their happiness and unlock their potential.

Yachting was something Ahmed hadn't covered in his resumé of the Prince. Mansur owned several yachts, of which the biggest and best was moored in Marbella. Again the ownership seemed of secondary importance to the enjoyment of sailing. Seldom had Penny heard anyone describe hobbies with such passion. Horses, sailing, music, theatre, books, food, wine and of course gambling. His interests seemed boundless, and all described with the vocabulary of an expert and the passion of an aficionado.

Suddenly he stopped talking and held his hand to his mouth. 'My goodness, I am talking constantly about myself, and I asked you here to get to know more about you. Now I bore you with my hobbies.'

'Please don't apologise, I'm so intrigued by all of them.' She clasped her hands as if in prayer, then put them back on the table.

'You know, the reason I'm talking so much is because I feel comfortable with you. Normally I cannot share my enthusiasm with people around me, they are nice, very loyal, but they don't understand the depth of feeling I have about things.' He patted her hand affectionately but self-consciously. She responded by clutching his hand ever so briefly before drawing away with a shy smile.

'Please tell me about your own interests and dreams.' He looked into her eyes.

'Oh, there's nothing much to tell, I'm afraid I've led a pretty boring life so far. Nothing interesting. Not like you.'

'I find you the most interesting - and can I say the most beautiful - woman I have ever known.'

Penny was experiencing a confusion of emotions. The pleasure she derived from the attention of this attractive man was undoubtedly sexual, but she could no longer think in those terms without a surge of guilt. Was she doing as she had done before, unconsciously sending a message she was available, even willing? Is that what had happened before? Had she contributed to her own fate?

'Would you excuse me please? I would like to visit the ladies.'

When she returned, another man was with Talal but he left hurriedly.

'Penny, I'm sorry I am going to have to leave soon, my driver will take you home. But I want to ask you something.' His seriousness made her fear the worst. Was he about to ask about that night?

'Would you agree to come to Newmarket at the weekend? You could stay at my house and see my horses. We can go riding.'

In the ladies' room she had resolved to allow the relationship to go no further, but his question, and the relief of it not being what she'd feared, caught her off-guard. She agreed, and on her way home felt glad that she had.

There was a steady trickle of visitors at this early part of the evening. One or two of the regulars exchanged greetings with Pat as he descended the carpeted stairs to the reception. Ollie, he could see, was taking a temporary break to study to something behind the desk. *Probably the racing section,* thought Pat.

'Greetings, Venturians! Something interesting there, Ollie?' Pat asked.

Elena and Mia smiled. Ollie looked up a little guiltily, then saw it was Pat. 'I'm working on a retirement plan,' he said.

'A retirement plan for you or your bookmaker?' Pat winked at the two girls. Elena laughed and Ollie nodded in recognition of an all too accurate assessment.

'Pat, I'm sorry I was so rude when you called,' Elena whispered, glancing sideways at her colleague Mia.

Remembering Mia was one of Trist's girls who, though apparently busy with a customer, would be all ears, he moved closer to Elena.

'For God's sake, forget about it. It was nothing.'

'I had a terrible hangover, and I felt so angry about what happened to Penny, the dice thing and all that…'

'I understand. By the way, I rang Penny several times but didn't get her.'

'Actually, I've been round to her place,' Elena said even more softly, 'and she's a lot better. But I was surprised to hear from her that Ahmed had called.'

Monaghan thought about this. He hoped he hadn't given Ahmed encouragement, but knew the little Arab needed none. 'He's obviously got Penny's number and address from the Personnel Department. What's she going to do in the long term, did she say?'

'She doesn't know, but I got a funny feeling she hadn't completely ruled out coming back to Ventura.'

'God! Under what conditions could she contemplate that?'

'I'm not sure, but the only conditions anyone can contemplate working under here is with proper representation.'

'Well, I don't know,' he said thoughtfully, 'I've worked with unions before. In fact the GWU, but never found them much use. They have their own politics and know nothing about casinos. Anyway, they wouldn't have been able to do anything about Penny since she didn't want to say anything.'

'So we shouldn't do anything?' Her voice rose, then she lowered it again. 'We can't just take whatever they throw at us!'

'I'm not sure what to do, but you saw the reaction to the dice sackings. Not enough people care. And a lot of girls know what happened to Penny but still go to the parties. I'm not sure what the answer is.'

'Well I know what's not the answer - to do nothing!' Elena said forcefully.

Pat could see that their discussion was beginning to attract attention. 'Okay, you're right but maybe this isn't the time to discuss it,' he murmured, nodding in the direction of Ollie and Mia.

Chapter Nineteen

Pellzer pulled on the old-fashioned doorbell of Morgan Trist's Victorian townhouse and a few moments later Elspeth, an ex-Chica now acting as his secretary and receptionist, opened the door to welcome him, in the same seductive way she'd previously welcomed members at Ventura. As he passed one of the rooms on his way to Trist's study, he could see catering staff from Ventura preparing what looked like a buffet.

'Hi, Dan, sorry to drag you from the club but I thought we'd meet here. I'm expecting a visit later from Ahmed – about Talal,' announced Morgan, who, even at this early hour, was already pouring himself a drink.

'I saw them preparin' the table downstairs.'

'Oh, that's for a party I'm throwing tonight for the title fight. I'm gettin' bored livin' like a monk since that screwy dame stirred up all that shit.'

'Morg, we gotta be careful after the publicity we got…'

'Think I don't know that? Why d'ya think I'm havin' it here? This time no rookies like that crazy Penny. They're all handpicked and know the score. Hey, you're free to come as always!'

Pellzer didn't bother to decline the invitation or pursue the matter further, it was futile to argue with Trist on this subject.

'Dan, the subject of credit's coming up again. Ahmed says some players, Talal in particular, don't like that we bank cheques every day. It looks bad going through official accounts, them bein' Muslims and all that. He reckons that if we don't help they'll go somewhere that will.'

'Hey, this is a hard one! You know the law's strong on this.'

'Yeah, but can we lose players like Talal because of it?'

'What d'ya have in mind?'

'All those guys have accounts abroad. If we give 'em credit, without officially registering it, they could pay us outside. Better for them and us.'

'But how…?'

'Wait! let me finish!' Trist held up his hand. 'We've already seen Ellis and Nidditch will work for reward. Get them to find a way.'

Pellzer thought about it. It would certainly be profitable, saving on tax all round.

'But we gotta talk to those guys before we agree anything with Talal, Ahmed or anyone and decide what they're gonna get out of it.'

'You're right. Let's get Ellis down here now. We'll give them a percentage of all markers paid out of the country,' Trist suggested. 'What the hell, we avoid tax… this way it's clean profit.'

Ellis arrived just under two hours later and was shown into the other downstairs room where Pellzer waited. Trist, by that time, was occupied with arrangements for his party.

'Hi Jim. Morg's busy for the moment. We've got a bit of a problem and wanted to consult with you.' Pellzer guided Ellis to a chair with a comradely hand. 'Seems our friend Talal might stop playing at Ventura because he's showin' too many losses through his official bank account. Naturally, Ahmed has a solution but it sounds like something that would present difficulties. He wants us to give credit that Talal pays through an overseas account at a later date. I know, the law in this country has us by the balls and though it sounds like an ideal solution we couldn't ask managers to do it, even if we knew how it could be done. You have to deal with these guys every day, what d'ya think we should say to them?'

'Well, it's not the first I'm hearing this. Ahmed mentioned it the other day. It's a problem for many punters. Sooner or later somebody will find a way around it,' said Ellis thoughtfully.

Pellzer was encouraged by Ellis's response. 'When they do, they'll take our business.'

'Yes, the problem's complicated and even if we found a way, can we trust them to pay?'

'Well, we wouldn't do it for just anybody and there are ways to minimise the risk. We'd take that risk if we could find a way to do it that wouldn't be detected. You sayin' it could be done?' Pellzer asked.

'It'd be difficult, but I think it… I'd have to speak to John. He's the only senior manager on nights who'd co-operate and we'd have to keep it within a small circle.' Ellis looked thoughtful.

'Jim, Morg and I would greatly appreciate if we could find a way not to lose those guys, and of course like the union thing, we'd be more than happy to reward such loyalty with a share in those benefits.'

'Okay, let me talk to John, see how it can be done. I'll get back to you soon as possible.'

'Jim, that's great. Before you go, let's see if we can raise Morg, he's around somewhere.'

Trist was in the large room that adjoined his study, giving instructions to a technician rigging up hi-fi speakers while another was mounting a large TV on the wall.

'Hi, you guys! What's new?' Trist called out as they entered.

'Morg, I explained this situation to Jim. Of course he understands the problem better than we do. It's complicated, but he's gonna try work somethin' out.'

'Jim, we know we can rely on you. Say, why don't you come to my shindig tonight. It's the Ali-Foreman fight. We might get Ahmed and the Prince across, maybe even Dan here?' Trist winked mischievously at Pellzer.

'Great, why not. When does it start?' Ellis had heard of the Chairman's notorious parties.

'We'll start late evenin', but the fight's not till early mornin' so we have time to get a little taste of this and that - you know?' Trist laughed.

Pellzer agreed to attend. He could see, as Trist had, that here was an opportunity to draw Ellis ever closer into their group.

Later that evening, Ellis returned to Trist's home to be welcomed by the party's hostesses, Elspeth and Katerina. The Ventura Chairman, resplendent in a white suede suit, was already in full flow, gyrating none too athletically to the strains of 'Waterloo' between girls in Abba costumes who Ellis recognised as cocktail Chicas. Pellzer, who was not dancing, rose to greet and channel him through double-doors to an adjoining room that was only a little less noisy. There were several sofas and easy chairs in the room but they were already taken by guests, some of whom Ellis recognised – a few sports' personalities, a politician and the film star Tony Salinas – so they sat on the ledge of a large bay window out of earshot of the nearest group.

'I talked with John about the credit,' said Ellis, anticipating Pellzer's first question. Pellzer merely nodded. 'We can see a lot of difficulties.' Still Pellzer said nothing, waiting for Ellis to continue. 'Whatever way we look at it, we'll have to involve several members of the staff and that's dangerous.'

'So you're sayin' it can't be done?' Pellzer asked.

'Well, we've got to talk about the problems, but I... er... I think this isn't the place right now.' Ellis indicated the approach of Trist, draped in Chicas. Pellzer agreed, he could see Trist was already in party mode and likely to be indiscreet.

'Hey, why you guys hidin', scared you'll be groped or something? Aha, you settling that stuff with the cheques?' Trist called out, confirming Pellzer's fear.

'Hey, Morg, come on, it's party-time. Leave that stuff to office hours!' Pellzer intervened loudly, in a passable imitation of Trist himself.

'You're right, Dan. Hey, Rye! What's going down here, get some stimulus over here for my friends!' Trist roared through to the other room. Another rush of commands brought up the volume of the music and a bevy of Chicas to surrounded Ellis and Pellzer, including Chica Rosetta in boxer's boots and shorts. Round her neck a pair of boxing gloves offered only minimal coverage of her impressive bust. She was taking contributions to the Big Fight sweepstake while serving as a prop for Trist's jokes about going the distance and taking shots below the belt.

A stream of Chicas delivered drinks, while Rye offered those needing other stimulants, a visit to the games-room on the other side of the main lounge. Ellis was feeling good. Clarissa, a cocktail Chica, was doing her best to distract him from the pre-fight build-up now being shown on one of two large televisions. She was succeeding.

By the time a dishevelled Ellis descended from an upstairs room, bottle in hand, Ali was cavorting around the ring in celebration as Pellzer and other guests discussed loudly and animatedly the course the fight had taken. Trist was stretched out on a chaise longue, a boxer's dressing gown covering a throbbing mound on his midriff. A stiletto heel could just be seen protruding from below the robe.

'Jim, my friend!' another recognisable voice called above the din of television and hi-fi. Ahmed was standing by the double doors to the games-room, a Chica costume in one hand and a drink in the other. Behind him on the large snooker table, other human forms were in various stages of undress.

'Hi Ahmed,' he said belatedly, his mind acting slower than usual due to the effects of alcohol and the distracting activities behind the Arab.

'Ah, I see you have interest in billiard.' Ahmed glanced over his shoulder.

'It's snooker, actually,' Ellis corrected him, 'but never mind, it's a table game.'

'I think maybe you also had game upstairs,' Ahmed winked. 'But have you good news for my friend the Prince?'

Ellis was still watching the antics on the green baize. 'There'll be some problems but we'll work something out.'

She woke from her reverie when the wheel noise from the limousine changed from a whisper to the crunching sound of tyres on a pebbled driveway. A blast from the car's horn ensured her attention, as well as the waiting reception party in the large red-bricked house. A fully uniformed, dark-skinned butler and traditionally attired maid scurried to the entrance, closely followed by a beaming Prince Talal.

'Penny, welcome to Newmarket! I am so happy that you have come.' The Prince kissed her hand and led her inside to a spacious hallway. On the first landing of the stairway, facing the entrance, the central focus was an enormous portrait of an Arab horseman. Penny stopped and looked up in wide-eyed appreciation.

'My father. He is a great horseman,' said Talal with pride, anticipating Penny's enquiry and pleased by her reaction. 'Please, let Ayesha show you to your room. Take what time you need. Come down when you are ready. I will be in the lounge here,' he smiled engagingly before giving instructions in Arabic to the maid carrying Penny's baggage.

The large bedroom was lavishly furnished. Penny excitedly unpacked her clothes and donned the riding apparel that she had hired for the weekend and when she joined Talal in the lounge, he was pouring champagne.

'I think we can have one glass to celebrate your arrival. We must not have more if we are to stay on the horses!'

She laughed, took the glass and kissed him on the cheek. 'Mansur, thank you for inviting me here.'

'You have never been to Newmarket before? But you do ride before?' he asked, suddenly aware that he may have assumed too much.

'I don't know Newmarket but yes, I do ride, though not for some time – I hope I haven't forgotten.'

'No, you never forget, but don't worry, you will have a friendly horse.'

They finished their drinks and made their way to a gate at the back of the garden where a stable-hand waited with three horses.

'Good-day, Ma-am, this is Rabasal. He's very respec'ful. You'll enjoy being with 'im.' The young man patted the horse and handed the reins to Penny.

'Thank you, John. Stay near us for a short while,' the Prince instructed as he helped Penny mount the sleek chestnut.

They took off slowly across the plain while the stable boy took up the rear. The mist was beginning to clear a little and the crisp November air fired her skin. She felt a strange exhilaration to be astride the tall mount and be riding alongside the handsome Prince. The fairytale aspect appealed to her.

'You are handling him as an expert. He is, of course, of pure Arab bloodstock,' Talal said proudly.

'Oh, thank you. I do feel comfortable. You were right, I haven't forgotten. Will any of your horses run soon?' she asked.

'Unfortunately the flat season has just finished so we must wait until March but we have had a good season. Next year I hope to have a real chance in one of the Classics which is run here, the Two Thousand Guineas. Do you think you could try a trot now?' he asked.

'Perhaps more than that!' she laughed, and took off at a gallop, leaving him standing and momentarily shocked. He caught up a few seconds later but reined in his horse to gallop by her side, laughing at her audacity. For the first time she was feeling life had some purpose. She felt liberated.

The day had been wonderful. He had planned everything to perfection. After dinner, served by his own staff who had now retired for the night, they were truly alone for the first time. She was feeling slightly tipsy from the wine, but in control. She worried what she might do, how she would feel, when the time came for intimacy. Would the thought of that horrible night inhibit her? There was now no doubt she wanted him to make love to her, but fear mingled with desire.

When he touched her, the fear dissipated.

Of this first time together, she would remember each pleasurable phase: his seductive touch and kisses, the feverish removal of their clothes, more kissing and his soft hands touching her body, followed by oral stimulation and, when neither could wait any longer, an urgent penetration and orgasm. They lingered longer on the second coupling, less urgency, more variation. A prolonged ecstasy, then…

She woke to find him still asleep and holding her close. Her renewal was complete.

Chapter Twenty

From Pellzer's office Ellis could see the grass in the park wore a blanket of November frost and even the tops of some cars retained a thin layer of white, although the sun was now lancing through the window. He turned to Nidditch, who sat reading the morning newspaper while they waited for Pellzer.

'So they stopped all the traffic in this area last night during this bomb alert?'

'Yeah, they thought it was the IRA, up to their tricks again.' Nidditch put the paper back on the desk. 'Fortunately, it was a false alarm. It didn't really affect business. But they reckon it's only a matter of time before the bastards strike again somewhere and…'

The door opened and Pellzer entered. 'Hey guys, sorry. Got caught up with people from the police advisory section. After last night's alert, they're giving advice to anyone with premises that attract a large volume of customers what steps to take if there's a bomb alert…'

'Fuckin' big ones, is my advice!' Ellis quipped as he took a seat. The others laughed, nodding.

'Okay, to business. What's the situation?' Pellzer looked from one to the other.

'Well, the more we look at this, the more problems we see,' Nidditch began, 'The only way, is to use handpicked staff to authorise chips at the table without putting up a marker, or putting it up, but quietly taking it off some time later.'

'The problem with every other method is the falsified documents needed,' Ellis added. 'This way there's no false or altered documents and in the worse case, if anyone spots anything, it can be put down to human error with the markers.'

'We still have to involve some others in this. There's no way to avoid that,' said Nidditch.

'Yes, and the more people we involve, the more risk. Security might also catch a transaction on camera.' Ellis could see Nidditch's look of scepticism. 'Okay, it's unlikely, but possible.'

'Okay. How do we deal with those problems?' Pellzer held out his hands to them.

'Well, security reports go to Bollard,' said Ellis leaning forward over the desk. 'If there's anything iffy he usually asks the duty manager to investigate, that's one of us. If he suspected it involved the manager or he didn't like the result of our investigation... I suppose it would eventually come to you.'

'Okay, we'll handle that. What about the others? How many people need to be in the loop?' Pellzer pressed.

'We'll have to use a pit boss, and a couple of inspectors at least on each shift.'

'That's quite a lotta people. Do you know who these people are and how we keep them happy and quiet?'

Ellis looked at Nidditch for confirmation before continuing. 'We've got people in mind. They wouldn't cost much. There's a couple of Morg's girls who've been made inspector and Chicas who we know are putting it about with the Arabs. We'll make sure they don't say anything. A lot of those birds don't have a clue what's happening anyway.

There are certain pit bosses we can convince with a bit of financial help in the way of overtime, and preference with scheduling. They'll make sure the right people are on the right tables.'

'Well okay, do we agree this can work?' Pellzer asked. They nodded. 'Well if you guys are happy... let's try it!'

Ellis looked at Nidditch. He knew that, like himself, he still harboured some doubts and felt he should qualify their agreement.

'The players we're talking about would only be playing on the VIP level and we'll only be able to do it day shift, because Draper and his team run the floor at night.'

'Draper's always interested in what's happening on other floors and other shifts,' Nidditch added, 'and it's his job to know what players are in for, and how much they've signed for. He could notice we're getting action but taking less cheques. He'll look at results and the cheque-cashing records and might ask awkward questions.'

'He's right,' Ellis nodded. 'Draper could twig and maybe even Bland if there's too great a change in results.'

All three sank into silence again.

'This guy always has his own agenda. What's he lookin' for?' asked Pellzer, cradling his head between thumb and forefinger.

Ellis shrugged. 'It's like a moral thing. He should be in politics or the church.'

'He shouldn't be in this business. How does he think he earns his money? We work with sex and gamblin', whatever way you look at it. Can you take a moral tone with this job?' Pellzer shook his head in frustration.

'Yes, he's got a fucking opinion on everything and from what I hear he's in support of the Union!' Nidditch added bitterly.

They all paused for a few minutes before Pellzer spoke again. 'You're right, Draper and his guys are a problem - not only with this but also on the union thing. We're gonna have to find a solution.'

'Anyway, the most urgent problem is Talal,' Ellis said. 'We should tell Ahmed, and him, that for now he can take credit this way, only on day shift. Let's see how it works before we push it further.' Nidditch nodded agreement.

'Okay. Let's get Ahmed and Talal in to iron out the procedures, including when and where we're gonna be paid. Important for you guys too, right?' smiled Pellzer. Then, as they prepared to leave, he added: 'Oh yes, Marta tells me that maybe Chica Penny's coming back. Seems Talal has somethin' to do with that. But listen, keep an eye on her.'

'That's a surprise,' Nidditch said as they waited for the lift. 'I didn't think we'd see Penny again.'

'Ahmed was trying to fix it because Talal has a thing about her, and for sure he was playing more when she was here.' Ellis pressed the button to go down.

'Could be good for us, but could also be dodgy, with all the publicity surrounding her,' Nidditch warned.

'She might be the one to push the credit out to him. I'm sure he could keep her legs open and her mouth shut.'

Although Elena had pre-warned him, Monaghan still couldn't believe that Penny, was coming back to Ventura.

'So when's our young friend returning?' he asked Elena as he perused the files on reception.

'Next Monday. Back on days, in the VIP.'

'I don't get it. How will she cope? Will she just forget about the whole thing?'

'Women don't forget that sort of thing!' Elena replied irritably. Pat knew she was annoyed, not with him, but the situation. He waited for her to continue. 'It seems she's in love, with Talal. Don't they say love conquers all?'

'You mean they have a serious relationship?' asked Monaghan.

'I mean he's screwing her. To the delight of the chief matchmaker, your friend Ahmed, and I suspect others within Ventura.' Elena seemed compelled to debunk Pat's idealised description of the affair.

Pat fell silent for a few moments. 'So, did you talk to her about this?' he said finally. 'Is there anything we can or should do?

'I can't see it lasting. For him it's just an another fling with a Chica, but she thinks it's serious. Of course I tried to warn her, but I don't want to fall out with her and destroy her confidence again. She thinks he'll protect her and he will - while it lasts. For Trist and his gang it's ideal. She comes back, killing off the negative publicity and Talal, their biggest punter, comes in more often because she's there.' Elena shrugged in resignation.

Pat had quickly found that people could be demanding of his time so it was necessary to prioritise. This meant he sometimes had to leave the justifiable complaint of a regular player to attend to the petty grievance of a high roller. So he had learnt the art of the diplomatic withdrawal.

Tonight he'd already avoided possible snarl-ups by missing out the Playa restaurant where several garrulous regulars were dining. On the same floor, in the casino, he'd successfully escaped from a potentially long discussion on the merits of a betting system devised by an Indian member who'd set up almost permanent residence on one of the roulettes.

As he started to make his way to the VIP level, Ollie met him on the stairs. 'Pat, just to warn you about Al Khazari. You're aware he's been doing money all week? Well, according to Jim, he's in even deeper today.'

There would be no avoiding Hakeem Al Khazari, a big player who'd only just returned to London after being away for some time. It was always difficult when players lost large amounts quickly without even momentary success. Pat prepared himself for the onslaught, but when he arrived on the floor Khazari seemed to be making a partial recovery. A quantity of high-value chips were stacked in front of him.

'Ah, Pat. Just on time!' Ellis greeted him. He was with Tony Roberts, the VIP day-shift pit boss, and Ian Lowe. 'We've a situation tailor-made for your skills.' The three men grinned. Pat waited for the joke.

'The "Lady" herself, Mrs Bahdazreh, wants to continue playing on punto. She's in for two grand but objects to the gentleman sitting opposite who's apparently pickin' his nose and doing other disgusting things with his false teeth. He's losing five grand, by the way.'

'Jesus! What the bloody hell can I do? Put the camera on him, catch him green-handed?' Pat joked.

'Oh Meester Pat! Please, I weesh to talk wiss you!' the offended woman rose from the table.

Though Pat usually managed to appease the constantly complaining Mrs Bahdazreh by some means, this complaint presented a particular problem. The gentleman of whose behaviour she disapproved was a recent arrival from one of the Gulf States and had become a frequent visitor to the club. His level of play increased with each visit and information obtained about him indicated he had considerable wealth.

'Okay, Mrs Bahdazreh, leave it with me!' He held up his hands to dissuade her from further protestation.

Criticising a member's conduct always required diplomacy. Comment on their personal hygiene was a veritable minefield. Here the problem was exaggerated by another factor - Pat knew the gentleman spoke and understood little English. He paused, wondering how to handle the situation.

'Patrick, please!' Another voice diverted his attention from the immediate problem. It was Mr Al Khazari. 'What they try to do to me? I am losing all day, all week. Just when I begin to recover, they take away the dealer to make me lose again. It is not fair. They try to upset me so that I will not come again!'

'No, Mr Al Khazari. It's not like that,' Pat answered instinctively, still considering the problem on the other table. He looked around to see the managers, including the newly arrived Draper, were some distance away, apparently involved in animated discussion. For the moment he was alone with both problems.

'Mr Al Khazari. It's the end of the day shift, so dealers are changing over. The night staff are coming on. It's happening on every table.'

'So, it doesn't matter I lose all this money? They go home without a care,' the player said bitterly.

'No, Mr Al Khazari. All the people here value your membership, but you've had a bad run of luck. The staff have no control over this. Perhaps you should try another table?' Pat knew a change of position would in no way guarantee recovery but could see no other immediate solution.

Mrs Bahdazreh was becoming impatient. 'What you weel do? I want to play but not wiss thees person here!'

'One moment, Madame! I'll be with you directly!'

'What she wants, this stupid woman?' Al Khazari asked audibly.

'Who you are, to speak of me thees way?' she shouted.

'Shut up! *Sharmuta*!'

'Agh! Pig! Don't dare to insult me!' she screamed at the top of her voice.

The insults began to fly back and forth in a mixture of Arabic, French and English while Pat tried vainly to mediate. Draper and Lowe hurried to the scene.

After several minutes Draper, all the while agreeing quietly with Al Khazari that the Bahdazreh woman was a virago, managed to persuade him to go to the Playa, where one of his favourite Chicas was dealing. This change, argued Draper, might break his run of luck.

Pat eventually guided the hysterical woman to a seat in the restaurant where, with the aid of the best cognac and canapes on the house account, he helped her compose herself.

A little later, unnoticed by her, Mr Nose-Picker passed their table on his way out. He smiled sympathetically at Pat, his eye moving on to Mrs Bahdazreh. A shrug of the shoulders and shake of his head indicated his incomprehension at her unseemly behaviour.

Draper had returned to the VIP casino floor and Pat, excusing himself from Mrs Bahdazreh, joined him.

'How is it with Al Khazari?'

'For the moment okay, but for how long?' Draper shrugged. 'She's a fucking pain as always, but Al Khazari's becoming a problem because they're letting him take credit way above his limit and he's feeling the strain. It seems anything goes here!'

'You'll have talked to Jim about this?'

'Yes, that's what we were arguing about before their fight,' Draper continued, 'it's a subject that's been in dispute for some time and problems I predicted are now surfacing. Another example of the general decline in standards in this place.'

'What's the answer then?'

'Well, between you and me, the answer's a new Chairman and Managing Director, but that's not going to happen,' Draper said quietly.

'So, what then?

'I'm not sure, but having union representation wouldn't hurt.'

'With Pettigrew and Potts as representatives.'

'Well… yes,' Draper grimaced. 'It might be better if your friend Elena was elected as a rep.'

'You're probably right, though I don't have much confidence in that Union in particular.'

Draper was about to respond but the reappearance of Al Khazari near the restaurant, where Mrs Bahdazreh was still sitting, diverted their attention.

Chapter Twenty-One

On Penny's instruction, Talal's driver pulled up a discreet distance from the Ventura. She felt she'd rather walk the remaining few hundred yards than arrive ostentatiously by limousine. Until that moment she'd felt confident in her decision to return, but as she rounded the corner and caught her first sight of Ventura, her nerve faltered.

Although she'd passed the electrical appliance shop a thousand times and knew there was nothing in the window to interest her, she stopped to view its contents. The pretext didn't give her time to bolster her courage as she'd hoped; instead, it allowed time for more doubts to creep in. The positive images she'd constructed with Mansur's help were now dissipating. She turned to retrace her steps away from the Ventura.

'Hi, Penny! Great to see you. How are you?'

She stopped, startled by the sudden intrusion. Tony Roberts was coming towards her.

'Oh… er… Tony, hello.'

'I heard you were back today. There'll be a few people glad to see you.'

'Really? Who'd that be?' she asked with genuine curiosity, finding herself moving involuntarily with the Pit Boss towards the casino.

'Quite a few of the players actually, not to mention the management.'

'Well, I don't know about the players, but the managers? I can't imagine they ever thought much of my ability.'

'Actually, your dealing was improving, but more importantly, you have rapport with players.'

Penny made a dismissive gesture, but was pleased to hear his comment. It was true she seemed to have fewer disputes with customers. By and large they reserved their tantrums for other girls.

They had now reached the front of the Ventura building. She felt confused as Tony stood back to allow her to pass through the staff entrance. How to escape now? What excuse to give?

'Penny! Hi! Nice to see you back!' The greeting came from Steve Lucas, an inspector whom she often felt had dreaded her appearance on his table.

She began to think maybe she could do this after all.

The reception she received in the Chica-room and on the casino floor was no less friendly. No one made reference to the real reason for her absence, some even asked her if she had now fully recovered from her illness. Unknown to her, it had been orchestrated. Marta Woods, on Pellzer's instruction, had briefed the senior day staff. They, in turn, had passed the message on.

When Talal arrived late that afternoon he came straight to her table. Given Ventura's oft quoted rule concerning relations between Chicas and players, she at first felt uncomfortable, but Jim Ellis even asked her to stay on the table longer than usual to please the Prince. It was all going better than she could possibly have hoped. It helped of course that she had Mansur's reassuring smiles, although her presence was not helping him - he was losing.

There were several other players at the table, but Penny was handling the game well considering she hadn't dealt for a while. In fact, she reflected, this was probably the longest time she'd been on a table without making serious errors. There was only momentary confusion over the procedure for giving chips against a credit marker, but the Inspector and Tony Roberts supervised this operation as there had been a recent change in the regulation.

By late afternoon Ahmed arrived, to pronounce undying affection for the lovely English *Wardah*, sending her into a fit of giggles - fortunately at the moment she was going on a long overdue rest period.

On her return to the floor, she found the Prince still playing and was surprised when she was assigned once again to his table. For a brief period he recouped some money, but his luck turned again and he was soon taking credit once more. At seven-thirty he retired from the table, still in good spirits in spite of what appeared to her to be heavy losses.

Jim Ellis permitted her to go home a little earlier as she'd helped them by staying on the table while the Prince was playing.

The casino opened every day of the year, and because of this, senior managers were expected to take their time off on what were considered to be the quietest days. Therefore Bland deputised for Draper on Mondays and Tuesdays.

Ellis regretted that Nidditch, at an earlier date, hadn't pushed his claim to act as night-manager. The implementation of their new credit policy would have been so much more simple - never more apparent than at this moment.

Bland, having just come on duty, was going through the change-over procedure as zealously as Draper might've done himself, asking in particular of the cashier a list of the day's transactions. He seemed particularly interested in Talal, obviously aware the Prince had been playing. The Pit Boss, on Ellis's instruction, had registered only a small loss by the Prince.

'So, Talal lost only a couple of grand in cash?'

Tony Roberts glanced at Ellis before responding to Bland. 'Yeah, he was up and down all day before finally losing only what he came in for.'

Bland didn't look totally convinced. 'Odd – I heard Lucas in the break room say he was doing bundles.'

Ellis could see Roberts was thrown by this, but surreptitiously signalled to his Pit Boss not to offer further explanation. They waited as Bland studied the rest of the day's information.

'We've taken a bit of a beating elsewhere. Pity we didn't catch Talal for more,' Bland added, as he scrutinised the pit sheet. Satisfied that they'd passed on all relevant information, Ellis and Roberts moved off as Bland liaised with his pit boss, Ian Lowe.

As he made his way out of the gaming area, Ellis stopped to say goodnight and have a last joke with some of the regular players, then he cheerily dismissed himself with a final wave but didn't leave the floor. Instead he moved to the far end of the restaurant, took a coffee and brooded over the exchange with Bland. It confirmed, even earlier than expected, what he and Nidditch had feared - operating this credit system was dangerous. As he'd just seen, an innocent piece of gossip in the rest-room could arouse suspicion and blow the thing wide open. It had long been a regulation that staff couldn't impart information about players to outside parties, but staff couldn't be prevented from discussing the actions of players with colleagues or, more specifically, with other managers. To attempt any such prohibition would only arouse more suspicion.

If their alternative credit system was to work, it required the involvement of all floor management; that was impossible with Draper. It all came back to the same thing - he'd have to be removed, and that wouldn't be easy.

Bland was another story. He'd got off too easily with the dice and punto incidents but maybe they could still be used as a reason for replacing him as relief manager. With Nidditch in charge when Draper was off, they would at least reduce the latter's control and influence.

Lowe completed the result for the first hour of the night shift and showed it to Bland. It was still negative although there had been a slight improvement.

'What's Jim hanging around for?' Lowe asked the manager. Ellis sitting alone in the restaurant was an unusual sight. Being a socialiser, he would normally be in the pub within half-an-hour from the end of his shift. When he did go in the restaurant, he'd be with customers.

Bland indicated towards the restaurant. 'I think that answers your question.'

Lowe groaned as Ahmed joined the day-shift manager, then changed the subject. 'I hear Penny Irwin was back today, you see her when you came on?'

'No. She'd already gone,' said Bland. 'If what we heard was true, I don't know how she could come back.'

'No, it's hard to understand, but apparently it's to do with Talal. Ah! Here's the man who'll know something about it!'

'Anythin' you want to know, ask Monaghan.' Pat ambled towards them, greeting customers with a wave and smile.

Bland gripped Pat's elbow. 'We're talking about Penny, how she could come back after what happened.'

'Ah, that's a difficult question. I'm not sure. I think she's a bit confused.'

'We reckon Talal coaxed her back,' Bland probed. 'But why would he want her to work here? He can knock her off wherever she works.'

'Maybe he thinks she's lucky for him,' Pat offered. Bland looked thoughtful.

'You don't think Elena had a hand in it?' Lowe asked. 'Maybe she thinks Penny could help embarrass the powers above and persuade Chicas they need union protection?'

'No, she'd no say in Penny coming back. Actually, she thought Penny should've gone to the police.'

'That would've really stirred up the shit. Oh no! Talking of shit-stirring – here comes our friend!' Bland grimaced as Ahmed approached. The two gaming men broke off to look to the tables while Pat waited for the Arab.

'Patrick, it's yerself!' Ahmed called out. 'Our beautiful Penny is back. I spoke with her earlier. She is so happy now.'

'Yes, I haven't seen her today but I hear she was alright.'

'I just speak with Jim. He said she worked perfect today. We have all missed her. There are so few people who know to treat customers properly!'

He shuffled to a roulette table where three young Arab men were playing. Pat could see several important players in the restaurant and went to check that they'd been given appropriate attention.

He was addressing the Chica serving them when he was interrupted by an explosion of shouting at a roulette table. Pat moved to investigate what seemed to be a heated discussion between the manager and the three young men Ahmed had spoken to earlier. The one saving grace for the moment was that Ahmed, although nearby, had unusually but thankfully not yet become involved. The three players, screaming abuse at Bland, now stormed across the casino area in Pat's direction. He prepared himself to intercept them, but at that moment Ahmed lurched across to delay their departure and begin his own inquest. Pat approached and attempted a polite intervention but was ignored as they continued an animated discussion in Arabic. Arms gesticulated towards Bland, who stood a little way off in frustrated readiness to re-enter the discussion. Pat wondered if he should ask the manager what had happened but thought it better to stay in close attendance to the Arabs.

Ahmed seemed to have taken some heat out of the discussion. He now attempted to include Pat by introducing him to the young Saudis. They gave him a cursory gesture of recognition and headed, still complaining, towards the exit. Ahmed stalled them again near the door, permitting Pat another attempt at conciliation. But the arrival of the impatient and frustrated Bland seemed to ignite their anger once again. This time Ahmed made no move to stop them and they departed, with a final tirade, down and out through reception.

Ahmed shook his head and looked at Bland with disgust. 'This man will lose Ventura all players.'

'Look, you don't know what—!' Bland started, but Ahmed gave a dismissive wave and left, muttering under his breath.

'That bastard will stir up more shit over this!' snarled Bland.

'What was it about?' asked Pat.

'They put on late bets, we removed them, and of course one of their numbers came up.' Bland shrugged and strode off, leaving Pat to fill in the rest for himself. He knew Bland to be a man of few words but feared repercussions if the management side of the story wasn't put across convincingly.

'Will you make a full report on the incident?' asked Pat when he caught up with him.

'If I'm asked, yes!' replied Bland sharply.

Pat took the hint. He decided to speak with Lowe who probably knew as much, if not more, about the incident than his floor manager.

Lowe had a sardonic smile on his face. 'Our "friend" Ahmed sort everythin' out?'

'I'm still not clear,' sighed Pat. 'What's your side?'

'They arrived a couple of days ago and have been playing on day shift. They're Saudi Princes.' Monaghan nodded, this much he already knew. 'When I came on duty they were playing quietly, no problem. Then the Inspector called me tae say they were placing late bets and occasionally playing over the maximum. As you know, this maximum question's always a problem. Are they playing with the same money or not? We decided it was the same money because only one of them bought in, and they're all placing the exact same bets. We told them politely, but the next spin same again - late and over the maximum – but this time it was the winning number. The tallest one, who seems tae be a kinda leader, went berserk when we refused to pay.' Lowe shook his head. 'I don't know why they started all this aggro, they were good as gold before.'

'Maybe security have it on tape?' Pat looked up to the camera.

Lowe gave a derisory chuckle. 'They *say* they were watching other tables.'

Pat could see there was no significant play on those tables.

'Okay, we'll see what comes of it. Hopefully it'll pass, but the big one in particular was in a rage.' Pat made some notes as he spoke.

'Yeah, he claimed Colin called him a cheat.'

'Really? Colin didn't do that, did he?'

Lowe shook his head. 'Not while I was there. They carried on arguing, but I'm sure Colin never said anything like that. The guy misunderstood or, like many people, made it up when he couldnae win the argument.'

Pat felt he could go no further. He hoped there would be no repercussions but had an uneasy feeling about this one.

Chapter Twenty-two

Bollard had hoped for a quiet Tuesday, but his work-day was only a few hours old and already the problems were mounting. On his arrival he'd been summonsed upstairs to hear the latest complaints about his department. Fortunately he'd not had to listen to Trist's rantings, the message being delivered in Pellzer's more rational terminology. It was, however, no less emphatic: Bland was an incompetent, and at the very least must not continue as deputy night-manager.

Frank hadn't yet had a report of the latest dispute from his own department but as Pellzer had reminded him, the same manager was in charge the night of the dice scam, the dispute with Bin Assaid and now with the Saudi Princes. All were embarrassing and financially damaging, and although Bollard's own investigation hadn't shown Bland to be wholly culpable, one thing had to be said - the man was certainly incident-prone. He was now being pressed to demote Bland, and there seemed little else he could do. But he still wanted the full story behind the previous night's affair.

Not surprisingly, Security had no tape of the incident. Monaghan's report took a neutral position, adding that he and Ahmed Hammoud had unsuccessfully intervened to try to placate the clients. Frank was sure that the source of Pellzer's knowledge would have been Ahmed, probably via Trist.

With no independent record, it was impossible for Bollard to say just what had happened. From experience he could imagine the gaming staff might be technically right, but in public relations that wasn't everything. There were always other questions. Had there been an intent to cheat or was it simply over-enthusiastic betting? Were the customers informed properly? Had the dispute been handled with diplomacy?

In the end the investigation was academic. That evening Bland was once again scheduled to be acting night-manager, but Bollard relieved him of those responsibilities.

It would've been more correct to advise Bland's immediate boss before demoting him, but Pellzer would not hear of any delay and Bollard feared a confrontation with Draper at this point could make matters worse.

Ian Lowe hurried to the first floor, fumbling with the catch of his elasticated bow-tie. He was still tucking his shirt into his waistband and arranging his jacket as he approached the triumvirate of Tony Roberts, Ellis and Nidditch.

'Miss your wake-up call?' Nidditch asked.

Joke or indirect criticism? Coming from Nidditch it was unlikely to be innocuous, but Lowe simply smiled, ignored the comment and turned to his counterpart Roberts.

'What's happening?'

'Well, as you can see, Talal's still here and with the chips he's got in front of him he's a bit in front, having come in for cash.'

Lowe frowned when he saw Penny dealing to Talal. It was common knowledge that she was involved with the Prince, or 'shagging the Sheihk', as the staff put it. Though official policy and casino tradition were being ignored, he decided to say nothing about it for now.

'The Saudis, the ones that disputed with Bland?' Roberts waited, Lowe nodded but didn't comment. 'Between them, they're losing seventeen grand. Khouri has lost a bit, but Fischmann's winning. Here's the fills and break list. Okay?' Barely waiting for confirmation, he gave Lowe the documents and signalled to Ellis, who was also ready to go, that the handover was complete.

'Colin not here yet?' Lowe asked as Roberts moved away.

'Er… I think John's relief manager tonight,' he said awkwardly, looking across to Nidditch.

Lowe was puzzled, he knew Bland was in that evening, he'd passed him on the stairway earlier.

Nidditch coming towards him, cleared his throat. 'Frank told Colin not to come on this floor tonight, because of friction with the Saudis. I'm night-manager.'

'I don't understand. They were pulling strokes, Colin hadnae any choice,' said Lowe.

'I don't know about that.' Nidditch shrugged. 'Jim says they were good as gold yesterday and again today, so somebody upset them last-night.'

Lowe shook his head. 'Na, they were playing with the same money tae pass the maximum and late-betting.'

'Well, they're not doing it now. Maybe it's the way you handle them. I suggest you leave them to me. They're losing money, I don't want them upset, specially as they're playing on the same table as Talal,' Nidditch said sharply and walked away.

Lowe was angry at Nidditch's assertion and was inclined to argue but the table staff had arrived for assignment to the tables, so he reluctantly postponed his discussion with the manager to attend to this duty.

Before he'd allocated anyone, Nidditch returned. 'Put Eva and Bentley on Talal's table,' he ordered.

Furious, Lowe was of a mind to hand him the break-list and tell him to do it himself. Quite apart from Nidditch's manner, his choice of team to run the table was questionable. Chica Eva was a bouncy, vivacious girl but a bit dim and the veteran inspector Bentley was an ineffectual time-server. To assign them to a table where Ventura's biggest punter and the problematic Saudis were playing seemed to be asking for trouble. Nevertheless, he carried out Nidditch's instruction.

'Hi, Ian!' shouted Penny as she came off the table, having been relieved by Eva.

'Hello, Penny. How's our big punter doing?' he asked mischievously.

'Oh… er… you mean the Prince?' She blushed and whispered, 'He's losing a lot, as usual.'

Lowe wondered how long Talal would continue playing now Penny was off duty. He wandered over to where the Prince was playing, and was quickly joined by Nidditch.

'Listen, if you want to take an early dinner I'll look after this,' said Nidditch in a more reasonable tone.

Normally Lowe wouldn't have taken his meal-break so early but it gave him a chance to stop at the second floor and hear Bland's version of events.

Bland was sitting in the Playa restaurant with a coffee. This was indicative of his mood, as normally he didn't move from the gaming area except for his meal-break. He glanced up at Lowe.

'So, how's your new boss?' he asked bitterly.

'He's a cunt as usual! What's goin' on? Why's he there?'

'Bollard thinks I can't handle the public relations side of the job so he's put Nidditch as relief night manager.'

'Oh aye! Because he's so charming?' Lowe laughed ironically. "Is this because of the Saudis?'

'Well according to Bollard, that was the final straw after the problems with Bin Assaid and the dice scam.'

'None of that was down to you.'

'I was in charge, so it seems it's my fault. Although I fancy that bastard Ahmed's put the word in upstairs. Bollard said he got a report. The only other person who would've been likely to report on this was Monaghan.'

'I'm sure he wouldnae have stuck it in for you.'

'No, I'm sure it was that bastard. It gets worse every day. It's getting to the stage where it's not worth working here,' Bland grimaced.

Lowe couldn't think of anything to say to make matters better. He left Bland hunched over his now empty coffee cup.

'Hello there. You about to partake of some sustenance?' called Pat when Lowe entered the canteen.

'No, I'm goin' tae eat something.'

'Ah ha, then you must try the porridge, tonight's special!'

'That's why I'm here instead of the VIP restaurant,' Lowe laughed, then, remembering Bland's words, turned back. 'I'll just grab something and join you. I've something to ask you.'

Carmen, a waitress Chica on her meal-break at another table, smiled to Lowe and looked disappointed when he joined Pat.

'You heard about Bland?' asked Lowe as he placed his tray on the table.

'I didn't get details, but I heard Nidditch's now covering the VIP while Draper's off.'

'Actually, he's been demoted after the ruck with the Saudis. Bollard said he got reports, one from the PR department, and that after the Bin Assaid and the dice incidents, this was the final straw.'

'The criticism would've come from Ahmed. I put in a report, but only the bare facts about a dispute.' Pat shook his head. 'I did suggest to Colin he file a report himself to tell your side.'

'He's a bit stubborn at times, but really, this wasnae his fault, they were pullin' blatant strokes and passin' the maximums.'

'Well they're back today. What are they up to now?'

'It's strange. They were so angry yesterday but are back today. Ellis says they're good as gold. It's as if last night, they went out of their way tae cause us a problem,' Lowe said thoughtfully.

'So Colin's in charge of the second floor?'

'Yeah, but the mood he's in, I don't know for how long. The way things are goin' none of us'll last. Fuck knows what Draper will say when he gets back.'

They both sat in silence for a few minutes.

'I spoke briefly to Penny tonight.' Lowe put down his glass. 'She's made a smooth return under the circumstances. Course, she's out of our league now. Trist's happy anyway, all those nasty rumours about the rape have gone away and as a bonus the Prince plays every day.'

'Yes, she says if he keeps on losing as he's done recently, she'll have to lend him her salary to see him through the week.'

'Yeah, I'll bet,' laughed Lowe. 'Actually he's lost practically nothin' recently.'

'Really? She says, he's lost a fortune these last few days.'

'I don't know why she says that. I know he's only lost a few grand in cash since she's been back, which is nothin' for him.'

Monaghan looked puzzled.

As they left the canteen Lowe whispered something in Chica Carmen's ear which she obviously found agreeable.

These discussions about Penny left Pat uncomfortable, particularly the mention of rape. He'd vowed to protect her reputation but it was becoming more difficult. Her return to Ventura was seen as an admission that there was no real complaint against Trist or anyone connected with Ventura. Now her affair with a rich Arab punter confirmed her, in the eyes of many, as yet another girl willing to 'put it about' for advancement.

Pat was disappointed with the choices she'd made. But he still thought of her as a basically decent girl and could not forget her distress that awful night. .

The VIP area had filled during Lowe's absence and now all the tables were being played. Although Talal had gone, the Saudis were still playing. Nidditch had given the task of supervising the break list and keeping the table count to Joe Staine, an inspector he'd brought from the upper floor. A surprising choice as he wasn't a pit boss, nor even a candidate for the position, and he certainly had little experience on the VIP level. If a temporary pit boss had been needed there were probably two or three better candidates within the regular first floor staff.

'Congratulations, is this a promotion?' Lowe asked, trying not to sound derisive.

'Oh... er... temporary, I think,' said the Inspector, embarrassed by his sudden elevation.

'What's happenin', anything exciting?' Lowe took the clip board before Staine could reply. 'Mmm, Talal didn't contribute much, did he? Funny, he seems to have changed his ways recently. I see the Saudis are losing. Any problems with them?'

'Er... no...' answered Staine, distracted by Nidditch, who was signalling to him.

'Thanks, Joe, I'll fill Ian in. Take a break.' Nidditch turned to Lowe. 'As you see, we're winning a bit more. Talal lost back the chips he had in front of him. Your friends the Saudis are still here and losing quietly.'

'Funny the way Talal's playing recently, he's not getting involved,' Lowe commented.

'Maybe his mind's on something else. Once he gets tired of her he'll come in strong again.' Nidditch directed Lowe's attention to a table inspector signalling for assistance. Lowe went to him.

'Take this bird off, please. She doesn't really deal blackjack and certainly not with this action.' The besieged Inspector, meant to be supervising two B.J. tables, was fully occupied correcting the mistakes of the inexperienced Chica.

Lowe replaced the girl, but it wasn't the only example of Staine's incompetence.

The result sheet was totalled incorrectly; a Fill had been left off the sheet and one Chica, left off the break-list, had missed her rest period. Lowe brought these errors to Nidditch's attention but received only a sarcastic reply. He could see it was going to be a long night.

Chapter Twenty-three

Bollard waited for Draper, having called to request that, before going on shift, he drop by his office to discuss Bland's position. A needless exercise in diplomacy, as he knew a furious Draper would have already learnt of the demotion from Bland himself, and would have had no other thought in mind.

On arrival, Draper dispensed with pleasantries and launched into the subject. 'As you might imagine, I've already heard the gaming department's side of the story. Something you apparently didn't think to ask for. Of course, I agree that listening to all sides makes decision-making more difficult, but some think fairer.'

'Ralph, this isn't the first incident Colin's been involved in. This time he didn't even see fit to make an incident report in spite of the fact that it involved three top players. Saudi Princes who can influence many others. Nor did he, after the earlier incidents, give instructions to Security to record their play. At least we might then have had something to argue with.'

'Who is it we argue with, or against? Ahmed, perhaps?' Draper asked sarcastically.

Bollard sighed. 'Ralph, you know how it works here. Stories get to those above who're already paranoid about losing customers. If I don't have anything to counter the criticisms, I have to take action. Colin might be okay technically but his PR skills are abysmal.'

'So, your answer to Colin's lack of P.R. skills is to replace him with Nidditch, who is of course well known for his charm?'

This time Draper's irony irritated Bollard, 'He may not be charming when dealing with staff but he does know the value of customers. He doesn't lose any, which is the problem we have with Colin Bland.'

Draper snorted. 'Well, no. As Nidditch and Ellis ignore every procedure we've ever made, of course they don't lose punters. The punters run their shifts. We get shit for applying procedures that they've shelved!'

Bollard fell silent for a minute, he could feel Draper was again getting up a head of steam. 'Some of what you say may be valid. But our bosses see other casinos competing ferociously for top players. They believe to meet that threat we must be flexible.'

Draper threw up his arms. 'Flexible! What is flexible? Does it mean - no rules? How close must we come to breaking the law, or does flexible mean illegal?'

Bollard closed his eyes and shook his head slowly. 'Ralph, please take my advice. Don't put yourself in a position where you look to be a danger to the interests of the company.'

'Oh, I see. Is this a threat I'm hearing?'

'I'm not threatening you. I have respect for the job you do. But I know this won't end well if you persist in taking a position...'

'Okay, Frank. You play it as you like but there's a limit to what we have to take. There has to be some rules.' Draper looked at his watch. 'For now I'm going to get on with the job... or are you about to demote or sack me too?'

'Not at all. That's the last thing I want. All I ask is that you calm down and think twice about what you say.' Bollard stood and was about to continue, but Draper was already opening the door.

'Okay, let's see if I get through the night without upsetting your boss Ahmed!'

Bollard slumped back down in his seat.

Draper made his way downstairs in impotent rage. He'd felt obliged to make his protest, but realistically there was never a chance that Bollard would stand up to Trist and Pellzer, even if he agreed that Bland's demotion was unfair. However, in one thing Bollard was right; Colin could have helped by making a comprehensive report on the incident.

When he arrived on the VIP casino floor, Draper was still wondering what to do next. Lowe, at the pit desk, raised his head. 'Hi, Ralph. So what did Bollard say?'

'That Colin didn't help himself by failing to make a report. It doesn't matter. This is coming from above. I'll have to speak with Pellzer when I can, and get it straight from him how they want us to run this place.'

'Well if they want us tae run it like Nidditch I'm goin' tae have a problem every time you're off.' Draper looked quizzical and Lowe continued. 'A big game with Talal, the Saudis and other useful players and he insists I put Eva and Bentley on the table. Earlier, Ellis has Penny dealing tae Talal as if nobody knew. Oh yeah, and during my meal-break, Staine's running the pit!'

'This is what I told Bollard. Policy, procedures and norms are going by the board. Strange things are happening in this place.'

'Yeah, I can tell ye I'm thinking of looking elsewhere. I'm ready tae move.'

Draper looked thoughtful. There was a time when he would have tried to dissuade Lowe or anyone he valued from leaving, but he could now find no convincing argument. Instead he concentrated for the moment on the more immediate tasks.

'How we doing anyway?' he asked Lowe, who was now studying the results.

'We're a wee bit in front. Talal went at the change of shift. Anyway, he's not playing like before, he's starting with cash, where before it was always cheques. Colin's Saudis haven't come in, thank God.'

'Right. I'll take a look upstairs, see how Colin's doing.'

Draper found Bland slouched across a restaurant table and curbed his inclination to comment.

'Don't tell me you've also been expelled from the VIP level?' Bland asked sardonically.

'Not yet,' Draper smiled weakly. 'I talked to Frank but as usual, he can't do anything. I've decided to see Pellzer about all of this.'

'It'll make no difference. This shit comes from Ahmed and his mate Trist. This fuckin' company's getting worse by the day. The only thing that'll help is a strong union,' Bland replied bitterly.

'You're probably right. But the union campaign will die on its feet with the two Ps running it.'

Bland nodded in resignation. 'Ralph, I think we have to involve ourselves in this campaign, we've got a better chance of persuading people than those idiots.'

'You may be right, but our position as managers makes that difficult.'

'They've pushed me off the VIP floor. Nidditch's giving Ian a hard time. How much more difficult can it get? Maybe they'll make the "Gimp" night-manager.'

Draper gave a twisted smile. 'Maybe you're right. It's time we took an active part in the union campaign. It could be the only protection we'll get.'

Chapter Twenty-four

The restaurant was full when she arrived. The maitre'd was occupied, but she didn't need his assistance. Mansur was at his favourite table. She eased her way past the other diners and could feel the appraising eyes of several groups of men, a large number of them of Middle Eastern appearance. At last his eyes broke off from the huddled group round his table and he rose smiling to greet her.

'My darling, you look beautiful as always.' He kissed her cheek. Two of the other three men whom she had seen before also rose to receive her. The third, an older man, remained seated and gave no acknowledgement of her presence.

A short, seemingly angry exchange in Arabic followed before Mansur turned to her again. 'My dear, I am sorry we are just finishing our business, then we can have dinner together... er... maybe you could...'

Penny excused herself and moved towards the ladies' room. The ill-tempered discussion resumed. This had been the first time she'd heard anyone talk disrespectfully to Mansur. It was also the first time anyone had shown disregard for her in his presence. She therefore dallied in the rest-room, hoping the man would be gone by the time she returned.

To her relief, when she came out only one of the other men remained and he was already standing, presumably about to take his leave.

'My sweet, I am sorry about all this,' he said after giving instructions to the departing man. 'I hoped they would be gone before you arrived.'

'Oh, it's alright,' she smiled. 'Who was that old man?'

'He is my uncle, but don't worry about him. He's very conservative, religious.'

'But what was the problem with him?'

'You should not worry about him, it does not change anything. Please, let us enjoy our lunch and not think about him.' He picked up the menu and looked for the maitre'd.

Penny took up the cue. The menu there was always enticing, but her thoughts returned to his words. Why did he say she should not worry about his uncle, that it did not change anything? What did he mean? Change what?

'Tell me, what have you been buying? Anything nice?' he asked after they had both selected from the menu.

'Well I did buy that dress and...' she took a book from her bag and handed it to him. *Arabic for Beginners* it said on the cover-page.

'Ah ha! You will now learn to say sweet things in Arabic, and maybe also not so sweet things!' he laughed.

'Well, I feel I should learn for your sake. Someday, if I go to your country, I can at least say something, even if it's only a greeting,' she said enthusiastically.

The Prince looked thoughtful but didn't reply. After a few moments he resumed. 'Very soon it is Christmas and New Year. We must organize some parties. Ah, yes and one must be at the stables for all my staff and managers. You will come down to Newmarket and why don't we go to my place in Marbella? My yacht is there.'

'Oh, I'd love to. But first I must see if I can get time off.'

'No problem. I will ask Ahmed to arrange with Jim that you are off.' He shrugged dismissively.

'I don't think it's as easy as that. They have a schedule and it wouldn't be fair to other staff.'

'Don't worry. This is no problem. They will do it. After all the money I have lost in the last few weeks, they will want to make sure I pay them,' he laughed.

'Oh, you don't have to pay immediately?' she asked.

He raised his forefinger to his pursed lips, to signify it was a secret, and laughed again, 'I have a little arrangement but they will get paid eventually,' he said, then added, 'unless of course I win it back before then.'

This 'arrangement', as he put it, puzzled Penny but she left it at that. What concerned her more were the arrangements he'd mentioned over Christmas and New Year. Worried as she was by what others might think, she did want to spend the maximum amount of time with him over this period. She had never been so happy. He bought her beautiful things and took her to expensive places, and there was no denying that was exciting; but for her, knowing that he loved her meant so very much more.

A sudden erotic thought brought a frisson of pleasure and she smiled. He didn't miss it. Could he possibly read an unintended message? It seemed that way. Reaching across the table, he took her hand and whispered, 'I am so happy you are not working today, we can spend the whole day together.'

Chapter Twenty-five

'Happy New Year!' the short fat moustachioed man called out in a general greeting to reception staff.

'Ah, thank you, and the same to yourself, Mr Al Khazari,' Ollie replied quickly.

'You shouldn't say that until after 12 o'clock, it's bad luck,' said Cara.

Both Ollie and Pat glanced at her reproachfully.

'Is this true, I will now have more bad luck?' Al Khazari asked with a look of genuine concern.

'No, that's an old wife's tale,' Ollie smiled and ushered him away.

'Old wife's tail? What means this?'

'It's okay, Mr Al Khazari,' Pat intervened, 'he means an old joke. In any case, it's not meant to be bad luck for the one who says it…'

'You mean it is bad luck for the people I say it to?' Pat and Ollie reluctantly nodded. 'Ah ha! This is interesting!' And he made his way up the stairs with unaccustomed vigour.

'Jesus, Cara, don't say things like that!' Ollie rasped, when the gambler was out of earshot.

'What'd I say?' She looked bewildered.

Ollie shook his head. 'Don't tell any gambler something's unlucky, especially him!'

Elena, listening from the other position at the desk, smiled at Pat. 'If his luck's bad he'll be complaining to you later.'

'He's always complaining so that won't be any surprise,' Pat shrugged. 'By the way, you coming to our drink-up at Gulliver's after work?'

'Of course. I'll need a drink by then, looks like it could be a hectic night,' she whispered, as a sizable queue had already formed in front of the receptionists.

Pat signaled to Ollie that he was going upstairs. A number of people were arriving and the reception manager nodded a welcome to each one as they entered. So far, not many were big players. Pat remembered Lowe's comment that a client's importance could be gauged from a distance by observing the level of greeting given by Ollie. The polite nod for ordinary visitors, a more pronounced incline of the head for regulars, a handshake and bow for medium level players, an effusive and flamboyant sweep for high limit players. Draper added that a renowned big tipper departing after a winning night might find the reception manager genuflecting by the exit. They were slightly exaggerated but astute observations and Pat smiled as he looked back down to see a young Arab, who had initially received a nod, getting up-graded to a bow as Ollie suddenly realised who he was.

Pat found Colin Bland sitting in the Playa restaurant. The tables were already busy for this time of the evening.

'Hello there. How's it going?' Pat approached cheerfully, waving a greeting to regular clients seated nearby.

Bland nodded a less than enthusiastic response.

'This is the first New Year's Eve I've ever worked, how about you?' asked Pat.

'Yes, we've always been closed. But they're so fucking greedy they had to squeeze the last drop out of the staff,' Bland replied, adding as an afterthought, 'But I don't see the favourites working. No Mr Nidditch tonight.'

Pat suspected Bland had taken a few consolatory drinks but chose not to comment. He looked around at the rapidly filling gaming floor. 'I think we're going to be busy.'

'Of course, all the other clubs are closed. They don't mind their staff having a New Year holiday, it's only once a year.'

Pat wasn't too happy himself about working New Year but had accepted it. He understood Colin's disenchantment but didn't want to hear another rant. He made his excuses and moved on down to the VIP level.

The Primero restaurant was busier than usual and the gaming tables were already almost full. Pat offered his greeting and handshake to members as he progressed towards the central gaming area, occasionally stopping to favour a more highly rated player with a few additional pleasantries, almost as a royal guest of honour might do at a national sporting event.

At the pit desk, Draper and Lowe were studying a staff work schedule.

'Hello there, no first-footing for you this Hogmanay then?' Pat directed at the young Scot.

'My first foot would like to go up Ellis's arse!' Lowe fumed.

Draper continued in more modulated tones but was obviously no less angry. 'It was agreed that we'd co-ordinate work-schedules on each shift and each floor during Christmas and New Year to try to give everyone some chance of being off at least one of the holidays. Ellis was given the job. What he did seemed workable, but in the last few days he's authorised so many changes, probably to accommodate the favourite girls of Trist, Ahmed and various punters. So we're now short on a night that's promising to be hectic... and us, the mugs who normally can't be relied upon the rest of the year, have to manage all three floors. But dear Nidditch, who couldn't be with us tonight, left his favourite Waites to help me run the Terraza.'

Draper was about to continue but was called to the cash desk where a customer waited. Lowe made some adjustments to his list.

'There's some known faces but not many of the big boys,' Pat mused, surveying the gaming area.

'No, nor in the afternoon shift. The big players have probably gone partying wi' their favourite Chicas, like Talal with your friend,' Lowe grimaced.

'Ah yes. I didn't see Penny. I thought she was off Christmas and working New Year?'

'That was the plan, but it seems someone pulled strings for her tae be off New Year as well. You can imagine, that's made her very popular wi' some of the girls.'

Draper rejoined them, smiling, 'Banks-Forbes's gone to play blackjack. He says Al Khazari's driving him mad calling out Happy New Year to the punto staff every hand.'

Pat was about to explain why, but could see the shoe had ended on punto and Al Khazari was rising from the table to stretch his legs during the break. Pat decided he'd avoid him for now and take a look at what was happening on the third floor.

His passage from Primero restaurant to the main public stairway past the second floor and up to the Terraza gaming area took longer than usual, due to the frequent stops to greet members and reply to their queries. The volume of people was greater than he'd seen before, even in Ventura, one of London's busiest venues. There were many members who were less frequent visitors, perhaps not having the financial means to play regularly. They had obviously chosen Ventura as their party venue for the night and were already in high spirits.

'Pat, thank God you're here!' exclaimed Waites. 'It's chaos, they're bringing drinks in hip-flasks and those stupid waitress Chicas are giving them alcohol in their coffee. They're drunk, causing disputes on the table, spilling drinks, we'll lose our licence, it'll get worse at midnight and—!'

'Bejesus! Take a breath man!' he interrupted in exasperation. 'Have you bleeped Ralph or a catering manager?'

'Of course, but he hasn't put in an appearance yet. The catering managers aren't answering, I don't know where they are, it's—'

Pat held up his hand to stem the stream of complaints and shuffled over to a waitress Chica at a blackjack table. Zeta was a new girl, he'd never talked to before.

She turned with a vacant smile, apparently unaware of who he was. 'Yes sir, what can I get you?'

'I'm Pat Monaghan of Public Relations. Is it true that alcoholic drinks are being served to the tables?'

'Yes, sir, what would you like?'

'No, you don't understand, it's illegal to... oh never mind. Who's your catering director?' The girl looked confused but smiled inanely. 'Oh for Jesus' sake, forget it!'

Pat in frustration went to look for the person in charge of catering. Waites was now shouting at a group of players, obviously drunk and causing confusion with misplaced bets.

Pat wasn't sure who to call first. A catering manager to monitor the activities of the Chicas; Security to look into the infringements of the Gaming Act; or Draper. He decided first to call Ollie at the door and warn him that members were entering drunk and carrying alcohol.

The phone on reception rang for an interminably long time before he heard Elena's voice.

'Elena, is Ollie there?' the din at the other end seemed like the crowd noise at a football match.

'He's here somewhere but I doubt if he can talk, it's bedlam here, you better come down, sorry!' she shouted, and hung up.

'For fuck sake!' Pat exclaimed in frustration and began dialling again. This time he asked the switchboard to bleep Draper, then he waited by the phone at the cash desk. An unruly group now entered and proceeded to shout loudly to friends on the other side of the room. The phone's strident call diverted his attention. It was Draper.

'Ralph, it's Pat. I'm on the third floor and Waites is having a problem with clients drinking alcohol on tables. Some brought it in, but Chicas are also serving it.' He rushed the words, sensing by the hubbub at the other end that he didn't have Draper's undivided attention.

'Yes, the whole place is in chaos. The management on the catering side seem to be off serving at Trist's house party and those left, are pissed. Until I can get up there, Brown-Trousers will have to keep a lid on it. Our first priority has to be to restrict entry in some way, because we're being overrun. Meet you at reception.'

Pat eased his way through the revellers to the stairway. He could hear the commotion below and looked out over the balustrade to see Ollie and two security-men remonstrating with people in the crowded reception area. Their appeals to the crowd to form an orderly queue and have patience were falling on deaf ears. Several were trying to skip by without passing through the mandatory entrance procedure. Draper appeared on the second floor landing and was immediately surrounded by irate regulars complaining about the indignity and inconvenience they'd gone through to enter the club. The manager broke off while offering apologies and pulled Pat to one side.

'This is a complete fuck-up! We've got to block entry or we'll be completely over-run. I'm sure there are already people inside who haven't signed in. We could lose our licence for that alone, not to mention serving liquor on the tables. Lock the door and say we're full. Ollie or somebody will have to go on the outside with security and if any VIPs show up, direct them quietly to the back entrance.'

'Bloody hell, that'll be difficult, they'll have a fight on their hands with some of the people we don't let in.'

'We'll have a fucking riot on our hands if many more come in. We should never have opened when all other casinos are closed, it's just fucking greed!' Draper shouted, not only from anger but because the din was becoming deafening.

'Okay, let's see what we can do!' Pat squeezed his way through the ascending visitors to the lower level.

Ollie saw the logic of the plan. Although he didn't like the part he'd been given, he could see Draper was in no mood to brook dissent. The doors were duly locked and he and an equally grumpy member of the security team took their positions outside.

Pat meanwhile attempted to instil some order among those already mobbing the reception desk where Elena and Cara battled on. Their well-practised company smile had faded after multiple disputes with visitors. Some with no membership cards could not or would not co-operate by giving proper identification. Others admitted they were not members but couldn't understand why, for just this one night, they couldn't be allowed entry. Some had actually been barred previously and were attempting to return, no other casino being open that night. With foreign visitors all the usual linguistic problems were multiplied by the noise levels in reception.

Draper, having answered a call, signalled he was on his way to a dispute upstairs. In the din Pat couldn't hear on which floor.

Ollie entered looking cold and harrassed, 'This idea's not working. The regular players won't go round the back even if I escort them and—'

'Bastards, Bastards!'

'*Sharmuta*. I kill you!'

An explosion of noise drowned out Ollie's words as bedlam broke out on the stairs, several levels above.

The sound of shattering glass and screaming formed part of the overall cacophony and projectiles ricocheted off the walls and banisters, crashing to the floor of the reception below. Pat, Ollie and several customers raced below the stair for cover. Other guests, who had been on their way up, descended rapidly to escape the conflict; clogging up the lower area once again. Following his instinctive act of self-preservation, Pat moved out from under the stair to see what was happening. A melee on the third floor landing was spilling down the stairs.

From the mix of languages, it was unclear who the combatants were. Pat could see two security staff near the centre of the battle. He also caught a glimpse of Bland and Draper. The situation worsened as the curiosity factor brought people spilling out on all levels to see what was happening and, as the conflict escalated, they too became embroiled in the fracas. Too many people were now involved for Ventura security staff or managers to even hope to contain the problem. As the scuffles spread down to the next landing onlookers, in their panic to escape from the violence and flying missiles scattered in all directions. Inevitably, someone stumbled on the stair and screaming bodies began to tumble downwards. Pat roared out a command above the din to Elena, to call the police and emergency services.

The battle died down and flared up again several times. It now seemed to be between Greek and Turkish customers although several Arab nationals were involved and a group of drunken locals that Pat had seen earlier had also joined in.

The police arrived after what seemed like hours, though in fact it had been just over ten minutes. Pat had opened the door several minutes earlier only to be caught in the cross current of people trying to get out and those trying to get in. Two police officers, the first to arrive, could not hope to control the entire conflagration but their presence had some immediate influence and as back-up arrived the scuffles diminished, if not the noise. The door was secured to prohibit the departure of anyone who might have been responsible for the disturbance or who might be a witness. It was now being opened only to allow the emergency medics to enter and identify those most in need of urgent assistance, perhaps hospitalisation. All this had to be done in what was still a volatile environment with the ever present danger that violence would erupt again, not only between the original adversaries but by the victims of the turmoil who, emboldened by the police presence, were eager to seek redress.

There were also members furious at being prevented from leaving and enraged by the management's failure to keep control within the club.

Draper worked his way down through the battlefield to the reception in spite of being challenged by several customers. He identified himself to the officer in charge as the most senior manager on duty. Only then, on taking note of Draper's dishevelled appearance, did Pat take stock of his own. His suit was torn in several places the knot of his tie dangled precariously by one strand at chest level. His hands were bloodied. At this stage he wasn't sure if it was his blood or someone else's. A quick look at Ollie confirmed that he had not come off unscathed either.

Suddenly another blood-spattered figure lunged towards him shouting, 'You, you! You lied to me, it was not joke! It was curse from old wife, like this girl say!'

Ollie moved to intervene as a policeman took the arm of the disturbed member. He resisted violently and his flailing arm sent the reception manager to the floor.

Two police eventually lead the agitated Al Khazari back to the medics who had been attending him. As Ollie slowly picked himself up Draper, who had briefly been outside, arrived to find him on one knee. 'Aha, still hoping for a tip?'

Pat caught the eye of Elena, who gave him a tired smile. He was making a further inspection of his hands to see where the blood was coming from when he noticed the time on his watch.

'By the way everybody, it's just gone twelve. Happy New Year!'

Chapter Twenty-six

Bollard entered like a schoolboy summonsed to the Headmaster for mis-behaving. On Pellzer's desk lay a copy of the police report. He was on the telephone and pushed the report with his free hand rowards Bollard, who didn't bother to pick it up.

'You've read this?' asked Pellzer angrily when he'd finished his call. Bollard nodded affirmatively. 'I haven't reached Morg yet, but he'll hit the roof when he sees this.'

After a New Year's party Trist would probably be unavailable for some time but that was little consolation; he would indeed hit the roof when he eventually recovered. Meanwhile Pellzer, in his absence, would look for the culpable or more likely, the blame-able.

'I don't know if you've read these, they're reports from the managers on duty.' Bollard offered the folder he had brought to Pellzer.

'Yeah I have, for fuck's sake, I suggest you get rid of them and any other copies there are.'

'I don't understand, they give us—'

'The give us it, right up the ass!' shouted Pellzer, 'Clients not going through reception, carrying in drinks. Chicas drunk and serving drinks to gaming tables, overcrowding… et cetera. Enough to close us down if they fall into the wrong hands!'

'Well, we're not going to let them fall into anybody's hands, but mis-takes have been made and we should conduct an internal enquiry to—'

'You're damned fuckin right there'll be an enquiry! I want to know why every time those guys Draper and Bland are in charge there's a fuck up!'

'Dan, that's unfair, the policy to open was—'

'You're not saying they handled this well, are you?'

'Well, Draper was senior gaming manager but it was understood that Harry Rye would direct catering but neither he nor his senior managers worked and—'

'Exactly, that left Draper as the most senior, and what happened?'

Bollard was frustrated at not being able to get his point across but he could see the mood Pellzer was in. However, if he didn't make some headway with Pellzer he'd have even more difficulty with Trist.

'I think, handled the right way, we can count on Draper not to say anything to endanger the licence,' said Bollard deviously.

Pellzer was about to say something again but stopped to consider Bollard's statement. Then: 'I want rid of those two, out of Ventura - they're damaging this business!'

'Yes, but I don't think this is the issue to do it on. We need support from everyone in case the police take this further. You're right, they could pass this to the Licensing Authorities. We need everyone on side in case they're called as witnesses.'

Pellzer paced around his office fuming. Bollard was relieved to see he was thinking about what he'd said.

'Make sure everybody gets it right. You're responsible. If there's a fuck up of any kind you're in the shit, along with your team!'

Bollard felt he'd once again prevented a gross injustice. But the effect could be temporary. When Trist became aware of the scandal he'd look for scapegoats. He wouldn't question their own decision to open when other clubs decided New Year's Eve was more trouble than it was worth. Or consider if it was wise to draw senior catering staff to serve at his private party, leaving Ventura catering unsupervised. No questions would be asked of Walker, who had left a skeleton staff on duty on a night when security should have been at a premium.

He hoped Pellzer would persuade Trist that it would be unwise to take precipitous action. Meanwhile, the police's club division, who would be calling to discuss the previous night's events, had to be persuaded not to take the matter further.

When Bollard returned to his office there was a note for him to call the company lawyer.

'Morning, Frank, and Happy New Year. Or is it? A rather inauspicious start, I'd say, wouldn't you?' the rich baritone voice of Larry Silverman boomed.

'Yes, quite. It must be serious to have you working New Year's day, Larry.'

'Well, I'm not exactly working, but I did hear about the to-do last night from a colleague. He was unceremoniously rousted from bed by a rich Arab client who wants to bring charges against Ventura, ranging from malpractice to dereliction of duty.'

'Do you know who this client is?'

'I'm afraid not. At this point my colleague wouldn't breach client confidentiality. You have any idea who might fit the description of an injured party?'

'I'll check the reports, consult our managers and get back to you.' Bollard was eager to tackle this new problem before it reached the ears of Trist or Pellzer.

'I'm not sure how serious he is, but perhaps an early gesture on our part might keep it from going further. I can intercede through my colleague, if you so wish.'

'Fine. Get back to you soon. Thanks, Larry.'

Bollard read through the reports again. It was impossible to say who might have taken this action. According to Monaghan and Draper, there were several people physically injured and although, fortunately, none were particularly, serious they might feel justified in bringing an action against Ventura.

So far he'd heard of this one action; he feared there might well be others.

The phone rang for some time and Bollard was about to give up when a female voice answered. It was Norma, Ralph's girlfriend and, if rumour was correct, his wife-to-be. She sounded only half awake but agreed to call Ralph, who hadn't yet progressed that far. After some time Draper grunted his presence.

'Ralph, sorry to disturb you, I know you're off today, but we're getting a lot of flack from police, lawyers and others about last night. I want to clarify some things before we respond. Do you think you could look in as soon as you can? I'm going to call Pat Monaghan as well.'

'Oh, for fuck's sake!' muttered Draper, then after an interval of several seconds: 'It'll take me a while to get myself together, but okay.'

While Bollard waited for Draper and Monaghan, he studied the entrance records of the previous night. He was relieved the club division had not asked for the reception file. Of the several people who had made statements to the police two of them did not feature in the records. This meant they hadn't gone through reception procedures. Pellzer was right on one thing, there was enough information to cause serious problems. It helped that it was New Year's day ; there were fewer officials, lawyers and reporters around than usual. Nevertheless, he'd have his work cut out to contain this.

Bollard hoped to disseminate all available information and formulate strategies to deal with all possible complaints. But to do this, he needed calm and minimum input from people who saw every problem as an opportunity to push their own interests. Alongside Ahmed and Rye, Walker figured high on this list. Though undoubtedly he could help smooth over concerns the police might have, there would, as always, be a price to pay for that.

Bollard's secretary was requesting permission for Walker to enter now but he was already squeezing his considerable frame past her.

'Well, what a balls-up last night, eh? They had to call our lads out in the end.' Walker always used the possessive when referring to the police.

'"Your lads" - and I refer to the ones employed here - didn't seem to detect the entrance of drunks nor the serving of alcohol on gaming tables,' Bollard replied, already irritated by Walker's predictable attitude.

'Bloody hell, if your managers don't see the liquor being served on the table...!'

'Our managers did, they put it in their report. The security department report doesn't say anything of these misdemeanours.'

Walker took longer to respond this time, so Bollard pressed home his temporary advantage. 'The greater part of the problem was caused by an excess of alcohol. Some who entered had already had too much and were served more in the casino. Quite apart from the questions of whether it was wise to open on such a night and why we were woefully understaffed in certain departments. Our licence requires us to make sure people under the influence of alcohol are not admitted and, by the Gaming Act, that no alcohol is served on gaming tables. Both are security concerns.'

Walker, never the quickest of thinkers, did possess an instinct for self-preservation and a well practised ability to deflect criticism, but he was obviously suffering from the celebrations of the night before and stumbled over a response.

Bollard pressed on: 'We must conceal those facts from anybody outside our organisation to protect our licence. We're probably going to have to say that rival Arab factions started fighting and others got caught up in it. Pellzer has already said we mustn't reveal infractions. You, of course, will know how to present us in a good light to the police.'

Walker grunted his reluctant agreement although his natural instinct would have been to finger the casino managers as culpable. Bollard was in no doubt that these views would be voiced upstairs, but for the moment he was concentrating on the authorities.

When Walker had gone, the secretary announced that Draper and Monaghan were waiting downstairs. When they entered, neither looked particularly bright. Bollard wished them happy New Year and received a subdued reply. His suggestion that the secretary bring them coffee won a more grateful response. Bollard brandished the reports and addressed them both.

'After last night's events, Pellzer wants to be sure we co-ordinate reports to avoid problems with the authorities. In your reports you point out various infringements and it's important we know about them, but no one else outside of here should. You understand what I mean?'

'Understood. We cover up that we had insufficient staff to deal with the public, a lack of security personnel and catering managers to control staff and prevent the sale of illegal drinks,' said Draper moodily.

'Ralph, I understand errors were made and we must investigate these internally, but to submit them in reports to the authorities would be asking for trouble,' said Bollard.

'We're not stupid, although it would probably be an asset in this company. Neither I nor anyone else in management made any statement to that effect, nor did we submit any report to the police other than the bare facts.' Draper looked to Monaghan for confirmation. Pat nodded.

'Yes, of that I was sure. Nevertheless, you may be asked to give a statement and there are some problems.' Bollard, unsure if Monaghan was fully awake, raised his voice. 'One is that on the list of those questioned by police are people who are not on our entrance records. Also a customer, as yet unidentified, may sue for injury or damages.'

'But nobody was detained in hospital?' Monaghan sat up.

'True, but superficial injuries or trauma can be cited, even inconvenience. He's apparently a member—'

'Wait!' interrupted Monaghan. 'I'll bet it's Al Khazari, he was injured and complaining. Said he wouldn't pay the credit he owed and would sue us!'

'Yes, he made a fuss, but then he always does. I heard him mention credit. But actually, he didn't take any and there's nothing outstanding on his card,' added Draper.

'Well, we'll look into that. But the company line is that the fight was between two foreign groups and others got caught up, it spread out to the stairway, making it dangerous and difficult to contain.'

'Right, I'll omit infractions in any statement but if I'm asked directly by police about specific instances, I'm not giving false evidence.' Draper again looked to Monaghan.

'I don't want to endanger our licence, but don't want to give false evidence either,' added Pat

'I don't think it'll come to that. Walker will talk to the police to smooth things over.' Bollard ignored the look of scepticism on Draper's face. 'We must hope that no one, such as Al Khazari, stirs things up by bringing a court action.'

'Perhaps I could make contact with regulars like him who were involved, and make some apology,' offered Monaghan.

'That's a good idea. At least you might get some warning if any have intention to take action,' Bollard said as he took notes.

Draper and Monaghan studied the reports again and began to make a list of regulars who might in some way have been involved. Bollard thanked them for coming at short notice and again wished them a happy New Year. Draper looked anything but happy. Bollard wasn't entirely sure what proportion of his discomfort could be put down to after-work drinks and interrupted sleep, and what could be attributed to his distaste with the politics of Ventura.

When they'd left, Draper took the lift down to the first floor restaurant where he'd agreed to have coffee with Monaghan before making his way home.

He was on his second coffee when Pat joined him. 'Well, I'm completely baffled now,' Pat said as he sat down. 'I called a few of the members, including Al Khazari. He *is* threatening to sue and said I could tell Jim he's not going to pay the credit. Jim said he's crazy, he doesn't have cheques outstanding, that I should leave it, he'll talk to him.'

'That's funny – I checked his card, he hasn't given cheques for some time, which is quite unusual in itself.' Draper looked thoughtful.

'I don't know. Anyhow, he seems to be the only problem so far. Of the other players I managed to get a hold of, none seem to be too upset although they had a moan. I'll try to contact others over the next few days. I called Frank to tell him we were right about Al Khazari.'

'Yes, I know we said we'd keep it to Talal for now, but Ahmed spread the word to other punters including him...' whispered an irritated Ellis into the receiver as he stood at the pit desk. Pellzer had phoned about Al Khazari. 'I've tried to get hold of him.'

'Well, keep trying, this guy's a problem. He's told his lawyer he won't pay what he owes because of what happened. Our lawyer phoned Bollard so he'll be checking his credit situation.'

'Yes, he already had Monaghan talk to Al Khazari yesterday, who said he wasn't going to pay. So far, I've convinced Pat and Frank that he's crazy, he doesn't owe anything. But if he reveals details, people will ask the questions we always dreaded. He's takin' the piss of course, hoping we'll write off the debt. I'll keep trying but maybe Ahmed should to talk to him.'

Pellzer agreed that could be an idea and rang off.

While Ellis was on the phone Nidditch had arrived on the floor to take over the night shift. 'I'm moving Bland to the Terraza. I'll make up Lewis to take over the Playa while I concentrate more on down here. That shouldn't be a problem, should it?' Nidditch asked.

Ellis was still thinking about his discussion with Pellzer. 'The problem I'm most concerned about is Al Khazari. He's going around saying he's not gonna pay the credit because of New Year's Eve.'

'Actually, it might not just be that that's got him annoyed,' said Nidditch. Ellis looked quizzical and waited for him to continue. 'I hear a few of the Chicas have knocked him back because he's a bit weird.'

'Weird?'

'He likes to get a bit rough.'

'Fuckin' hell! If that's the problem we'll look for a bird who likes a bit of rough. We can't have him putting us in the shit because he can't get his nooky the way he'd like it.' Ellis shook his head in disbelief.

'I think that's the reason. He was upset before New Year, but I thought it would pass. I'll talk to Rye. He knows which Chicas put up with a bit extra for a bit extra.'

Ellis nodded thoughtfully and returned to the phone to make contact with their troublesome client.

On his way off the casino floor Nidditch came upon Talal and Penny in animated conversation by the staff exit. She had been on her way to the change-room after finishing her first shift back since her holiday. He had temporarily stopped playing on the table where she'd been dealing. Officially, she was in breach of regulations by stopping to talk to a customer. But Talal wasn't just any customer. Nevertheless, even Nidditch expected girls to keep up some public appearance of compliance. He positioned himself behind the Prince so only Penny could see him, hoping his presence would encourage her to terminate the discussion. Already irritated by her conduct, he now became aware of the subject in dispute. She wanted Talal to stop playing and leave with her. Nidditch was about to intervene – something he'd been reluctant to do for fear of the Prince's reaction – when Penny abruptly broke off, stormed out through the staff exit and Talal returned slowly to the game. Nidditch pretended not to have seen anything and decided against admonishing her as it would undoubtedly carry to Talal. However, their relationship needed to be monitored. Only a short while ago the girl had been a timid trainee; an attraction, an asset. Now she was getting above herself and could become a liability. As if to confirm this, the Prince was now cashing out. As Ellis moved to talk to him, Nidditch returned to his original objective to consult with Rye.

'So Talal didn't stay?' Nidditch asked when he returned. Ellis was sitting in the Primero restaurant.

'No, and he was winning. That fuckin' Penny's becoming a problem. He said she loved Spain and wants to move there. That's all we fuckin' need.'

'Yeah, she really had a go at him out here. I wasn't sure if I should interrupt or not.'

'Yeah, she wanted him to go for dinner. He's got a thing about her at the moment but let's hope it doesn't last. It's not like an Arab, especially the top ones, to be bossed about by some bird. We've got to do something about her. I'll speak to Ahmed. Anyway, I got Al Khazari, he's coming tomorrow. What did Harry say?'

'He thinks he's got the Chica for him. I'll tell him to have her available tomorrow.'

Chapter Twenty-seven

Penny chose a small restaurant in Shepherd's Market to avoid Talal's usual haunts at the Hilton and Dorchester hotels, where he'd be approached by an endless caravan of Arabs and the ritualised greetings and impromptu meetings would take up almost the entire night. During these encounters the Prince's supplicants would either ignore her completely or leer at her salaciously.

He hadn't spoken much since picking her up outside the Ventura and she sensed he was upset by their disagreement in the casino. But as their relationship deepened, she was becoming increasingly uncomfortable with the management's perception of her as bait to squeeze money from him. Her annoyance had been all to do with their attitude, not his.

'Mansur, I'm sorry, but I really feel bad about them using me to take your money. Today, when you were winning, they wanted me to stay so that you'd continue playing and lose again.'

'Yes, but you should not worry, this is small money.'

'Yes. for you it may be, but it's the principle. I don't like them using me to do it, no matter what the amount is.'

He paused while studying the menu. 'I will in future not play at your table.'

'It doesn't matter, they'll assign me to deal wherever you play.'

'I will tell them not to put you to my table,' he said decisively.

Penny thought about this. It could be the answer. If she wasn't dealing to him she'd feel happier. She smiled and grasped his hand. He responded by raising her fingers to his lips.

Nidditch announced Bland's banishment to the third floor with obvious relish. Though in essence the work was the same on the Terraza as on the second floor Playa Casino, status had always been accorded to areas which attracted the heavier gamblers. Although the Terraza had more tables, staff and visitors each night, its lower minimum and maximum table stakes meant the big players frequented it less. To Nidditch's visible disappointment, Bland concealed his displeasure and accepted the assignment without comment.

For Bland the move provided opportunity for contact with employees with whom he rarely talked. He could now listen to their grievances and implant the idea that only by union representation would their concerns be addressed. He reckoned that Nidditch's autocratic approach and insensitive attitude towards people on this floor had created fertile ground for the Union case. He was also sure that Norman Brown Trousers would've been primed by Nidditch to report on any union activity. However, Waites's eagerness to ingratiate himself with Nidditch by continuing his autocratic policies also helped the union cause.

The walk from the car park to Ventura was as much exercise as Bollard got in a week, now that he spent little time on the gaming floors and more behind his desk. When he reached the office gasping from the exertion, his secretary greeted him with the usual look of resignation and a list of callers. Among that list of salesmen and suppliers the names of Mitford and Silverman stood out as potentially problematic. Surprisingly, there was as yet no call from Pellzer.

Neither Mitford nor Silverman was available when he returned their calls. The lawyer, Bollard assumed, would have rung about the threat of an action from Al Khazari and the GWU's Mitford about the union recognition question. Bollard decided to contact Pellzer, rather than wait to be called, but his secretary said he was in a meeting. When he rang the VIP Level to ask for Ellis, the Pit Boss said his manager was at a meeting upstairs with Pellzer.

Ellis and Pellzer. *What could that be about?* he wondered.

The meeting in Pellzer's office had been delayed while Ellis took Al Khazari through the back entrance for a discreet meeting with Rye.

Ahmed was discussing the Talal situation when he returned.

'The Prince has many interests, gambling only one. Now he has this girl as a new friend…'

'Yes, the guys think that's the problem,' Pellzer indicated to Ellis, 'but you explain, Jim, I'm talkin' to Ahmed about Talal's recent lack of action.'

'Yes, we think it's down to this Chica Penny. We've heard her telling him he should stop playing. We could pull her up about it, but when she tells him he'll get annoyed. What d'you think?'

Ahmed gave it some thought. 'Maybe you are right. Western girls they start off sweet but when they think they have position, they become a problem. He likes her too much, at the moment. But I will find how it can be finished. There are ways. He is Muslim and the first son. She has no future. Don't worry.'

Pellzer looked to Ellis; these words seemed to reassure him, so he changed the subject. 'Jim, Al Khazari, what can Ahmed do about him?'

'Well, as it happens I think we've solved that one. It seems he was upset because he was losing a lot of money but our girls weren't treating him too well, or at least not the way he likes.'

Pellzer looked puzzled and Ellis anticipated his question. 'What I mean is, they weren't coming across because he's got a bit of a reputation for being a bit… er… kinky. Anyway, I got Rye involved. He's found him a Chica who's a bit more adventurous. I think he'll forget about the other problem now,' Ellis winked.

'Good, but let me know if you need help. He may become tired of girl very fast. I know this man, he can be problem to keep happy,' Ahmed laughed.

'One thing this has shown – the danger of this credit system, if players talk to others about it. I said this would be a problem. I'm still worried about Draper,' said Ellis.

'Yeah, we have to be careful with Draper until we find a solution. But now his number two is upstairs maybe it'll be better,' replied Pellzer.

'But what is the plan, this Draper will go or not?' Ahmed asked.

Pellzer sighed. 'Jim will tell you. With the Employment Law it's not easy to sack someone if they've been with you a long time. But we'll find the way.'

'Why you don't offer him money to fuck off?' Ahmed threw his arms up.

Pellzer looked to Ellis to respond.

'He's strange, Draper, he's likely to cause even bigger problems if the company did that.'

Ahmed looked puzzled, 'Then you must say he's stealing or something. It's easy, get somebody to say he took money…'

'Ah well!' Pellzer glanced at Ellis, who like him looked uneasy with Ahmed's simplistic solution. 'Don't worry, leave it to us, we'll find a solution. Listen, guys, if we could leave it at that for now. Don't forget, Jim, we've this union shit to clear up. Ahmed, keep me posted on Talal. Gentlemen, thank you.'

'Hello Mr Al Khazari, nice to see you again, how are you?' Pat hoped the Arab wouldn't answer in tiresome detail, being apparently unable to recognise a polite rhetorical pleasantry for what it was.

Al Khazari gave a half-smile, mumbled a reply, but didn't stop. He made his way to the elevators that served the apartments. Pat shot a quizzical glance at Elena on the reception desk.

'He's booked into an apartment, authorised by Jim Ellis. Don't ask me why,' she said in response to Pat's unspoken question.

'Ah, maybe his old wife has turfed him out,' quipped Pat, to the obvious amusement of Ollie and Elena. Mia, the other reception Chica, looked puzzled. Ollie began to tell her the story.

Pat moved across to Elena. 'What's new with you? Heard from your friend Penny recently?'

'A brief word here and there, but she's totally occupied with you-know-who. It's real love, poor cow. I can't talk sense into her. But then talking sense into most Chicas is an uphill struggle.' She glanced at her colleague Mia, now laughing at the story of Al Khazari's New Year greeting. Pat knew Elena was referring to the Union recognition issue.

'How's the campaign going?' he asked quietly.

'As you can imagine,' she sighed, 'none of those close to Trist, Ahmed, Rye et cetera want it. But others might support us if they weren't intimidated by their floor managers. And you? Still against?'

'I'm not against worker representation, it's the GWU I'm not sure about, especially for a business like this.'

'But we need someone to back us, if it's not the GWU...'

Monaghan signalled the approach of a customer. He was glad of the distraction before the quiet discussion moved to animated debate. The early evening lull over, several members were now arriving so he could justifiably take his leave and go for his usual reconnaissance tour.

On the VIP Floor there were various small groups of people dining, none of whom were particularly big spenders. Pat greeted several, one of whom was Mrs Galton.

'Good evening, fair lady, what brings you to these parts? Have you cleaned out the tables upstairs?'

She giggled, and pointed to the strawberry gateau. 'I came down to wish Sharon happy birthday and I'm afraid I saw this cake,' she said, pretending guilt.

Pat couldn't think who Sharon was but it was undoubtedly the real name of one of the Chicas working there. There wasn't much Mrs Galton didn't know about staff as she attended almost every night, and chatted to all of them while waiting for her husband, a moderate but regular player, to satisfy his gambling need.

'Well, that's a good way to celebrate her birthday,' Pat smiled and made to move on, but she gestured for him to come close.

'That young man just leaving was asking everybody about Penny,' she whispered.

Pat turned to see a tall youth come out of the casino area, and cut through the restaurant towards the front stair.

'Maybe he's family or a friend,' Pat suggested. Her nod indicated probable agreement, and she returned to tackle the gateau. Pat took the opportunity to move on.

As usual in early evening the tables were fairly well attended, mainly by players who had survived from the afternoon. Lowe and Nidditch, who might have supplied an update, were in animated conversation behind the tables. Pat could see neither was happy. Rather than interrupt them he went to the cash desk to enquire if there had been much movement on day shift, and since the changeover.

'Nothing much,' said Keith the cashier, 'Talal lost a couple of grand in cash and cheques. It's funny, the smaller players seem to be increasing their cheque action but the big boys seem to be playing less.' He continued to check the chips on the tray in front of him.

Pat could see Lowe and Nidditch had now finished their discussion and the Pit Boss had come out to the centre of the gaming floor. Nidditch passed Pat, giving him only a cursory nod of recognition before disappearing through the staff exit.

'Everything alright?' asked Pat disingenuously of Lowe.

The Pit Boss shot him a look which seemed to say: what do you think?.

After a few seconds he broke his silence. 'I've had my fill of this place. You're not supposed tae think, just do what you're told, without question. Something funny's going on here. I didn't think it before, but union recognition's maybe the only answer. Either that, or look for another job.' Lowe continued without input from Pat. 'When he comes back in a few minutes I'm tae go upstairs and break the pit bosses and Bland as well. He wants me off this floor. He didn't say it, but that's what he wants. Then he'll put somebody who doesn't know what he's doing, like Staine… I don't get it…' He shook his head in frustration.

'Yes, even in the time I've been here I see a change in atmosphere and not for the better. I'm told the bigger players are playing less, maybe they're getting fed up as well.'

'Of course, if people like Bennett and Staine run the games, punters will get pissed off wi' their mistakes. But there's something else, I'm no sure what. Where Talal's concerned, I'm told Penny keeps him away. Apparently, he's told them they've to keep her off his table. By the way, there was a young guy in here looking for her.'

'Yes I saw him, who was he?'

'Don't know. He asked if she was working here. I told him she was on dayshift, he'd missed her. He seemed a bit pissed off. Later I had tae tell him not tae talk tae the girls. He was asking questions about her, but wasn't playing. After that he went anyway.'

'I'm not sure, but she once told me about a boyfriend she used to have back home, maybe it's him. Lucky Talal wasn't around,' Pat laughed.

'Yeah that would've been interesting. Oh, here comes his Highness,' Lowe smirked, referring to Nidditch. .

'Okay, take your meal first before you break the others. I'll take the lists,' Nidditch announced officiously, taking the clip-board with staff break-list and hourly result estimates. Lowe indicated to Pat he would see him later but said nothing to Nidditch. Neither bothered with the usual changeover procedure.

'How's it going, John?' asked Pat when Lowe had taken his leave.

The manager grimaced. 'Nothing brilliant, we might have got more from the Prince if he didn't have to run away to service "our Penny". The others are in and out,' he replied, moving away.

Monaghan followed him towards the cash desk. 'I see Al Khazari's back and upstairs in an apartment. What's the story there?'

Nidditch seemed reluctant to answer, 'He seems to have got over his tantrum, but in any case, Jim comped him to a room for a little entertaining he wanted to do. He'll be alright.'

'They say some bigger players are playing less these days, what do you think's the reason?' asked Pat, as they reached the cash-desk.

'Who says?'

'Well several people, including Keith here.'

'We get a few days' lull and all these experts draw conclusions.' Nidditch cast a dismissive look at the cashier.

'No it's just that the—'

'Excuse me, but I've got work to do. I can't stand here blarneying with you all night,' Nidditch interrupted. His smile suggested jocularity but the message was clear. Pat moved away without further comment, to continue his reconnaissance on the upper floors and, deciding he needed the exercise, took the internal stairs. As he reached the first landing he could hear a conversation on the next level. He couldn't see who the girl was but there was no mistaking the voice of Harry Rye.

'… so what d'fuck's the matter now, you can usually handle any guy?'

'Look, I'm telling you, it'll take a lot more than I'm getting if I'm to put up with his shit… and even then, you or someone better warn him – there's a limit!'

'Okay, enough, we'll talk about it later. So where is he now?'

'He's gone down to play in Primero.'

Pat quickly resumed his ascent to see if he could identify the girl. He caught sight of Rye and a waitress Chica called Marietta as they moved off to the service and kitchen areas. He was curious to know what it was all about. If a player was being abusive towards a Chica, the manager or pit boss on the floor would normally handle the complaint; so if she was complaining to Rye, obviously she wasn't happy with their response. Was this an example of the incompetence Lowe had been talking about? He decided to go back down and see what it had been about.

Fortunately Nidditch was occupied, so Pat went to Staine who was standing at the pit desk poring over his lists.

'Hi, Joe, how's it going?' said Pat cheerily. Staine gestured, so-so.

'Tell me, was there some problem with a punter and the waitress Chica?' asked Pat.

'What punter, what Chica… this one you mean?' he said, directing Pat to the waitress who had just made an appearance.

'Hold on, I'll ask her about it,' Pat said, leaving Staine to continue with his list. The Chica wasn't Marietta, it was one of the newer girls but she would probably know what happened to her colleague.

'Hello, Pia,' he said, looking at her name-tag. 'Tell me, did Marietta have a problem tonight with a punter down here?'

'Marietta? Marietta's not working tonight,' she said, looking puzzled.

'Really? But I saw her talking to Harry Rye a short while ago, on the stair.'

The girl thought about it, then remembered. 'Oh yes she was in, but not here, I think she's doing something in the apartments upstairs.'

Pat was now even more curious than before. Marietta had a problem with someone, possibly in the apartments. He looked round the players on the tables. Who? Ah yes! Al Khazari had appeared in the few minutes

Pat had been gone. He had an apartment courtesy of Jim Ellis. Staine laboured on with his paperwork, so there was no need to return to him on the subject.

Nidditch was now sitting in the restaurant and Pat wondered again if he should mention the incident with Marietta; he decided to leave it for now. He was coming to understand more and more Bland and Lowe's intense dislike of this man.

Chapter Twenty-eight

Bland, like Draper, considered that the prospects of winning union recognition had improved by the inclusion, in the campaign committee, of Elena Spencer. Relying on the crude advocacy of Ray Potts and the monotone drone of his colleague Pettigrew had at one time prompted Bland to consider his own participation in that group, but Draper advised against it, suggesting instead he liaise closely, but unofficially, with Elena. In keeping with that policy, Bland was now waiting for her as agreed at a pub near the Union offices where, for the first time, she had been meeting the rest of the committee and the GWU official, George Mitford.

'What'll you have, sister?' he asked when she entered, briefcase in hand.

'Oh, don't you start! I've had that *Brothers and Sisters* stuff from Mitford,' she said, and asked for a lager. He quickly downed the remainder of his whisky and chaser and returned with her drink and the same again for himself.

'You're starting early,' she said, as he took a shot of the whisky. 'Off tonight?'

'No, I'm working later, this is just to start the motor.' Elena nodded without comment, so he continued. 'So, d'you think we've got a winning team and plan?'

Elena gave him a wry smile. 'Well, you know the two Ps. Then there's Carmen, not the brightest but we don't have many supporters among waitress Chicas, at least she has the guts to stand up to Rye. Roland's the best of them, as Chef he gives us insight into what's happening back-of-house. He also gets a lot of stick from Rye.'

'So what about the GWU, what are they saying?

'Mitford's their man,' she sighed and shook her head, 'a typical factory-floor negotiator. He reckons their entry onto the scene brought the reinstatement of the dice crew and agreement on the ballot for recognition. He didn't like it when I said it was the negative press and worry about their licence that brought them to talk, hoping that GWU would help them dampen it down.'

'No, he wouldn't like that opinion,' Bland laughed. 'So, the plan: what are they doing to get recognition?'

'I asked him that. He waffled. Basically the answer is - nothing. It's all down to us, what we can do,' she shrugged.

'So, during the campaign what are we allowed to do in Ventura?' asked Bland taking a pen from his pocket.

'Well, without recognition, we've no right to conduct union business during work-time, use company notice-boards or distribute union information, without permission. Nothing must interfere with normal work practices.' Elena looked up from her notes. 'As manager you must be especially careful. Legally, they couldn't sack you for being a union member, but they can if the activity interferes with your job.'

'So they've got us all ways.' Bland downed the remainder of his drink. 'What about intimidation, what are the GWU doing about that?'

'Mitford agreed intimidation is illegal. If we have witnesses we could use it in a Tribunal or in a court of Law. But when I asked if GWU would bring the case, he waffled again.'

'So basically we can only use rest breaks at work, and the pubs and clubs outside, to do our campaigning,' Bland said. He stood up and pointed to Elena's half-full glass. She declined and waited while he again ordered his engine-starting materials.

'So, it's going to be difficult to get enough support,' she said when he returned.

'We might just get a majority in gaming, some cleaners and maintenance people, but support from the catering side is low, from admin and security, nil.'

'Sounds like we need a miracle.' Bland slumped back in his seat.

'We might have to use other weapons…'

'Such as?' Bland looked sceptical.

'Well, during the strike, the press coverage embarrassed them into making concessions. So we know they're worried about anything that might damage business or attract the attention of the gaming board or licence authorities. So, we keep our ears and eyes open to find things. Actually, Roland says they sometimes break hygiene regulations. Under the Law on Health and Safety at Work, if two employees request it, a safety committee has to be set up within three months. The committee would at least be some kind of representative body for the staff.'

'Yes, if we get the right people on the committee.' Bland sat up. 'As a matter of fact, the committee could investigate the New Year's Eve fiasco, when some people, including staff, were injured.'

'Actually, Roland told me a cleaner he knows personally got caught on the stair and is so bad she's still off work.'

'My God, they've kept that quiet!' Bland was now taking notes.

'Perhaps if that story attracted attention, Ventura might think a GWU-backed safety committee would convince the authorities that safety was being taken seriously,' Elena smiled, also taking a note.

'And if the committee was to get compensation for the cleaner it might sell the idea of union representation,' added Bland.

'Okay, Colin, I've got to go. I'll put this idea to the committee.' She rose, said goodbye and left him looking as if he might order another drink.

The hotel in Bayswater Talal had chosen for lunch would be more discreet than his usual haunts, he said. So far they'd been interrupted only five times by messengers and well-wishers. She supposed it was something she'd have to get used to if she was going to make her life with so important a man. The latest interruption was on the way; one of the Prince's drivers stood nearby, waiting for permission to approach. He delivered a brown envelope, from which the Prince took a large photograph, smiled and handed it to Penny. It was a picture of his favourite mare, Desert Lady, with the foal she had just produced. Below, the caption read: *Pleased to announce the Birth of Princess Penny.*

'Oh Mansur, how wonderful, she's beautiful! Oh, thank you!' Penny cried out in excitement, then rushed around the table to give him a hug and kiss. Even he was surprised and delighted by the extent of her reaction.

'Unfortunately, we were not there for the birth. I wanted to go but you were working and... You know, I think it not necessary that you work. When I return from my trip I want to talk to you about...' He was distracted by the arrival of another retainer.

Penny looked at her watch and was shocked to see it had gone 12.15. If she didn't leave soon she'd be late for work.

'I'm sorry my love, these people have arrived...'

'It's okay, Mansur, I have to go or I'll be late. If you can ask the driver to drop me near the Club?'

'Yes, of course. When I finish I will come to Ventura.' He rose and beckoned the driver.

Penny, smiling broadly and clutching the photograph to her heart, mouthed a thank-you, pecked him on the cheek and moved off toward reception.

'Hello, long time no see, where've you been? Don't you keep up with old friends?' smiled Elena as Penny entered the Chica's rest-room.

'Oh Elena, sorry, I've been so occupied! I wanted to see you, I've so much to tell you.'

'Actually, I'm not working today, I came in to talk to some people.' Elena led Penny out of earshot of the other girls. 'Someone told me you've been sent to work on the second floor, what's that about?'

'Yes. I don't know. Tony Roberts says it's because Talal said he didn't want to play on my table. But he could play on another table so why...?' Penny seemed upset by the sudden change.

'He was happy to play on your table before, no?'

'Yes, but we agreed it's better he doesn't, so he told them. It used to be the rule anyway.'

'Rules, what are rules in here? There'll be no rules until we get a proper voice. Here, take this and read it later.' Elena thrust a Union pamphlet into her hand. 'Anyway, what else's been happening? How's your love life?'

Penny smiled, asked Elena to wait and went to her locker. She returned with the photograph. 'What do you think?'

'Very nice, lovely.' Elena could see Penny was excited but was a little unsure how to respond.

'You see she's called "Princess" Penny?'

'Oh yes. D'you think maybe that has some special significance?' Elena said, trying not to dampen Penny's obvious delight at this detail.

'Not only that, but today he told me that he thinks I should give up work.'

'Oh, and do you want to?'

'Well, if we're going to be permanent it's better I'm not here… you know what I mean?'

Elena wasn't sure how to handle this. She knew how impressionable and naive Penny was. It could well be that the Prince had a genuine affection for her. But by all she'd heard of Arab dynasties, it seemed unlikely he'd be allowed to continue this relationship, far less legitimise it by marriage; which was what Penny seemed to be imagining would happen. But how to put it kindly without shattering her illusions or souring their friendship?

'Well, you won't lose much by not working here. It's great you get on well together… but you always have to remember you're both different nationalities and religions. There could be difficulties… I hope not, but be aware problems can arise, not so much from Talal himself, but maybe his family.'

Elena could see Penny was thinking about what she'd said. Her smile had evaporated and Elena wondered if once again her cynicism had spoilt someone else's day.

'Yes, we had a bit of a problem with his uncle…' Penny frowned, then broke into a smile '… but I think Mansur will sort everything out. He's so intelligent and very powerful with all his people.'

Elena decided to leave the subject for the moment. 'Look, we need more time to talk, why don't we meet some day for early lunch before work. You're not giving notice yet?'

'Oh no, we've only just talked about it. No, Mansur's going on a trip I'll call you in a couple of days and we'll get together.'

'Great, got to go. See you soon… Bye!'

Since returning to the floor after her break, Penny had been unable to concentrate and had made several errors. The Inspector had been patient, but the game on her table was building up. Games on this floor were different in character to those on the Primero level, where there were usually only a few players per table and being high rollers they were given more time to place bets. The cash value of the chips being played was high but the volume of chips was normally low. Also, because many of the players had accounts or cheque-cashing facilities, fewer cash transactions took place across the table.

Here in the Playa, the activity was perpetual, at times almost frantic. Players were coming and going and would throw cash or chips on the table while the ball was spinning, leaving little time for them to be placed or exchanged. The Inspector, with a tone of resignation, kept instructing Penny to remove wagers that had been placed late. This inevitably led to noisy protest, making her even more nervous and prone to error.

She prayed for her next break and was in no doubt the Inspector was doing the same.

Relief came with a tap on her shoulder from the incoming Chica and she hurried through the restaurant towards a welcome break. But suddenly felt someone grasp her arm.

'Caught up with you finally!' said a loud voice.

She swung round to face her ex-boyfriend.

'Martin… what?' She withdrew her arm from his grip. 'Look, I… I'm not allowed to talk to customers on the floor.'

'What do you mean? I'm not your fucking customer. I'm your boyfriend, remember?'

'No, you're not! Don't shout, or swear… you'll get us both in trouble. I'm sorry, I have to go.'

She wriggled free and rushed through the staff door, ran up the stairs to the restroom, and headed straight for a toilet cubicle, stifling tears and fearing she would attract unwanted attention. The day had started so well. Now, on top of her disastrous performance on the table, she had this to cause further embarrassment. What was she to do? Martin had so obviously been drinking. She should report him, but for what? Maybe he'd be gone by now; but if not and he came to her table…?

She thought of saying that she'd taken ill and couldn't return to the floor. But there was already talk that she'd taken advantage at New Year; now they'd say she was avoiding work on this floor because she couldn't handle the games.

She was so weak and stupid! Emotions took hold and she began to cry.

'Hello, everything alright in there?' a voice called through to her.

She grabbed some toilet paper, wiped her face and blew her nose. 'Yes, I'm… I'm okay… just a bit of a cold !' she eventually answered. There was a sympathetic comment from one voice while another mumbled something about not spreading her germs. She waited.

After a few minutes, when they'd gone, she came out. Although still nervous about going back, she set about repairs to her make-up. If she didn't go down now, she'd be late and that in itself would provoke an inquest.

From the stairs, Penny could see there was considerable traffic in and out of the door leading to the casino and restaurant from both gaming staff and cocktail Chicas. With the door propped open, she could see through into the casino area. There was no sign of Martin.

A voice in her ear made her jump. 'Hello, me-darlin' you hiding or something?'

'Oh Pat!' She sighed with relief to see Monaghan. 'As usual I have problems. My ex-boyfriend's around, and he's drunk. I have to go on the table and I want him to stay away from me. I don't really want to report him, I'm scared he'll make a scene and… anyway, I have to go out now,' she said in a flurry of words.

'On you go. I'll look out for him, don't worry!'

She made her way nervously out to the Pit Boss who was already look-ing for her. Fortunately, he'd taken note of her earlier problems and had decided to give her a less demanding assignment. To her relief she was told to chip on the roulette table in the corner.

When the volume of losing chips was too great to permit the dealer to quickly pick them up, stack them in their corresponding values and colours and still carry out the other duties efficiently, a chipper was needed. Speed was essential; more spins meant more turnover meant more profit. Though the volume of chips wasn't excessive, it was enough to keep Penny's head down. She glanced up only now and again and was just beginning to relax when she heard his voice once again. He was arguing with Pat.

'Hey, is this Paddy your boyfriend, could that be it? Is that your fucking interest, Paddy?' Martin cried, so that Penny and everyone else could hear. Pat tried to lead him away but he violently brushed off his arm and approached the table.

'You look like a tart in that costume! Is that what you are now, a fucking tart?'

Penny hid her face in her hands. Pat looked apologetically towards her. He'd tried to handle it discreetly but now this guy had gone beyond the limits. The Pit Boss and Inspector moved to restrain him from going behind the table to where Penny stood. Then, when two burly security-men appeared, he mounted a brief and rather pathetic display of bravado before discretion took hold and he allowed himself to be led, still shouting abuse, off the floor and out of the building.

Pat, in agreement with the pit boss, took the tearful Penny to the nearby office to compose herself. She'd stopped crying and now just sat staring at the floor.

'I'm sorry, Penny. I tried to talk to him but he was drunk, and... well you know...' She just shook her head. 'Can I get you something, coffee, tea...?'

'You always seem to be the one who has to help me, like the night—' Pat moved quickly to comfort her. The memory of that dreadful experience was, unsurprisingly, just below the surface.

'Pat, I can't carry on working, I'm absolutely useless anyway. Mansur wants me to leave. He's right, I should.'

Pat wasn't sure what to say. Talal was undoubtedly right, but what was he proposing she do? Did he intend to marry her? Pat doubted that. So was she going to be a 'kept-woman', as his mother would put it? There was much he could say; all of it wrong at this moment. He just patted her shoulder and said nothing.

'Do you know if Mansur's here yet?' she asked.

'I don't know, I'll find out.'

He picked up the phone, dialled reception and asked if Talal had come in. He also asked what had been done about Martin. After a few seconds he put down the phone.

'The Prince came in a few minutes ago and went to the VIP.'

'Can you get a message to him?' she pleaded.

'Well, yes I suppose so,' he agreed, though he wasn't sure where he stood with this request. She took a pen and paper from the desk and scribbled something.

'I've told him I'm not well and have to go home.'

'Yes, but what's he to do, meet you downstairs or what?'

'Yes, I've said that in the note.'

'One thing, they've thrown your ex-boyfriend out, but they didn't call the police, just barred him. He might wait outside.'

She seemed to think about this but didn't comment. 'Oh, can you ask Jim Ellis if it's all right if I go?'

Pat once again felt uncomfortable with this request. Strictly speaking, she should ask the pit boss first. But her recovery seemed fragile and he felt he should do what he could to keep her calm.

On the way downstairs he informed the pit boss she was unwell and had asked to go home. The man seemed neither surprised nor concerned and simply removed her from his list.

The Prince was already playing on roulette. Ellis was standing by the table talking to the Inspector. From the other side of the table, Monaghan made eye contact and indicated he wanted to speak to him.

'Yes, Patrick, what's up?' Ellis asked

'It's Penny, she's had some problem upstairs with her ex-boyfriend. He was drunk, we threw him out. Now she's taken a bit queer and is going home. She wants me to give this message to yer man here.' He nodded towards Talal and showed Ellis the note.

'For fuck sake! We haven't seen much of him lately, now when we get him in for some money, she's calling him away!'

Pat shrugged and waited. Ellis looked at the note again. After a few seconds he gave it back to Pat.

'I suppose if we don't give him the note, we'll be in bad with him any-way when he finds out. She's becoming a real fucking pain, that bird!'

'So, I should I give him it?'

Ellis nodded reluctantly. Pat waited until the spin was over and indi-cated to the Inspector that he was about to interrupt Talal's play.

'Hello, Prince Talal. I'm sorry to disturb you, but I have this message for you.' He gave the Arab Penny's note.

'Pat, what does this mean, what happened to her?'

'Well, as I think she said, she's not feeling well because of certain things and has to go home. She's getting changed now and will wait for you by the staff entrance.'

The Prince looked puzzled but after a few minutes, during which he made a rough count of his chips, he called Ellis who was standing near-by. 'Jim, I have to go out. Please keep them on my account.'

The Manager nodded and stifled the urge to say something.

By the time Penny reached the back entrance, the Rolls was waiting. The car door opened before the driver could come round and the Prince slid out.

'My darling, what is the matter?' He held out an arm.

'Oh Mansur! I've had a terrible night.'

The driver held the door open and they both assisted her to enter the limousine.

She sank into the soft leather seat and snuggled up close as the Prince instructed his man to take them home. For the first time that night she felt safe.

'What has happened?' he asked quietly.

'Oh, they sent me to work upstairs because you said you didn't want to play on my table. I wasn't prepared and was nervous, it's very different, you know. Then this boy I used to know came in drunk and started to annoy me. Pat tried to take him away but he became abusive. Eventually they threw him out but I was very upset and… I'm sorry.'

'No, no my sweet, we go home now, don't worry. I will find out why they send you up there, this is not what I asked. And this bastard, who is he to come doing these things… why do they let in such people?'

She snuggled up and they sat quietly for the rest of the journey. It gave her time to reflect that, upsetting as the incident with Martin was, it was only one component of her distress. Her earlier discussion with Elena had awakened fears about her future with Mansur. The unexpected transfer to the Playa level and her inability to cope with the action there had destroyed what little confidence she had. On top of that her ex-boyfriend's appearance had revived memories of home and the fractured relations with her parents.

But worse – all this anxiety had re-awakened the trauma of 'that night', which she'd tried so hard to dispel but knew was always waiting to re-surface.

Chapter Twenty-nine

'Mr Pellzer wants you to contact him as soon as possible. Several other call-ers, including your wife, are noted on your desk,' his secretary announced when he entered. Bollard nodded acknowledgement, hung has jacket over the chair and sat down with a sigh to prepare himself for another day.

The list, by normal standards, was fairly short. Mayfield, on holiday, had left his contact number – invaluable, should something sufficiently frivolous come up that no one else wanted to deal with. Mitford - no doubt wanted to know when and where the ballot would be held, perhaps imagining that Bollard might have some part in formulating these plans. Mrs Bollard - no message except to call her, possibly about plant seeds he should pick up on his way home. Pellzer. What could he want? Not to congratulate Bollard on the fine job he was doing, of that he was sure.

Bollocks to them! he thought.

That bit of mental dissidence out of his system, he picked up his papers and headed for Pellzer's office. By phone he'd only get the latest instruction or complaint and very little response to his questions. Face to face, he had a little more chance of constructive dialogue. Only a little.

'Frank, your department's New Year fuck-up is still costing us! We've just had to fork out a sizeable sum to a fuckin' cleaner, of all people, for some supposed injury!' Trist assailed Bollard the minute he entered Pellzer's office.

Bollard hadn't seen Trist for a while, probably due to the Chairman's heavy social programme, but Pellzer hadn't failed to pass on his continuous criticism and displeasure. It was no surprise to hear the New Year's "fuck-up" was now solely down to him.

Trist continued, 'Those mother-fuckers in your department are pushing this union thing. This Bland guy's got to go!'

Pellzer took up where Trist left off: 'Yeah, they seem to be getting more active. Fortunately we've someone on the inside, otherwise this thing with the cleaner might have caused problems. They're calling for a safety committee now, apparently by law we've got to grant their request.'

'Yeah, make sure that committee is loaded with our people or they'll cost us more money.' Trist stomped around while he spoke.

'We have people with First Aid Certificates who're not militant. Logically they'd be members of this committee,' Bollard offered.

'Who are they?' asked Pellzer.

'The public relations people Monaghan and Keane completed a short course. And Gordon has several certificates for first aid and health and safety.'

'Mayfield ! Fucking perfect. He's a must for the committee, he'll bore the balls off everybody.' Trist rubbed his hands together and Pellzer laughed. Bollard smiled and made a note to call Mayfield. He'd no doubt spend his holiday preparing, meticulously and exhaustively, the agenda for the first meeting.

There was a brief silence while Pellzer took notes. Trist poured himself some black coffee. No doubt recovering, as always, from the night before, thought Bollard.

'Was there something else, Dan?' he asked as he pulled up a chair.

'Yeah, this Mitford guy from the Union will call to agree a date for the ballot, and the procedure. There are rules about these things which we have to stick with, but we can still organise this to our advantage. We'll get regular news about who's supporting this union thing. It's to be held over two days to let everybody get a chance to vote. But maybe we can make it that waverers or potential supporters of this fucking union get days off or holidays on those days and have to make a special journey to be here. Jim Ellis'll look at that and then we'll decide dates.'

'This Union, there's no way waitress Chicas are gonna vote for those idiots, the problem's the game-staff,' grunted Trist. 'You gotta make sure the bastards who're stirrin' this shit, get the message about their future.'

Bollard shifted uneasily. 'Yes, I see your point, Morg. Although I must also say that, as always, we have to be careful not to give them cause to claim victimisation and run to a tribunal. Recently, laws protecting the rights of employees to be members of a union have become stronger.'

Trist mumbled an expletive and returned to his coffee. Bollard had thought to discuss Al Khazari's length of stay in the apartments, but felt it might provoke a return to the subject of his New Year fuck-up. The reduction in the drop figure seemingly due to a decrease in cheque-cashing by bigger players was another matter he decided to postpone. In the presence of the unreasonable Trist, this would also be a failure of Frank's management. Bollard tucked his notes away and, seeking Pellzer's permission and noting Trist's indifference, he took his leave.

'You think it's worth keeping that guy?' asked Trist, when he'd gone.

'We need an innocent face to put in front of the Gaming Board, the Licence Authorities, press and the like. Both he and that bozo Mayfield can stand up before any of those guys and sound believable,' answered Pellzer.

'You think Ellis or Nidditch couldn't pull that off?'

'Maybe, it's doubtful, but there's another reason. We need deniability, in case one of those guys gets in trouble and decides to tell all. We can say they were lower down the management chain, so any instructions would've gone through Bollard and Mayfield. They'll certainly back that up and deny any such policy was in place. Without off-shore bank records, nothing can be proved. Those punters sure as hell are not gonna go in court to talk about gambling debts. Lots of them are Muslims, and those who're not wouldn't divulge details of off-shore accounts.'

'Maybe. But surely Frank or even Mayfield's gonna figure out what's going on eventually?'

'It's possible, particularly Frank, but don't forget we chose those guys because they need and want the job. Where else they gonna get this salary and position? As far as Mayfield's concerned, I don't think he's sharp enough and sure as hell nobody's gonna tell him. Frank, if he found out, would make a lotta noise up here, but in the end he's not gonna stir up shit that'll make himself look bad. He'll swallow.'

'Maybe you're right. Anycase, how's it going result-wise?' Trist slouched across to get himself another coffee.

'Well, we gotta small problem with Talal, according to Jim. It seems your old friend Chica Penny, who he's screwing, has been talking him away from the tables.'

'That fuckin dame! We should've found out a way to get rid of her before!'

'It was okay at first, when she was attracting him in, but now she's a pain. Anyway, Ahmed'll find a way to get him to dump her. Apart from that, we're getting more in from the others, including Al Khazari. Since he's been given an apartment with a bit of entertainment, he's been contributing more.' Pellzer smiled, not only because of increasing returns but also at Trist. He'd finally succumbed to the temptation of the drinks cabinet. The meeting was at an end. Trist's concentration limit had been reached.

Back at his desk, Bollard looked at his notes. Al Khazari's comped stay in the apartments was perhaps not worthy of any great concern. The reduction in drop, particularly the amount taken in cheques from high rollers, was worrying. Curiously, the policy Draper had criticised - the relaxation on cheque-signing limits – hadn't developed in the way he'd feared, nor in the way Trist or Pellzer had hoped. In the recent period the bigger players were actually playing less. Was this a temporary statistical blip or was there another explanation?

But for now Bollard's pressing problem was his bosses' dislike of Draper and Bland and their management methods. It brought him again to the question - why fight to retain managers so obviously unpopular with his bosses? For a quiet life he could comply with their wishes and find a way to dispense with their services. But no. Apart from his sense of fairness, and the legal difficulties, he had another motive for retaining them: self-preservation. They represented the last vestiges of a management structure.

Argumentative and critical as they'd always been, they did at least re-spect a chain of command. Bollard knew instinctively that with Ellis and Nidditch running things, he'd be left out of the lines of communication be-tween Trist, Pellzer and the operations. He'd become - in fact had already become - like Mayfield, a willing workhorse with a title but no authority. Draper and Bland, and through them others such as Lowe, offered at least some guarantee against autocracy. For the same reason, though he could never voice the opinion, he now also hoped - but was not confident - that those campaigning for union recognition would be successful.

Penny woke to find Mansur had risen earlier. She pulled on a silk robe, took a critical look at herself in the mirror and decided repairs could wait until after she'd revived herself with a strong coffee. In the large kitchen and breakfast room of the Kensington apartment, the Ceylonese maid was busying herself. When Penny entered, the maid assumed a position of def-erence and awaited instruction. Still unused to this type of attention Penny felt embarrassed.

'Good morning. May I have some coffee please?' she requested.

'Yes, Ma'am, where will I bring it?'

'Oh... er... the Prince is in the lounge?' Penny was unsure what to call him when addressing staff.

'I think the Master in his office,' the maid answered, and Penny under-stood she was referring to his study.

'Okay. Put my coffee in the lounge, I'll take it there, thank you.'

The door to his study being slightly ajar, Penny could hear he was talk-ing on the phone to someone in his own language. Somehow, he always sounded angry in Arabic yet gentle when he spoke to her in English. She knocked, popped her head in and gave a wave to indicate she was up and around. He replied with a cursory signal of recognition but continued in animated conversation. She therefore went through to the lounge and picked up the morning paper.

'Ah, you are there. How are you this morning?' he asked when he en-tered a few moments later. A little formally, she thought, but perhaps be-cause the maid was now bringing in the coffee.

Penny waited until she'd left before replying, 'I'm fine, but I think you were right. I shouldn't remain at Ventura, I don't feel happy there.'

'We should talk about this when I return.' He looked distracted. 'I have to go on a business trip and also meet my father.'

'Oh... then you're going home?'

'Yes, but I have to go to other places on the way.'

'I will miss you terribly, can't I go with you?' She rose from the sofa to go and snuggle up to him.

'I am afraid that would be impossible, it is very complicated,' he replied, seeming to back off.

She moved closer, putting her hands round his waist on the inside of his jacket. His response was minimal.

'Your coffee will be getting cold,' he said, leading her back to the sofa.

'Is everything all right? Are you upset with me?'

He took a few seconds to answer. 'No, no it is some business problems, it will be all-right.'

'I hope so, I don't like it when you are upset. I love you so very much. I hope you love me?'

Again he seemed to hesitate before answering. 'Yes, of course, don't worry. But now I have to go,' he said. He gave her a perfunctory kiss on the cheek before rushing off downstairs to his waiting driver. Penny watched from the study's large bay windows as his driver opened the door of the Silver Cloud. She waited to see if Talal would look up, and raised her hand to wave, but the limousine moved off quickly and was out of sight within seconds.

Somewhat dispirited, she picked up the coffee and went through to the study to make a call. As she leant across the desk, something caught her eye. The name Martin Atkinson was scribbled in English on a notepad, followed by Arabic writing; further down were more Arabic symbols and amounts of money. Who had given him her ex-boyfriend's name and why did he want it? Her head was a flurry of confused thoughts. What should she do? Should she tell Mansur she'd seen his notes and ask him what it was about? Was that why he was a little strange before he left? Could it be Martin was causing more problems? When would she get the chance to speak to Mansur? Surely he'd phone when he arrived wherever he was going. The only people who would have known Martin's surname were Pat, those on reception, or the security personnel who threw him out and barred him. But why would anyone at Ventura tell Mansur?

Penny didn't know what to do or to think and wanted to speak to someone, but to whom? Suddenly she noticed the photocopier and, after fiddling about with the controls, finally managed to make a copy. She wasn't sure what she'd do with it, but had a vague idea that she'd find someone to translate the Arabic and give her some idea what it was about.

The idea of returning to work filled her with dread, she'd have to call in sick again. Why couldn't she be strong like other girls? Like… Elena.

It was just like Elena to suggest a pub lunch. Penny hadn't been in a pub for ages and felt conspicuous as most of the early lunchtime patrons were men, and the few women were accompanied by men. Penny had intentionally arrived a little late, hoping Elena would already be there, but by sods-law she was also late. The option was therefore to ignore the admiring attention she was getting, the occasional come-on, and simply wait for her friend, or take a walk round the block in the cold drizzle. She ordered a lager and lime, declining the offer from one of a group of young men to pay for it, and hoped Elena would soon join her.

To her relief, a few minutes later her friend scurried in, offering apologies. 'I'm so sorry, I've been held up in my bloody bank, they're always understaffed!'

'It's alright. I've already had several offers,' said Penny, trying to be a little more upbeat.

'Nothing in here worth taking,' Elena said, looking around. They both laughed.

'So, how are you? You sounded a little down when we spoke on the phone,' said Elena when they'd taken some food from the buffet, ordered drinks and sat down.

'Oh, everything seemed to be going fine when I met you before the shift yesterday, then…' Penny swallowed hard, trying not to get emotional again. Elena waited. 'I'm sorry, I always seem to be in a state when I see you… I'm a real disaster.'

'Don't worry. It's not what you are, it's what other people do to you. Take your time.'

Penny composed herself and retold the story of her nightmare evening on the second floor and the experience with her former boyfriend.

'Anyway, Pat had the security throw him out. But I was so upset, Pat called Mansur to take me home. I don't know what happened, when I woke this morning Mansur was a bit strange, like he was angry or something. Later I found a note on his desk with my ex-boyfriend's name on it. I don't know what it means and I don't know who gave him it. But I'm worried, just when things between us were going so well. I don't know what to do,' said Penny in a rush of words, as if eager to get them out before she broke down again.

'Talal knew about the scene your ex had made?'

'Yes, that's why he had to take me home.'

'Did he know about him before last night?'

Penny thought about this before answering, 'No, I never talked about him and even last night I didn't say what his name was.'

'Talal must have asked someone at Ventura about him. Maybe he asked Pat last night.'

Penny considered this and supposed it was possible. 'Maybe, but I wondered why he wrote it down and…' She laid the copy she had made on the table.

'I don't know what the rest of it means, do you?' asked Elena.

'No, these figures below… I don't know if they're connected.'

'Will I get someone to translate it?' asked Elena.

'Yes, but I don't want anyone who knows Mansur or who might talk…'

'Don't worry, I have a friend who was at uni with me, she doesn't know anyone at the club.'

'Oh, that would be great!' Penny squeezed her friend's arm.

'But this Martin, why has he suddenly come on the scene? Does he live in London?'

'I don't know. I thought he was still in Tadley, where my parents live. Maybe someone told him I was in Ventura.'

'Your parents perhaps?'

'No, definitely not. My father refused to talk to him and even threatened to get the police if he didn't stop harrassing me after I split with him. Maybe one of my old school-chums found out and told him, I don't know.'

'He sounds like a nutcase.'

'He's jealous, was very angry when I broke up with him, but the main problem's his drinking.'

'You're well shot of him.'

'Well, I thought so. Everything seemed to be going so well with Mansur. He's so wonderful. I know you said… about the religion and things, but I really think we could work it out. I could even take his religion.'

Elena tried to conceal her horror at the suggestion of Penny subjugating herself to the role women played in Islamic society. 'I don't really think that's an option. It's much more difficult than you could ever imagine.'

'Well, as they say – love makes everything possible.'

'I'm going to have to go, I have a meeting this afternoon,' Elena said, looking at her watch. 'Are you staying at Talal's place then?'

'Oh, no, I just stay there sometimes. I've kept my flat on, although Mansur did ask me to give it up before. I'll go back there while he's away.'

'It's to know where to reach you when I get some news on the note, I mean if you're not working…'

'Oh yes, you can get me there, I'm not sure yet if I can face work, I'll see.'

Elena was about to give further advice but decided it could wait and gave Penny a goodbye peck. 'Sorry I have to leave you, but be in touch soon.'

Penny left almost immediately after her, before she attracted unwanted company.

As meetings had to be conducted outside work, the Astley Pub was chosen as the venue. It was close to the Ventura but being less popular with the casino crowd, they were unlikely to be interrupted by other colleagues. Elena had hoped to report some progress with the cleaning lady who'd been injured at the club on New Year's Eve. But Roland, who knew her and had previously arranged for her to meet Elena and Carmen, had called earlier to say she had now decided to forget about the whole incident. Elena had also just learnt, from one of her reception colleagues while on a brief visit to Ventura for a uniform fitting, that Ollie of the PR department would be a member of a new Health and Safety Committee. It was too much of a coincidence for both matters to be resolved within a few days of them being discussed. Was someone in the committee a management plant or had idle gossip reached the enemy? Now they would view each other suspiciously. Elena recognised the creeping paranoia. This thing could affect all of them and destroy their unity of purpose.

'So what's this about the cleaner and the Health and Safety Committee?' Potts asked Elena as soon as they had all sat down.

'Someone's close to management, it seems,' added Roland, looking at Elena. The others also seemed to be looking in her direction.

'Oh no, if you're talking about my contact with Colin Bland, you're way off track. He's more in support of our cause than you could possibly imagine.' She wanted to sound convincing but a doubt was also creeping in to her mind. Could an excess of alcohol before work have loosened his tongue?

Chapter Thirty

Nidditch watched Ellis work on Al Khazari and was glad it was Jim who had the task and not himself. The man was a nightmare. When winning, Al Khazari was boisterous and arrogant with no respect for other players around him. When losing, as he was now, he was belligerent and abusive towards staff. Ellis would sit and sympathise with him on his incredible run of bad luck and encourage him to talk about the one subject that would take his mind off his losses: sex.

After some time the player made his way to the lift and, presumably, to the apartments. Ellis went to the internal phone. When he'd made the call he joined Nidditch by the cash desk.

'Jesus, that was painful, I thought he'd go on forever about his luck and how the Chicas on the tables are trying to make him lose. I wouldn't mind but he's got more fuckin' money than Switzerland. He lost eighty-five grand in the end, which is a good result for us but a drop in the ocean for him, you'd think he was going broke to hear him. I persuaded him he needed a bit of pussy to take his mind of things, so he's gone upstairs.'

'Good, anyway, the result's holding up, even increased. Li Kim and Al Jahallad are now in for a few grand.' Nidditch handed Ellis the break-down.

'Oh, another thing,' Ellis remembered. 'Ahmed called in earlier, Talal's gone to the Emirates and he won't be back for a week.'

'Oh I see, that's why Penny's called in sick. She's gone with him?'

'Apparently not. Ahmed said he's already working on ending that affair. Anyway, I'm off for a beer or two now that everything's quiet, see you tomorrow.'

Nidditch moved across to speak to Lowe who'd just arrived on the floor. 'Ian, I want you to take Lewis off upstairs in the Playa and let him do the swing.'

'He'll break Staine, down here?' Lowe looked incredulous.

'He'll take his own break first, then break Waites on the Terraza, then you. After that we'll see what's happening down here.'

Lowe, though perplexed, nodded and made his way upstairs without further comment.

Interesting, thought Lowe, Nidditch preferred not to leave Staine on his own on the VIP level, as he was spending more and more time down there himself. If the staff were unable to do the jobs, why had he recommended them? Was it that he trusted no one but himself to make the decisions there? Lowe objected to being categorised with Staine and Lewis. Not only did he feel better qualified than either of them, but also better than Nidditch. He'd made up his mind anyway – he'd go for the position offered by Ladbrokes. it was time to get out.

When he returned later that evening, the VIP level was as busy as he had seen it recently. Staine was behind the tables looking harassed, while Nidditch, by the cash desk, was attempting to explain something to the Chinese player Li Kim. Lowe moved closer to hear without interrupting, but the phone rang on the pit desk nearby and he moved to answer it.

'Is Nidditch there?' The voice was unmistakably Harry Rye's.

'He's a wee bit busy at this minute, It's Ian Lowe here, can I help?'

'If he's there put him on, it's urgent!' shouted Rye.

Lowe was disposed to tell him to fuck off, but with Rye what could you expect. He put down the phone on the table and called to Nidditch, 'It's Rye for you, says it's urgent!'

The manager, relieved by the interruption, excused himself to take the call.

'Nidditch here. You what? You're fucking joking?' he paused, listening, then continued, 'Where are they now?'

Lowe, attracted by Nidditch's exclamations, now watched the look of shock cross his face.'Jesus Christ ! Okay, I'm on my way, you'd better call Walker!'

Nidditch put down the phone and, without pausing to explain, made his way off the floor, calling back to Lowe, 'Keep an eye on this for now!'

Lowe followed his path across the gaming floor, hoping to get some idea of what was happening, but Nidditch exited quickly through the staff door. Lowe looked around him. What did "keep an eye on this for now" mean? Was he in charge? Was he to relieve Staine for his meal-break? What kind of emergency, reported by Rye, would require the attention of Nidditch and Walker? The IRA threat again, perhaps? He began to feel nervous.

Mr Li Kim, unhappy with the interruption, came to ask why Nidditch had run away. Happily, Pat Monaghan suddenly appeared. Maybe he'd some idea what was going on, or could find out.

'What's happening Pat, any idea?'

'What d'ya mean?'

'Rye called Nidditch and he went running off in a panic looking for Sid Walker.'

'Another bomb threat?'

'That's what I was thinking but...'

'I'll see if I can find out. Where'd he go, downstairs?'

Lowe shook his head, he wasn't sure. Monaghan went to the phone.

Li Kim was now looking decidedly grumpy so Lowe called to Staine: 'Joe, Nidditch had tae attend tae something in a hurry. If you know what Li Kim's problem is, can you talk tae him?' Staine nodded reluctantly and Lowe indicated to the Chinaman that his colleague would take up the complaint.

Monaghan returned. 'Well, they're not downstairs, it seems there's some problem up in the apartments. I'll go see if I can make it any worse,' he said with a chuckle.

Staine was in protracted discussion with Li Kim, so Lowe, although distracted by events taking place elsewhere, reluctantly began to take himself round the tables; to keep an eye on things, as instructed. Play was fairly heavy on all tables. The faces on punto-banco were all familiar to him and apart from the dispute which Staine was hopefully resolving, everything else, including the win result, seemed to be moving along nicely. The relief dealers were now filing in to the casino after their break. Fortunately at that moment Staine having apparently placated Li Kim, returned to active duty, break-list at the ready. Lowe continued his overview of the tables.

'So, what's going on with Nidditch, Ian?' Staine asked, when he had allocated the staff.

'I'm not sure, Rynckwicz called with some emergency, I don't know yet what it is.'

'Fucking hell! Not another bomb scare!'

'No, I don't think it's that, it's in—'

The pit phone started to ring. Staine moved first, towards it. 'It's Pat for you.' He handed Lowe the phone.

'Yes Pat, what's happening? Oh really, well that's a relief.'

Staine was waiting to hear what emergency they had.

'It's not a bomb. It's apparently a dispute with Al Khazari in the apartments.'

'Oh well, that's not surprising.' Staine turned towards an inspector who was signalling for assistance. As was Prince Al Jahallad. Lowe moved to talk to the player.

'What I should do, I am losing. I should have no chance to win back my money?' the Prince protested.

'Don't worry, Prince Al Jahalled, I'll call the manager now.' Staine's appeal for patience met with a typical gesture of frustration from the Arab. Lowe followed Staine to the phone at the pit desk where the latter called the switchboard to have Nidditch bleeped.

'What's the problem, has he passed his limit?' asked Lowe.

'Er… yes… Nidditch told me he should refer to him if he asked for more.'

Lowe shook his head. It was another indication of how little Nidditch was prepared to delegate. This was okay provided he was always in attendance, but at times like now they risked upsetting a valued customer because no one else could make a decision.

After a few minutes the phone rang and Staine grabbed it. 'Hello... yes, it's Al Jahallad, he's asking for twenty grand. Well... yeah he's right here... Oh, right...'

While Staine was on the phone Lowe decided to check at the cash desk how the bigger players present stood with their cheque-cashing allowance. This way he could anticipate who might be next to request an extension to their cheque limit. The cashier looked unsure if he should pass him the records but eventually slid the cards under the grill. Al Khazari, being on top, was the first one Lowe opened. He was puzzled by what he read so left it to one side to take up Al Jahallad's, since this was the one currently being discussed.

Staine put down the phone and came across quickly. 'Nidditch says you better go up and break Bland for his meal,' he said, hurriedly gathering the cheque records.

Lowe looked at him with surprise, 'Bland's no problem, he takes a quick bite on the second floor and just leaves Waites with instructions to call him if something comes up.' Lowe was still holding Al Jahallad's file.

'Well, that's what Nidditch said.' Staine fidgeted uneasily and held out his hand for the file.

'What did he say about Al Jahallad?'

'Oh... er... don't worry, I'll handle that. If you want to get up there... maybe Bland's complaining.' Staine still held out his hand for the file.

'I'm not worrying, just as a matter of interest I'd like to know how Nidditch wants to handle it.'

'Oh he's coming down soon, I expect he'll... er... sort something out,' Staine blustered.

Lowe could sense his colleague's discomfort. Once again Nidditch's policy was puzzling. His actions indicated a lack of confidence in Staine's ability to run the floor, but he was sending Lowe where he was not exactly needed, and leaving Staine to handle a delicate situation with a major player. Lowe felt tempted to probe further but realised Staine wasn't going to give him answers. He smiled and handed him the file.

'Okay, I suppose I shouldnae look for logical reasons for what he does! 'Lowe could see Al Jahallad coming to find out what had been decided, so he side-stepped this confrontation by moving out round the back of the punto banco table.

As he went up to break Bland, the questions mounted in his head. Why did Al Khazari's file have no record of him signing cheques today when Staine had him on the daily result sheet as a substantial loser? Lowe could never remember the man playing cash. Was this part of the problem Nidditch was supposed to be having with him? Why was Al Jahallad being kept waiting when according to his file, he hadn't yet reached his limit. Lowe wasn't sure what he should do with these questions. The Ventura, it seemed to him, was sinking rapidly in a swamp of incompetence and dubious practices. It was definitely time to get out.

Sid Walker was coming out of a sixth floor apartment when Pat finally caught up with him. He'd been looking for at least one of the three - Nidditch, Rye or the Security Chief - but none of them had answered their bleepers. He was finally told by one of the switchboard operators that there had been a problem on the sixth floor. Walker was his usual laconic self but finally told Pat in a hushed tone that Al Khazari had been arguing with Rye about service in the apartments and it had got a bit out of hand. Nidditch then opened the door of the apartment and confirmed, on Walker's prompting, that it was as he'd described, but that everything was now in hand.

Pat offered assistance but both assured him there was no need and he could return to his casino duties. He phoned Lowe from the PR office to assure him there was no bomb threat and had just completed the call when he heard the outer office door open. He waited to see who had entered but when they didn't come through he opened the door to startle Marta Woods, who was rummaging through the First Aid cupboard.

'Oh, it's you Pat, what a fright you gave me!'

'You're working late, eh? What's up, what are you looking for?' Pat moved to assist her.

'Oh nothing really... I... ah... just one of the Chicas has hurt herself.'

'Oh yeah, well I'm your man. I'm on First Aid duty, you know, should I take a look?'

'Oh, that's not necessary, it's fine. I'll just take some cotton wool and some other dressings.'

'What injuries does she have?'

'I… I'm not sure… it was Harry Rye who asked me to get… some dressings.'

Monaghan could see she was being evasive and was curious to know what was going on.

'Is it to do with Al Khazari?'

'Oh, you know about it?' She looked surprised.

'Yes, Sid just told me.'

She looked relieved, 'Well I just wanted to get something to soak up the blood a little and maybe an ice-pack for the swelling, then we'll get her to the hospital.'

Monaghan was shocked to hear it was a girl and to learn how serious it was but tried not to show it. He didn't want Marta to clam up. The memory of Penny's experience suddenly returned.

'Okay, let me get this bag, and the ice-packs are in the small fridge there. Where is she now?' asked Pat as he crouched down to get the medicine bag.

'She's still in apartment six with Harry.'

At that moment the phone rang and Marta, being nearest, answered. 'Yes, I'm with Pat Monaghan, he's helping… no, no… Sid! Okay.' She looked anxiously at Pat. 'Yes, I don't know… I can't help it if… it's not my fault… yes, alright!'

She swallowed hard and turned to Pat, who was waiting with the equipment. 'It was Rye. He said everything's now in hand, we don't need anything. I thought it was a girl who was injured but it's a guest.'

Pat looked at her sceptically. 'Really? And how did it come about?'

'I don't know, he didn't say.'

'If it's a client I should go up there, public relations an all that, eh?' Now he was sure what her reaction would be.

'No, no he said the client's embarrassed about it, so we should steer clear.'

'Yes, yes, we don't want to see something we're not suppose to see, do we?'

She didn't respond, nor did he expect her to. After a few seconds' embarrassed silence she said, 'Right, I'd better be going.'

There was little doubt that the problem involved Al Khazari. He'd had trouble with someone – Harry Rye, a Chica or another customer – and whoever it was, they were embarrassed about it and wanted to keep it within a small circle. With Marta included in this group, the odds were in favour of it being a Chica. Pat remembered Marietta's complaint to Rye about Al Khazari, but surely she would've kept clear of him.

Pat felt disturbed by the thought that this sort of thing was going on and a little aggrieved that he wasn't thought capable of helping to resolve the incident. But in truth it was better not to be involved.

Having been on duty since early afternoon, Pat felt this was as good a time as any to knock off and go for a pint. He called Ollie to inform him that he would now be the one on call if the PR department's presence was required anywhere. The staff elevator was taking forever so he took the stairs down to leave by the staff exit where he could deposit his bleeper and inform switchboard he was going off-duty.

Descending the last flight of steps, he rounded the corner past the staff lift to be met head-on by the burly figure of Fred, who normally manned the glass-fronted security booth. He was about to give Pat some hurried instruction or warning when the doors of the small express lift from the apartment floors suddenly opened. Sid Walker, who Pat hadn't seen at the end of the corridor by the exit door, roared a command and Fred stood in Pat's way. But the lift's occupants were already in view.

Marta and Rye supported a girl, wrapped in a large raincoat, who was almost in a crouched position. Her face was swollen and damaged almost beyond recognition - but not quite. It was Marietta.

Rye looked furiously at the security-man while Woods, startled and mortified, averted her eyes. They hurried along the corridor, Marietta groaning in pain, to where Walker led them to a waiting car.

Pat's path was still blocked by Fred, but it didn't matter; completely immobilised by what he had seen, he was going nowhere.

Rye now returned to berate the security-man for not following instructions to block the passageway of anyone coming down the stair. Fred, offering apologies, skulked off to his booth.

'Listen, we're handling this, you've gotta keep this to your fuckin' self. Not a word to anybody, d'ya hear?' Rye addressed Pat, who didn't answer.'Hear what I'm sayin?' Pat nodded eventually. 'We're sortin' this out but we don't want every fucker talkin'. Before we know it the police and the press will be round, know what I mean?'

Pat once again nodded. Rye gave him a long hard look and turned to open the lift door.

'What's happened to Khazari?'asked Pat as Rye stepped inside the elevator.

'I told you. We're handlin' it. Just keep it…' He made a sign of sealed lips.

The doors closed and Monaghan stood there, not knowing what to do next.

Lowe had relieved Bland so that the manager could go for his meal and had been going through the motions, nothing more. He wandered aimlessly up and down the floor, from pit to pit, stopping briefly to look at one table then another, taking nothing in. Instead he turned over in his mind what had happened on the VIP floor and was becoming more and more convinced that something was going on. On top of that, the manager who he might have expected to confide in was in a strangely detached mood. Lowe suspected he might've had one too many at the pub before work, but was surprised it hadn't worn off by now. Bland had actually been gone more than an hour and should have returned by now.

Lowe was considering dropping downstairs to look for him when he suddenly appeared by the entrance in uncharacteristically cheerful mood, even stopping to joke with punters on the way.

'You enjoyed your break then,' said Lowe with some irony.

'Aye Lowesy, I wiz a wee bit thursty!' Bland called out loudly in a poor imitation of his colleague's accent.

Lowe looked around to see if anybody might be taking notice of his behaviour.

'Er… Colin… I suspect you've had a few and that's a dodgy situation. You've got enemies about. Why don't you get a few coffees and I'll cover for a bit?'

'Fuckin' nonsense! I'm great, no problem. Piss off back to your ayne wee pit!' Bland laughed and moved off towards Waites, who was now standing only a few yards away.

Lowe could see it was pointless to argue with him and it wasn't the only thing that was pointless. Working at Ventura was completely pointless. As his mother might say, it was 'time tae get a proper job'.

Chapter Thirty-one

When Nidditch entered, his face, never bright at the best of times, had a particularly sour look. Only four hours' sleep hadn't helped. Ellis held up the percolator to offer him coffee; Nidditch nodded sullenly. Rye sat in the corner muttering something to Walker while Pellzer talked on the phone.

Finally Pellzer put down the receiver and sighed deeply. 'Morg can't make it.' He didn't say but they had a pretty good idea why. 'Well, I've got most of the story, I think. But you better fill me in on all of it.'

They looked around at each other. Walker took up the story. 'About nine-thirty, the security on the back door phoned to tell me Al Khazari had gone out cursing about something that had happened in the apartment. I didn't know what it was about, so I called Harry here.'

Rye took over. 'When Sid called, I went to the apartment and found Marietta on the floor, semi-conscious, in a bad way, seems this fuckin' nut had beat her and left. I called John, also Sid. We decided we'd better keep it under wraps, but needed help so we called in Marta. We got the girl round, cleaned her up a bit, but she needed hospitalisation. Sid arranged transport and we took her to Charring Cross.'

Walker continued. 'I'd to call in a few favours because the hospital's obliged to report incidents to the police. I've smoothed it over, they'll be no report at the station, if you know what I mean?'

Pellzer knew exactly what Walker meant; he was emphasising his own importance. 'Good Sid, but what happens now. How's the girl?'

'She's got a broken jaw and nose, concussion, some stitches and multiple bruising.' Walker read the report to a chorus of expletives.

'What do we do about her, and of course him?' Pellzer looked around the room, but his questions were directed mainly at Walker.

'We can't take legal action against this guy. If this came out we'd be in deep shit. We have to hope we can get her to keep shtum,' Walker said, looking at Rye, who shrugged and opened his palms in a non committal gesture.

'We have to bar him, no?' Ellis looked around for their response.

'I think so, don't you?' said Pellzer

'Yeah, the guy's a fuckin' nutcase. But he owes us a hundred and fifty grand,' said Ellis.

Walker and Rye whistled in amazement. Pellzer was shocked. He hadn't read the previous day's income report yet.

'Tell him we'll only work to keep this quiet if he pays up,' suggested Pellzer.

'We could, but we have to be careful,' said Ellis, 'he's a screwball, there's no telling what he might do.'

'I think only Jim could talk to him, anyone else and he's liable to blow up,' said Nidditch.

'Right, Jim, see if you can get to him. Gauge his reaction. Tell him we gotta pay off certain people, including the girl, but won't unless he pays up,' Pellzer suggested. Ellis, looking far from enthusiastic, nodded.

'What about the girl, will she talk?' Walker asked Rye, who was pacing back and forward across the floor.

'Don't know, she was pretty mad last time he came on rough. I thought I'd got through to him to cut that out. He gave her a gift as an apology. How's she gonna react now? Who knows, but it don't look good.'

'You mean this guy's got a history of this?' Walker looked incredulous.

'Look, this is why we chose her, she knew the score. She'd normally handle this kind of guy!' Rye seemed irritated by Walker's implied criticism.

'Okay, never mind that,' Pellzer intervened, 'What do we do to ensure she doesn't talk?'

'Well, far as I know, she's sedated and will sleep for a while yet. But I suggest we move her to a private ward. When she wakes we tell her we're prepared to take action, but the fallout could be bad. We could lose the licence and she her job, as well as being accused of prostitution.' Rye paced the floor again as he spoke. 'Tell her we'll get him to pay a sizable amount in damages, if she keeps it buttoned. But if we can't get it off him, Ventura has to pay her.'

There was a silence while they considered this plan.

'I don't think we've got much choice. It's as good a plan as any.' Pellzer looked to the others. Nidditch and Ellis seemed to agree.

'Well, there's a couple of problems. Marta Woods and Monaghan,' grunted Walker.

'Marta, shouldn't she speak to Marietta? And Monaghan what…?' Pellzer asked.

Rye frowned and shook his head, so Walker explained what Pat had seen.

'Fuckin' hell! So what, will it already be all over town?' Pellzer slumped back in his chair.

'He doesn't know the whole story, but we have to agree on a story so that we're all singing from the same song-sheet,' said Nidditch.

They agreed. A story was concocted, Pellzer authorised Walker to arrange a private room and a carefully selected nurse to monitor visitors. Rye would instruct Marta, and Ellis would attempt to resolve the matter with Al Khazari.

'Oh yes, I almost forgot…' Nidditch stopped as he and Ellis were about to leave. 'I think we've got rid of Bland. I sent him home on suspension last night, he was pissed.'

Pellzer made a praying gesture. 'Thank God, some good news!'

It seemed the whole world was under the influence of alcohol. She had downed a few after work and was considering a pointless resolution to make it her last when Carmen phoned to tell her Bland would probably be dismissed for being drunk on duty. Elena was absorbing this not entirely surprising news when Pat called. Curiously, he also sounded drunk and most upset. He'd fed a coin box several times and mumbled about a scandal at Ventura when he ran out of money. Elena waited, and when he rang

back she quickly ascertained his whereabouts. They agreed ⸗
near Pat's apartment and also conveniently near where she
the translation of the note Penny had taken from Talal's des

She found him huddled over a coffee in the corner of the ₚₒᵣ café
she knew as a greasy spoon, but which basked in the glorious name of The
Kilburn Royal. The waiter didn't bother to rise from his seat behind the
counter as she joined the crumpled Irishman, instead asking loudly in some
foreign accent what she wanted to drink. She ordered a coffee and then another when Pat held up his empty mug.

'So, you here looking for new clients for the VIP level?' she asked flip-
pantly. He barely smiled.

After a pause, he tried to put some words together, 'There's shome-
thin'... not right, I heard her... Marietta... shay about trouble,... to Rye.
Then she did,... I'm sure, with Al Khazari, at the apartment, although
they tried to cover it. I shaw them and her... a real mess... blood and
everything—'

'Pat, take some more coffee, I'm not making sense of this,' Elena
interrupted.

'Oh shorry, I'm... I've bin, drinking a bit, and...'

The fat waiter lumbered over with the coffees and put them down with
a thump on the formica-topped table. Elena waited. Pat took several large
swallows, then continued slowly.

'Al Kha... zari beat up Marietta... I think. They took her out shome-
where... she was bad... ly cut and every... thin'.'

This time Elena understood the main point and took time to apply it to
some of what she had deciphered from Pat's previous mutterings.

'Who else was involved, Rye and who else knows about this?' she asked
slowly.

'Rye, Shid Walker, Niddi... and Marta Woods and... dunno.'

'Everyone a winner,' Elena grimaced. 'Do they all know you know?' Pat
nodded. 'They obviously didn't call the police?' He shook his head. 'No,
they wouldn't, would they?'

Elena thought about the situation while they drank their coffee and was
about to ask the very question Pat now seemed to anticipate.

don't know why I'm tellin' you… I'm not shure what…' He lost the train of thought and his head was beginning to drop.

'You've obviously been drinking since you left work. Pat, why don't you go home and sleep it off? Meanwhile, I'll discreetly find out what I can, and we'll talk later.'

After a few seconds he seemed to nod agreement. 'Have you told anyone else about this?' He shook his head. But Elena wasn't totally convinced. 'Where were you drinking?' Who with?' Eventually Pat shrugged his shoulders and shook his head almost in one movement.

There was little point in continuing, he wasn't responding. Elena distracted the waiter from the Sun newspaper just long enough to pay for the coffees and helped Pat to his feet to attempt the tortuous two block journey to his flat.

Lowe had slept reasonably well. The events at Ventura no longer angered him unduly, he'd made his decision to move on. Nevertheless, as he sat at his kitchen table with his second cup of tea, he considered if he should discuss the discrepancies he'd noticed on the cheque-cashing records with someone. Probably not Ellis. So, should he report to Bollard? Something told him no. The things going on either had Bollard's blessing or he had no power to prevent them. Draper, who as yet he'd been unable to contact, was really the only person with whom he felt safe to openly discuss his findings. More urgently, he was eager to assure Ralph that there was nothing he could have done to save Bland from his fate.

He dialled Draper's home number again and at last heard the educated tone of his senior manager.

'Ralph, thank God, I've been trying tae get you since last night.'

'Sorry. I've been at my mother's, I should've left you the number. What's up?'

'Oh, you havenae heard then? It's Colin, he was pissed at work last night. Nidditch sent him home. I'm afraid it looks like the end for him.'

'Fucking idiot! I was afraid that would happen. He's played right into their hands.'

'Well yeah, and there's other things going on. I'd like tae meet before you go in, tae explain.'

They agreed, at Lowe's request, to meet in a pub seldom frequented by the Ventura crowd.

Pat's confused story about Marietta hadn't been simply a product of alcohol-fuelled imagination; something had indeed happened to her. Through a friend who worked in the Health Service, Elena had found out where Marietta had been taken, and that she had subsequently been transferred to a private section. Carmen couldn't add anything to the sum of information when Elena called her. But later, dressing room gossip revealed that Marietta had been *'seeing'* Al Khazari, but had thought about ending it because he was getting a bit too *'physical'*.

No one wanted to dig deeper because Rye's name kept popping up and he'd already warned them about gossip. Elena agreed they shouldn't attract his malicious attention.

Cara, who dealt with apartment guests, confirmed that Al Khazari was no longer on the room register, although there was no actual record of him having checked out. This was not unusual or significant, because players comped by the casino, having no necessity to clear their account before leaving, often left by the rear entrance. However, the apartment key had not yet been returned. Elena discovered another interesting fact: a cleaner informed her that the room used by Al Khazari had been cleaned, but not by them.

As Elena began to piece together the background to the story, it was difficult to feel much sympathy for Marietta, no matter how badly she'd been hurt. It was, however, another example of the corruption at the heart of Ventura, and it forced Elena to revisit a dilemma. Should she resign or stay and fight? If she stayed, she should expose everything that she understood to be illegal and corrupt. But this could lead to the revocation of the licence, closure of the club and loss of employment for her friends and colleagues.

For the moment her natural doggedness dictated her actions. She'd see how this latest development might best be used to further their recognition campaign.

As she rummaged through her bag in the Chica-Room, she came upon the translation she'd picked up on the way to see Pat. Being in a hurry all day, she hadn't even looked at it yet, nor had she spoken to Penny, whom she assumed had not returned to work.

Elena's head was in turmoil: Penny's continued problems; the Marietta incident and Monaghan's part in it; Bland's dismissal; a traitor in the committee; the union campaign. How was she to deal with it all?

'Ralph, I'm sorry about Colin but he just wouldnae listen.' Lowe brought the pints to the table.

'No, silly bugger gave them the opportunity they were looking for. I doubt if anyone can do anything for him now.' Draper looked disconsolate.

'It's become impossible tae work there. I've got a couple of job interviews this week. Anyway, there's things going on I just don't understand.' Draper waited once again for the young Scotsman to continue. Lowe explained the events of the previous evening, the mysterious incident with Al Khazari, the discrepancy between his apparent loss and what was on his record and the even less understandable problem with Al Jahallad.

Draper listened with interest and growing concern. When Lowe finished, he didn't reply for some time, then finally: 'If everything you say is true, this could be serious. Have you told anyone else about it?'

'No, but Staine saw me looking at the credit records.'

'But you didn't ask him about them?'

'No, I wasn't sure what tae ask him, anyway, he never seems tae know anything.'

'It's best you don't say anything to anybody for now, let me think about this.'

'No, I won't mention it again. I hope to be out of there soon, away from it all.'

When Lowe had gone, Draper thought long and hard, but was unsure what to do. If there was something fishy going on, did Bollard know about it? For all his faults, Draper was sure Bollard wouldn't be party to anything as dodgy as this sounded - a gross infringement of the Gaming Act, a tax fraud. It had to have come from Trist and Pellzer. Ellis and Nidditch couldn't contemplate such a scam without their order, approval and support.

But why? This to Draper was the equivalent of a petty cheat move on roulette - the chances of eventual discovery by someone far outweighed the possible rewards. The problem was that if it was true and it came to light, not only would the company lose its licences but all senior managers would come under scrutiny and risk prosecution. Even if that could be avoided, the stigma of having worked as a senior executive in a company charged with such misdemeanors could blight a person's career.

Draper now had to ask himself – did he want to be the one to provoke an investigation and all that followed? At this moment he did not. But neither could he afford to wait until someone else blew the whistle. First he had to confirm the suspicions beyond doubt, and how to do that, God alone knew.

Lowe was relieved to have the next two nights off. By the time he returned to work on Friday he might already have another job and could happily tender his notice. But for now, he had more interesting things on his mind. He'd arranged to meet Carmen, who had also managed to get the night off by switching with another Chica. They agreed, for convenience, to meet in The Coach. It was still a little early but a couple of pints would go down well while he waited for her to finish her shift.

Having downed their pre-work drinks, the night-shift staff of Ventura and other nearby casinos had already gone. The pub would therefore be free of casino staff for a while before the day-shift people started drifting in. It gave Lowe temporary respite from questions about Bland and other casino related themes. In fact, he thought, if Carmen arrived early they could take off immediately and have a night free of casino-talk.

It was not to be. He was on his second pint when Davis, a third floor inspector, appeared.

'Hi, Ian, you wouldn't be waiting for a dusky beauty, would you?'

'Aye, but you're not dusky and you're no beauty.'

Davis laughed and sidled up to whisper in Lowe's ear, 'Actually, a young lady asked me to tell you she'd be a bit late, perhaps an hour. I suggested if you didn't want to wait I'd take your place.'

'That's okay, you came up so close, for a minute I thought you were goin' tae offer tae take *her* place.'

Davis laughed again.'A tempting offer, but no. Although I will let you buy me a drink.'

'Oh no! Buy a drink! You know how tae hurt a Scotsman. Lager, is it?'

Lowe caught the barman's attention and was about to order when another casino group arrived, led by Mick the cashier, who called out, 'Aha! Lowesy's getting them in, two bitters and two lagers!'

Everyone found this hilarious, including the barman. Lowe paid with a look of feigned anguish.

'Hey, they didn't take long to replace Colin, not even a day,' said Davis. 'They've already got Staine in a suit as floor manager.'

'You're fucking jokin!' Lowe was incredulous.

He thought of walking to Ventura to meet Carmen, thereby extricating himself from the tiresome discussion on management policy, but was worried she might take an alternative route and he'd miss her.

At last Carmen appeared in the doorway, gave a little wave and he hurriedly excused himself to a chorus of catcalls and comments about illegally fraternising with a Chica.

'Ian, I'm sorry. Elena wanted an emergency meeting during her break...' said a breathless Carmen '... some union things.'

'Okay, in the restaurant you can tell me about it,' he said, hurrying her away from the pub.

In the restaurant; Carmen began asking who he thought would support the union campaign and if he'd help. Lowe was barely listening. Even now, the Ventura was hijacking his night out. He resolved to change the subject as soon as he could.

Chapter Thirty-two

Penny wasn't sure why she was coming back to work. Was it a new-found determination to overcome her fears? Or a faint hope that Ahmed or one of Mansur's circle would come in to give her news of his return? She'd sat at home waiting for a call from him but it hadn't come. He was no doubt busy, with a tight travel schedule. Yes, she was sure that was the reason. Anyway, she was now in the building making her way up the stairs rather than wait for the lift.

She'd almost reached the Chica's room when she caught sight of a familiar figure clutching the handrail on the level above.

'Pat, what's wrong? You look terrible.'

'Ah, me darlin' Penny. It's the curse of the demon drink!'

'Oh, have you just come in?'

'Yes, I'm going up to see Bollard about something...' Pat looked as if he might add to that, but instead simply asked, 'How are you, everything okay?'

'Oh, I suppose so. As always, could be better.'

'Yes, I can agree with that. Listen, can we get together later, maybe we can have a chat during your break?'

'Great, until later, bye.' Penny watched as he continued his wearisome journey, then went into the rest room, Elena was already there watching a news item on television.

'What's the world coming to? A woman in charge of the Conservative Party? Next they'll be suggesting a woman for pit boss!' commented Elena loudly.

Someone else shouted, 'What d'ya mean, we've already got some old fucking women as pit bosses!' This prompted a barrage of profane comments. Elena smiled and guided Penny to a quieter corner. She was amused to see how embarrassed her young friend could be when girls used bad language.

'Hi, Pen, glad you came in. I was meaning to call you, but I've been so involved with one thing and another.'

'Oh, it's okay. I know you're doing so many things. I just saw Pat out there...'

'Oh, what did he say?' asked Elena, worried that he'd talked about the Marietta incident.

'Nothing really, he seemed to have a hangover. He was going to see Frank Bollard.'

Elena wondered what his meeting with Bollard might be about, but changed the subject. 'I got the translation. To be truthful, I haven't even looked at it. Hold on.' She scurried to her locker and returned, looking at the note with a worried expression.

'What's wrong?' asked Penny.

'Well, nothing really about your ex-boyfriend except his name.' She handed the note to Penny, but continued to look at it over her shoulder. 'Those other items clearly refer to debts Talal has with Ventura,' Elena added quietly, glancing around to make sure no one was listening.

'No, it doesn't help me understand. Unless he was upset about the money he owed,' Penny said.

Elena was still looking at the paper. 'Penny, I don't think you should tell anyone else about this.'

'Of course not. If Mansur found out he'd be angry.'

'No, it's more than that. This note refers to money owed out of the country and...' Elena suddenly felt she shouldn't go into this with Penny and changed tack. 'Anyway, it's personal finance and people like that to be private.'

'Well... yes... yes, of course.'

'Here, I'll destroy these, case you forget.' Elena took the notes. 'My God! It's time I got back!' she said, flying out the door.

Penny still didn't understand why Mansur had been so cool towards her before he left. Was it connected with Martin? Was it to do with her calling him away before he'd had the chance to recover the money? Although a huge sum to her, she knew that two hundred and eighty-five thousand pounds to him wasn't so important. She just didn't know. Perhaps when he returned she'd wonder what all her worrying was about.

Shouting broke her train of thought. The rest-room was now a hive of activity, as girls arriving late fought for positions at the mirrors, some borrowing make-up and accusing others of taking theirs. Penny hated this aggression but had to get ready or she'd be late and start off on the wrong foot again. Her few weak 'excuse-mes' made no impression on her jostling colleagues and she was bundled aside as they prepared for the 'Cattle Parade' - a brief inspection by the Mama de Chicas to see if hair, make-up and general appearance matched the company's profile of a Ventura Chica. In spite of arriving early, Penny was going to be last on the floor again.

When Monaghan had gone, Bollard sat dejectedly at his desk. Where would it end? All around him things were happening over which he had no control, but for which he could ultimately be held responsible. He'd turned a blind eye to Rye's procurement of Chicas for Trist's parties, he'd even ignored Rye and Ahmed's brokering of girls for 'promotions' outside of Ventura. But this, although they'd deny it, was blatant prostitution on company premises. How interesting that Rye, Walker, Nidditch and Marta Woods had shown inter-departmental co-operation rarely seen on legitimate operations. There was little doubt this had been initiated, or at least approved, by Pellzer and possibly Trist who, even if he did not actively participate, wouldn't find it objectionable.

Here he was again, at the crossroads. What to do? Confront them and threaten to report their actions? Resign? Ignore it once again and carry on as best he could? All three options had some appeal. Which one had the strongest? Actually, he'd already taken a fourth option: complicity.

Rather than admit to Monaghan that he knew nothing about the incident, he pretended he'd received a report and, though serious, it wasn't quite as bad as it appeared. However, a full investigation was in process.

He urged Monaghan to keep it to himself because gossip would hinder a proper examination of all the facts and a satisfactory resolution. Pat had seemed, at least for the moment, a little more re-assured by his words. But Bollard was less happy in his new role of accessory. He considered his next course of action. But at that moment it was already being decided for him.

Ellis had been trying to reach Pat for most of the afternoon to 'clarify' the situation. Monaghan, in an alcohol-induced coma, had been oblivious to the ringing phone. But Security alerted him to the fact that Monaghan was now in the building and he found him on the stair.

'Pat, me old mucker, what's going on? John tells me you got sight of that sickening incident last night. What a carry on, eh?'

'Yes, I've just been discussing it with Frank. He says there's an investigation going on so I shouldn't say anything about it for the moment.'

'Yeah, that's right, we shouldn't talk about it, in case it gets to the ears of those who like to stir up shit. Who else knows about it?' Ellis was already wondering what should be done about Bollard knowing.

'I'm not sure, those involved last night - John, Walker and his guys, Marta and of course Rye. If they've included anyone else I don't know.' Pat omitted to mention he'd told Elena. Ellis noted that he emphasised Rye's name with distaste, but decided to leave that for the moment.

'No, according to them they've kept it quiet. I just wondered if you knew of anyone else,' said Ellis. Pat shook his head to indicate he didn't. 'The whole thing's a crying shame. I don't know what got into him. He's such a good punter,' Ellis added with a pained expression.

'Pity about the girl too, how is she?' asked Pat, aware that little concern was being shown for her.

'I hear she's okay,' he replied, then as an aside: 'To be truthful, the things I hear she gets up to, I'm surprised this hasn't happened before. Pity it had to happen here.'

'Yeah, she needs a new agent.' Pat turned to go downstairs. 'See you later, I'd better see if we're looking after our other punters.'

Ellis noted the sarcasm in Monaghan's voice but assumed that, for the moment, the incident would go no further. Curiously, Bollard had done a good job in damage limitation. But what to do about him knowing? Ellis decided to pass that task to Pellzer and went to the nearest internal phone.

How would he play this? Pellzer had called him to his office, without saying what it was about. He sounded grave, and Bollard suspected the time had come for them to impart, even to him, the privileged information on the Al Khazari incident. This, of course, in case there were any probing questions from the press or, even worse, from the police. Pellzer wouldn't know Bollard already knew and there was no reason to tell him; at least not until he'd heard their explanation. On the other hand, if he'd been wrong in assuming that Pellzer had given approval for this arrangement with Al Khazari and, like him, had only just found out, he'd face awkward questions about his casino managers' involvement. Rye and Walker would no doubt have their stories ready but he could only say he knew nothing of the matter. There was also the possibility that Pellzer's summons was nothing to do with this subject. In which case, Bollard had to decide if he should bring it up anyway.

When he entered the office, Frank was happy to see they were alone. Pellzer was on the point of finishing a phone call and seemed to be talking to his wife, hence his impatience to be finished. Bollard looked for tell-tale signs of a report on the desk.

'Frank, we've a potential problem,' began Pellzer as soon as he came off the phone. 'Harry told me that one of the cocktail Chicas, Marietta, looking to make money for herself visited a member in an apartment last night. The full story's by no means clear, but it seems she demanded more money, it got heated, and he ended up getting a bit heavy with her. He stormed out, complaining to security as he left the building. When they took a look up there, she was in a mess. Harry and Sid arranged for her to be taken to hospital, and reported it to your night guy Nidditch, because this guy's a big player – Al Khazari. Naturally, they tried to keep all this under wraps but a few people know about it, including the PR guy Monaghan, and Marta Woods who they called in to help with the girl. I don't need to tell you how serious this could get if the press or the police get wind, Frank. So far, Sid has managed to keep the police out. We seem to have lost contact with Al Khazari so we don't know what he'll do. This Chica could cause us problems depending on what she chooses to say or do. At the moment we're paying for her treatment in a private medical centre to keep her out of the public eye. We don't of course owe her anything - she broke the rules and brought this on herself, but she could blab to the press.'

The story sounded believable. It would still be embarrassing and problematic if it got out, but it did sound credible - at least to those who didn't ask why Al Khazari was invited to stay in the apartments when he had a luxury flat not five minutes from the Ventura. Or those who didn't know Marietta was one of Rye's favourite girls for private entertainment. Bollard didn't put this to Pellzer; there was no point. Neither did he bother to say that Monaghan had told him of the incident. However, he had to say something, if only for effect,

'This is very serious. A lack of effective control over those girls could cost us our licence.'

'Frank, you're absolutely right. I've asked Harry and Sid to review all our procedures. We have to learn from this.'

Once back in his office, Bollard tried to evaluate the situation. There wasn't much that could be concluded from the meeting with Pellzer except that, so far, they'd done a reasonable cover-up job. A lot depended now on how the girl would react but that would probably be simply a question of how much. Al Khazari would be unlikely to cause trouble. He'd be barred at considerable cost to Ventura. Anything he had going through in cheques might be cleared, but the real cost was his potential future losses.

So now here was Bollard, like the people he worked for, evaluating the damage to the company in financial terms while disregarding the fact that within the Ventura, prostitution, criminal assault and complicity to conceal criminal acts had taken place. Where would it end? How low was he prepared to sink to retain his position?

Chapter Thirty-three

Nidditch waited, the number was ringing. He was about to put down the phone when at last someone answered.

'Hello, Pellzer here.'

'Hi, Dan, Nidditch in the VIP, Jim suggested I call you because we have a surprise visit from Morgan down here.'

'Really, who's he with?'

'Samantha Dee, the actress, and another three people… thing is, he's asking about Al Khazari and we don't want to talk in front of people. He's a bit… loud.'

'Fuck!' Pellzer understood loud. It meant stoned. 'Okay, I'm on my way down, don't say anything.'

The Primero VIP restaurant was fairly busy and Trist had positioned himself and his guests in the middle of the room. He'd noisily called for service and then when the room director and serving Chicas hurried to his table, trooped off into the casino area to demand, 'How much we winning tonight?'

His equally inebriated guests giggled and shouted to him while the catering staff waited to take their order. Nidditch and Ellis tried to head off the rampaging Chairman, who was by now shouting across tables at the newly promoted and beleaguered Staine. They managed to divert him back into the restaurant and away from gamblers, who were beginning to look irritated by this interruption.

After Trist had disturbed a group of Arabs in the restaurant by asking loudly 'Was it one of those fuckin guys who did the business on the Chica?' Ellis had suggested a call to Pellzer.

The two managers attempted to keep Trist and his guests occupied by having the room director offer them cocktails and invite them to choose from the buffet. Pat, advised by Ollie that the Chairman had come in and gone up to the Primero, arrived by the public stairway almost at the same time as Pellzer entered from back-of- house.

Pat stood almost mesmerised by the spectacle of the company Chairman shouting at the group of Arabs.

'We set you up with girls and what d'ya do? Treat them like fuckin George Foreman! Are your fuckin' names Al or Ali!' Trist was laughing and doing a poor imitation of the boxer.

Pellzer, alarmed by this outburst, moved to steer him towards the exit, 'Morg, Morg, come with me. I want to show you something.'

Trist resisted stubbornly but good humouredly. 'Hey, Dan, where d'you come from? I'm havin' a party with Sam and—'

'Morg, I got something good for you out here,' Pellzer whispered, moving him towards the staff exit. 'Call Rye!' Pellzer shouted to Nidditch as he hustled Trist out through the door to the corridor.

Ellis looked around. All attention had been on this performance. Fortunately, although everyone recognised outrageous behaviour, few recognised the perpetrator as the Chairman of Ventura. Even fewer understood the significance of his jests.

One who did still stood transfixed.

Ellis called to him. 'Pat, get around, see the punters are okay!'

It took a moment to sink in, then Pat nodded and moved towards the tables to smooth ruffled feathers. Not being easily diverted from their mission, almost all the gamblers had already resumed playing. Only a few people in the restaurant seemed to be disturbed by the events, but they too were soon pacified.

Rye, on taking Nidditch's call, scurried down the stairs and arrived at the first floor service area to find Pellzer and Trist doing what seemed like a waltz. Trist was intent on returning to his guests, while Pellzer endeavoured to keep him anywhere out of the public area. A bus-boy and several Chicas stood watching the company's two most senior executives with amused fascination.

'Get on with your work!' screamed Rye. They scattered in all directions. 'Hey, Morg! I've been lookin' for you,' he said, moving between the two bosses as if it was an excuse-me dance. Pellzer gratefully stood off.

'Rye! What the fuck… what's going with this guy?' Trist said, staggering and gesturing at Pellzer.

'Dan asked me to organise a surprise for you upstairs,' Rye said, then continued quietly in Trist's ear, 'I got some great stuff, let's go!'

Trist hovered for a minute, then pointed to the door. 'I got S… Sam and Don…'

'They're on their way up. They're waiting, let's go, it's party time!'

They moved across the corridor. The lift door had just closed. Pellzer reached quickly to press the button and catch it, fearful that any loss of momentum would allow Trist to change his mind again. The doors re-opened and they bundled inside, almost crushing three croupier Chicas, against the back wall of the elevator.

'Hey, you guys… this is one of the best Chicas!' Trist stumbled towards a blonde girl, who stood paralysed with fear.

'Christ!' exclaimed Rye, suddenly realising who the Chica was. He attempted to slip himself between Trist and the girl. A little too late. As Trist reached to touch her, her mouth dropped open, her eyes rolled and she slithered down the wall in a faint. Both Pellzer and Rye made a frantic attempt to catch her but succeeded only in knocking themselves and Trist off-balance, all of them falling in an ungainly heap on the floor. The other two Chicas shrieked in alarm.

'Jesus fuckin' Christ, what th—!'

'What the fuck…!' the two men roared.

'Okay, okay, okay, calm down!' shouted Pellzer, first to steady himself.

Rye struggled to his feet to help Pellzer lift the cursing and abusive Trist off the legs of the unconscious girl. The lift shuddered to a halt and the doors opened to another group of staff waiting to enter on the next floor.

'Take the fuckin' stairs!' screamed Rye, enraged and humiliated. The lift doors closed again.

The girl was only semi-conscious when they got to the apartments. Rye opened an apartment with his master key, then diverted a thoroughly confused Trist to his own suite, while Pellzer, with the help of the other two Chicas, placed her on the bed. She was conscious but in an almost catatonic state. A few moments later the seamstress from the Chica-room arrived to assist with her recuperation.

Pellzer left them and made his way slowly down the stairs to the Primero level, stopping on the way to light a cigarette, compose himself and dust down his clothes. He gave instructions to a catering supervisor to escort Trist's guests upstairs to the suite where Rye was 'entertaining' Trist, then signalled Ellis and Nidditch to join him at a table in the corner.

'Things okay down here?' he asked, exhaustion showing on his face.

'I think so, but we could've done without that,' answered Ellis.

'Yeah.' Pellzer wore a look of resignation. 'There was another incident with that Chica Penny in the lift. I don't think she'll be coming back on the floor.'

'Oh no! You mean Talal's bit. That bird again, she's only just come back!' Ellis looked to Nidditch. 'I thought we put her upstairs out of the way?'

'She was down here chipping while Talal's away.' Nidditch shook his head in frustration.

'Anyway, how do we stand with this Al Khazari thing? I see our PR guy's here on the floor, he said anything?' asked Pellzer.

The two managers looked at each other to confirm nothing more had been said by Monaghan and shook their heads.

'Hopefully that's a good sign. I spoke to Frank, told him our story, he wasn't too happy but seemed to accept the situation. Although he didn't say the PR guy had already told him. As for the Chica, Marta told her the score, and that we'd get Al Khazari to pay compensation only if there was no police, no scandal. She's considering it. The biggest problem is Al Khazari, there's no trace of him, far as I know.' Pellzer looked to them to confirm this.

'He's left London,' said Ellis, 'we'll have to get Ahmed to ferret him out wherever he is.'

'He won't pay now. He knows we can't take action,' added Nidditch.

'We've got to impress upon him this can only be hushed up with our help, otherwise he can't return to London,' said Pellzer sharply, already angry at the events of the evening but also with Nidditch's negativity. 'You gave this guy eighty-five grand, set him up with this girl, now you're telling me we can't trust him, and we should just write this off?'

Nidditch was about to reply, but Ellis grabbed his arm and intervened. 'Okay, let's talk to Ahmed, he should be here in a bit.'

'Okay,' Pellzer said getting up. 'Oh, and check up on that Penny girl.'

Nidditch waited until he'd gone. 'What d'you make of that? This whole fucking credit thing's his idea. Now it's all going arse up, he wants to blame us!' He slammed his palm on the table. 'And what about that other arsehole Trist! He'll have us all in the shit!'

'Cool it. Let's talk to the little fella, see what he says about Khazari,' said Ellis thoughtfully. 'Oh, and Pat can check up on Penny, he's a mate of hers, isn't he?' He added, on seeing Monaghan at the far end of the restaurant.

Nidditch rose to talk with Monaghan and Ellis signalled to the waitress Chica. He needed a drink. They were both stopped in their tracks by a shout from the door.

'Where he is, 'The Greatest', Muhammed Ali? They told me he was here!' Ahmed appeared, doing a shadow-boxing movement like Trist, although his feet were letting him down.

'How the fuck did you know about that?' asked Ellis under his breath.

'My friends, I know about everything in Ventura,' he laughed, then changed his expression. 'Tell me now, what is the problem with this Marietta and Hakeem Al Khazari?'

The Mama de Chicas and the seamstress were in close attendance when Pat knocked and entered the apartment. Penny showed no awareness of his presence though she was sitting up and conscious. He moved to the bedside and could see that she was trembling.

'Penny, it's Pat, Pat Monaghan.'

There was a brief eye movement, then she bit her lip. The seamstress, holding her hand, also took note of this slight response and made way for him to take her place.

'What happened? he asked the two women, quietly. 'She fainted in the lift?'

The Mama shrugged and looked to her colleague, 'We weren't there, the Chicas said she fainted and Mr Pellzer brought her here.'

'Mr Pellzer?' Pat repeated incredulously. 'He was with...' He stopped. A sudden alarming vision came to mind. Pat took her hand. 'Penny, listen now, you're with friends, there's nothing to be scared about.' He kept repeating the words like a mantra.

After what seemed like ages, tears started to trickle down her face. Her breathing became pronounced but regular.

'Will I get Elena, will I ask her to come?'

Again there was a long pause then a barely perceptible nod of her head. Pat turned to the two women, who were waiting with anxious anticipation. 'Please, find Chica Elena, ask her to come, she's her friend.' They seemed to be deliberating who should go. 'It's okay, I'll wait with her.'

They both sped off.

Pat waited, patting Penny's hand as she sobbed quietly.

Just then Elena rushed into the room, closely followed by the seamstress. 'What's the matter? What happened?'

'She fainted in the lift, I think she ran into you-know-who,' said Pat in a whisper, as Elena almost pushed him aside to get to the stricken Penny. She turned as if to ask: who's you-know-who? Her eyes widened, then closed in horror as she remembered Trist's earlier drunken arrival at reception.

'We asked if we should call a doctor,' said the seamstress, 'but Mr Pellzer said we should wait a while.'

'Yes, I'm sure he did.' Elena grimaced as she spoke. The woman looked a little puzzled. 'It's okay, I know Penny's problem. I'll call if we need any help. Thank you, Jill.'

'Penny, it's alright now, you're with friends.' Elena pulled her over gently until her head rested on her shoulder. 'Come on, it's over, you're with us.'

Chapter Thiry-four

Lowe was surprised to learn from Bollard's secretary that her boss was somewhere on the casino floor, he himself having seen him there recently on only a handful of occasions. He asked her to inform Mr Bollard on his return that he would be in the male rest-room.

The job offer from Ladbrokes, a position of General Manager in one of their provincial casinos, was even more than he'd hoped for. Now the announcement of his departure would be doubly pleasurable. His new employers accepted his continued employment at Ventura in a position of some responsibility as a testimony to his worth, removing any immediate need for a letter of reference. Nevertheless, knowing it did not pay to leave enemies behind, he decided against voicing his suspicions about the credit policy to Bollard, lest he alienate him or become embroiled in an investigation.

Draper called the male rest room 'Dresden'. The carpet's original colour was indeterminable, a rich mulch of dirt, food, chewing gum and cigarette ash, which had been applied regularly and liberally. The chairs had all been broken and repaired so many times that little was left of the original material. The three coffee tables/ footstools had decorative rings of cigarette burns to add to the stains and scratches. One item stood unscathed amid the carnage - the television - because, in an uncharacteristically resolute moment, Bollard had laid down the law that, if broken or damaged in any way, it would not be repaired or replaced.

Two inspectors and Ventura's token black male trainee did their best to maintain the room in its traditional condition by lounging across several units of furniture and dropping ash while they watched a news programme.

Lowe's arrival provoked only a nod of recognition and moments later the unexpected entrance of Bollard almost ignited a spark of curiosity but this quickly died as the news reader announced the next item: football.

'Evening, gentlemen, please, don't bother to get up.' Only Lowe acknowledged Bollard's ironic greeting. 'Ian, you wanted to see me? Let's go to my office lest we distract these gentlemen.'

Bollard walked quickly, as he did when traversing the casino floor. He sat down and beckoned Ian to do the same. Lowe, wasting no time on ceremony, handed him his resignation letter.

Bollard read it. At this point he knew he should give his managerial speech about Lowe's bright future with the company, and ask him to reconsider, but he could find no convincing argument why a young ambitious manager should remain at Ventura.

'I assume from this you have another position?'

'Yes, Ladbrokes have offered me the position of General Manager in one of their provincial casinos.'

'That's an excellent opportunity,' said Bollard, envious of the younger man. 'Though we'll be sorry to see you go, I can understand why you don't want to pass up this chance.'

Lowe nodded, 'About the procedure... should I tell Nidditch? Work the notice... or...?'

'Yes... er... as you know, people in this business often don't work notice. Let me call John about your decision.' Bollard picked up the phone and dialled the VIP. 'Hello John, Frank... yes, fine... I've got Ian Lowe here and he's just given his notice... I see. So... er... if I let him go now you've got cover? Okay... fine, bye.'

'Well,... I'm sure he'll be sorry to lose you...' Bollard began, but he could see Lowe was smiling .

'Yeah, that'll be right. I've made his day.'

'Why would you think that?'

'I'm not sure. Maybe I ask too many questions. There's always the risk I'll ask how the credit system works,' Lowe replied and immediately regretted it, having resolved not to mention that subject.

'What do you mean? You think something's wrong with… the administration of the cheque-cashing allowance?' asked Bollard.

Lowe smiled at his avoidance of the word 'credit'. 'Well, I'm sure you'd know if anything was wrong so I'll leave that…' He was now anxious to terminate the conversation. 'So can I clear my locker?'

Bollard looked thoughtful, 'Er… yes. You know the drill? I should really call security and let them know.'

'Great, that's fine. I'll wait in the rest room till they come. So…' Lowe hovered.

Bollard seemed distracted but after a brief pause extended his hand. 'Ian, very best of luck with your new appointment, and I'll inform admin about your wages and papers.'

'Thanks, bye.'

Lowe left looking as happy as he'd seen anyone at Ventura look for some time.

Bollard felt envious. The young Scot had secured himself a great opportunity; helped in no small way by Nidditch and Ellis's sponsorship of Staine over his more serious claim for promotion. They had never given any concrete reasons for this preference. But why would Nidditch be happy to see Lowe go because he 'might ask how the credit system works'?

Bollard knew he'd lost touch, abdicated responsibility a long time ago, divorced himself from operations and let others dictate policy. For some reason Pellzer had formed an alliance with Ellis and Nidditch to bypass him. Was it his plan to replace him or was he simply to be left as a kind of… Mayfield? The fact that the latter option didn't immediately fill him with horror was an indication of how low his spirit had sunk.

'Hello, it's Pat,' he said on hearing Elena's voice. 'Is Penny's still with you?'

'Oh yes. Wait a moment please,' she said formally, returning seconds later.

'Sorry, she's next door, I didn't want her to hear. Yes, she's a lot better, but quiet. I'm not sure how to play it.'

'I've just had a visit here in Ventura from Talal's driver. The Prince's back and looking for her.'

'Really? I suppose I'll have to tell her. Actually, he's all she's talked about, so perhaps he can cheer her up. Okay, Pat, I'll handle it. Anyway, how are you?'

'I'm well. I've come in to organise a trip to the racing for some punters. I suppose for the moment I'll just carry on. According to Jim Ellis, Marietta's dropped her complaint against Al Khazari because she struck at him first and is scared she'll be accused of prostitution.'

'Bullshit, she's been paid off! What about him, he coming back in again?'

'Jim says he doesn't think so, because he abused our hospitality by taking a girl to his room.'

'Ho ho! Pull the other one. Did he keep a straight face when he said that?'

'Yes I'm afraid so. Anyway, what can we do?'

'You know one thing we can do… fight for our rights and everyone else's who works at Ventura.'

'Well maybe, but I don't think you're going to get enough support. That Union is doing nothing. You're trying to do it all by yourself, and what if you fail, what then?'

'Don't worry, I've still got a few tricks up my sleeve. I know a lot about them.'

'Be careful. They won't let small people like you or me get in the way.'

'Small people? Speak for yourself, you're the leprechaun! There's no small person here.'

Pat laughed and said he would see her later. Elena went to break the news to Penny.

'This suit, you have borrowed it? asked Ahmed maliciously.

Staine, familiar with Ahmed's ways, smiled and tried to look nonchalant. However, as intended, the comment amused the Chicas round the punto table.

'Stop! The manager's rented suit is not a laughing matter!' Ahmed pretended to be serious. The giggles increased. Staine skulked away, forgetting he was supervising the addition of a 'fill' to the table. The cashier, the inspector and the croupiers stood immobile, waiting to see if he would remember.

Nidditch shook his head in disbelief. 'Staine! Haven't you forgotten something?'

Staine returned to more sniggering as Nidditch signalled an appeal to Ahmed to leave him be. The Arab managed to restrain himself although his wide grin continued to provoke giggling amongst the Chicas. Nidditch signalled again that they were waiting upstairs but Ahmed appeared, as usual, in no great hurry, stopping off at various tables to salute clients and potential clients.

'That man is very good gambler, we can make deal with him,' he said when he finally joined Nidditch to go upstairs.

'After Al Khazari we should be careful about making deals,' replied Nidditch sourly.

'Ah! On this I have some good news.' The little man looked smug.

'Oh yes, what's that?'

'Ah ha...' He waved a finger that said: *you have to wait*. Of course, thought Nidditch, he needs the full audience.

Pellzer and, surprisingly, Trist, were waiting with Ellis when Nidditch arrived with Ahmed.

'Morgan! Or is it Muhammed Ali? I don't see you for long time,' Ahmed announced.

'What the fuck you on about - Muhammed Ali? 'asked a bemused Trist.

Pellzer threw a reproachful look at Ahmed. He didn't need that incident dragged up again, having already had a heated argument with Trist over his indiscretions.

'Listen, guys, let's get on with the business in hand, you can joke later,' Pellzer addressed them quickly.

'You were saying, Ahmed, you've some news about Al Khazari?' Nidditch prompted him.

'I spoke with him, he's very upset about this girl. She made him very angry, saying things like - he wasn't paying enough money. He said also that Ventura uses girls as temptation on the tables and make sure he always loses—'

'His usual crap,' Ellis interrupted, 'but is he saying he won't pay?'

'I told to him the girl and her family reported to the police but I can get my friends at Ventura to fix this to be no scandal or problem. In the end he say he will give me fifty percent now, to pay you. To show he is willing to find solution. Then I should act for him, to see that nothing bad come to him.'

'And the rest of the money he owes?' asked Pellzer.

'I can get it, but maybe we have to wait.'

'Where is he?' asked Ellis

'He… does not want to say and—.'

'No, but you must fuckin' know?' intervened Trist.

'I know but… he ask me not to say. It will not help if I tell you. Trust me, my good friend.'

They were all silent for a minute.

'If I trust you and I'm your good friend, does that mean I don't have to pay you for this?' Trist asked, without looking up from the coffee he was pouring. They all smiled.

'Morgan ! I am a poor man, I have costs. Everyone takes my time with these things. I have to live.'

'How much?' Trist paused with the cup to his mouth.

'Morgan, it will not be much.'

'How much?'

'Small, maybe ten per cent… small.'

'That's not fuckin' small! Five percent's okay. But I want all of it. That fuckin' flake beat up one of our girls. Now we have to pay her off. We're not losin' the money he owes as well.'

'We've lost his business also. He'll go to another club and lose fortunes,' added Pellzer.

'If he pays he can not come back?' asked Ahmed.

'That's a problem.' Ellis shook his head. 'Other people know about it – Bollard, Monaghan, maybe more.'

'Maybe that's squared with them,' Pellzer said, 'anyway, let's get the money first then we'll look at that.'

'If the story's got around, there's no way he could come back in, people like Draper would stir up all kinds of shit,' Nidditch added.

'That fuckin' guy's still here? I thought I heard he was supporting this union shit. We got fuckin' enemies in the camp we can't get rid of - Draper, Bollard, Bland…'

'Bland's gone, we got lucky there. Bollard… well, as I said before, we need somebody there.' Pellzer felt uncomfortable discussing this in front of the others.

'Why don't we just keep the other prick May… flower, or whatever his name is?' Trist grunted.

'Mayfield,' corrected Pellzer, as the others sniggered. Then, to divert the conversation, he added, 'You mentioned another problem, Ahmed?'

'Yes, Prince Mansur Talal. He has returned from the Gulf. There is no problem for him to pay, but for security he wants to pay through another company, not his own. My company maybe?'

'Aw Jesus! Don't tell me you want ten per cent for this now?' Trist spat out the words as well as tobacco flakes from his cigar.

'No, my friend, I am talking only my costs – one, maybe two per cent. He does not want his family to see and ask why big money go to a Western account. His father and uncle are very strict. His father is sick, maybe will die soon, his uncle don't like Western things - gambling, women and other. This way he will not have problem with him.'

Trist sighed and looked at Pellzer who seemed to be looking for the answer on the ceiling. Nidditch smiled knowingly at Ellis, who directed himself to Ahmed.

'Maybe you can get him to spend more time in the casino? He spends more and more time with that bird.'

'You are right, this girl is a problem and he likes her too much. She is problem also for Morg, no?' Ahmed glanced mischievously in Trist's direction.

Trist looked up from preparing a new cigar, unaware of who they were talking about.

'Penny, I speak of Chica Penny!'

'Oh, that fuckin' dame! Set her up with this Khazari guy, do us all a favour!' This provoked a chorus of laughter.

'This is difficult,' Ahmed laughed, 'but I work to get Mansur to forget about her, his uncle already does not want him with this girl.'

'Maybe she won't come back after this latest… incident,' said Nidditch, glancing briefly at Trist as he directed the remark to Pellzer.

'Yeah, but what will she tell him?' pondered Pellzer, also glancing at Trist, who was pouring yet another coffee. 'How will he take it, and if she's not here, will he gamble elsewhere?'

'Well that's Ahmed's fuckin' job! You've gotta earn the fuckin' money you're squeezing out of us,' said Trist. Suffering as always from his previous night's activity, he staggered with his coffee and spilled some of the hot liquid over Pellzer's defensive outstretched hand.

'Look, your Chairman "floats like butterfly but stings like bee"!' Ahmed laughed again. 'Okay my friends, I go now to do my job.'

Ahmed took his leave. Pellzer sat down with tired resignation and put a handkerchief round his hand. The two floor managers tried to contain their amusement.

'What's this shit about Muhammed Ali?' mumbled Trist. No one bothered to let him into the joke. Nidditch suggested that if there was nothing else he'd get back to the casino, and left to accompany Ahmed.

'I don't suppose we've any choice but to go along with him, but it's giving him a lot of power,' said Pellzer when the Arab had gone.

'I don't like it, but how else we gonna get our fuckin' money? You guys sure made a bad call with this Kazi guy,' grunted Trist.

'We can only deal with the punters we've got. This system's always going to be dangerous,' said Ellis angrily. Pellzer signalled surreptitiously to him to be calm.

'Hey, that's why we're cuttin' you guys in,' answered Trist.

Pellzer, seeing that Ellis was becoming even more angry, held up his hand for him to leave it.

'Morg, let's leave this for now, we'll find solutions to everything. Didn't you say you wanted your driver for ten o'clock?'

'You trying to get fuckin rid of me?'

'That's right, I got work to do.'

'Okay.' Trist rammed his cigar in an ashtray, 'I'm glad somebody's fuckin' working in this place. See you guys.'

Ellis waited in angry silence until Pellzer had seen him out.

'Jim, look, don't bother about what he says, you know Morg, he just blurts out stuff, he—'

'No Dan, this is serious! We agreed to do this, of course we want something out of it, but it's for the company's benefit. We said it wouldn't be easy, but we don't need him coming in stoned to shout his mouth off—'

'Wait Jim, he was only talkin' about Al Khazari and the girl…'

'No, before you came down he was shouting about how much Al Khazari owed us… and if we'd got him the girl. Both things are fucking illegal!'

'Okay, okay, I know it's a problem when he's… had too many…'

'Too many, when he's had too many? That's every fucking night! We're breaking laws everywhere and he's announcing it publicly. He'll have us all in the shit!'

'Okay, let me promise you, I'll see he doesn't do that again. Right?'

'We don't know what he says outside either.'

Pellzer knew that was a concern. 'If he doesn't get all the information he won't be able to talk about it.'

Now Ellis took time to think. 'Then you better tell Ahmed not to tell him things during their sessions.'

'No problem,' agreed Pellzer, although he wasn't sure he could control this, 'I'll handle this end. Anyway, it'll be a little easier now you've got Bland out of the way and Lowe's given his notice. Both Draper's men.'

Ellis returned to the Trist factor, 'We'll see, but if anything happens like the other night we'll have to stop or we'll all end up in jail.'

'Hey Jim, come on! It was an embarrassment, but from now on it'll be controlled.'

Ellis left, unconvinced by Pellzer's assurances.

Chapter Thirty-five

Her excitement was mounting. He was back at last. She could see his car in the street below her window. The doorbell rang and she raced down the stairs, opened the front door and threw her arms around him before he could get out his first word.

'Oh Mansur, Mansur I've missed you so much!' she cried. His reponse was smothered by another embrace. At last she stopped and leaned back, smiling, to look at him.

Now he smiled, and although at first it seemed strained, it warmed as he looked at her. 'Penny my dear, you almost threw me back down the steps!'

'Oh, I'm sorry, but I'm so happy to see you!' She locked arms and guided him in to the hallway. 'When you didn't call? I was so worried.'

'I was very busy, but the last few days I have been calling, and looking for you, where have you been?'

'Oh, I... was a little unwell. I went to stay with my friend Elena, because...' She faltered and tried to expel the dark thoughts. 'Anyway, I'm fine now.'

'You are more than fine, you are even more beautiful than I remembered,' he said as drew her to him gently.

Her fear that the re-awakened memory of that fateful night might inhibit her relationship with Mansur immediately evaporated. Instead of fear, she felt excitement. Desire vanquished doubt. He eased her towards the sofa but it was too far away. Her clothes seemed to melt away but to shed his required some frantic tugging. She eagerly assisted. Twisting, turning, writhing, thrusting on the carpeted floor. Tremors: then erruption!

Now, with slow, undulating movements, he stayed within her, caressing, stroking, washing away all thoughts of the outside world. After some time, she felt new pleasurable tremors and an explosion of ecstasy.

They lay entwined for some minutes before he gently disengaged, rolled over and lay breathing heavily and contentedly by her side, one arm still locked below her.

She was reluctant to break the spell, but he rose first.

'You are not working tonight?' he asked.

'Er… no. I decided to leave Ventura.' She rose and began collecting her clothes.

'Why, something happened again?'

She noted the 'again' but decided not pick up on it or say anything that might destroy the present feeling.

'Nothing happened, my love, I just don't like it there. I'll find something else.'

He was quiet for a few moments then, to her relief, smiled. 'So, you are free to go out tonight? I know a very nice restaurant.'

'Wonderful, but I have to wash my hair… do things… you know?'

'Please, do not make yourself any more beautiful, I cannot bear it!' He put his hands together in mock prayer. She laughed and prodded him gently.

'I will leave you, and send the car in two, no… three hours, yes?'

She agreed. He tucked in his shirt, stepped into his shoes, grabbed his jacket and pecked her gently on the forehead before leaving.

The Ford Capri drew up. Carmen climbed out, blew a kiss to the driver and it was only as she turned to enter the club that she noticed Elena standing in the doorway.

'Oh hi, Elena! I didn't see you there.'

'Well no, you were too busy throwing kisses. Wasn't that Ian Lowe?'

'Yes, we've been going out for a few weeks now.'

'Nice. Nice new car too.'

'Yes, a company car. He's going to work for Ladbrokes, did you know?'

'Yes, lucky sod. Lucky to be getting out of Ventura and with a good job. So is this something serious then?'

'Oh, I don't think so. He'll be leaving London. It's just some fun. What about you, no special guy yet?' added Carmen as they went inside.

'No, still waiting for Morgan Trist. We've so much in common.' They both laughed. 'Anyway,' said Elena, 'We need a meeting soon to discuss our campaign and how to ensure no more information leaks to the enemy.'

Carmen seemed to think. 'You sure it wasn't something you said to Bland or maybe just coincidence?'

'I don't think so. We can't ignore the possibility that there's a spy in our camp.'

Carmen nodded but did not answer.

Bollard had good news for Mayfield on his return from holiday; he would have additional responsibilities. Not only would he chair the new Health and Safety Committee but also carry out a long overdue audit and review of all casino operational procedures. The latter was one of Bollard's initiatives and he congratulated himself on choosing the time and the arguments to get Pellzer, in an unguarded moment, to endorse his proposal. He used the dice scam and several minor incidents to suggest that the distraction of the union campaign had caused some staff to neglect important operational procedures and, following Mayfield's review, confirmation of this might give the company grounds to initiate disciplinary procedures.

Bollard had an altogether different motive for launching his assistant on this abortive mission. Mayfield, with the MD's approval, would attack this assignment with his usual diligent attention to detail. Frank would suggest he pay particular attention to those areas covered by legislation. Ellis and Nidditch would refuse to cooperate and Pellzer, at their insistence, would probably cancel or limit the review. Bollard would then have, should he ever need it, a witness in Mayfield that he'd initiated an internal audit only for it to be cancelled by Pellzer.

Mayfield, having heard about the new committee while on holiday, predictably returned with a briefcase full of material. Bollard reluctantly allowed him to explain what he'd prepared, in the unrealistic hope that he'd be brief.

'Excellent, Gordon, but being a bit pushed for time I'd just like to stress that the audit authorised by Dan Pellzer is of crucial importance to ensure total compliance with the Gaming Act in such things as cheque-cashing.'

'Of course, I'll start an assessment of compliance immediately. It will mean that I'll have to make unannounced visits and inspections. Naturally, I will try as far as possible not to interfere or disrupt normal operations.' said Mayfield.

'Good,' smiled Frank. 'Now if you'll excuse me, I have to call the GWU to discuss ballot arrangements.'

'Ah the GWU, you may be interested to know they've made a proposal to the Government on Health and Safety at Work, they—'

'Yes, yes I know about it,' lied Bollard, almost nudging Mayfield to the door.

Ahmed left Talal in the hotel lounge with a group of his compatriots. They'd slowly congregated around them as he briefed the Prince on what had happened during his absence. When he saw they'd no longer be able to talk privately, he took his leave. Some matters were too delicate to share with others. He'd touched briefly on the credit arrangement with Ventura, but the other matter required a slower and more subtle approach. He risked fracturing the relationship if he openly criticised the 'English *Wardah*'. There was little doubt the Prince was still captivated by her.

Nevertheless, Ahmed had again brought up the matter of her ex-boy-friend, given that Talal had previously asked him to investigate Martin Atkinson's sudden appearance. There was nothing new to relate but, hoping to revive doubts which had originally surfaced, he invented a 'report from contacts' which revealed that Atkinson had moved to an address near Penny's. Ahmed offered to keep tabs on him, to make sure he did not harass the Prince's lady. Actually, as far as was known, Atkinson had made no contact and probably did not know where she lived. Ahmed felt it was time to rectify that, and bring them together. He could then report their meeting to the Prince before she did.

'What's this prick Mayfield doing here? He says he's got your approval.'

Pellzer hadn't failed to notice the recent change in attitude of both Nidditch and Ellis. A disrespectful almost hostile tone was creeping into their exchanges with him.

'What exactly are you talking about?' he replied.

'Mayfield's on the floor doing what he calls "a review of internal procedures" and says you authorised it.' Nidditch's enunciation was slow and deliberate.

Pellzer considered this for a moment, then remembered Bollard's suggestion. 'Yeah, with the recent dice scam, various other problems and reports that some staff pay more attention to union matters than security procedures, Bollard and—'

'This is bullshit… I want this arsehole outa here!'

'Now, just a—'

'No, fuck it, he's—'

Pellzer tried several times to intercede but he ranted on. He could now see it might have been a mistake sanctioning Bollard's review but Nidditch's overreaction was infuriating. He was stepping completely out of line.

'What's the big fuckin deal? He's only looking at table procedures!'

'Yes, including our credit procedures!' grunted Nidditch.

Now Pellzer grasped the problem. He'd have to speak to Bollard but didn't want to back down.

'Put him on, I'll tell him to do it upstairs. You're not giving anything up there, are you?'

'It doesn't matter, I don't—'

'Just put him on, Jesus! Don't make a big deal outa nuthin'!'

Nidditch cursed and slammed the receiver on the desk top. A few minutes later Mayfield spoke. 'Hello, Gordon here… yes hello, Dan. It seems there's some resistance from John Nidditch to our review and I—'

'Yes, Gordon, it's a misunderstanding. I'll sort it out with Frank. For now, better to leave the VIP and start upstairs. There's plenty to be getting on with on the upper floors.'

'Well okay, but I'll have to say something in my report to Frank about Nidditch's attitude,' Mayfield said sniffily.

'Yeah, do that Gordon.' Pellzer put down the phone. He too was wondering what to do about Nidditch's attitude.

Had Mitford put on weight since she'd last seen him, wondered Elena, or was it just that the broad grey pinstripe had been bought when he'd been smaller?

'Morning, Comrades.' Mitford placed his briefcase on the Union meeting room table. 'What's new with the campaign?'

'The ideas I told you about have been scuppered. The company got wind of our approach to the cleaner and also formed their own Health & Safety Committee, from so-called volunteers,' answered Elena.

'Sounds a bit iffy, somebody been talkin?' The Union man looked at them for an indicator. Their shrugs signalled only doubt. Mitford continued. 'Well, let's hope it was just loose talk. Anyway, let's see where we are with this.' He opened a file taken from his case. 'The company proposes a pre-ballot meeting on 17th February at the Grosvenor Hotel where both sides can put their case and explain how the ballot will be run. The question is – do we agree with this proposal?'

Elena wasn't sure but had no reason to contest the venue. The others offered no counter-proposal.

'So I take it we agree.' Mitford scribbled a note on his file. 'So how's support going for the campaign?

'Not so good. Thanks to the leak, we haven't made the impact we'd hoped. Now they've changed my shift, and Carmen's, so we don't have the same access to the staff. It's discrimination and intimidation all the way. So much for the protection of a union!' Elena said with bitterness.

'Well, without recognition that's difficult. Unless you're getting specific threats, intimidation's also difficult to prove.'

Elena gave him an ironic smile.

'Now I hear the company's going to introduce a new salary and bonus scheme to sweeten up the staff before the ballot,' said Carmen.

'Naturally, but none of that would have happened without the threat of the Union.' Mitford looked smug.

'Maybe, but many think they can get improvements with the threat of a union, but without actually voting them in,' said Elena.

'Also, unions don't have a good image,' added Carmen. 'Casino people don't think of themselves as workers, like miners and dockers.'

Mitford looked irritated. 'Maybe, but just because they wear fancy dresses and suits doesn't mean the bosses don't think they're workers and won't screw them when they can.'

'In more ways than one,' said Elena. 'The problem's to convince them. They don't have much solidarity with each other.'

'Well, that's your job, bring 'em together,' said Mitford, a little too dismissively for Elena's liking.

'You don't think since GWU are trying to get recognition, you might do a little bit more?' answered Elena sharply.

'What you suggest we do?'

'You, an official of a Union with a long history of campaigns, are asking me? Even the literature we requested came two weeks late, and not enough. You could've organised a mass meeting yourselves to put the Union's case. Your lawyers could've seen the cleaner who was injured, or something. Everything's down to us, is that what you're saying?

'Look, I know it's difficult, but we don't have a mandate yet to represent.' Mitford took a softer line in the face of Elena's criticism.

'You need a mandate to provide information and get publicity in the press?'

Mitford sighed, 'I'll see what can be done.'

'Who'll speak at this meeting at the hotel?' asked Elena.

'I don't know who'll speak for them. You should speak as representative of the workers.' Mitford looked at Elena, then the others to see if they registered any disapproval

'Yes, that's clear, and you'll speak for the GWU?' asked Carmen.

The union man paused before answering, 'Yeah, I can do that.'

'What time's the meeting? How long will the session be, how many speakers are permitted and is there a time limit on speeches?' Elena lifted her pen to take notes.

'Well, that we don't yet know,' said Mitford.

Elena shook her head with frustration. 'Haven't they suggested a time?'

'They just proposed 17th February and Grosvenor and asked if we agree. Which's what I asked you,' he replied testily.

'We need to know all the arrangements.' Elena made a face.

'Well, of course they've got to agree certain terms,' Mitford sounded as if everything was in hand.

'Shouldn't we take a lead? Not allow them to do all the running,' suggested a frustrated Elena. 'For example - to make sure everyone can attend, insist they close for a day, suggest three speakers from each side and a time limit per speaker and insist the meeting is thrown open to questions.'

'Well, course we're gonna impose terms - that every worker gets to take part - normal union conditions,' Mitford smiled patronisingly. But Elena noted he was now writing as he spoke.

'And if they don't agree to fair terms, you've got to scream about it - to the newspapers, radio, television. Use your power, your contacts, that's why we wanted the back-up of a big union. You and your "brothers" brought down the last Government, so Ventura shouldn't be a problem.' Elena took her turn to be patronising.

Mitford made to reply, instead shook his head and took more notes before answering. 'We'll do all we can, I'll get back to you with the Company's response to our demands. Then we'll see. Right?'

They nodded in unenthusiastic agreement. Mitford rose, collected his papers, creased his face in a pretend smile and, with slight bow of the head as a goodbye gesture, led them to the door.

'Bye, Comrade!' Elena called out as she left. He didn't answer. Carmen stifled a laugh.

Once outside, Pettigrew muttered a quick goodbye and broke off.

'I know Pettigrew's never been articulate, but hasn't he been quiet?' asked Elena when she and Carmen were alone.

'Yes, I'm not sure what's wrong with him. Ian calls him "the drone",' answered Carmen.

'Speaking of Mr Lowe, how is he, and how's the romance going?'

'For the moment it's still on,' Carmen smiled, 'he's meeting me at the Coach. I didn't know how long we'd be.'

'I'll run you there. I've got to go to the club.'

'Oh, that would be great! You've got the car back then?'

'Yes, the banger's back but I don't know how long it'll last. The mechanic said it's already a miracle it hasn't fallen apart.'

Elena pulled the red mini into the mews to allow Carmen to get out just outside the pub door. 'Look, you can park here. Come in, have a drink and say hello. Come on!' insisted Carmen.

Elena was reticent, then remembered she'd a question that Ian could probably answer. 'Actually, I will, but just a quick one, then I'll leave you two lovebirds alone.'

Carmen gave a dismissive laugh.

Ian rose as soon as he saw the two girls. 'Hello there, comrades!'

'Oh no!' Elena looked to the heavens.

'Anyway, what will you girls have?'

Lowe returned after a few minutes with the drinks. 'So, how's the campaign going?'

'To be truthful, not too well. And I'm not impressed with GWU's part in it so far,' Elena grimaced.

'No, it's not their usual battleground. Probably they don't give a stuff if they win this one or not,' Lowe said, putting down the drinks.

'We don't have that luxury, we'll have to keep fighting or look for another job. What about you, how's your job going?' asked Elena.

'It's good tae be out of there, away from those bastards!' he said bitterly, then changed his tone. 'Matter of fact, I'm really enjoying it.'

'Carmen asked me to come for a quick one to say hello. But I must confess I also wanted to ask you something about the Gaming Act... about credit,' Elena said looking a little apologetic.

'Fire away... about credit, you say?'

'Yes. It's just something I heard and wanted to clarify. Can a player take credit and pay it back in instalments... from abroad, say?'

Lowe was intrigued that the subject of credit, something that had figured greatly in his last days at Ventura, should be raised by Elena. But for the moment he answered without enquiring what had fired her interest.

'Well, in the Gaming Act, credit isn't actually allowed. A player must establish a cheque-cashing facility with the Casino and then can only sign cheques up to the limit requested and authorised by his bank. The cheques taken must be banked within two banking days. Even if the player wins, he can't buy back the cheques. The casino, when it takes a cheque, has got tae bank it.'

'Aha, so there's no way a player would be paying in instalments?' Elena nodded in understanding.

'Only if his cheques had bounced and he'd reached an agreement tae re-pay or replace or re-present the cheques.'

'Oh, now I see. I heard something about credit being paid back. I didn't think about clearing cheques that had bounced.'

'You look disappointed. Is this somebody in particular you're referring tae?'

'Oh… er… no. It's just something I was talking about with someone, it doesn't matter.'

'Funny you ask about credit, because I'd a feeling before I left that something was going on at Ventura with credit,' said Lowe.

'In what way?'

'Oh, just a few strange decisions with various people, a few things didn't quite add up.'

'Oh, Ian, you're out of it now, you don't need to care what they do, you're lucky,' Carmen intervened for the first time.

'You're right, darling.' He sensed she was becoming bored. 'How about another drink?'

'Oh no, I'm driving, I really must go.' Elena downed the last drop and stood up. 'It was great seeing you again Ian. I hope everything goes well.'

Chapter Thirty-six

Normally he'd be concerned that the Managing Director was question-ing his judgement and cancelling policies he'd initiated, but Bollard left Pellzer's office feeling strangely satisfied.

They had chosen to bypass him, but they were going to find that this was easier said than done. He wouldn't risk open defiance, but by judicious use of the Law, labour unrest, company procedures and the 'guardian' of them, Mayfield, he'd frustrate their plans and cover himself against future problems. He'd now suggest to Mayfield he request written confirmation that the audit had been cancelled.

Penny juggled with her groceries while trying to find the keys in her purse. She finally set down the bags, unlocked the front door of the apartment block and, holding it open, reached behind her for the shopping. A voice startled her and a hand reached out from behind to take the bags.

'Let me help you with that.'

She turned to see her ex-boyfriend snatch up the groceries.

'Martin, what are you doing here?' she said, trying to recover from the shock.

'I came to see you and apologise for my behaviour at the casino.' He stood with a bag in either hand.

'It… it's not necessary. Who told you where I live?'

'It doesn't matter. Well, are we going to stand here or will you invite me in?'

'I would prefer you didn't, my flatmate's sleeping,' she lied.

'Come on, Penny, you don't have a flatmate.' He pushed his way into the hallway.

'How do you know… what do you want?'

'Don't be anxious, I'm sober and won't make a scene. I just came to be friendly, explain, then if you still want me to go, I'll go, promise.'

She paused, unsure of what to do, then made her way towards the stairs without comment. Martin followed. On the first floor she paused again, then reluctantly opened her apartment door. Martin looked around the lounge appraisingly. Penny took the groceries from him and went into the small kitchen.

'You have a boyfriend then?' he asked, when she returned.

'That's not really any of your business.'

'I heard you were going with one of them rich Arabs, s'at right?'

'Okay, you promised. I want you to please now go and leave me alone!' she pleaded.

'It's true then… got yourself a rich guy. Now you don't want to talk to an ordinary guy like me, is'at it?'

'Go, or I'll call my neighbour or the police!'

'Okay, don't get hysterical. I'm annoyed, that's all. You ditched me and came here when I thought we were serious.'

'We were over before I came to London. I'm sorry but I don't want to talk about it, please.' She held open the door.

He waited a long time before moving grudgingly to the door. As he moved to pass through, he leant across to kiss her. She recoiled and pushed him out into the hallway.

'What's the matter? You want me to pay like the Arabs you fuck?'

'Leave!' she screamed, slammed the door shut and waited behind it, shaking with emotion. He shouted obscenities for some time but eventually she heard the front door downstairs slam. She ran quickly to peep out from behind the curtain but had to pull away quickly as Martin was looking up from the pavement outside.

After ten minutes she dared to look again. He was gone.

'Hello, me darlin', you're on days now, I see?'

'Hi, Pat. Yes, I've been shunted to day shift and given weekends off. It'd be nice if I didn't know it was done so that I'd come into contact with fewer people. Your colleague here won't admit it, but when he was recently given the job of doing our work schedule, he was told what shift to put me on.' Elena was referring to Ollie Keane, who was standing by the door talking to a car jockey.

'Well, that's what happens in here. Anyway, apart from that, how's it going?'

'Not well, but interesting.' She moved closer to speak quietly. 'I'll be knocking off soon, we could have a chat, in the canteen perhaps, or are you scared to be seen with a militant?'

'Nonsense, see you there in half-an hour. I'll be the one with the big hat, false moustache and dark glasses.'

She was sitting at a table at the back of the room when Pat entered the canteen. Nodding a greeting to several people, he sat down at the table next to Elena while she finished a conversation with two other Chicas.

'You couldn't find the disguise then?' she asked when she slid in beside him. He turned up his collar and looked around furtively. She laughed, but quickly turned to more serious matters.

'I wanted to ask you about some things.' He nodded and waited attentively. She pulled up close. 'There are so many weird things going on, I don't know where to start, but first about credit. Ian told me that the only way someone can owe is if their cheques bounce and they're given time to redeem them.'

'That's right, if the original cheques bounce the managers try to make arrangements for repayment. Who are we talking about?'

She hesitated. Then, in even more of a whisper: 'This has to stay between you and me.'

'Of course.'

'One is Talal and the other I've heard about is Al Khazari.'

'No, you've got the wrong story. Talal I would've known about. Al Khazari I checked when we had the problem with him. In Public Relations we have to keep track of these things.'

She looked thoughtful. 'Could you check again, to be sure? Would it take long?'

Pat agreed and left her to go downstairs. Twenty minutes later he was back. 'Sorry I took so long, I met a few people on the way. Well, neither owes or has ever owed anything. Whoever told you got it wrong.'

'That's funny,' Elena said, deciding for the moment not to mention Talal's notes, feeling it to be a betrayal of Penny's trust, even if Pat was her friend.

Penny put down the phone. Although still upset, she'd tried to sound as normal as possible so he wouldn't detect anything was wrong. Remembering Mansur's reaction after the last incident with Martin, she'd decided not to mention the latest encounter.

The car was coming soon to take her to him, so she made an effort to pull herself together, not daring to consider what might happen if Martin came back.

Although expecting Mansur's driver, she jumped when the buzzer sounded and moved hesitantly to the window. Relieved to see the short, dark man, she knocked on the window to attract his attention and signalled - five minutes. He smiled, nodded and went to wait by the black Rolls Royce. Ten minutes later she slipped quietly downstairs, pleased that none of her neighbours were around to comment on her earlier visitor's language and behaviour.

They had agreed to meet at the restaurant in the Hilton Hotel but when she arrived, Mansur was in the foyer with several men, including his uncle. They were engaged in what appeared to be another heated argument. The old man shot her a glance but made no sign of recognition. Mansur beckoned to his driver while continuing with his animated discussion. The driver darted forward, received a hurried instruction and returned to Penny. His message was unnecessary; she was already making her way to the lounge bar, out of sight and earshot.

Some minutes later Mansur joined her, looking disgruntled. 'My dear, I am sorry, shall we go to the restaurant?' He bent to kiss her lightly on the cheek.

During the time it took for them to be seated at the table, order the aperitifs, study and choose from the menu, he addressed her only to establish her preferences in food and drink. She didn't ask him what was troubling him, although she knew by his demeanour that something was. All the more reason, she thought, not to tell him of her unexpected visitor. They sat in virtual silence except for uncharacteristic small talk from him. Finally she could stand it no longer.

'Mansur, what's wrong. Has something upset you?'

'It is nothing, don't worry about it.' He looked away but at nothing in particular.

She waited, then stretched across to take his hand. He didn't respond at first but then, to her relief, he squeezed affectionately. 'You know, I have a lot of responsibilities to my family and they expect from me that I live in a certain way. Their ways are very different from how I live when I am here. They do not understand.'

'It seems always when your uncle is here, he upsets you,' Penny said sympathetically.

He thought for a moment before answering, as if reluctant to discuss the old man.

'He is the representative of my father, who does not travel. He is a traditionalist, he sees that we younger members do not... er... lose our way. I will one day succeed my father who is old and sick. He worries that I will not uphold the Islamic principles and family traditions.'

'And this is to do with me?' she asked tentatively.

He was slow to answer. 'This is not the only problem, but yes. He thinks a Western woman cannot follow our traditions.' He shook his head in frustration.

'He's wrong, I'm willing to do whatever's necessary, because I love you.' She grasped his hand again with both her hands.

He didn't reply at first. Two waiters now approached with the food.

Then he smiled. 'Don't worry, my darling Penny. I will find the way.'

'Penny, what are you doing here?' Elena was surprised to see her friend at the pub.

'I rang Pat, he told me you were here.'

'Yes, I took a bank holiday they owed me. I'm meeting the committee. This pub has become my office, a place we can meet without being harassed. So what's with you?'

'Oh… as usual, I've got problems.' Elena put down her folder and listened attentively. Penny continued, 'Martin, my ex, turned up at the flat and made a scene. He's also been calling. I'm scared he's…' She paused to compose herself.

'Okay, don't worry.' Elena clasped her friend's hand. 'How did he get your address and phone number?'

'I don't know. I haven't told Mansur after his reaction last time. I was going to stay with him to get away from my flat. But his horrid uncle, who doesn't like me, has arrived, so I can't.'

'Then stay at my place. But longer term, what are you going to do about this Martin? You'll have to call the police if he doesn't stop pestering you.'

'Oh, I'm so sorry to always come to you with my problems!'

'It's no problem for me, you can stay as long as you like. What are you doing about Ventura?'

'I'm still on sick leave, but I don't want to go back. I should give in my notice, but I suppose I haven't even got the courage to do that. But I'll have to go, to collect my money and things from the locker.'

'When you want to go let me know, I'll go with you.'

'Oh thanks, thanks for everything. I really wish I could be strong like you, then I wouldn't have these problems,' said Penny.

'No, you'd have others. Your problem is getting rid of men, mine is to get one and keep him more than one night!' Elena attempted to lighten the atmosphere.

'Oh, that can't be true, you're so pretty!' Penny smiled for the first time.

'It is. No man wants a bolshie cow like me. One night out and they're off. I can't keep my mouth shut long enough.'

'Oh, I'm sure you'll find someone nice,' Penny reassured her, and Elena smiled at the sudden role reversal.

'Anyway, here's the spare key. Do you want me to come with you to your place, to pick up your stuff?'

'Oh no, that's not necessary, I'll get a taxi.'

'Well if you're sure... I've got to see some people, see you later back at... our place.'

They hugged and Penny left. Elena looked around; Roland was now at the bar with Pettigrew and Potts, who waved to Penny as she left. Neither Carmen nor the new self-appointed union representative had yet come, but it was still early.

To Carmen's surprise, when they both arrived simultaneously at the pub, Draper joined them in the corner. Elena had already advised the others of Draper's participation, but she could see Carmen's questioning look.

'Ralph's here to assist with our campaign.'

'Oh... right.' Carmen looked across to Draper. 'The company won't be happy with you.'

'I don't give a damn, since they don't give a damn about me. It's a way of distancing myself from their increasingly dubious policies and hopefully win some protection for people who work there,' said Draper.

'Yes, Ian told me about your views. I'm just surprised you've decided to campaign openly.' Carmen gave a half-smile.

'I don't think I've got anything to lose now. By the way, how is Ian?'

'Oh... yes, he seems to be okay...' Carmen seemed a little distracted.

'Anyway, to business,' said Elena. 'We've confirmed the pre-ballot meeting's at the Grosvenor, starting 2pm on 17th February. The Club won't open until 5pm to enable everyone to be present. After the meeting, from 5pm until 8pm the next day, anyone can vote in the canteen at Ventura.'

'So how will the meeting be organised?' asked Pettigrew.

'Up to three people from each side can speak. But the speeches should last in total no more than thirty minutes from each side. After that, the representatives will take questions from the floor. The meeting ends 4pm.' Elena read from notes.

'Who'll be on the table?' Carmen asked.

'Well, we couldn't find out who'll represent the company. Mitford will represent the Union. He suggests I also speak,' answered Elena.

'Shouldn't Ralph speak for the senior staff?' asked Roland.

'Actually, I think it's better I don't,' answered Draper. 'Instead I could ask some pertinent questions from the floor. It might have more impact.'

'Yes, it's important we prepare questions that will cause them embarrassment.' Elena continued to add to her notes.

'But who do you think will represent the company?' asked Potts.

Elena looked to Draper.

'I'd assume Pellzer, but I'm not sure who else. I think Bollard won't want to speak. If I was on their side, I'd put Mayfield.' Draper could see they were amused.

'No, actually he's just the guy for this sort of event. He'd give a dispassionate viewpoint and wouldn't be phased by questions. But I don't imagine they'll ask him.'

'Mitford should've insisted they say who'll be speaking,' said Potts.

'That Union should've done a lot of things to put pressure on this company. They've been getting away with murder. Every day that bastard Rye's threatening people...' Roland threw his pen on the table angrily.

Potts nodded agreement. 'Nidditch and Ellis also give stick to anybody they think supports the Union.'

'Yes, but GWU aren't going to do anything until we've won the vote. If we don't, we'll all have to look for another job, so make this next period count,' said Elena.

They began to compare notes while Roland went to the bar for drinks and Draper made for the gents. Elena rose to go to the ladies' and walked with him to the other side of the pub.

'Ralph, I hoped we might have a private word, I've some information you might be able to make some sense of,' Elena said quietly.

'Really, well actually I also wanted to ask you...' Then, seeing Pettigrew approach: 'We could meet later at the Red Lion?'

She agreed, with a quick nod.

'This past year the Health and Safety at Work Act was enacted. A copy was sent round to each of you. I'm sure by now you've all read it.' Mayfield looked to his three fellow committee members. Marta hastily confirmed this fact, as did Ollie, who nudged Pat to do the same. This didn't stop

Mayfield from covering each point, thereby ensuring their complete inattention.

Ollie was writing out his selections for the next day's race meetings, Marta's eyelids drooped. Pat's thoughts also wandered; but as Mayfield again emphasised the Company's responsibility under the Act, he could not resist the temptation, and interrupted him in mid-sentence.

'Excuse me, under the Health and Safety Act, is the company obliged to make sure members don't beat up the Chicas?'

Mayfield looked puzzled, Ollie amused. Marta looked up with alarm and quickly intervened.

'I don't think that's a matter for this committee.' She glared at Pat.

But Mayfield took up the question. 'It's our job to explore every possible problem, however unlikely, and propose solutions. Naturally, some gamblers take losses very badly and…'

'I'm not talking about bad losers, I'm talking about what happened to Chica Marietta.' Pat ignored Marta's efforts to distract him.

Mayfield looked to Marta who, as Personnel Manager, would have known of any such incident.

'He's talking about a cocktail girl who had an illegal relationship with a client and a dispute with him, in her own time,' said Marta.

'She was beaten up by him,' Pat added, before Mayfield could respond.

'The girl was terminated and the player barred,' Marta stated firmly, shooting warning looks at Pat.

'Well… I suppose under the circumstances, the company acted appropriately.' Mayfield looked thoughtful. 'If she has any complaint, it must be against the gentleman in question. Although obviously, her conduct contributed to the whole unfortunate event.'

For once, one of Mayfield's pronouncements satisfied Marta.

Pat, surprised after his discussion with Bollard, that Mayfield didn't know about this incident, was about to challenge Marta's version, but considered for a moment the motive behind his outburst. He supposed it was a feeling of impotence. Twice he'd been exposed to the consequences of reprehensible behaviour but didn't know how, or worse, didn't have the courage, to deal with it. Here again, they'd closed ranks, tidied up the mess and he was expected to pretend, like others, that nothing had happened. Whatever he said would be pointless but he couldn't quite bring himself to let it lie.

'This player whose behaviour was so questionable was a VIP client comped to stay in our apartments and she was one of our staff. This incident happened on our premises. Is that not our concern?'

Mayfield absorbed this information with a look of incredulity and turned once again to Marta for comment.

She gestured dismissively. 'The matter was investigated. Dan Pellzer was satisfied that the right action had been taken.'

Mayfield nodded, but to her dismay proceeded to take copious notes. They would now undoubtedly appear on the minutes of the meeting.

'Ah, Habibah, you are more beautiful every day. Please, go and serve my friend Prince Mansur Talal. Look, you see, he is about to sit with the Manager,' Ahmed instructed the new waitress Chica and watched approvingly as she sashayed up to the table. This might just be the girl, he thought, to divert the attention of his most important client away from the troublesome Penny. He'd made a mistake with her, she had looked so beautiful, so innocent. The problem was, she had been too innocent. Instead of simply having fun and taking what she could get while his interest lasted, she wanted love and marriage. Now his attachment to her had caught the attention of his family, already concerned about his Western habits, he would have to mend his ways or threaten his inheritance. Yet although Talal knew this, he was still reluctant to end it with Penny.

The earnings Ahmed had previously derived from providing the Prince with discreet services had dried up, due to his infatuation with her. Now, with his visits to Ventura becoming infrequent, the percentage he had negotiated on the credit deal was also in danger. Should his client incur the displeasure of his father and be disinherited, Ahmed's total investment in him would be lost.

Ellis was discussing with Talal his selection for the big race when Ahmed joined them. 'Sorry I interrupt, but I must ask Jim about this Lebanese man playing on punto banco, his name is Azzad. He is good client and comes here for first time. He asks for credit and I can guarantee him.' Ellis looked across at the player. 'Jim, if you can explain procedure to him, I will come in one moment. I must speak with Mansur.'

Ellis had watched the man in question earlier and agreed he was worth cultivating. He excused himself, after making a quip about Rita the approaching waitress, and went to speak to the player. The shapely, long-limbed Chica arrived smiling broadly with tea the Prince had requested and Ahmed, taking a cue from Ellis, advertised in Arabic her assets. He was happy to note Talal was not unappreciative.

After this pleasant diversion, Ahmed reported on a more serious matter; the follow-up to an investigation the Prince had previously asked him to carry out.

Ellis noted their conversation hadn't lasted long. The Prince returned to the roulette table but his pattern of play had changed; whereas before he'd played with no discernable purpose he now placed maximum bets with a brooding deliberation.

Ellis made no attempt to diagnose the cause but was happy with the consequence. By change-over he reported to Nidditch a record win for the day shift, due mainly to Talal's apparent determination to lose as much as he could.

Draper was now sure he had no future with the Ventura. From what he'd heard from Elena during their meeting at the pub, he was convinced they were operating the illegal credit scheme which Lowe had suspected. But what to do? If he reported it, he'd have to furnish proof, and however convinced he was of their guilt, he wasn't sure he could obtain concrete evidence. Nor did he have the option to stay and ignore it. But how did they expect to get away with this, with him present? They did not. They would have to get rid of him. But who were *they*? Who was involved at Ventura? Trist, Pellzer, definitely Ellis and Nidditch. But was Bollard a party to this? Mayfield definitely not. A number of pit bosses, cashiers, inspectors, presumably dealers? The whole thing was crazy. Fuelled by a cynical belief that most people were as greedy and corrupt as themselves and the remainder were either too stupid to notice or, even if they did, too apathetic to care.

The few like himself who did care, such as Bland and Lowe, they'd forced out in one way or another.

So what was his next step? He'd already nailed his colours to the mast by advertising his support for the Union. If the GWU won recognition in the ballot the company might well find it difficult to sack a union representative but in reality his days as manager, a job he loved, were numbered.

After his discussion with Elena he could see the ballot result provoking another action he feared. A disillusioned or threatened union supporter in possession of damaging information, such as Elena herself, could release information to the Press or authorities and precipitate an investigation. If irregularities came to light, he as a senior manager could be faced with the task of proving he had no knowledge of them; something under oath he could not now truthfully claim.

His course of action seemed clear - resign and take up one of the positions he'd recently been offered abroad, thus distancing himself from their actions.

But why not stir things up a little before he went? He decided to confront Bollard at the earliest.

Chapter Thirty-seven

'Look, Morg, everybody's here to go over our plan for the ballot-meeting... okay... no! They're not... no listen! Okay, but when we're finished...' Pellzer was obviously angry and frustrated but, being conscious of Bollard's presence, tried to conceal his difficulty with Trist. Ordinarily, Bollard might have derived quiet amusement from Pellzer's discomfort but after the conversation he'd just had with Draper, he could find nothing amusing about his bosses.

Like Draper's, his career at Ventura, built on self-delusion, was over. He might just be able to convince the authorities that he had no knowledge of the procurement of girls and had no part in a cover-up of serious assault; but how could the Casino Manager seriously claim to be unaware of a systematic policy of giving illegal credit? Not unreasonably, they'd contend that it was his job to know. Unlike Draper, he couldn't take off to foreign parts and leave the scandal to break at some future date. For a start, his wife would be unwilling to go and his heavy financial commitments would necessitate him finding a similarly highly paid job in the UK - something he wasn't confident of doing. But he had to do something other than just hang on, hoping for a miracle.

Pellzer finished talking, or more probably Trist hung up. He put on a brave face.

'Morg can't get across, but I'll brief him later.' He picked up a note-pad. 'There's a couple of things I wanted to touch on before the rest of the guys get here.'

Bollard sat impassively, for once not even pretending to be interested.

'Your man Mayfield's at it again.'

'He's employed by the company, not by me,' Bollard replied in a tired voice.

'Okay, don't split hairs. He takes instructions from you,' Pellzer answered irritably.

'He takes some instructions from me. What matter are you referring to?'

'In the minutes of this goddam Health and Safety meeting he's put something about that Chica that got herself slapped about. What the fuck's that gotta do with him?'

'I imagine he was responding to a question about the health and safety of the Chicas.'

'Listen, this committee was supposed to be hand-picked. Now this Monaghan guy asks a goddam question like that; even worse, Mayfield treats it seriously. We can't show these minutes to anybody now. Get him to take this item out and tell this Monaghan guy to wise up. He's supposed to be public relations. Or is he one of those fuckin' union people?'

Bollard didn't respond, but after a brief moment of reflection: 'Dan, maybe you should have a word with Gordon yourself. He's under the impression that company operating procedures and the health and safety of employees are subjects to be taken seriously.'

The reply hit a nerve with Pellzer but he wasn't sure how to read Bollard. Was the man actually being sarcastic or did he just not get it? Pellzer was about to make it clear to him when the secretary knocked and entered with Larry Silverman, the company lawyer. Bollard rose to greet him.

'We'll come back to that subject later, Frank,' said the frustrated Pellzer.

'Good afternoon, gentlemen!' boomed Silverman, 'Where's Morgan, not up yet?'

'Morg's got something on and can't make it, I'll brief him later,' answered Pellzer testily. The lawyer smiled knowingly to Bollard.

A few moments later the others started to arrive. The secretary brought chairs for Rye and Sid Walker who, along with Ellis, Nidditch and Bollard, made up the full complement of those invited.

Pellzer composed himself to address them. 'I've asked Larry here because I want him to be on the table Monday. There's a number of legal questions which might come up. Anyway, I'm sure we've got a majority, in spite of a traitor in our camp - that right, Jim?'

'Yes, Dan, I'm sure most people don't want a union in spite of Draper stirring them up.' Ellis looked at Bollard, who sat impassively.

'Which is a question I'll put to Larry. First, the plans for the meeting and ballot.' Pellzer gave the papers to Walker to pass around. 'You'll see there are six on the table: Morgan, Larry and myself; for the Union, Mitford, their legal guy and this Chica Elena, who's set herself up as staff representative. Two will speak for each side, afterwards the meetin' will be thrown open to questions. I'm hopin' you'll all make sure the right questions get asked from our side.'

'You're saying Morgan will speak?' asked Nidditch. By their reaction, he was also echoing the concern of the others.

'Yeah, as Chairman and founder of Ventura—'

'Is this a good idea?' interrupted Ellis. 'Let's be honest about this, he's not always in the best of—'

'Don't worry, Morg knows the importance of this,' Pellzer came back quickly,

'He actually has more experience at public speaking than any of the people there. He really wants to do this.'

Nobody looked convinced. Bollard wondered if Pellzer believed this himself after the phone conversation he'd overheard.

Pellzer continued: 'Some awkward questions we should ask are on the last page. I leave it to you to choose who asks them. Naturally they'll also try to plant embarrassing questions. Some of them we can answer, some we should avoid and if I understand Larry correctly, some we might prevent from being asked.' Pellzer indicated to the lawyer that he should explain.

'Well, when we invite questions from the floor, someone is going to ask or say something that causes embarrassment or damage to the Company. However, I think we can get agreement with GWU on some ground rules before we start. We can also give notice to the floor and to certain people that legal action will be taken against any individual who makes unsubstantiated allegations or statements which might bring the company or its executives into disrepute.' Silverman waited to see if there were any questions.

It was Pellzer who spoke once again. 'I don't need to tell you who in your departments is likely to ask or say something. It's up to you to advise them what'll happen if anything dirty comes up. We have the case of Draper, a Manager campaigning as a union rep. Larry, where do we stand with this guy?'

'Well, in theory a manager has the right to union representation like other employees. But being a representative? That's a grey area. He has to perform his duties in accordance with his contractual obligations. He cannot divide his time between the two. He can only canvass union support or conduct union business in his own time. There's no recognition agreement so he's not an official representative. Of course, in a practical sense it's difficult to see how he can reconcile his obligations as a manager with a union position. But if you dismiss him for failing to perform his duties, he'll undoubtedly claim discrimination because of his union affiliation. If you can't prove repeated dereliction of duty, a tribunal may find in his favour.'

'When a manager's in the building he's on duty. So if he's campaigning, it's on company time and property, isn't it?' said Ellis.

'This, in essence, may be true but I still think the burden will be on the company to prove his union activities inhibited him in his contractual duties. They may also ask if he was given notification of any breach of contractual obligation, and an opportunity to correct his behaviour. Has he received an official verbal and written warning?'

They looked to Bollard, who hesitated before answering, 'No. I had to see where we stood legally, and as Larry said, we need very specific evidence of a breach of contract.'

There followed a series of vague allegations of Draper's misconduct from the others and suggestions on what action should be taken. Bollard could see from the lawyer's smile that none of it presented the company with a strong case.

Pellzer finally intervened. 'Okay, maybe we're not yet on secure ground with that. But we have to make sure he doesn't say something damaging at the meeting or after it. Can that be done?'

'As I said before…' the Lawyer looked relieved '… we should advise him directly that legal action will be taken if he makes any unsubstantiated allegation.'

'It'll have a bit more weight if you tell him directly, Larry,' said Walker. Pellzer gave a curt nod.

'So, that's what we do. Larry, you talk to GWU's legal guy about ground-rules and warn Draper. The rest of you, get the message across in your departments and ask the right questions at the meeting.' Pellzer, remembering his earlier words with Bollard, addressed him directly. 'The warning should be directed at the two people I mentioned earlier.'

Bollard gave a perfunctory nod to indicate he understood.

Pellzer thanked them for coming, more as an indication that the meeting was over. Bollard didn't bother to wait for more complaints and slouched off. Only Ellis and Nidditch dallied.

Ellis was first to speak when the others had gone. 'You see we cleaned up with Talal?'

'Yeah, Ahmed said the Prince lost five hundred grand in a couple of hours. That's great. Apparently he's about to dump that problematic Chica,' Pellzer smiled with satisfaction.

'I hope so, when she's not around he's a real punter,' said Nidditch. 'But going back to Draper… why don't we just sack him and if he wins a tribunal, so what? The company pays the fine or pays him off, whatever it costs. Isn't it cheaper in the long run?

Pellzer shook his head. 'It's not that easy, according to Larry. There's a new law that they can order you to reinstate anybody they think has been unfairly dismissed and after that it's almost impossible to sack them again.'

'Yeah, and he's just the one who'd like that, awkward bugger,' Ellis grunted.

Pellzer, changing the subject, handed Ellis the minutes of the H&S meeting. 'This Monaghan was asking fuckin' awkward questions about Al Khazari. Is this PR guy gonna be a problem now?'

Ellis read the underlined item 'Well, as you know he went to Bollard about the incident and he told him it was being investigated. If he didn't get any more information maybe he's still thinking about it,' said Ellis, 'and apparently Rye gave him stick that night when he got in the way. Pat was upset by that, Rye's not always the most diplomatic.'

'That's for sure,' agreed Pellzer, 'nevertheless, we can't have Monaghan going around asking those questions. Talk with him before the meeting.'

Ellis nodded. .

'You're serious about Morgan speaking at the meeting?' Nidditch seemed incredulous.

'Look, believe me, Morg can be silver-tongued. He could sway a lot of people, if he's in the mood—'

'If he's not swaying himself,' interrupted Ellis.

Pellzer sighed. 'Listen, if he can't or won't do it, someone else will. Don't worry about it,' he said with a tone of finality. Ellis and Nidditch left it at that.

As Elena entered her apartment, Penny all but pounced on her. 'Hi, you haven't seen or heard anything of Mansur, have you?'

'Er... well... I know he was in yesterday and apparently lost quite a bit. But didn't you meet him last night?'

'He didn't come to the hotel. I waited and waited but neither he nor his driver turned up. I've been calling his place constantly but his butler says he doesn't know where he is. I don't know what to do,' Penny said nervously; then, realising what Elena had just said: 'You say he was at Ventura last night?'

'Well... yes, he came in the afternoon. As far as I know he was still there when we changed shifts.'

This disturbed Penny even more. 'If he was there why didn't he come down? He knew I was waiting.'

Elena could see she was becoming upset. 'You know what gamblers are like, maybe he got involved and...'

'No, he's not like that, he's never left me waiting.'

'Well, maybe something came up, something with his family, you never know...'

'Then he should've called or left a message with his driver or... it's not right.' Penny paced nervously about the room.

Elena guided her to a seat. 'Penny, be calm, it's probably nothing. I'll try to call Pat, see if he knows anything, but calm down.'

After a few minutes Penny seemed more composed and mouthed a silent thank you. Elena waited while the switchboard bleeped Pat. Then she heard his soft brogue.

'Pat, Elena here, I'm phoning for Penny. She's worried because Talal was to meet her yesterday and didn't turn up, and hasn't been in touch today.' She paused, watching Penny. 'Yes... maybe you could check... yes, we're here... okay, bye,' she finished quickly before Penny could ask to speak to him.

'Pat'll see what he can find out. If anything, he'll ring back,' Elena lied, not wanting to tell her that Pat had said the Prince was in the VIP level at that moment. Then, as an afterthought: 'Does Mansur know you're here?'

'Yes, his driver brought me here, remember?'

'Oh yes, of course. Anyway, have a coffee or maybe a little drink, yeah?' She reached for a Bacardi bottle. Penny didn't look too enthusiastic but as she hadn't refused, Elena poured two large ones and went to the kitchen to get a coke.

The phone rang. She almost dropped the bottle in her haste to get through to the other room to answer it, but Penny had already picked it up.

'Hello, yes, Pat, it's me... yes I'm... I see, okay. Thank you anyway... yes just a minute, bye.' She handed the phone to Elena.

'Hi, Pat.' Elena listened while keeping an eye on her troubled friend. As she'd imagined, Pat had dissembled, not daring to tell Penny what he was now telling her: that when he'd given Talal his girlfriend's message of concern, the Prince had been dismissive.

Elena, seeing Penny approach once again, cut short the conversation. 'Look, thanks Pat, I'll speak to you soon. Let us know if you hear anything, bye.'

'I don't know what to do. D'you think I should go to his house and wait?' Penny slumped back in her chair.

'No, definitely not. Remember, you said he had trouble with his uncle, maybe it's something like that. You'd make it worse. Leave it tonight, we'll get to the bottom of it tomorrow, I promise.' She put a drink in Penny's hand.

Elena had planned to spend the entire evening preparing her speech for the pre-ballot meeting but instead spent hours stealthily feeding drinks to her naive friend while diverting the conversation away from past traumas and current concerns. Penny, unused to much alcohol, finally succumbed and retired to bed. Elena knew she'd only postponed the inevitable. Tomorrow Penny would learn what her friends already knew, that her lover had abandoned her.

A busy, perhaps momentus day would soon be upon her. She needed to be fresh. But what would she do tomorrow about her sleeping friend? Elena deliberated, bottle in hand, and finally poured herself another drink.

Chapter Thirty-eight

The hall was filling. On the stage the speakers' table, with eight microphones and eight empty seats behind, awaited the protagonists. Like contending boxers in the red corner and the blue corner, the two sides were keeping a respectable distance apart in the wings.

As she scurried down the centre aisle, to her right Elena could see Mitford and the GWU legal expert in animated conversation with Draper while Carmen, Potts, Pettigrew and Roland lingered nearby. On her left, for the opposition, only Ellis, Rye and the company lawyer were at that moment present. In another part of the hall stood Bollard, Mayfield and several pit bosses. Glancing quickly at those already seated, it was apparent to her that someone on the company side had been drumming up support. Never had she seen so many waitress Chicas in one room without a rich Arab in sight. Although today, she imagined, Trist would be providing the remuneration.

Draper was stamping around angrily. 'So you, the great defenders of the working man, are party to this gagging order?'

'It's not like that. We simply agreed we'd stick to the issues that are important for our members,' Mitford sighed, looking to the ceiling. Draper threw up his arms and stalked off a few paces in disgust before returning.

'Sorry, I'm late, I miss something?' Elena said, looking at Draper, then Mitford. Carmen and the others now came to join them. Mitford made to speak but Draper beat him to it.

'Silverman, Ventura's lawyer, made a point of warning me that the company would take legal action against anyone who makes any reference or statement which might suggest the company or its Directors had infringed any law or regulation or knowingly permitted any law or regulation to be infringed,' Draper read from his notes. Mitford tried to interrupt, but he continued. 'Now it seems these great defenders of free speech and the democratic rights of the workers have made a pact with Ventura that we will not ask any questions which might prove to be embarrassing.'

A chorus of opinion came from all present. But Elena held up her hands to silence them. 'Is this right?' she asked Mitford.

'No, not as he puts it.' Again there was an outburst from Draper and the others. Elena gestured to them to let Mitford finish. Instead he indicated the lawyer would speak.

'Our job is to get union recognition, not prove malpractice. To say something which might spark a negative press campaign or an investigation of the company would be counter productive. Therefore we've agreed the campaign should be fought purely on whether this Union can offer workers a higher level of job protection and participation in policy-making decisions and, as such, the prospect of better conditions.'

'How do we convince them they need union protection without highlighting the terrible things that have gone on?' asked Elena. Draper and the others agreed.

'You highlight the positive advantages of having the support of a large Union to address workers' grievances. What we must not do is make unsubstantiated allegations that might have to be proved in court. If anyone does that, this Union cannot back them,' said the lawyer. Mitford nodded approval.

'So we can waffle on about how good the GWU is, but not mention any of the real grievances, because if we do, you'll run like scared rats!' said Elena angrily. This time she walked away. Draper, Roland and Potts continued to exchange heated words with the GWU representatives. Carmen and Pettigrew followed Elena,

'You think we could prove any allegations we make, if we have to?' Carmen asked. Elena, still seething, made no comment. After a few minutes, Draper joined them; Potts and Roland followed. They were all talking at once. Elena regretted her alcohol consumption of the previous night; her head was thumping and she was not looking forward to making a speech in support of the GWU.

At that moment Pellzer arrived with Morgan Trist.

'Well, there's a surprise, our esteemed leader has come to give us the benefit of his wisdom,' said Draper.

'Ralph, what are we going to do now, what tactics do we take? Do you think they're serious about this legal action?' Elena asked, turning with distaste from the sight of Trist receiving welcoming kisses from several of his favourite Chicas.

'I'm sure they are. If we talk about corruption, credit irregularities, abuse of girls or any of these things, I'm sure we'd be forced to prove it. Without the back-up of the GWU I don't think we'd be able to fight them. We'll only get support if they win recognition. It's catch 22,' he said dejectedly.

Trist and Pellzer were now shaking hands with Mitford prior to taking their seats at the table. The two lawyers also exchanged pleasantries. Surprisingly, Mayfield took a seat on the company's side. Though they still didn't know who would speak for the company, someone had obviously concurred with Draper's view that Mayfield's dispassionate approach would be an asset. To his left followed Trist and Silverman. Mitford sat next to him with the GWU lawyer on his other side. It had been agreed Mitford and Elena would present the case for recognition.

They waited as the last few employees took their seats. Marta flitted back and forward nervously with messages between Pellzer in the front row of the audience and Trist on the speakers' table, while on either side of the assembled employees, Walker and Rye patrolled the aisles intimidatingly. Woods, at a nod from Pellzer, shushed the audience. Mayfield stood to open the proceedings.

'Good afternoon, ladies and gentlemen, thank you for coming. A few months ago, a group of employees exercised their legal right to join a union and in turn this organisation asked that a ballot be arranged to permit our employees to register their opinion, on whether or not they want a union to represent them. Although quite clearly the managers of this company do not think an Industrial Trade Union would be the best representative of our employees, we nevertheless agreed that you, yourselves, should decide. Although I'm sure many of you have already formed an opinion we thought it right to have this meeting, prior to the ballot, to put our respective positions. From four o'clock this afternoon until 8pm tomorrow you can register your vote in the Ventura canteen. To have official recognition GWU need a mandate from the majority of all employees of the company. Not a majority of the vote. Is that clear?' Mayfield waited. No one stirred so he continued.

'So, today we have with us Mr George Mitford of the Union for General Workers and Mr Richard Wonk, their legal representative. They and their appointed representative in Ventura will be talking about the possible advantages of being represented by a Trade Union.

'For the company, our Chairman Morgan Trist wanted to address you himself and I will be here to answer any questions you might have later. We also have Mr Larry Silverman, our legal expert, to clarify any legal questions. But first, we invite Mr Mitford to take the floor.' He gestured towards the GWU man.

Miford slowly hauled his portly frame upwards, patting his greasy hair with the palm of his hand. He shuffled his papers then stooped to confer with the lawyer before beginning. Elena silently prayed he would not address the audience as 'comrades'.

'Afternoon, ladies and gentlemen. We at the GWU were first contacted some time back by a number of your fellow workers concerned about the management's lack of consultation with the workforce on important decisions which affect your jobs and future. They were particularly worried about the unfairness of a system that hires young women as crupers and…' The lawyer nudged him and whispered. 'Sorry, hires young women as croup-i-ers, and then doesn't give them proper training to enable 'em to move up to more senior positions.

'They were also worried about job security. It seems once girls reach a certain age, they're in danger of being paid off because they lose their looks. Apart from the question of job security, there's also been a loss of income in real terms because there's no allowance for inflation and no recognition that you work unsociable hours. Job security also affects male workers and this came to a head some months ago when members of a crap table...' the lawyer again advised Mitford as sniggering broke out '... a *craps* table were made redundant and called for industrial action to support their claim for reinstatement. The bosses claimed the strike was illegal. It's our position that the redundancy was illegal, because there was no consultation and no attempt to reach a negotiated settlement with the workers. In fact, an unfair dismissal. This could have gone to Industrial Tribunal and dragged on but fortunately we managed to get the management to the table - the result being that the workers were reinstated and the crap... *craps* is in production again, proving redundancy wasn't necessary in the first place. During the industrial action. tempers got frayed and a lot of adverse publicity was generated in the press. So it was agreed that recognition would be put to a ballot after a cooling off period. It's now time to decide: will you continue to accept that bosses make policy without consultation with workers, or do you want the strength of a Trade Union behind you to ensure your grievances are heard?'

Mitford paused, scanning the audience as if gauging their reaction before continuing.

The silence was broken by one girl shouting out, 'No, we don't want a union!' and other voices followed, echoing her sentiments, while some supporters of the union shouted 'Shut up!' and this provoked even more forceful comments. Mitford attempted to resume several times but now the hall was in uproar.

Eventually, Mayfield intervened. 'Please, ladies and gentlemen, let's have order! Each speaker must be allowed to speak without interruption. There will be an opportunity later to have your say and to make your position clear on the ballot paper.'

Silence restored, Mitford continued. 'The history of the trade union movement...'

Elena tried to concentrate on what he was saying, even if he was the most un-inspiring speaker she'd ever heard. But her thoughts kept drifting to her own speech. Should her ill-prepared notes be edited to make sure there were no sensitive references to the abuse or exploitation of girls? Could she really put forward a convincing case for the GWU when her personal opinion of them was close to zero? God, she wished she hadn't drunk so much the night before! With this thought, her mind drifted to Penny and how she would be coping today.

Surprisingly, as she rarely drank, Penny felt little effect from the alcohol Elena had fed to her the night before. The source of all present discomfort remained the continuing uncertainty of her relationship with Talal. So, in spite of her friend's view that it could possibly make matters worse, she could not resist the temptation to go directly to his London home in the hope that she could find a reason for his absence.

His maid answered the door and, on seeing Penny, seemed to be in doubt as to how to respond and relieved when the butler appeared behind her in the hallway to take over assertively.

'I'm sorry, Ma'am, Prince Mansur bin Talal is unavailable. Would you like to leave a message?'

'Not available? But he's here in London!'

'I cannot confirm where he is, but I will certainly inform him of your visit.' The butler was smiling but his extended arm left no doubt that he expected her to leave.

'Please tell him I must speak with him, I'm at this number.' Penny tore off Elena's number from a note she had written earlier. The butler received it, smiled and again stretched his arm to take the door in a dismissive gesture disguised as good manners.

Penny, even more confused than before, wandered down the street, unsure of what to do next. She had gone less than a hundred yards when, realising that she should be walking in the opposite direction, she turned to catch sight of Talal's Rolls pulling up at his entrance. She paused momentarily but when she saw him alight with two others, broke into a run.

'Mansur, Mansur!' The calls alerted him and with outstretched arms, he stepped swiftly in front of the other men to intercept her.

'Mansur, where have you been, why didn't you meet me or call me?' she pleaded breathlessly.

'Please, one moment!' he commanded and led her to one side, before calling out something in Arabic to his companions. One of them, his uncle, paused to look across disapprovingly before continuing with the other towards the house.

'Mansur what's going on, I...'

'Please listen!' he shouted. 'We cannot continue, our lives are different...'

'What do you mean, how can you do this... you know...'

'Stop!' he called to silence her frantic tearful pleas. 'I already had a problem with some of my family and tried to convince them but then I hear you have been seeing this Martin at your apartment—'

'He came only once... who told you this?' she intervened desperately.

'That's not important, what matters is you did not—' His words were interrupted by a call from his uncle, who was still standing by the door.

'Mansur, I didn't tell you because—'

'No matter, enough!' he barked. 'People are waiting, I must go. There is no point for us to continue, we are different, goodbye.' He turned and moved quickly up the pathway, leaving her momentarily stunned. When she did respond, he was already entering the house.

'Mansur, Mansur, please! I want...'

He had gone, leaving the butler to intercept her on the pathway. 'Can I arrange some transport for the lady? If you tell me where you would like to go...' he asked, doing his best to ignore her distraught pleas.

A general sniggering broke out in the audience once again.

'... no, no what I mean is that without the strength of a major union none of you will have any voice. With representation, grievances can be resolved and conditions made better for the workforce. The GWU has a long and impressive history in the struggle for better conditions for workers. With our experience in industrial relations and negotiating skills you'll get a better deal. Vote for recognition for the Union of General Workers. Thank you bro— Thank you.'

A ripple of applause, initiated by the GWU lawyer, welcomed the end of Mitford's address. Elena reluctantly joined in. Draper and the other Committee members grudgingly put their hands together in embarrassed solidarity. A brief moment of confusion followed because no one quite knew who should follow Mitford; then Mayfield rose.

'Ladies and gentlemen, I would like to call on our Chairman, Morgan Trist, to say a few words.' In the best traditions of stage-managed gatherings, vociferous applause broke out. Trist, waiting until the noise abated, smiled benignly, as if indulging boisterous children.

'Well, how do I start? Is it "Hi there, guys and gals", or "Hello, good evening and welcome"?' Trist's supporters laughed, but his accurate mimicry of two popular broadcasters even brought a smile to the others including Mitford. 'Maybe I should now refer to you as comrades? Actually, I'm trying to bring a lighter mood into the proceedings, but I know it's a serious business. And believe me, it's more serious than you think. Every day we face increasing competition in a business that's restricted like no other. In no other industry would you be prohibited from marketing your product, of going out and looking for new customers. In no other would you be restricted from allowing half the staff from accepting gratuities for services that clients so obviously feel they deserve. Prohibited from offering even a drink on the table to our best players. All these and more we live with day by day. It's the law. We must comply and of course we always will. But what it means is that we're constantly experimenting, trying to find new ways, within the law, to sell ourselves or get more financially efficient. Sometimes we make mistakes. Perhaps a example of this was the incident with the cra*ps.*' Trist's emphasis on the 's' brought more laughter.

'But let me explain a little about that decision. You may not know but we cannot easily extend or change our gaming facilities. To add a table, we have to request permission and prove there's a demand. It sounds strange but that's the way it is. So, with restrictions like that, naturally we have to make sure that every table gives maximum benefit. After calculations were made, it could be seen that the craps table gave less benefit than a roulette. On top of that, on a number of occasions, one in particular, the table was turned over by cheats. Clearly the staff on this game had allowed efficiency and security to fall to unacceptable levels. Rather than wait till things got worse and be obliged to sack those guys as incompetents, in which case they'd have difficulty getting another job, we took a decision to close the table and make them redundant. It was a miscalcualtion, perhaps it wasn't handled in the right way. But I have to say, since that little scare this table has given better results. Surely it shouldn't have to take that?

'Another criticism - that girls don't get a chance, they're exploited for their looks and discarded when they lose them - well this is just, excuse me, bullshit! We, like some of our main competitors, Playboy and Penthouse, don't make any secret of the fact that we employ attractive girls. It's a major part of our image. Hell, all you girls answered the advertisement. You were happy to be selected knowing that one of the qualifications was your attractiveness. It's true, some girls have gone, but not because they lost their looks through the natural passage of time - we haven't been operating long enough to worry about that. No, it was usually because they'd let themselves go, lost interest or stopped giving the service our customers expect. Some say more girls should be promoted. They're probably right. We haven't given enough opportunity to the ladies. Frankly, I'd be happier with women in every department at every level. I look forward to the day when I can replace ugly guys like Harry Rye with beautiful women!' This brought laughter and cries of 'Yes, yes!'. Rye played his part by looking stunned by the suggestion.

Elena could see it was stage-managed but the ease with which Trist addressed a audience of young people contrasted vividly with Mitford's prosaic shop-floor rhetoric. She could see the fight was being lost. Trist must have sensed the same as he continued. Improvements in consultation were promised; the Union's ignorance of the casino and night-club business was highlighted; more references to 'crupers' and 'crap, sorry, craps policy' followed. Trist contrasted the lifestyle and salary of the average GWU transport or dock worker with casino staff and asked, if in pursuit of a croupier's pay deal, they expected the bus drivers to bring London to a halt, or if they'd be 'downing chips and cards' in support of a dock workers' demarcation dispute.

Trist's performance had become a cabaret; he was visibly enjoying himself.

Elena tried to concentrate her mind on what she'd say to return the waverers to the real issue of Ventura's unfair practices. As she stared off to some indiscriminate point at the back of the room, her eyes suddenly focused on a figure moving slowly down the centre aisle towards the stage. Although still someway off, it was unmistakable. The person Elena least expected to see.

Trist had returned to a more serious note. 'No one has more interest in the welfare of the staff than me, I —'

'No! No! You're lying! You don't care about anyone, you know what you did to me. Now I'm going to tell everyone!' the woman screamed out; stopping Trist mid-sentence.

Mayfield appealed for silence. Marta Woods and Sid Walker rushed to intercept the intruder.

She was now screaming. 'Rapist! That's what you are!'

People stood to see who was causing the uproar. Elena dashed off the stage and down the passageway.

'Get that crazy girl outta here!' Pellzer shouted to Walker and Rye.

Penny Irwin continued to cry out but in her condition the message was now even more incoherent. Her initial resolve having faltered, she allowed herself to be hustled slowly towards the exit. Elena struggled through the crowd that surrounded her and, brushing off the officious attention of Woods, Walker and various other people, took over the supervision of the now sobbing girl; leading her to a sofa in the reception area. Walker stood with several security-men in a ridiculous line of defence across the door as if expecting the distraught girl to charge through once again. Their line was broken from the rear by Pat and Draper, who had come to offer support. Elena gestured to them that she had the matter in hand. So they waited in front of Walker's formidable barrier as Woods and Rye craned their necks from behind it to see if the danger had passed.

The disruption caused by Penny Irwin brought the proceedings to an inconclusive end. Mayfield called for an adjournment while calm was being restored after what he called 'a perplexing incident', later announcing that Morgan Trist, upset by the 'outrageous allegations of the disturbed girl', would not resume his address. He suggested that in the absence of Chica Elena, who was to have been the next speaker, he and the representatives of GWU would answer questions on the ballot process, procedure for counting votes, announcement of the result and the official implications once a result was known. Mayfield's convoluted answers to Pellzer's pre-arranged queries took up the remainder of the time, thereby avoiding awkward questions.

Elena could make little sense of the lachrymose mumblings of her friend, except the fact already known to her: that the Prince had terminated their relationship. This, aggravated undoubtedly by another unaccustomed intake of alcohol, had led to the astonishing outburst, but there was no point in going into that now. Elena's immediate objective was to get Penny fit enough to be escorted home, and to do this she needed help. Carmen would've been her best bet but she hadn't seen her since leaving the conference room, so once again she signalled Pat.

'Yes, me darlin', what can I do?'

Elena whispered quietly, 'Pat, can you sit with Penny while I go get my car?'

'Of course, me dear.' He looked down at her forlorn charge. Penny looked up and said something, made incomprehensible by racking sobs. Pat quickly sat down and put his arm around her. A nod and wink to Elena indicated it was okay to continue with her plan.

She managed to avoid the departing crowd by going through a side exit and some minutes later returned to find Roland but no Penny. Pat had also gone.

'It's okay, Pat had to find someone to take her to the toilet, they'll be back in a minute,' said Roland quickly to allay her concern. She nodded and they fell silent for a few minutes.

'I don't know what to say. It's been a disaster.' She looked apologetic.

'It was a disaster before Penny entered, that was just the final touch.'

'How did it finish?'

'Well, at least she shut Trist up, he didn't continue. Mayfield waffled on until time ran out,' he said disconsolately.

'So nobody spoke for us.'

'You're right, nobody spoke for us, including Mitford.'

'I'm sorry, I had to help her... anyway, I doubt if it would've mattered, we were muzzled anyway.'

'No, you're probably right. I suppose we should look for another job... oh, they're back,' Roland indicated, as Pat and Carmen appeared with Penny locked between them. She looked only slightly more composed.

'Er... if you like I'll drive and you sit behind with Penny,' Pat offered.

'Oh, would you,' said Elena, pleased by the offer. She glanced at Carmen. 'Of course, you and Roland are working tonight.' Carmen nodded and grimaced.

'If this ballot goes the way I think, it's maybe our last shift,' said Roland.

'We'll see. If that's the case I've plenty on them, maybe they'll all be out of a job,' said Elena bitterly.

'What do you mean, what have you got?' asked Carmen, who seemed to be sniffling from a cold.

'Oh they'll see.'

By the time they reached the parking space near her flat, Elena had heard, and only just understood, Penny's tearful and faltering description of events. She wasn't sure what had been the most harrowing, her distressed friend's story or Monaghan's driving. She walked them to her apartment building through a passageway carpeted with the shattered remains of the lamps that by night were meant to illuminate the area. On one side, paint-smeared railings enclosed a disused factory yard and on the other, the remains of a fence that bordered a litter strewn scrubland; once intended as landscaping, to enhance the appearance of the adjacent tower blocks.

'You walk through here at night?' asked Pat.

'Actually, I normally run,' Elena said. He nodded understanding. 'I park there because it has easy access to the main road. My street's a cul-de-sac, so it doesn't always have a place.'

The plan, once inside her apartment, didn't differ greatly from the previous night's – get her anguished friend to sleep as soon as possible. Then, in spite of her oath of life-long abstinence earlier in the day, Elena found herself looking forward to a drink. Even Monaghan, she was sure, could be persuaded.

It was about an hour before Penny slipped off. When she'd finally gone, they sat for several minutes, not saying anything, just drinking.

'I know Talal broke it off but what was his reason, something to do with Trist?' asked Pat finally.

'No, he apparently found out her ex-boyfriend had been at her apartment… and she'd kept quiet about it. She couldn't understand how he'd found out, since as far as she was concerned, I was the only one who knew. She obviously had a few drinks then decided to come and ask me about it, not knowing that Trist would be there. Being already in a state, when she saw him she just cracked.'

'So how'd he find out this Atkinson had been to her apartment?'

'I'm not sure. I didn't say anything to anyone… it's strange.'

'Didn't she explain the guy was pestering her?'

'She tried, but he was suspicious when she kept his visit secret from him. Actually, I suspect he's using it as an excuse, that he wanted to finish it anyway.'

Pat nodded thoughtfully.

Elena poured them another drink and began to search for food in the pantry. In a way it was intended to delay his departure. After the events of the day she needed company; she didn't want to eat and drink alone again. She needn't have worried. Pat was of a like mind.

The coffee couldn't possibly live up to what was expected of it. It was meant to inject life into her alcohol-ravaged body and stimulate her brain cells. She could then begin to make sense of the conflicts going on in her mind and consider why she had created yet another. Two people, sleeping in the adjoining rooms, would soon wake and she'd have to respond to them, but in what way? Elena poured another coffee, this time stronger.

Why had she slept with Pat? She liked him very much as a person, but… The alcohol had played a part but she knew that wasn't entirely the reason. Sexual frustration? Desperation? A temporary diversion from other problems? Whatever it was, it now created another problem. What would his reaction be? Would he look upon it, in these liberated times, as just a one-night-stand? She hoped he'd not think it the start of a serious relationship. She hoped it wouldn't spoil a much valued friendship.

Then there was Penny; what to do about her? Since Pat first brought her into Elena's life she'd acted as her counsellor. With a sense of guilt, she had to admit it was becoming a burden. Particularly as there seemed no end in sight. Penny was an extremely sensitive girl who'd had a horrendous experience from which she'd never fully recovered. Each emotional upset brought a new crisis. Elena wasn't sure if she could continue to deal with this and still lead her own life. But did she have a life? She formed no relationships and now she had slept with a friend in the absence of a lover. Her time seemed to be spent agitating for causes not enough people cared about; and the current campaign, after the previous day's debacle, would undoubtedly end in bitter failure.

The loss of her job wouldn't be the hardest thing to take; that would be the triumph of corrupt and unscrupulous people.

The coffee wasn't doing its job; she was no nearer to answers so she prepared herself an even stronger brew.

'Good morning… I think.' A dishevelled Pat appeared in the doorway.

'You think it's good or you think it's morning?' asked Elena.

'Now don't be asking difficult questions, except whether I'd like it black or white.'

'With sugar, or not?

'Black with sugar please,' said Pat. 'Penny still sleeping?'

Elena nodded, and put the coffee in front of the pallid Irishman. Neither of them knew quite what to say.

Eventually Elena spoke. 'I'm not sure what to do about her, I have to go to work… but don't know if it's right to leave her.'

'Yes, I see the problem. I'm supposed to go in myself or I would help…'

'No, it's okay. I'll see how she is when she gets up.'

They fell silent again.

'Pat… about last night, I got a bit drunk… and, well I didn't plan for that to happen.'

'Er… no… I didn't either… er… I hope you don't think I took advantage?'

'No, no it just happened. I wanted to say…' she searched for words '… I wanted to be clear that I look upon you as my friend, I wasn't intending… or… don't intend to have a relationship,' she blurted out, then waited with concern for his reaction.

He was nodding some sort of acknowledgement; she wasn't sure what, and waited for him to reply. Finally he said, 'It's okay, that's fine, although, you don't mind if I put you down as a reference if I need one?' He laughed, and she did too, with relief.

Chapter Thirty-nine

She had posted her vote at the canteen-cum-polling station. Unlike national elections there were no exit polls to predict the result, but the outcome seemed in little doubt. Penny's dramatic entrance was a major talking point but only as a delicious piece of scandal. Elena found it disturbing that so few girls seemed to be alarmed by the possibility that their boss, Trist, might have been guilty of a rape.

Some colleagues asked how Penny was feeling and what she planned to do. The management and personnel department had so far made no such inquiry.

Penny had said very little when she eventually rose that morning. In the end, with some reluctance, Elena left to go to work, extracting a promise that Penny would call if she was feeling particularly bad. Several times Elena had been of a mind to phone her from the break-room call box, but hadn't for fear of triggering Penny's suppressed grief and then being obliged to leave work to go comfort her. Apart from anything else, she'd get no approval for an early departure and her absence would provide the company with ammunition to, at the very least, serve her with a warning.

In her brief impromptu meetings before work and during rest periods with Roland and Carmen, she heard no encouraging news on voting intentions. In effect they were waiting for the axe to fall.

Bollard also worried about the axe falling. He'd continued his campaign to distance himself from irregularities by accumulating documentary proof in the shape of memos, minutes and reports, from himself and Mayfield, which would underline his disquiet with Ventura's policies. In particular, he'd just sent a memo to Ellis and Nidditch, copied to Pellzer, asking them to comment on puzzling trends in the cheque-cashing records. They would of course avoid answering or give some nonsensical reply leaving Frank to content himself with the filed document. If he pushed things too far they'd have to sack him. He could then, of course, take his findings to the authorities. But with a reputation as whistle-blower, no references or previous management record and the prospect of being embroiled in a Gaming Board investigation, his chances of finding another suitable position would be difficult, if not impossible.

Bollard had privately hoped the Union might win recognition. The legitimate right of employees, backed by an independent outside agency, to question and monitor areas of company policy, might have helped to curtail some of their excesses. But the campaign would inevitably fail. Unfortunately, the shocking but probably truthful accusation from the Chica Penny would have no adverse affect on Trist's reputation. Being thought of as something of a hysteric and having returned after the alleged incident to conduct an affair with one of Ventura's biggest punters was never going to win her many sympathisers.

Leaving those murky waters, Bollard's thoughts returned to Mayfield's report on the inconsistencies in cheque-cashing. Their response would be interesting. Bollard was beginning to get some mischievous pleasure from these jousts.

'Hey, you're the one who told me to come over at this time,' said Pellzer.

Trist grunted and dismissed the two naked girls, who ran giggling to the adjoining room. 'Yeah, I guess,' he said, rubbing his bloodshot eyes and inspecting himself in the dressing table mirror. A tuft of hair pointed defiantly skywards in spite of his efforts to pat it down. 'Gotta watch where I'm putting my head in future.'

'Better than Brylcream,' said Pellzer. 'Anyway, to business. I bring good news. The ballot gives us a substantial majority. The union thing can now be put to bed. Draper resigned before the result came out. I think we can soon begin the rest of the clean-up.'

'Great. All those jerks who supported this union thing, I want out!'

'Well yeah, but there's still laws which give 'em protection. We have to be clever about the way we do it.' Trist looked unhappy with Pellzer's observation but let it go. 'Couple of things. Larry Silverman says he can prepare a slander case against that Chica who made the fuss at the meeting...' Pellzer paused to see Trist's response.

Trist shook his head. 'That fuckin' broad. She goes to a party, gets stoned then complains about being screwed. This from a chick who's puttin' it about with the Arabs!'

'Okay, but personally I think we should leave it, the publicity wouldn't do us any good.'

Trist looked thoughtful again. 'Maybe. But if she continues to shoot her mouth off, I'm gonna have to do something about her.'

'Okay, but for now let's watch the situation.' Pellzer pulled out a bundle of papers. He had to retain Trist's attention just long enough to get some things signed.

Carmen's call the next morning only confirmed what Elena already knew: their recognition battle had been lost. In a few hours she'd have to go in to face the sneering and belligerent presence of people like Rye and listen to snide comments from the likes of Ollie Keane. The thought daunted her but she wouldn't give them the satisfaction of resigning or taking time off to hide away.

In any case, there was a more immediate worry - she had awoken to find Penny gone. That in itself could be an encouraging sign that Penny had thrown off the torpor that had seen her moping around the flat for the last two days; but Elena wasn't convinced. She was about to call Penny's apartment when she heard the key in the door.

'Hi, I'm sorry, I was going to leave a note, but...' Penny entered, smiling. 'I've been with Mansur...' She paused for effect and Elena could guess what was coming. 'We're back together.'

'Really?' said Elena, at a loss for anything else to say.

'Yes. I managed to catch him at the hotel. I convinced him Martin came to my flat only once and that's why I moved to your place, and that I didn't tell him because I didn't want to bother him with it.'

'Oh right,' said Elena. still considering how to react, then remembering something. 'You didn't tell him about the note on his desk, or…?'

'No, I didn't talk about that. Anyway, I wanted to pick up some things, so he took me to my apartment, and… well, you know…' She hid an embarrassed smile.

Elena couldn't help feeling the inevitable had only been postponed, but tried to look happy for her friend. 'Great,' she said, then as an afterthought: 'Who told him Martin had been to see you?'

'I'm not sure, he didn't say. Maybe his driver or…' Penny looked puzzled, as if she hadn't really thought about that.

'Okay, never mind,' said Elena, 'so what's the plan now?'

'Well, if you don't mind I'd like to stay here for a little while. I don't want to go back to that apartment and his horrid uncle's still at his place. Mansur will help me get another flat.'

'Great, stay as long as you want,' Elena said, then warily added, 'and what about your position at Ventura?'

'Yes, I should give in my notice, shouldn't I?'

'Yes, you won't be the only one, we lost the vote.'

'Oh, I'm sorry,' Penny said, 'did I spoil things at your meeting?'

'No, absolutely not. It was lost for many reasons, but not that. I was surprised your story didn't have the opposite effect, but those girls never learn.' Elena looked at her watch. 'Hey! If I don't get moving they'll sack me today.'

As Pat exited through the restaurant door to the stairs at the back of house, he could hear Rye in the kitchen berating the chefs and wait-staff. He sympathised with anyone in that department who might've expressed even a passing interest in union recognition; their life would now be a living hell. Pat was ashamed to admit to himself that since his run-in with Rye on the night of the Marietta incident, he'd also stayed out of his way. Now he hurried down to the Primero level and studiously avoided the restaurant area, where Ellis and Ahmed were sitting in what looked like conspiratorial conversation.

Tony Roberts was poring worriedly over papers at the Pit desk. He gave Pat only a cursory nod of recognition but the punto table-staff, as yet untroubled by any player, greeted him loudly. Pat moved across to talk to them but as he did, the Inspector indicated the approach of someone else. Pat turned to see Ahmed.

'Ah, my friend, top of the morning!'

'Hello, Mr Ahmed, how are you?'

'I am well. I have been appointed shop steward by GWU,' he announced loudly, to a ripple of laughter. Pat smiled but noticed not all the staff within hearing found this funny.

Ahmed took Pat to one side. 'I hear our friend Penny made a big scene, and was very upset. She is okay now?'

'Ah, well… yes, I think so.'

'But where is she, she has disappeared?'

'Well… I think she fell out with your man, the Prince. She's gone to stay with Elena her friend. I don't think she'll be back here.'

'Aha, Elena… she is Chica from reception?' Pat nodded. Ahmed also nodded understanding, then smiled. 'Well, then I am happy she is now fine.'

The call hadn't been long in coming, she'd been working only two hours. On her next break, Elena was informed, she should see Marta Woods. Could it possibly be they were going to sack her? In a way she rather hoped they would. They couldn't possibly have valid grounds and a tribunal would surely find it discriminatory. As a precaution, Elena asked Roland if he could arrange to be available as a witness.

The front office in the personnel department was, as usual, in chaos: Chicas coming and going, papers strewn everywhere, a phone continued to ring unanswered and an overweight ex-Chica, 'promoted' to the department, typing with one finger.

'Hello, Marta wanted to see me,' Elena shouted above the surrounding noise to an assistant who sat reading a magazine.

'Really? Wait a minute.' The assistant went to the door of the inner office, poked her head in, then turned to Elena, 'Yes, come through.'

Elena signaled Roland to wait. Woods asked her to close the door and take a seat.

'I've been asked by management to speak to you,' she said. 'As you know, the ballot was overwhelmingly against union recognition.'

Elena smiled at her exaggeration but didn't reply.

Marta continued, reading from notes, 'This means you have no mandate—'

'Excuse me for interrupting,' said Elena, 'but I've a representative here who I'd like to be present.' She rose to call Roland.

'I asked to speak to you, not a committee,' Woods said sharply.

'I know, but I don't want any misunderstandings. Roland isn't participating, he's just listening.'

Woods unhappily resumed. 'The vote was overwhelmingly against union recognition. This means you cannot under any circumstances conduct union affairs or organise meetings on these premises either during or after work. Is that clear?'

Elena nodded, more to indicate understanding of the statement than agreement.

'You must not do anything to damage the reputation or standing of this company in any way—'

'I think I can safely leave that to you and the management,' Elena said quickly before she could finish. Roland sniggered.

'Be warned. If you step out of line, you'll not only be out of here, the company will also take legal action against you,' said Woods angrily.

'You're departing from your script. Is this an official warning? What action would they take against me... for what?'

'Shut up, smart arse! Nobody liked that stunt you pulled with Penny Irwin...'

'Oh, I see! You accusing me of that? If you are, you're on dangerous ground.'

'Okay, maybe it's not official, but I'm telling you. Your days are numbered here, you better think about getting yourself another job, if you can... with a bad reference.'

'Before you threaten me, think about the skeletons you have in the cupboard, the dodgy things that've gone on here. Do you really think I'd go quietly?' Elena rose to leave. 'Sorry, we have to get back to work. Thanks for the little chat. Byeee!'

Elena walked out as calmly as she could. Roland followed. Woods was visibly seething with anger but didn't respond.

'Well, that's the start. We know where we stand,' said Elena as they walked down the stairs.

'That was a friendly chat compared to the rant from Rye when I first came in,' he replied.

Elena left Roland at the third floor and made her way down to reception through the casino and the public stairway. She could see Pat below at the desk talking to Ollie. They both looked up expectantly as they caught sight of her.

'Hello, me darlin', what's going on?' asked Pat with concern. Elena looked at Ollie, who waited for her reply with unconcealed anticipation.

'Sorry to disappoint Ollie, I'm still employed... for now.' Pat showed relief. Ollie feigned misunderstanding.

'So what did Woods want?' asked Pat.

'Nothing really, an enquiry by tax authorities into reception staff's tips.'

'What? Oh, you're joking,' said Ollie, trying to conceal his initial alarm. Pat made no attempt to hide his amusement.

'Don't worry, Ollie, your secret's secure with me...' she said, as he went to greet a member, then added '... for the moment.'

He glanced back and she smiled falsely.

Pat waited while Elena carried out the brief take-over procedure with the outgoing reception Chica, then asked quietly, 'What did she want?'

'To convey a threat. They're waiting for me to step out of line, then I'm for the chop. And they think I put Penny up to that scene at the meeting.'

'You're joking?' he said, but knew she wasn't. They both fell silent then Pat remembered. 'Oh, message from Ralph Draper... his farewell drink-up's at the Coach tomorrow night, hopes you'll make it.'

'Why not,' she smiled. 'Lucky Ralph, getting out with a good job before the shit really starts to fly.'

Pat greeted a regular player and Elena processed his entry, wishing him an enjoyable evening.

'How's Penny?' Pat asked when the member had gone upstairs.

'You didn't hear? She's made up with Talal again… for now.'

'God, after all that! Well we'll see,' said Pat, looking at his watch. 'Got a meeting with yer man Mayfield. And Ollie, can you manage without him for now?'

Elena gave him a 'what do you think?'look.

Only a few minutes later Elena was surprised to see Pat back. 'Seems I'm not needed, they've cut the H & S committee to three to allow me to get on with my job,' he said, before she could ask.

'Really, you sure that's the reason?'

'Nah, bullshit! It's because I ask the wrong questions. In the minutes that item about Marietta's been taken out. Mayfield says Ventura's lawyer advised it. Anyway, I don't care, but I'll really miss Mayfield's talks on hygiene.' He rolled his eyes, and took the stairs on his way to the first floor.

'You're days are numbered, better look for another job!' Elena called out after him.

'Please God, not back to the building site!'

His appeal wasn't entirely in jest. At long last he seemed to have found a job for which he was suited. As a natural communicator, he enjoyed engagement with the public and the salary was the highest he'd earned in his working life. But if he was to leave Ventura, he doubted if an uninspiring CV, with his brief stint in public relations tagged on the end, would interest another casino operator.

He resolved to avoid controversy and simply get on with what he had to do. Others could worry about the politics.

The VIP Salon was busier than it had been earlier. Talal was playing roulette, Mr Chidiac had been joined by some Lebanese friends on blackjack and the faces round the punto-banco table were all recognised gamblers.

Ahmed was alongside Talal and Ellis stood next to the Inspector on the same table. The Prince appeared to be cashing out and Ellis was going through his repertoire of jokes and congratulations, but by the glances he was giving Ahmed, he was undoubtedly unhappy. The departing pleasantries over, the Prince signalled his driver who was waiting near the door and stopped briefly to receive Pat's greeting and thanks for his visit.

Ellis threw up his hands in frustration. 'He's been here less than an hour, took a hundred grand and now says he's got to meet Penny! I thought you said that was over?'

'I hear only now that he sees her again…' Ahmed's attention was diverted to the approaching Monaghan.

Ahmed nodded a greeting to Pat and on his way out called back to Ellis, 'Don't worry, I will finish it…'

'Finish it, finish what?' Pat asked Ellis.

Ellis gave a dismissive gesture. 'Oh, nothing important.'

Chapter Forty

Elena left the pub early, and alone. Pat had invited her to go on to a disco but she wanted to avoid the result of previous piss-ups. Apart from the problem of drinking and driving, she worried about the effect alcohol might have on her resolve not to sleep with him again. He could end up as a convenience and she didn't want that. She suspected that in spite of his assurances to the contrary, he now had somewhat of a thing for her and she didn't want to give him false hope or take advantage.

When she arrived home a note on the kitchen table informed her that Penny had gone out with Mansur and would be back late. She folded the Guardian open at the crossword section and filled the kettle. Just when her information retrieval system seemed to be lumbering into active service, the strident interruption from the phone re-buried the answer to three across.

'Hello, Hello... hel... lo!' No reply. She was about to put the receiver down.

'Hello, Penny?' answered a male voice eventually.

'Who is this?' she asked.

'Oh... just a friend,' the man said hesitantly.

'Penny's not here... who gave you this number?' Elena suspected he was Penny's ex-boyfriend.

'Oh, it doesn't... sorry.' And he rang off.

It had to be Penny's ex; but how did he know she was here and who had given him the number? Could only be someone at Ventura. Elena, worried about the effect this would have on Penny, thought to keep it to herself.

But if he called again, or worse still, if he managed to get the address from the same source…?

She wasn't sure what to do. The tea and crossword now offered no comfort or distraction. Instead, she went to the cupboard for some alcohol. This was becoming a habit, she thought. Nevertheless, she poured herself a large vodka and found some orange juice in the fridge.

Although Elena hadn't heard her, there were signs that Penny had come in after she'd gone to bed, whenever that had been. Surprisingly, having drunk a considerable amount, Elena didn't feel much after-effect. Which was as well, for the day promised to be a challenge, followed by another alcoholic finale - Draper's going-away party.

She lifted the mug from the table to make coffee and the unfinished crossword below it reminded her of a problem that remained to be solved. What to do about the previous night's phone call? She was going out soon. If Penny hadn't risen by then she'd have to hope that he wouldn't ring again later.

By the time she parked her car to walk round the corner to Ventura, Elena had recognised in her own recent behaviour two disturbing and inter-linked tendencies: chasing problems with alcohol and postponing them with bogus rationale. She resolved to return to her former decisive self.

Roland had suggested a meeting at the pub. She'd made little contact with committee members over the last few days, being anxious not to give the company anything that might be used against them, so Roland took responsibility for informing the others. The intention was to discuss where they now stood after the ballot, though 'in the shit' was the phrase that sprang to mind. While waiting for the others, she used the pub's call-box to phone the apartment and check if Penny had replaced the receiver. She'd left it off the cradle to ensure Penny wouldn't wake to the shock of hearing her ex-boyfriend on the line. The number rang, so she'd obviously replaced it, but there was no reply.

The others started to arrive as she put down the phone. Potts and Roland were already carrying drinks to a table.

'Didn't know if you already had a drink. Anyway, I got you half a lager,' said Roland as she greeted them.

'That's fine,' Elena said, taking a seat, 'you both off tonight?' She addressed Potts and Carmen, knowing that Roland had been on early-shift. Potts nodded as he pulled on his pint.

'I don't start until later, someone's covering for me,' said Carmen.

'You didn't say why you'd be late, I hope?' said Elena.

'Course not. I said I was going to the doctor,' Carmen said.

'Good. Anyway you've had a bit of a sniffle for some time, you got a cold?' asked Elena. Carmen nodded uncertainly.

'All the same, it's a bit dangerous. If someone sees you here with us...' Roland had a quick glance around.

'Yes, they're looking for anything. Your union affiliation can't interfere with work. Be careful,' said Elena.

'Right, so what's the purpose of the meeting, or is it a wake?' said Potts.

'Yeah, you're right, we've certainly seen the death of GWU at Ventura.' Elena made a sign of the cross.

'Well that's what I wanted to talk about,' said Roland. 'I'm getting a lot of stick from Rye. Is there nothing we can do or should I look for another job?'

'Theoretically, by law, they can't victimise a member of a union, but in practice...' Elena sighed and shook her head. 'How's it been for you two?' she asked Potts and Pettigrew.

'Not too bad,' answered Potts, 'all the guys on dice supported the union. We get stick from Nidditch but Chris gets worse. He and a few others, even myself, are thinking about Bahamas, they're looking for dealers.' He looked at Pettigrew, who nodded.

Elena turned to Carmen for her current experiences as Roland signalled the barman to serve the same again.

'Yes, I'm getting comments and things. Nothing really bad, but I don't know what'll happen from now on,' said Carmen. 'We can't do anything about getting a union now... what you think?' She looked to Elena to answer.

'To be truthful, no. Things can only get worse. Now they know they can do what they like. People will put up with it to keep their jobs.'

'I thought the business with Penny would've scared more girls into getting representation,' said Potts.

'Sorry to say this, I know she's your friend,' said Roland to Elena, 'but if you don't want this kinda thing to happen, don't go to those parties.'

'Nobody, not even Penny, knows exactly what happened...' Carmen began.

'Oh yes, I do!' Elena intervened angrily. 'I was there immediately after the rape, if she hadn't been frightened and ashamed to report it, we'd have proved it. In fact, I still think we could.'

'I'm sorry, it's just that... others say she was drunk and invited it. You know the way they...' Carmen looked to the others for support.

'They might say that, but if I could persuade her to use the doctor's report we got that morning they wouldn't be able to say she consented,' Elena lied, feeling the need to defend Penny against these slanted views.

'Well, that would be the answer, wouldn't it?' said Roland. The others nodded in agreement.

'Was she ready to do that, was that what the scene at the Grosvenor was about?' asked Carmen.

'Yes, but she's got cold feet again and I have to respect her wishes. Anyway, there are many other examples of their misuse of employees, especially girls. Girls fired because they wouldn't perform for Trist, Rye or punters, or because they put on a few pounds. And Marietta, beaten up by Al Khazari, then threatened and paid to shut up. Don't worry I'm preparing a dossier. If they want to get tough they'll see how much I know, even about flagrant breaches of the Gaming Act,' she rattled off in an explosion of pent-up resentment.

'Woah! I can't wait to see that report, please make it before I go to the Bahamas!' cried Potts, and the others laughed. Roland and the other two guys went to collect the drinks.

'Elena, I'm sorry if you thought I was insulting Penny, I didn't mean...'

'It's okay, Carmen, I'm a bit touchy, don't worry.' Elena patted her colleague's arm. 'How's it going with Ian anyway, everything okay?'

'Well, I'm not sure... you know. I haven't seen much of him recently.' She looked uneasy.

'Oh, I'm sorry, maybe with his new job he's a bit occupied,' said Elena as they returned with the drinks.

'I must… I have to go,' said Carmen, showing some agitation.

'Yes, watch your back,' said Roland. 'On the other hand, we're just warming up for Draper's drink-up, right? Elena held up her glass in confirmation.

The preliminary session of celebrations or going-away parties were traditionally held with an early start-time. This permitted those who couldn't be off that night to pass by before work for a quick one.

The remnants of the union movement didn't have far to go. Ralph held court at the bar with Monaghan and Chris Russell in supporting roles. Close by, in the corner, sat Ralph's girlfriend, several inspectors and Chicas. The host welcomed the 'Red Brigade', as he called them, and directed their attention to the grateful bar manager, waiting to put up the drinks.

'Your friends Morg and Dan should be here any minute.' Draper's jest drew laughs and jeers. But just then two surprise guests did enter, Lowe and Colin Bland. 'My God, it's the rogues' gallery here tonight!' Draper extended his hand, pointing to Lowe. 'I knew he'd know about this piss-up but who told you, Colin?'

'I told him, he's working for Ladbrokes now,' said the young Scot. Draper looked surprised.

'Don't worry, I'm off the sauce. I'll just have a lemonade,' Bland said, indicating to the barman he was serious. 'We came to wish you and the young lady the best of luck.'

'Oh yes, I better explain to those who haven't heard.' Draper beckoned Norma across. 'This is a double celebration, Norma and I are getting married before we take off to foreign parts!' he announced to noisy congratulations from all around.

Elena rationed her drinks, knowing the night would be long. She was pleased and surprised when Bland, true to his promise, took his leave early to avoid temptation. In her brief conversation with him, she'd been interested to hear that competitors were taking a keen interest in Ventura's methods and interpretation of the Gaming Act. He didn't say, but she guessed that people such as himself and Lowe had encouraged this interest. When Colin left, she accepted Pat's earlier invitation to join him and Ian at the bar. Draper stepped aside to host a flying visit from Bollard, which caused a momentary stir.

'Cheers, Ian, by the way, how's the romance going?' asked Elena as Lowe handed her a drink.

'I thought you'd know, you probably see her more than me!'

'Well yes, she said you haven't been able to get together much. I hope it's only temporary,' Elena said.

Ian avoided this and asked, 'What about you, anybody break through your defences yet?'

Elena glanced at Pat. He looked uneasy, but she was sure he wouldn't have said anything.

'Only when I'm drunk,' she grinned.

'Ah, in that case, what'll it be,' said Pat, holding up his hand in jest to call the barman.

'You'll be lucky, you haven't got enough money.' She gave him a pretend punch. 'And you better hold on to it, you could be out of a job soon.'

'Yes, that counts for a few of you,' added Draper, who'd rejoined them.

Norma, seeing signs that the night could turn political, came across with some other girls to change the mood.

The taxi driver wanted directions to her address but she wasn't at her most coherent. Eventually, after muttering several 'bleeding's and bloody's', under his breath, they finally stopped at the passageway to her block. Elena scrambled out, fumbled through her bag and slapped the fare in his hand with an instruction to keep the change, all ten pence of it. He looked down at it with disdain, and mumbled what sounded like *'fuckin' drunk slag'* and screeched off. To the accusation of being drunk she could offer no defence, that was why she'd left her car and taken a cab. The other part was inappropriate; no recent fucking had taken place. She'd ended up going home with Pat in a breach of her vow not to use him. However, he'd fallen asleep before copulation. But as the effects of the alcohol wore off, so had her disappointment. She'd slipped out before he woke, having slept only a few hours, and now amused herself with the thought that if he remembered anything at all, his disappointment would be greater than hers. Especially since the reference he'd previously requested would now be withheld.

She could see by the tidyness of the apartment that Penny had been back, but a note on the table confirmed she'd gone with Mansur to look for an apartment. Elena, deciding she needed more sleep, closed the curtains to block out the morning sun, kicked off her boots, shed her mini-skirt and, too tired to remove anything else, collapsed on the bed.

When she woke, the first stage of her revival tasted sweet and strong, the second sounded loud and shrill and she raced to pick it up.

'Hello… Elena here…' She waited: no reply: then dialtone. *Oh no, not him again*, she thought. She downed the receiver and moved back to her coffee. She was considering what to do about him when it rang again.

'Yes, hello?' It sounded like a call-box.

'Driver, Prince Talal, I come now… Miss Penny!'

'Sorry, I don't understand?'

'Driver, Driver Prince Talal, I come… Miss Penny no leave car!'

'Sorry, I still don't understand, Penny's not here…'

'Penny in car! I come now… need help!' The voice shouted louder, then put down the phone.

Elena's mind was in turmoil. What did he mean, Penny in the car, need help? She ran to the window, realised she was in her underwear and raced into the bedroom to pull something on. By the time she got back to the kitchen, a car horn was blasting outside. Looking down, she could see the Rolls and a nervous driver halfway out, looking up at the building.

The lift normally moved at snail's pace, when it wasn't broken or had its door jammed open with an empty beer bottle, so Elena took the stairs instead. When she emerged, breathless, at the front, the Arab seemed to recognise her; in any case, he showed signs of great relief.

'What's the matter?' she called out.

The driver opened the passenger door and pointed inside. Penny was lying along the back seat, face down with her hands up round her head in obvious distress.

Oh not again! 'Penny, what's the matter?' Elena called out, moving quickly to her side. 'Penny… what's wrong, what's happened?'

Penny's body was convulsing. Elena had seen this anguish only too often before. The driver pushed his head inside and made a soundless questioning gesture.

'What happened to her?' she demanded of him. He recoiled in surprise, shaking his head. 'What happened to her?' she persisted.

'I no know, Prince tell me take girl home. She no want go.'

Elena moved back to her desolate friend. 'Penny, Penny listen to me, look at me!' she said firmly, this time levering her friend's head gently off the car seat. 'Tell me what happened, what's this about?'

Penny's eyes were swollen and red, her hair wet and matted around her face. She began to make barely intelligible sounds but at least she was now beginning to respond.

'The… they…' Her words were contorted by sharp intakes of breath. Elena still propping her upright, waited.

At that moment the chauffeur popped his head in again. 'She must to go… I leave…'

'Fuck off!' screamed Elena. He recoiled in shock that a woman should speak to him in this way. Penny also jolted by this sat up. The driver was now preoccupied with the attendance of several locals, including scruffy youths looking over the car. Two women, one with a pram, now approached to see what was going on inside the fancy vehicle.

'Penny, please tell me what happened!'

After a short period she began again in faltering voice. 'They… told him I was… a whore, and… I did… perverted things at a party and… made a scandal at Ventura.'

'Who said this?'

'Mansur… somebody told Mansur this… He says I will shame his family… he doesn't want to see me again…' She dissolved once again into pitiful weeping.

'Bastards!' muttered Elena under her breath. She could see more people were congregating around the car in curiosity. The driver was becoming agitated at their ever closer proximity to his master's vehicle.

'Penny listen, we need to go up to the flat, if you're ready? Please hold on to me.' Elena pushed open the door while still keeping one hand on her stricken friend.

The driver, seeing this, held the door then danced gingerly around them as they exited, not quite knowing if he should assist or not. The locals looked on.

One of the women ventured across, 'She awlright, love?'

'Yes, thank you,' said Elena, nudging Penny onwards. The relieved chauffeur dived into the Rolls and raced off.

Once upstairs in the apartment, she sat Penny down at the kitchen table and, drained herself by the exertion and nervous tension, collapsed onto the chair opposite, making no attempt to re-open the painful discussion. Her tormented flatmate slouched across the table, face in her hands, silently weeping.

At a certain level Elena felt an urge to reproach her, as one might scold a child who hadn't learnt from a previous painful experience. *Well, what did you expect people to say after you took no action and even went back to work for the very man who'd raped you? Did you really expect a fabulously rich heir of a conservative Muslim dynasty to marry and take home a mini-skirted dolly-bird he picked up in a casino?* But she knew this would be cruel and would serve little purpose.

The first stage in Penny's recovery would be in getting her to talk and that couldn't be postponed much longer. Starting in the traditional English way, Elena rose to put on the kettle.

By evening she had progressed from tea and sympathy through coffee and motivation to gin and retribution. Penny now sat quietly drinking gin and tonic, nodding at Elena's assertion that it was time to fight back. But her recovery was fragile. For that reason Elena was now doing the talking, having earlier drawn out from Penny, in agonising detail, what the man she loved had said to crush her morale so thoroughly. It seemed he, having been confronted with the evidence of her loose morals by his own family members, and having no convincing arguments to refute the allegations, had finished the relationship for fear of bringing shame to his family.

Elena didn't know who had fed the lies and distortion to the family but the content could surely only have come via Ventura. Like all the best lies, it had elements of truth which could easily be verified. From what she'd heard of Talal's family, and in particular his uncle, it was logical to assume they would have been looking for material to discredit her and someone connected with the casino had obliged.

Even if Elena was on the way to convincing Penny that it was time to fight back, she herself was unsure of what form this would take.

They'd both have to eat something otherwise the alcohol would take its toll. Elena rose to look in the fridge, just as the phone rang. Penny jumped like a startled cat from her reverie. Elena moved quickly to take it in case it was the very person Penny least needed to talk to at that moment.

'Yes, who is it?' she answered curtly. 'Oh, Pat. Yes… er… sorry. It's been a difficult day,' she said with relief.

She listened while he struggled through an apology. On another occasion it might have been entertaining to pull his leg about the previous night but she wasn't in the mood. Penny was looking tremulous again so she interrupted Monaghan's flow.

'Excuse me a minute…' she covered the speaker '… it's Pat, you want to talk to him?' Penny shook her head. 'Should I tell him anything?' After some time she again signalled no.

'Sorry Pat, I'm a bit tied up at the moment, can I call you tomorrow?' He agreed, she hung up and was about to return to the fridge when the phone rang again. This time she lifted it without thinking.

'Hello?'

'Hello, is that you, Penny?'

'No, this is Elena, there's no one of that name here!' she said angrily and put the phone down, even more enraged because she couldn't say what she wanted to say for fear of upsetting Penny.

'What was that?' Penny looked concerned.

'Nothing, it's a wrong number,' Elena lied. Something would have to be done about him too but now was not the time.

*

Penny hadn't yet risen or at least hadn't emerged from her room. Elena took the opportunity to call Pat. The phone rang for some time before he answered.

'Aha, is it yerself, Elena? I'm sorry, I was sleeping late.'

'Yes, I know you can sleep through most things,' she smiled to herself.

'Ah, well, yes... I'm sorry about that...'

'It's okay, I was pretty drunk myself. I did say I wouldn't let that happen again and of course it didn't,' she laughed. He was about to make another apology, but she continued, 'Forget it. Although I'm not sure about that reference now.'

'Bejesus, I'm off the booze for good now.'

'Listen, Pat, on a more serious subject... I couldn't talk last night because Penny was present and in a terrible state. Talal ditched her again. He said he'd been told that she got wild on drink and drugs at a party, screwed several people, then afterwards claimed she'd been raped, causing a scene at the meeting by accusing Trist without proof.'

'My God, who told him that bloody shite?'

'I don't know. But someone's also given her ex-boyfriend my number and he's been phoning here. I haven't told her because that'll make her worse. I really don't know what to do about it.'

'Right, I'm working this evening, I'll check the file at Ventura. If he gave a phone number I'll call and threaten him with the police if he doesn't leave her alone.'

'Pat, that's great, you're fantastic.'

'In that case, do you think maybe you could put that in the reference?' They both laughed. 'I'll let you know how it goes,' he said, 'you're off tonight, yes?'

'Yes, thank goodness, otherwise I don't know what I'd do about her, I don't like to leave her alone.'

'Maybe, I could stop by for a little while on my way to work, see if I can cheer her up,' offered Pat.

'Well, I don't want to put you to...'

'No problem. Around three-thirty, would that be okay?' he insisted. Elena agreed and was relieved to share some of the burden.

It was almost two o'clock in the afternoon when a pale and red-eyed Penny drifted into the lounge and gave a weak smile.

Elena poured the coffee and attempted to lighten the atmosphere with some unimportant chatter which brought only minimal response. The suggestion that there might be jobs for both of them at Ladbrokes had a similar effect, although Elena was of no doubt whatsoever that making a complete break, finding another job and new friends was the way for Penny to recover from her recent traumas. Slowly she moved again to the subject of Talal, hoping to bring Penny round to accepting that the romance was over for multiple reasons, unconnected with her. But Penny clung desperately to the belief that when he learnt the truth, they'd be together again. Fearful that questioning this belief would provoke another crisis, Elena dropped the subject.

Pat's arrival brought some relief to Elena but in spite of his best efforts, Penny remained in subdued mood. Taking advantage of Pat's presence, Elena left them briefly to run to the local store, as she'd probably have to stay home to baby-sit her morose friend and the fridge was empty. On her return, Penny was visibly more animated. She wasn't sure if the coffee was working, the effects of alcohol and sleeping pills were wearing off, or Pat in his inimitable way had lifted her spirits. As Pat was now about to leave, she would no doubt find out.

'She seems to have opened up a bit, how did you find her?'

Pat shook his head, 'I had a little talk, she's in a state…' He stopped as Penny called out.

'Will you call tomorrow, Pat?'

'Yes, me darlin', we'll speak tomorrow!' he replied. Then, seeing the quizzical look on Elena's face: 'I'll explain later, bye!'

So far that day Talal hadn't appeared. For Pat it was just as well, because he didn't know what he'd do or say. In a moment of weakness he'd not only agreed to give him a letter from Penny but had also said he'd speak on her behalf. He now regretted these rash promises. There was every chance the Prince would reject the letter and be annoyed by Pat's intrusion, and in these politically delicate times, this could threaten Pat's position. What could he hope to achieve for Penny anyway - a rehabilitation of her reputation? Another temporary reconciliation? A pointless exercise. At least now he could truthfully say he'd been unable to deliver the letter.

Nor had he been successful with his other mission. Martin Atkinson, Penny's ex-boyfriend, had given a telephone number on his Ventura application that was now disconnected. These preoccupations Pat pushed to one side as he made his way through the Primero restaurant towards the VIP Casino area.

'Is it himself?' The voice from behind caught Pat unawares. He turned to see Ahmed, accompanied by two other Arab players.

'Aha, good day, gentlemen,' Pat welcomed them. 'Ahmed, you're getting more Irish every day.'

'Yes, I must to stop to drink Guinness.' Pat laughed, the others looked quizzical. 'We go to eat, they play later,' Ahmed winked to Pat.

'Bon Appetite.' Pat then remembered. 'Oh Ahmed, Prince Talal, will he be coming tonight?'

'No, I think maybe he will come after two days. You want something from him?'

'No, it's a message from Penny. He has a box at the apartment reception, I'll leave it there.'

'Okay, I will tell him,' Ahmed nodded, then asked, 'Penny, she still live with this other Chica?'

'Yes, but she's not coming back to Ventura.'

Ahmed had a faint smile on his face. 'No, of that I am sure.'

Chapter Forty-one

Elena's two days off had been quite the most boring she had spent in a long while. But by Sunday there seemed to be a slight improvement in her flatmate's spirit. Penny had agreed that Elena would, on her behalf and with her letter of authority, terminate her employment at Ventura. This involved collecting outstanding salary and documents and removing personal items from her locker. She also agreed that Elena could look into the possibility of them both finding work at Ladbrokes, as suggested by Ian Lowe. Encouraged by this new resolve, Elena readied herself for work.

Later that day she entered the canteen to find Pat practising his blarney on two Chicas fresh from the training school.

'Catching them early?' Elena asked impishly when he broke off to join her.

'Ah you know, just making them feel at home.'

'Sorry, what did you say you were making them feel?'

'Now, now, don't be naughty.'

'Actually, they don't know it, but you're about the nicest bloke they'll meet in this building.'

'Yes, and they don't know that when I ask them to sleep with me, that's exactly what I mean.'

Elena laughed but didn't respond in case it took her into the subject of their relationship again.

'Anyway, I have a confession,' Pat sighed. 'When you were out yesterday Penny got very upset and in a moment of madness I agreed that I'd try to talk to Talal.'

'Pat, for God sake, you can't!'

'I know, it was stupid. In any case, I haven't seen him. But she also gave me a letter. He has a mailbox at the apartments' reception, I left it there.'

'And she told you not to tell me, I suppose?'

'Yes, she reckoned you'd be against it.'

'She's right. It's horrible the way it ended, but it would've ended anyway. She'll only get hurt again. She's so naïve, sometimes I can't stand to hear her. You're not still thinking of talking to him?'

'No, I called and told her I didn't see him, but have left him the letter. Oh, and sorry Elena, I'd no luck either with her ex-boyfriend, the number he gave is disconnected.'

'Well, he hasn't called over the last two days, maybe he's given up.'

'I hope so. How's it going for you here, any problems?'

'Nothing I can't handle so far. They've changed my days-off again without asking me, so I'm off again tomorrow and Wednesday. They probably thought this would annoy me but actually it suits me better, I can get more done during the week. Everything I do is being monitored by your mate Ollie and his reception colleagues. They're waiting to catch me out.'

'Yes, we'd both better show our faces,' Pat said, rising from the table.

The personnel office buzzed with activity, none of it essential to the operation of the business. Sally was displaying cosmetics she was hoping to sell from a catalogue, Lana showing photographs of her recent holiday, while another ex-nightclub Chica was cooing and giggling on the phone. Woods was herself fully involved with coffee and a fashion magazine when Elena knocked and entered her inner office on a nod from Sally.

'Hope I'm not disturbing you,' said Elena. Marta put the magazine to one side and looked up questioningly. 'You received a letter of resignation from Penny Irwin, and earlier I sent authorisation for me to pick up her papers, salary and things from her locker. Would that be alright?'

Woods looked thoughtful then shuffled through papers on her desk before answering. 'Actually, I tried to call her. I was about to send her this letter,' she said, handing the already sealed envelope to Elena. It bore Penny's old apartment address.

'What number did you call her on?' asked Elena, looking at her for signs of deception.

'I don't remember.' She flicked through a diary and read out the number.

'No, she's not there now,' Elena, still watched her face for giveaway signs.

'Oh well, she didn't tell us she'd changed her address.'

'What does the letter say?' asked Elena. Then, anticipating the Personnel Manager's answer, she added: 'She's given me authority to settle all matters with you.'

'I don't know about that, she's given you authority to pick up...' Marta stopped when she saw Elena opening the envelope.

'Well, since you've taken the responsibility on yourself,' said Marta, 'you'll see the company considers that she left without giving notice... Article 12 clause (b) – if an employee does not give a satisfactory justification for absence after—'

'Yes, yes, don't bother quoting it. You knew of course why she was absent...'

'I had no official...'

'Okay, when will her papers, the P45 and the money you do owe her be ready?'

'Well I'm not sure this power of attorney is enough, we still need a signature of receipt from her,' said Woods.

'You're surely not interested in her coming in here, are you? If you give me the details of the settlement and make out the paper, I'll take it for her to sign. Then tomorrow I'll pick up the lot, including stuff from her locker, okay?'

Woods grimaced, nodded reluctant agreement, then as an afterthought added, 'This document should have her current address, no?'

'Yes, she's staying with me, it's on my file,' she said. Woods accepted this information with what seemed a look of surprise and no indication of prior knowledge.

On her next and final rest break before finishing, Elena called Penny and pretended it was simply to relate her conversation with Woods. Though a weakness could still be heard in Penny's voice, there was no obvious deterioration in her mood - an indication that her ex-boyfriend hadn't made any further attempt to contact her.

Her next call was to Ian Lowe. Apart from picking his brains on credit procedure anomalies, she also wanted to ask him how an application for work at his company might be made. Her first thought was to find a job for Penny, but she was now convinced she should also find herself another position. Ian suggested they meet the following evening, and meanwhile gave her the number of their personnel office, insisting he put in a word for them with the manager.

For the first time for days she felt she'd actually done something positive, however small. To the obvious consternation of her appointed monitors Eva and Ollie, she returned smiling to her work place. It was to prove difficult to maintain. Moments later Prince Talal entered, showing no recognition of who she was, although he most certainly knew. Her colleague quickly processed his entry while Ollie paid appropriate homage. In spite of her advice to Pat, she almost succumbed to the temptation to address him.

The following morning their drive into central London was unusually quick. During the trip her passenger had been curiously talkative and was now actually humming to The Bay City Rollers' *Bye Bye Baby* on the car radio. Elena decided, in spite of the dubious taste in music, that this was another positive sign. Persuading Penny to come into London to Ladbrokes' offices had been the first big step. As agreed, Elena, armed once again with authorisation, planned to visit Ventura first to pick up Penny's salary, papers and personal things. But although they'd seen little traffic on the way, there was a lengthy queue of cars to enter the car park. Elena tapped on the wheel impatiently.

'Would you like me to park the car and you can go straight up?' asked Penny.

'I didn't know you could drive,' said Elena.

'Yes, I've had a licence since just after my eighteenth birthday,' Penny said proudly.

Several minutes passed but nothing seemed to be moving.

'Maybe you're right, there seems to be a problem here. If you're sure, I'll press on and meet you at the café,' said Elena, pleased to see her new-found confidence.

At Ventura the personnel office seemed to be doubling as a nursery; with two toddlers crawling around the floor and another in the process of having her nappy changed.

Elena shouted above the din. 'Excuse me, but I arranged to meet Marta here at eleven. Is she around?'

Eventually Woods's assistant, who was crawling on the floor with one of the children, answered, 'She's not here at the moment.'

In frustration, Elena picked up the nearest phone, dialled and asked that Woods be paged. A few moments later the phone rang. It was Woods, obviously irritated. 'Something's come up, you'll have to come back later.'

'I'm off today, in case you've forgotten. Can't anyone else give me the stuff?'

'No, they're all busy.'

Elena tried to contain her frustration. 'Yes, I can see that. I'll be back but I'll call first. I want to do this today,' she said emphatically, while realising she had no leverage to make this happen.

The interview at Ladbrokes seemed in sharp contrast. Their personnel manager, undistracted by the diverse activities that ate into the time of Woods and her staff, explained his company's policy and the fairly rapid expansion that had created opportunities around the country. He was especially interested not just in Elena's reception experience but, more importantly, in her academic attainments. Elena confessed that, soon after starting at Ventura, she'd begun to regret not having pursued a professional career, but somehow hoped she'd be given training and the opportunity to advance. The manager smiled knowingly when she said that it was now apparent that at Ventura, advancement for a young woman didn't lie in knowledge or academic ability. He concluded the interview by saying he was happy to hear that she wanted more responsibility, and with that in mind he'd consider the positions available and come back to her with a proposal.

Tempting as it was, she was careful not to make any reference to the scandalous events at Ventura and had advised Penny, whom he'd agreed to see next, to also avoid that subject.

Penny's interview seemed brief but she returned beaming. 'He said they normally train their own croupiers but could offer me some re-training before I start.'

'That sounds good, doesn't it?'

'It's even better than I thought. I feel better going into the training school first. You know how nervous I get.'

They both returned in good spirits to the café before Elena made her next attempt at finalising Penny's connection with Ventura.

After Ladbrokes it was back to reality with a thud. Although she'd agreed that Elena should come at four o'clock, predictably Woods wasn't in her office, nor was anyone else. Elena was about to page her when she shuffled in munching a doughnut and, without apology or comment, moved to her desk, leaving Elena to follow.

Rummaging through a drawer, Woods eventually produced an unsealed envelope. 'If you've got the letter of consent from Irwin I can give you this.' She waved the envelope teasingly like bait.

'You show me your contents first, then I'll show you mine,' said Elena in a child-like voice, mimicking the wave with her own envelope.

Woods glared at her then threw the envelope down. 'It's the P45 and the cheque, what do you think's in it?'

Elena snatched it up without releasing her envelope. Inside it contained the tax document and a cheque. But there was also another letter, stating that the total previously calculated had assumed the return of the uniforms, the dealer's manual and locker keys. None of them having been received, this value had been deducted and would be repaid only on receipt of them.

'What pettiness! You knew I'd bring the keys to her locker,' spat Elena.

'We thought you would, but couldn't be sure the items were there.'

Elena shook her head. 'I have here the keys, you want to join me at her locker?'

'Wait in the rest-room until I get someone to come up,' Woods said sternly.

To supervise the removal of personal effects and the return of company property from the locker of a departing employee, Woods, in the absence of female members of security, always called an assistant to accompany her. Elena, knowing this, also wanted an independent witness and was happy to learn that Carmen was on duty and would shortly be on rest-break. She arrived in the rest-room a few minutes later.

'Hi, Elena, what's going on? I heard you were here…'

'Hi, Carmen. Penny's not coming back, I'm here to collect her things.' Elena patted her bag.

'Nice, very nice,' Carmen said, admiring the bright patchwork bag.

'Yes, it's corduroy, a Salaminder. Anyway, I'm glad you're around, I wonder if you could be there when we clear out Penny's locker? Just to make sure they don't say later I took something I shouldn't?'

'Oh, okay,' Carmen agreed, then asked, 'I hear Penny's also finished with Talal?'

'Yes, seems they got to him with their lies. Although I didn't think that relationship ever had much future,' said Elena.

'What happened?'

'They told him the Ventura version of the rape. I suppose they were worried he and others might get to hear the truth first,' said Elena bitterly.

'So he believed their story?'

'Yes. Well, he is a Muslim with worries about his reputation back home and all that.'

'Didn't you say she had a doctor's report or something?'

'Er… yes, I have.' Elena had forgotten her earlier fabrication, but now continued, 'I think she decided that if he could believe their story without hearing hers, it was pointless trying to persuade him. Now that it's over and she's left Ventura, she might take a different view about bringing home the truth to everyone.'

'What about your plans? Fighting on?'

'Well, I don't like to give up, but there's no future here for anybody with integrity. They'll be trying all they can to get rid of me and anyone who stood up to them. But don't worry, under my arm here I've enough stuff to close this place,' she whispered, clutching the fashionable bag closer.

'Like what? You mean about Penny?'

'Well that, yes... and Marietta and... a breach of the law on credit, shsh! Careful, here comes the KGB!' she said as Woods and her assistant appeared.

'Right, let's sort this out,' said Marta with an air of authority.

Elena dangled the keys. Woods snatched them and, opening the locker, instructed her assistant to remove items as she listed them on a notepad. There were two uniforms, one which Penny had last worn and a laundered spare; and several artificial flowers with pienetes, the decorative combs used to hold them in place on the Chicas' hair. On the shelf, a training manual completed the items to be returned to the company.

'The rest are personal things.' Elena moved to take them.

'Let's complete the hand-over officially, if you don't mind,' said Woods curtly.

'Two pairs of shoes, assorted cosmetics, a mirror, comb, brush and an envelope,' announced her assistant.

'Containing what?' asked the Personnel Manager.

Elena moved again to intervene. 'That's not your business...'

'It's security procedure,' demanded Woods. 'It's a photograph of a horse... Princess Penny from Talal with...'

Elena grabbed it before she could finish reading the inscription. 'It's a personal item, haven't you people got any shame?'

'It's a personal item from one of our clients, who she wasn't allowed to go out with,' said Woods.

'Don't give me that bullshit! Bar him then - when you've collected the illegal credit you've given him!' said Elena angrily, then asked, 'You finished here now?'

Woods, angry but perplexed, looked to her assistant who nodded confirmation. Elena stuffed the items in her bag.

'You're witness to the fact that the keys, uniforms and manual have been returned,' said Elena to Carmen, before addressing Woods, 'No excuse now for not sending the money you owe. We'll expect it at my address within the next few days.'

Woods scowled, made no reply and left.

'Well, that shocked her,' said Carmen. 'What was that about Talal and illegal credit?'

'Yes, I've got stuff on that…' she patted her bag '… but I shouldn't have said anything at this point. Anyway I'll explain later, have to run, bye, and thanks.'

'You working tonight?' Carmen called as Elena headed downstairs.

'No, they've changed my days-off. Maybe I'll see you at the pub later, but I'm having a quiet night.' Elena suddenly remembered she'd be meeting Ian, but decided to avoid that subject. Later she'd find out if he and Carmen were still seeing each other.

Chapter Forty-two

The Red Lion was full. Elena recognised some as regulars but fortunately no one from Ventura. Lowe had already taken a table and sat with a beer.

'Hi, Elena, what'll you have?' he said as she greeted him with a peck on the cheek.

'Half a lager. Oh, can you get me a packet of crisps?'

'They've food at the back if you're hungry...'

'No, that's all I want. I'm meeting Penny later for dinner,' she assured him.

He returned a few minutes later with her drink and crisps. 'So, you two girls are going out later? How is she, and how did the interviews go?'

Elena gave a brief explanation of events with Talal. 'And my interview went well,' she added, 'they seemed interested, said they'd contact me.'

'Great, I'm sure they will, they're expanding rapidly. Actually I've bin offered the new unit in London so I'll be back on the scene myself soon,' said Lowe.

'Fantastic! The only cloud on the horizon is, you might get us as employees!' They both laughed. Elena continued, 'Is it still on with you and Carmen?'

'Well, you could say it's not officially off, but she's bin a wee bit strange lately,... volatile.'

'Actually, I saw her today, I didn't mention you, nor did she. She did say she might see me down the pub later.'

'Well there you go. I asked her tae a wee party for a friend of mine at

Gullivers later tonight, she said she was working,' he said with a look of resignation.

'Oh, but maybe she's changed her shift or something,' Elena said, somewhat unconvincingly. Lowe smiled.

'Anyway, what's bin going on at the funny farm?' he asked.

'Well, now there's no chance of representation they do just as they please. The only way I think anyone could get at them is on points of law. I'm sure they break all sorts of laws – on health and safety, employment… But remember, we talked about credit? You mentioned something then, did you think they were breaking the law?'

'Yeah, I'm sure that's why they don't want people like me and Draper around because Ellis and Nidditch give credit without cheques and…'

'But are they doing that on orders or just for themselves?'

'I'm sure it comes from the top. Ralph reckons Bollard's isn't in on it, that Pellzer bypasses him and though he knows, is too scared tae say anything. That's possible.'

'Even if somebody wanted to do something, what could they do?'

'I suppose report it tae the Gaming Board, but they need proof. Otherwise anybody who'd some kinda grudge could say anything against their employer or ex-employers,' he smiled.

'Like you or me you mean?' she asked, smiling back.

'Exactly. Actually, I've thought about taking it tae the bosses of my present company, because the word is that the big London companies are already at war. Accusing each other of infringing Law tae attract punters.'

'So why haven't you?'

'I don't know. Although I'm sure, I don't have absolute proof and I suppose… although I hate the bastards, I've never quite seen myself as a grass.'

Elena wasn't sure how to respond. She could furnish him with proof. She wanted to say that he shouldn't feel squeamish about reporting a group that included a rapist, procurers of young girls, and accessories to serious assault. But she wasn't sure she wanted to provoke Ian or anyone else into doing something she should do herself, since she felt so strongly about it.

Instead she asked. 'What kind of material do you think the Gaming Board would act on?'

'I suppose they'd want customers' names, amounts, dates, and then they might launch an investigation. But I've no doubt there'll be nothing tae substantiate this on Ventura's accounts. Unless somebody's willing tae talk who's been involved in it. Why, you heard something from somebody?'

'Oh, gossip.' She still didn't want to say. 'If it got to the Gaming Board and they asked people like you and Ralph about it, would you confirm your suspicions?'

'Well, I suppose tae keep ourselves in the clear we'd have tae say we left because we were worried, but couldn't prove anything. Why, you heard somebody's going tae do that?'

'No, but with so much talk, someone might. I would, if I could get enough proof.'

Lowe looked thoughtful, then flashed the smile that the Chicas always talked about in the rest-room. 'Come on, let's have another drink and forget about the place for five minutes.'

'Okay, but only a half pint.'

'A half, what you worried about? You said your defences came down when you were drunk, surely you're a few away from that?'

'Ah, you remembered! No, actually I'm driving and had planned to have a quiet night.'

'No, don't say that. I was hoping you'd come tae the party at Gullivers.'

'You mean in place of Carmen?' She threw him a coy sideways glance. 'But maybe she'll still come?'

'Forget about her. It's dead, we just havnae announced the funeral. Anyway, no commitment, just come for a drink. It'll be a good night, we've a live band.'

She thought about it. 'I told you I'm meeting… oh, I get it, you want me to bring Penny!'

'I wasn't thinking about her. Really! Ease up, you're always suspicious of everybody! I was asking you,' he said emphatically.

'I'm sorry, it's just that I thought you used to fancy her,' she smiled, trying to 'ease up' as he'd suggested.

'A lot of guys did, she's a good-looking bird, but too much of a problem for me.'

'Well I do have to meet her and we said we'd go for something to eat, so…'

'Okay, our "thing" doesn't start until after eleven. If you want tae come, with or without her, you'll be welcome. Now, about that drink?'

'Okay, a large rum and coke, to ease up,' she said laughing.

She hurried on the short distance to the Coach, being already a little later than they'd agreed and knowing Penny would feel uncomfortable in the pub by herself. One drink had turned to three and the alcohol, mixed with Lowe's boyish charm and story-telling abilities, had almost caused her to forget her previous plans. When she got there, Penny was standing outside.

'Sorry, I'm a bit late.'

'Actually I don't know why I agreed to meet here. I don't really want to see any Ventura people, I'm… well… you know?' Penny shrugged.

'I understand. We'll go somewhere else, but I need to go to the toilet, can you wait a minute?'

'Of course. But… Carmen and the rest of your committee are in there. They didn't see me, I saw them go in as I came round the corner,' Penny said, adding, 'if you want I can meet you later?'

'No, I didn't agree to meet with them and I'm starving. Walk round to the restaurant, I'll catch you up, promise. I'll just say hello, I can see them another time.' Elena danced off to the pub toilet.

Before leaving the ladies', she paused by the mirror, combed her fingers through her hair in the pretence that this would improve it, and dabbed cologne here and there as she'd perspired a little in her haste to get there. While doing this, she considered why Pettigrew, Potts, Roland and Carmen should be in the pub together. The committee had all but disbanded and only the two Ps had ever been close friends. In her earlier conversation with Carmen she'd made only a throwaway suggestion that they might see each other in the pub.

When she exited, Roland was standing by the bar, waiting to ask her what she would drink.

'No I can't stay,' Elena said, moving across to their table. He followed her. 'What are you all doing here, another strike?'

'No, Carmen mentioned your proof about Ventura's lawbreaking,' said Potts.

Elena looked quizzically at Carmen.

'Well, you said you were coming to the pub with the stuff. I thought they'd be interested,' said Carmen, looking as if she'd already had a few drinks.

'I'm sorry but I'm really in a terrible hurry, I can't wait. I've got to do some things then go collect my car,' she said, making it up as she went along.

'You're off tonight, yes? You going out later?' asked Carmen.

'No, I'm going home fairly early, once I've done a few things. You going anywhere, out with Ian?' she asked.

'No, he's working. Anyway, you still got the stuff you were telling me about?' asked Carmen, looking at Elena's bag.

'Yes, but I'm sorry, I've really got to run.' She looked at her watch. 'You'll hear about it in the next few days, I promise.' And she rushed off, leaving them grumbling to each other.

A quiet night she may have been planning but after a bottle of wine, of which her companion only drank two glasses, the thought of quietly going home was becoming distinctly unappealing.

'Do you feel like a party after this?'

'Not really, why don't you go. I'm alright to go home,' said Penny.

'Actually, Ian Lowe told me about it, it's probably all his people – our new work-mates perhaps.'

Penny smiled but shook her head. Earlier she'd been talking excitedly about the opportunity they'd given her. She seemed to be on the road to recovery, although very occasionally she took on a wistful look.

'I won't be able to drive us home, I've had a bit too much to drink. I've been stupid,' Elena said, trying to break the mood that was taking hold again.

'No, you're never stupid Elena, not like me. I have to tell you something,' Penny said, her voice faltering. 'I sent a letter to Mansur and put really stupid things in it. I said I thought I might now be pregnant and... I was going to the newspapers about Trist raping me… and…' She put her head in her hands. Elena stretched across to comfort her and the waiter approached with some concern.

'It's okay,' she said, to both Elena and the waiter. 'It's okay, I'm sorry.'

Elena said nothing. The waiter was still hovering so she asked for the bill.

'Mansur didn't reply, of course. You were right, he's more worried about his reputation than me. I have to make my life. Not always be so weak. You give good advice, I have to start taking it,' Penny said, summoning up a determined smile.

When they got outside Elena put her arm round her.

'Why don't you go to the party. I'm all right to go home, really!' insisted Penny.

They continued walking in the direction of the car-park.

'Tell you what, I'll take your car home, you go to the party. You can't drive it anyway,' Penny said, 'go on, please.'

Elena thought about it. 'Are you sure you can drive it back?'

'Yes, I'll take it easy. Anyway, there's less traffic at this time. Go on, say yes!'

After another ten yards Elena overcame her guilt and re-ignited her excitement. It might have been the alcohol but she suspected her interest in Ian had intensified, so much so that she'd been delighted when Carmen had, by her blatant lie, confirmed it was over.

When they reached the corner, she stopped. 'Okay, if you're sure, you might as well take this.' She handed Penny her bag. 'It's mostly your things anyway. I'll just take my purse and my flat key, here's the car keys, don't wait up.' Elena's smile still betrayed some guilt, but Penny skipped off, grinning broadly.

Her night might have been complete if she could only expunge from her mind the nagging feelings of guilt. Guilt that she'd left Penny, against her better judgement, to drive home, although she had obviously not driven for some time and certainly not in anything as volatile as Elena's banger. To a lesser extent there was also the feeling that she'd been a little calculating in her dealings with Carmen, interpreting her and Ian's comments to her own advantage.

For the moment, she thought, *I'll live with the guilt*. Maybe it was time to be a little selfish and certainly the end justified the means. She couldn't remember a more enjoyable experience than the night she'd just spent.

Nevertheless, when Ian returned from the kitchen with the coffee, she suggested maybe she should use his phone to call Penny. 'I'm worried because she's not used to driving and—'

'Naw, come on, she'll be sleeping, it's the early hours o' the mornin'.' Ian pushed across the coffee.

'I suppose so.' Elena conceded. 'Anyway, I'm afraid I'm going to have to get home.'

'That's a pity, I'm off tomorrow, we could've done… things…'

'Oh, and what is it we could've done?' She edged nearer to him.

'More of the same, but skipping the party bit,' he grinned.

'Well, you'll just have to do more of the same before I go,' she murmured.

He put down his coffee cup and gave her a delicious smile.

Ian had suggested he drop her home, but as he'd been drinking quite a lot, Elena convinced him it was safer to take a taxi. She directed the driver to the parking area she normally used, with the intention of verifying that the car and therefore Penny was safely back, then, rather than redirect him to her address, she decided to walk through to her block. That way she could inspect the front of her car and avoid testing another black cab driver's 'knowledge' to the limit of his patience.

'Mind how you go in the dark, love!' the driver advised as she got out. 'It's a bit rough round 'ere!'

Elena was relieved to see the banger parked there and as far she could make out by the light from the one street-lamp that wasn't broken, there were no new dents. She picked up her pace and headed for home.

Chapter Forty-three

The phone was ringing as Pat turned the key in his door. He entered the sitting room, hurriedly dumped the milk, bread and newspaper on the armchair and picked up the receiver.

'Hello, Pat? It's Ian Lowe here...'

'Oh hello, Ian how's it going?'

'Er... okay. I'm sorry tae trouble you but... I know you're friendly wi' Elena and Penny and... er... I've been trying tae ring Elena. Thing is, it's probably nothing but... it was on the radio that the police have found the body of a young woman in Venter's Lane...'

'Jesus! That's the bloody place Elena goes through when she parks her car!'

'Yeah, I thought it was near when they were describin' the area of West London...' Some time elapsed and Pat hadn't responded. Lowe spoke again. 'I'm sorry, Pat, I just thought maybe you...'

'What did the report say happened to the girl?' Pat suddenly found his voice.

'The police say there are suspicious circumstances...'

'Holy...!' Pat took a deep breath and tried to collect his thoughts. 'I'll try to find out something. Ah! We're probably thinking the worst, when... I'll get back to you.'

Now Pat also tried Elena's number and listened to it ringing for some time. There was no reply. Now what? He sat back down again. Could it be Elena or Penny? The thought sent shivers through his body.

He wasn't sure how long he'd been sitting there but now felt he had to do something; anything. Somehow he had to find Elena or Penny. He turned on the local radio and waited for the news report.

Eventually the item came on the air. It stated that Hammersmith and Fulham Police were investigating the suspicious death of a young woman whose body had been found by a passer-by in the early hours of the morning in the undergrowth by the gate to a disused rail-yard on Venters Lane. *Yes, that was the lane Elena passed through to get to her apartment block after parking her car.* Police were asking for anyone who had heard or seen anything suspicious to contact them, and gave a number.

Pat had no information to give them but should he call? He nervously dialled the number given. A switchboard operator answered and after he'd stumbled through his explanation about possibly having some information on the Venters Lane thing, she asked for his name and the number he was calling from, then asked him to wait.

A few moments later another voice came on. 'Good evening, sir, I'm Detective Sergeant Faulds, I believe you have some information that might help us in the investigation into the death of a young lady in Venters Lane?' Pat was about to explain but the officer continued: 'First, let me confirm your full name and address, telephone number and the number you're calling from now.' Pat gave him the details. 'Thank you, sir. Now, what can you tell us?'

'Er… well… I'm not sure. Thing is, I've got two friends, girls, who live near there I'm worried 'cause I've been unable to reach them.'

'Excuse me, sir, may I ask you how you found out about this incident?' asked the policeman.

'Er… yes, it was on the radio.'

'That's okay sir. Now, please, can you tell me their names and address, and perhaps a brief description age, height, et cetera?'

Pat gave him the details.

'Thank you, Mr Monaghan. Now, can I ask you, is there any reason why you should think this might be one of your friends?'

'Well, er… no. It's just that it's near where they live and… I was worried, because I haven't heard from them and can't get them on the phone.'

'I see. Well, I can tell you sir, that as yet there has been no formal iden-tification of the deceased, but the investigation is ongoing and we will undoubtedly be doing a house to house request for information in that area. I'm afraid that's all I can tell you at this stage. Hopefully, we'll have no need to contact you again and that you will hear from your friends very soon.'

Pat hung up, none the wiser and even more worried.

The doorbell was ringing. Before it had been the phone; it had rung twice, once to wake her and then again later when she was in the shower. She had got there too late on both occasions. The silhouette behind the glass of the front door seemed to be that of a policeman. She opened the door with the chain still attached and gingerly looked out.

'Afternoon, Miss, I'm Sergeant Wallis of the Metropolitan Police, this is my colleague, Detective Inspector Blanchard.' The uniformed policeman's plain-clothed colleague held out identification. 'We're investigating a seri-ous crime in the area and are asking assistance from the public. May we ask you some questions?'

'Oh, yes, just a moment.' She closed the door, removed the chain and reopened it.

'Sorry, to disturb you.'

'No, it's okay,' she said, self-consciously pulling the belt tighter on her dressing gown and running a hand through her hair.

'Do you live here alone?' asked the Detective Inspector as they entered.

'Er... no. My friend's...' She gestured behind her down the passage.

'Is the other young lady at home?' he asked, as they followed her into the lounge.

'Er... actually I'm not sure, maybe... I haven't checked... What... is it you're investigating?'

The two policemen glanced at each other before the Detective an-swered, 'We're investigating the suspicious death of a young wom-an.' She inhaled sharply and shuddered. The policemen waited a few moments observing her reaction. 'Can you just check if your flatmate is here?'

'Oh pleasssss no!' she cried out in trepidation and went to check the other bedroom. 'She's not there!' she cried, returning to the lounge to look around the room. 'I... I don't see...'

'We don't as yet know the identity of the young lady. Would you happen to have somewhere a photograph of your flatmate?'

She thought for a moment, then rose unsteadily to go back to her bedroom, returning a few minutes later with a photograph clutched to her breast, afraid to let go, afraid of the outcome.

'May we see it... please?' asked the uniformed policeman gently. She handed it over grudgingly. Both looked at it, then at each other.

'W... we... well?' she pleaded.

'There would have to be a formal identification... before I could say...'

'It's her... it's her, isn't it?'

The uniformed policeman moved forward to comfort her as he nodded. 'It matches the description but...'

'Ohhhhhh no, no, no no, no!' And she crumbled in a heap on the sofa.

'Call for a WPC!' the DI ordered his constable.

Chapter Forty-four

While waiting in his office for Ellis and Nidditch, Pellzer tried to assess where they now stood with what was becoming a huge damage limitation exercise. Since Walker had informed him that a girl, said to have died in suspicious circumstances in West London, had been identified as Penny Irwin, the Chica who'd accused Morg of rape, Pellzer had been meeting with everyone who might conceivably be asked questions by either the police or the press, to agree on the best approach.

Meanwhile, Walker used his contacts in the Met to find out what was known so far about the girl's death. What he'd found out was that the police, following the pathologist's report, were treating her death as an unlawful killing and that the estimated time of death had been between midnight and 2am on Thursday. The case had been referred to the coroner, who would suspend the inquest until an autopsy had been done and the police had made further enquiries.

More disturbing news was that the police had already taken a statement from the dead girl's flatmate, the Chica from reception, Elena Spencer. Undoubtedly, in recounting her friend's recent history, Spencer would have mentioned the alleged rape, and certainly would have told them that Prince Talal, Ventura's biggest player, was the girl's recent lover. The only crumb of comfort was Sid's observation that the police, at this stage of the investigation, would have advised Spencer that she should not to talk to the press.

But by far the biggest worry of all was the man, whose action justified most of this concern, Morgan Trist. When the news came through, Pellzer found him in the apartment above, not yet fully recovered from his previous night's activities. In his befuddled condition, the immediate implications of the investigation and publicity which would follow the Chica's death seemed to escape him. Pellzer hoped his initial reponse – 'That'll keep the bitch quiet' – wouldn't be repeated and, as the day wore on, he would see the enormous danger to Ventura in all of this.

The Managing Director was in no doubt, and Walker agreed, that they would soon be visited by the police, if only to establish certain facts. It was therefore of utmost importance that Morg get himself together and though Pellzer's first instinct had been to get him out of the building, on balance it seemed more prudent to keep him within reach. Pellzer was pleased to learn that Tony Salinas, who'd been with Trist when the girl had supposedly been violated, was in Los Angeles. As a precaution, he called to inform him of the development, suggesting he cancel any impending trip to London for the time being.

An agreement on a unified approach towards police and the media was complicated by the fact that not all senior figures within the company had the same knowledge of that particular incident, nor other matters that might come to the fore in the glare of publicity that would surround the Chica's death. Rye knew most, probably more than Pellzer himself; Walker and Woods less; Bollard a little and Mayfield probably nothing. Pellzer preferred to keep it that way. Although time-consuming, he would meet them separately, starting with Ellis and Nidditch.

'Well, isn't this a fucking shock, Dan!' Ellis said, as he entered the office, closely followed by his colleague.

'Hi, guys. Yeah, this is really gonna put the spotlight on us for some time. So I thought we'd better review what we know so far, and how we're gonna treat the rumours and shit that's gonna fly.' Pellzer offered them a seat.

He briefed them first on Walker's information.

'So they don't yet know how she was killed, or who did it?' asked Nidditch when he'd finished.

'They may have an idea how, but Sid reckons they won't say until after the autopsy,' answered Pellzer. 'He also says the signs are, they don't have a definite suspect. But they've already talked to our favourite militant Elena, so she's no doubt put Morg and Talal in the frame. Whichever way, we're gonna get some unwanted attention.'

'What about this ex-boyfriend who made a fuckin' scene in here?' suggested Nidditch.

'Sure, they'll look at him as well,' agreed Pellzer.

'That could be another fucking problem because Ahmed put him on to her again, to piss off Talal. Said he did it through somebody else, but if the police start digging…?' Ellis added.

'You're right. You seen or heard anything from Ahmed, or Talal?' asked Pellzer.

'No, I tried earlier but couldn't get them,' Ellis answered.

'I couldn't get Ahmed either. If you hear from him or Talal, I want to speak with them. Meanwhile, I don't need to tell you guys, we don't want anybody talkin' to the press. Anyone snooping around, they're to be referred to me. Loose talk could mean loss of business and jobs, remind everybody. The police is a different matter, they'll come officially and maybe Sid will get wind before they arrive,' said Pellzer

'The one likely to be the biggest problem we've no control over and as you say she'll have already spouted her mouth off,' intervened Nidditch.

'One other problem,' Pellzer addressed Ellis, 'is our PR guy Monaghan – he hasn't turned up for work. He also has knowledge that in the wrong hands could cause difficulties. I don't know what your relationship is, but maybe you could give him a call. Convey sympathy or something, what d'ya think, Jim?'

Ellis thought about it, then nodded, 'I'll see what I can do.'

At that moment someone else was calling Pat Monaghan. The Detective Sergeant paused to allow him to go to the phone but had almost to prod the dejected Pat to get him there.

'Oh, yes… er… hello, Ian.' Monaghan stumbled over the words. 'I… I don't know, Jesus… I'm sorry.' He paused, nodding as he listened.

'I… er… I don't know where she is, but I know she's okay. Well not exactly okay… but she talked to the police…' Pat suddenly remembered the detective was in the room and looked round. The man was certainly taking an interest, 'Okay, Ian, if I find out I'll call you… yes, bye.'

Pat, his mind in turmoil, couldn't think why Lowe would want at this time to talk to Elena but dismissed it from his mind to return to the officer's questions.

'May I ask you, sir, who that was?' asked the detective.

'Oh, a friend, an ex-colleague at Ventura, Ian Lowe, he now works with the Ladbrokes Company. He's heard about Penny… and was asking about Elena Spencer,' answered Pat as he slumped back in his chair.

'I see.' The policeman took some notes. 'He had no special connection with the deceased?'

'No, just an ex-workmate of Pen…' Pat gulped back the tears. The policeman nodded sympathetically.

Before leaving, the Detective Sergeant went over the notes he'd taken to verify their accuracy and see if Pat wanted to add anything. When he'd gone, Pat returned to his thoughts which were only slightly less confused than they'd been earlier. One thing was clear: he could not now remain at Ventura. But the decision as to where he'd go and what he'd do he postponed for another day. It all seemed so unimportant now.

The response from staff at Talal's residences, that he was out of the country, was on balance good news. Pellzer wasn't sure if the Prince's trip had been prompted by the events or his absence was a convenient coincidence. Whatever the reason, it was certainly preferable, both from his own and from Ventura's point of view, that he avoid police questions and the inevitable explosion of press interest. Ahmed's absence was a bit more puzzling, his daily routine being fairly predictable. For those who did business with him, he provided several telephone numbers where he might be reached at various times of the day. However, no one at those numbers had seen or heard from him.

Pellzer pushed that to the back of his mind on hearing Walker in the outer office. As feared, the police had interviewed both Morgan and Marta Woods. Walker had used his ex-Met credentials to enable him to be present during both interviews and had now come to make his report on those proceedings.

'Right, Dan, the lads are still here. I've left them downstairs, invited them to a bite and a cuppa, but don't like to leave'em long on their own. Anyway, the situation's like this...' Walker took out a notebook. Pellzer got the distinct impression he was enjoying the drama and the chance to play cop again.

'They interviewed Marta first, to establish the facts about the deceased's employment here and ask for her file. Here, I've got to say, Personnel made a bit of a cock-up. There's no mention on her file of the problem at the party or the meeting. I know we didn't want to give credence to the accusation, but they're major incidents in her employment history. To not enter anything's a bit sus.'

'So they asked about it?'

'Well, not in so many words, but from their line of questioning with her and Morgan... and later, in a little chat I had with them, I gleaned that our union friend told them her version.'

Pellzer grimaced. 'So, what did they ask Morg?'

'The D.I. asked him if he knew the deceased, to which he answered that he made a point of meeting all staff. Actually his statement concerning the girl was...' here Walker began to read from his notes– '... *Although we didn't know it when we employed her, this poor girl seemed to have some psychological problem. She was invited to attend a cocktail party, which we hold from time to time for promotional purposes. There were some famous people, she had too much to drink and it all became a bit much for her. I myself had to help her out of the party then get our Personnel Manager to look after her and get her home. Later she made outrageous allegations about several people including myself. None of it official. Against our better judgement we let her to return to work but the poor girl had further problems with boyfriends, one of whom we had to eject from the club after an unpleasant scene. There were also rumours that she was seeing at least one of the members outside, something which is strictly against company rules. Just before this tragic incident she had actually given in her notice. We were relieved, because there seemed to be no end to the poor girl's emotional problems.*'

Walker closed his notebook. 'Anyway,' he continued, 'Morgan added that the Personel Department could give them details of the girl's work record and information about the boyfriend who was ejected. They confirmed Marta had given them this information. Morgan was then asked if he could give any details about her relationship with a client of Ventura. He said he wouldn't like to say because it was rumour and he couldn't verify it. They didn't press this point. That was it. They thanked Morg for his and his company's cooperation and I took them downstairs.'

'So where do you think they are with the investigation?' asked Pellzer.

'Well, I had a quiet word with them, and my contact at HQ. It seems the autopsy will confirm the girl died as a consequence of several blows to the head. There were no indications of sexual assault nor were articles of clothing removed. However, some personal items are missing and she may have put up some resistance...'

'Does that mean it looks to the police like a mugging?' interrupted Pellzer.

'Well, they'll consider that, but also they won't discount the possibility that someone wants it to look like a mugging and—'

Pellzer interrupted again. 'Okay, where do we stand with all this?'

'Well Morg, I think, handled it well, considering that bitch Elena put him in the frame. Marta, apart from the cock-up with the file, was a bit nervy and too eager to answer questions they hadn't asked. I gave her a little help here and there but on the whole it went okay,' said Walker.

'But, are they gonna make a thing about this rape allegation or be snoopin' around to ask about Talal?'

'The girl never made any formal complaint or accusation and she returned to work here... but of course they're going to look at anything that might point to motive. Talal's name has been mentioned so they'll look at him. But I'd think her former boyfriend will be their next port of call.'

'Our urgent problem's the press, when they get their teeth into this, there's no telling where it could end.' Pellzer rubbed the back of his neck.

Walker raised his burly frame with a groan. 'Yes, that's a major worry. Anyway, I'd better get down to the lads, make sure they get a proper send-off.'

Chapter Forty-five

Even in the safe-haven of the family home with the loving attention of her parents and sister, Elena was only slowly emerging from the anguish that had taken over her entire mind and body. Several days before, the WPC, seeing the effect the shattering news was having on her, had persisted until Elena gave her a number of someone who could offer support. The policewoman then personally called her mother to enlist help. It was a wise decision; Elena couldn't have coped alone over these last few days.

Although mindful of her distressed condition, the police had interviewed her several times during this period. She remembered they'd asked her questions but had no idea if what she'd told them would help catch the person who'd killed her friend. This thought prompted the entry of another emotion to join her grief and guilt: anger. But while there was obvious focus for both grief and guilt, channelling her anger was somewhat more complicated. For one thing, she didn't know who had committed this hideous crime. Could it conceivably have been conspired by Trist, or had Penny somehow provoked or embarrassed Talal or his family into committing this outrage? The frightening calls from her jealous and heavy-drinking ex-boyfriend seemed to place him as prime suspect and this probability reinforced Elena's feeling of guilt. Why, when she knew he'd found out where Penny was living, had she allowed her to go home on her own? Why hadn't she warned her that he'd tracked her down and pressed her to call the police, instead of telling only Pat?

Pat. What must he be thinking or doing now? Pat, who'd first called on her to help the poor, beautiful, tragic Penny. The tears welled up in her eyes again. Her mum and her sister Sarah, cleaning up in the kitchen around her, hadn't dropped their guard and moved swiftly to engage her in restorative conversation. But Elena wasn't listening to their comments; her need to make contact with Pat, the one person who'd shared their friendship, had become urgent.

She rose purposefully, picked up the phone but couldn't recall his number. Her private address book was still at the apartment and the thought of returning there, however briefly, to be confronted everywhere with remembrances of her friend brought on another emotional crisis.

'Elena, what's wrong, who did you want to call?' asked her sister.

'I wanted to… it doesn't matter.' She slumped back in her seat.

'Yes it does. Let me help you. Who is it?'

Her mother now took her hand, 'Who is it dear, let Sarah get the number for you.'

'It was my… our friend Pat, Pat Monaghan, but his number's over… there,' she said tearfully.

'Maybe it's in the book.' Sarah snatched up the telephone directory. 'Or I'll get it through enquiries. If not I'll go over and get it, and whatever else you want from there.'

'That's a good idea, you go and get all her stuff from that place. Dad'll drive you over,' said their mum, only too keen to bring to an end Elena's association with that flat.

The call was most welcome if upsetting. When he answered, after a long pause Elena spoke, then seemed to lose her way before a voice, which turned out to be her sister's, took over. Sarah didn't elaborate, saying only that Elena had been extremely distressed but would be very pleased if he could pay her a visit at her parents' house. He assured her he would and took note of the address.

To fulfil his promise he should now have called Ian Lowe, who'd phoned no less than five times during the last few days. However, under the circumstances, Pat couldn't presume Elena felt the same urgency to make contact with Ian, so he decided to keep her whereabouts to himself for the time being. Nor would he inform the others, including the members of the Ventura Union Committee, who had individually called seeking news of Elena's welfare and where she might be located. Then there were the calls from the personnel department.

The calls were not just about Elena, although everyone asked about her. Ellis made contact to commiserate with him on the loss of his friend -'a lovely girl' - and asked how he was bearing up after 'this fuckin'awful crime' and of course, how Elena was taking it. He suggested they go for a pint but Pat postponed it for another time.

Bollard, when he called, assured Pat that he was free to take the time off he needed, but suggested that being at work with friends around him might also help. Pat thanked him but made no commitment. He'd decided he wanted the solace and tranquillity of home, but the telephone hadn't stopped ringing - though in a way, the calls and his anticipation of them had given him something on which to focus his mind; a duty, to be available when she eventually made contact.

He patted down his hair, pulled on a jerkin, lifted the note with her address. As he made for the door he could hear the phone again, but he could now ignore it.

Pat rang the doorbell of the smart semi-detached house and an attractive middle-aged woman opened the door.

'Ah hello, I'm Pat Monaghan.'

'Hello Pat, I'm Elena's mother, we're so pleased to see you,' she said ushering him in, 'and pleased she finally wants to speak to somebody after this terrible, terrible business. She's been in a dreadful state and still is. Nice of you to come so quickly. It must have been an awful shock for you too. Elena told me you were all friends?'

'Yes, I... I'm not sure if I'll be much comfort. I haven't really come to terms with it either, but...'

'No, of course you haven't, who could? But it's enough that you're here,' she said, showing him in to the sitting-room, 'This is Elena's sister Sarah, who spoke to you on the phone.'

Sarah stepped forward, smiling. 'Hi, Pat, great you could come. Elena's upstairs, I'll get her... or maybe you should go up yourself?' she said, looking at her mum for agreement.

'Yes, good idea. You two might find it easier to deal with this on you own at first. What do you think?'

'Er... yes... I think that might be best.' Pat followed Sarah.

'Good. Sarah can bring some tea in a while or, when Elena's Dad comes, maybe you'll join us for a bite,' Mrs Spencer said eagerly, so obviously hopeful that a step on her daughter's road to recovery could finally be taken.

Upstairs, Elena stood to face him as he entered her bedroom and he thought he caught a momentary flicker of happiness before her lip quivered. The resolve they'd both practised disappeared as they interlocked in a trembling, sobbing clinch. Pat attempted to regain control and searched with one hand for something to wipe the tears and mucous from his face.

'My God, Pat! Do you know, I must have passed her lying there... I walked past the very spot! When I came in I didn't check if she was there, I just assumed she was home and went to bed! How... why did I let it happen... why did I let her...?'

He was becoming aware of the main focus of her despair. Her anguished cries had a recurring theme. 'Why did I let her come home herself...? I knew she wasn't safe... I should have told her... I should have known...!'

Pat understood guilt, he himself had felt some, but this was disproportionate.

'Please, Elena, listen, you must stop this, it wasn't you're fault...'

'I brought her to that awful area... I let her go home alone... I should...'

'Stop it! For fuck sakes, stop it!' he shouted, grabbing her shoulders. 'This was the work of some bastard! It wasn't your fault. You're letting Penny down by taking the blame instead of helping to pin the blame on the right one. She wouldn't want you to be like this, she always looked to you for strength. A lot of people do. You have to continue to fight. D'you hear?'

The violence of his reaction shocked her into a momentary silence. It shocked him too. But seeing some positive effect, he continued cajoling, though in a quieter, more gentle tone.

'Pat, I know what you're saying but I can't help feeling that if I had...'

'Stop! You couldn't possibly imagine anybody doing a thing like this. You're not guilty. The guilty party's the bloody bastard who did this!'

She was silent. Some of what Pat had been saying was beginning to register. She'd allowed the murder of her friend, and the search for the perpetrator, to be overshadowed by her own personal guilt. So much so that she wasn't even sure where the police were with the investigation.

'Do they... have the police... found out anything new?' she asked, trying to adhere to Pat's advice.

'Well, they've got what you and I told them,' said Pat. 'They've been to Ventura and, I'm told, interviewed Woods and Trist. Talal seems to have been out of the country. It said in the paper they've questioned her ex-boyfriend. But nobody's been arrested.'

'I'm sorry, I haven't even followed the news. I...' She began to lose her way again, but held up her hand to indicate she was collecting herself. Pat waited; she began again. 'I should find out if there's something more I can tell them.'

He was relieved to hear some of her old resolve. They both sat quietly on the edge of the bed for a few moments before she spoke again. 'You know... I don't even know how... how she died... or anything.' She choked back tears. He waited, encouraged by the fact that she was now fighting the emotions. 'What do the police... the papers say?'

Pat wasn't sure if she was ready to discuss the known circumstances and details of Penny's death. He wasn't even sure if he could. During the last few days he had accumulated information from TV and radio and some of his callers had contributed snippets of news, but he'd evaded discussion with them on what might have taken place that dreadful night.

'Ah well, the... er... evidence doesn't seem to point to anybody in particular.'

He would have been happy to leave it there but after a few seconds thought, Elena returned. 'What were the circumstances?'

The pain was still visible in her eyes but her teeth were making indentations on her lower lip, a visible sign of determination to control her emotions. It seemed he couldn't avoid the subject.

'The report said she was... struck several times about the head... and seemed to have made some attempt either to protect herself or her belongings. She died of a massive brain haemorrhage. She had no jewellery, purse, handbag or money, or even the car keys. So they think the motive was robbery... unless someone wanted it to look like robbery.'

'Oh my God! Could it really be just some robber? I should've moved out of that area, my mum always said I should...'

'Elena, you're starting again!'

'Yes, but the police... I can't remember what I told them.'

'Was anyone with you when you spoke to them?' asked Pat

'I don't think... but when they came here, my mother and maybe Sarah...'

'Let's check with them, then if you think of something else that might help we'll call them,' said Pat, eager to maintain her progress.

She seemed to be considering this. 'You're right, let's do that.'

From then on, her determination to find something that could aid the investigation may have helped Elena come to terms with her guilt and grief; it certainly cheered Pat and her family to see her return to somewhere near her old self. But in reality it brought the police no nearer to a breakthrough. Acting on the information received from Elena, Monaghan and others, the crime team had pursued several lines of enquiry.

The post mortem ruled out any sexual element to the attack and though undoubtedly violent, the crime-scene and forensic investigation detected no telltale signs of an act of passion. The motive appeared to be robbery.

Aware that opportunist attackers often quickly discard things which they cannot convert to cash or use personally, the police made an extensive search of the surrounding area. None of the items listed by Elena as missing, and assumed to have been taken during the attack, were found. These included Elena's Salaminder bag, its contents and the car and apartment keys. As the keys had apparently not been used to enter the car or apartment, they would have been items of no value to a random attacker. The bag would've been of nominal value only and its contents, or at least those that Elena knew of, would likewise have been of little use to a robber ignorant of their significance. The objects of value Penny had been carrying or wearing, such as two rings (one a diamond given to her by Prince Talal) and a watch, would've given the thief the kind of reward he was looking for, but also something the CID could work on through their contacts in the clandestine market. Her purse probably had contained some money but this was the least traceable.

The investigating officers didn't entirely discount the possibility of theft being a tactic to conceal the true motive. They interviewed Martin Atkinson, Penny's ex-boyfriend, several times, following verification that he'd been threatening and abusive towards her at the Ventura and had tried several times to make telephone contact with her at Elena's apartment, in spite of being told that she did not want his attention. One question put to him remained unsatisfactorily explained – who had given him her addresses and telephone numbers? He said he'd obtained the information from a person called Eric, whom he'd met in his local pub, and who'd claimed to have worked with her. He could provide no further information on this individual nor could anyone else. In spite of this loose end, and his previous pattern of behaviour, no incriminating objects were found in a search of his apartment and no evidence had been found at the crime scene to link him to the murder.

The continued absence from the country of Prince Mansur Talal was also viewed initially as suspicious. But being a first born heir to a Muslim fiefdom, his and his family's desire to escape the inevitable publicity which surrounded the death of a girl who worked in a casino, and with whom he was said to be having an affair, was not very surprising. Representatives of his family invoked the privilege accorded to him as a registered diplomat to avoid the embarrassment of police interviews in the UK, which in turn would provoke more press speculation. But an interview was arranged with him and his representatives in Spain where senior CID officials were able to verify some facts. No evidence, except for his reported affair with the deceased, pointed to him as a serious suspect.

During the early days of the investigation, the police had jealously guarded their information and the media honoured this unofficial period of grace. Only police statements and confirmed facts were reported, but when no arrest seemed imminent, the prospect of a story on the death of a glamorous Ventura Chica, said to be the lover of a handsome oil-rich Sheik, was too much of a temptation even for the more serious reporters. By the time the coroner, to the relief of her parents, had released Penny Irwin's body for burial, all the unseemly slants that could possibly be put on the story had begun to appear.

At the funeral, the anguish and guilt of parents who'd never fully understood their daughter was all too visible, and Elena Spencer and Pat Monaghan were the only representitives of her recent life who could offer them the comfort of a positive image. Fortunately Monaghan, after consultation with Mr Irwin, had managed to dissuade the Ventura from sending Marta Woods or any of her assistants as company representative to the funeral. As it was, a few unwanted guests still turned up - several reporters.

Pellzer looked on developments with increasing concern. Though no formal complaint of sexual assault had ever been made by the deceased girl, the CID were able to question Trist on this matter because several people confirmed that the girl, at a meeting in Grosvenor House, had made a highly public allegation and the events of that meeting had appeared in newspapers.

The position taken up by Ventura's lawyer was that the girl had been emotionally troubled, having had several unsuccessful affairs. The statement also pointed out that though many people were present at the party on the night of the supposed assault, none had reported anything untoward. Her continued employment at Ventura even after the supposed violation was also cited.

Throughout this period, Sid Walker used his contacts within the force to keep Pellzer apprised of the progress of the investigation and give him time to formulate responses, not only to the CID but also to the media. But the press's voracious appetite for anything vaguely connected with the murdered girl was uncovering all kinds of information about Ventura, its Directors, employees and customers that were beginning to damage business. Publicity-shy Muslim clients and business people who preferred to avoid questions about their social habits began to avoid a club that seemed to be constantly in the news for the wrong reasons. Competitors, encouraged by the effect this was having on an aggressive rival, fuelled speculation and called for the authorities to investigate Ventura's business methods.

As weeks turned to months, the police investigation ran out of steam and became another on the unsolved crime file. Not so the Ventura story; new titbits emerged daily. It seemed that the person who had taken Penny Irwin's life had indirectly threatened the life of The Ventura itself.

Chapter Forty-six

2006

Pat's reintroduction to the casino world had been therapeutic, not least because the Europa Club was vastly different from his recollection of the Ventura. Not only in the obvious architectural changes but more importantly in the way it was managed. Draper had given him a complete briefing on the corporate as well as the operational structure of the company. He'd been only too happy to highlight the contrasts between the responsible and transparent policies of the building's new tenants and the corrupt shenanigans of the people they had worked for many years before. It was also refreshing to hear that people who Pat had liked and trusted in those earlier traumatic years had in the end prospered. He wanted to believe that this would also be the case with Elena, whose name had come up several times, but of that he could not be sure.

However, something that Draper had mentioned in passing gave him an idea – he'd said that he'd made contact with a former colleague through the website Friends Re-united. Pat was doubtful if Elena would communicate with ex-Ventura colleagues through this medium but, having studied at university, there was an outside chance she'd maintained contact with student contemporaries.

Two days later, he checked his inbox to find, along with normal business-related mail, a response to his probe.

This is a message from Elena Spencer – email: espencer@aol.co.uk who is contacting you through http://www.friendsreunited.co.uk

The message is as follows:–

'Dear Pat, a brilliant piece of sleuthing. So pleased to hear from you, please call me at 0161 650 2365. Love, Elena

'Is it me darlin' Elena?' he asked when she picked up the phone.

'Pat, how wonderful!' she said excitedly. 'Where have you been for so long? I can't believe we lost touch!'

'I don't know, the time just seemed to go by. I kept saying I'd get in touch but when I tried, you'd moved and so had your family.'

'Yes, I've been in Manchester for some time now and Mum moved when my father died a few years back.'

'Oh, I'm sorry to hear about your father. Are your mother and sister well?'

'Thank you. Yes, they're both well. My sister's married and living in Canada.'

'And you, Elena, you married?'

'Afraid not, same old me, scared off every man I've ever met. And you?'

'No, I've managed to fight off all those women pestering me for a ring,' he said with mock seriousness. Elena laughed.

'Oh, so neither of us have changed, at least not in that sense. So where are you, Pat, what're you doing?

'London at the moment, though next week I'm off to Spain for a few days to complete a contract. After that, a new job back in London.' He didn't at this stage want to tell her where. 'And you?'

'Well, I went back to study and now I'm doing what I said I'd never do when I left uni – I teach.' Her tone sounded like resignation.

'What's wrong with that? That's great! What're you teaching?'

'Special needs. Teaching teachers to teach to special-needs children.'

'That sounds like you - something worthwhile, helping people.'

'Just hiding from the real world,' she replied. 'Anyway, will we get the chance to meet?'

'That would be great, will I come up there?'

'You're welcome to, but I'm thinking to go to London to see my mother at the weekend, we could meet if you're still around?'

Pat happily agreed on Saturday. Neither wanted to explain feelings or motivations on the limited medium of the telephone. That could keep for the weekend.

The initial embrace and preliminary greetings over, Elena began to take a closer look at her old friend. The years had taken no toll on Pat Monaghan, he looked the same, if not better . Slim figure, slightly fuller in the face, a complete head of grey-speckled, close-cropped hair, the same easygoing manner and winning smile. Perhaps a little more self-assured, she thought, but that was no bad thing. She feared that in spite of taking a little more care with her appearance than usual, his appraisal of her couldn't, in all honesty, be as generous.

She wasn't entirely right. Pat saw a more mature woman but the attractive features of the girl he'd worked with remained. There was, however, a weariness about her.

'So, you were telling me about your teaching?' Pat was still steering clear of a painful subject.

'Yes, I went back to university not really knowing what I wanted to do. I'd a vague idea that I'd follow an academic career. Instead, I've moved into lecturing on special needs teaching,' she said, without much enthusiasm.

'That's essential work, no?' Pat said, eager to endorse her lifestyle choice.

'I'm not even sure I agree with the received wisdom I'm putting across. I sometimes wonder if I'm doing any good at all.'

'Well, you're trying to do good, that's something in itself.'

'Yes, it doesn't matter if I actually do good, I salve my conscience with what they call "conspicuous compassion", a need to be seen doing the right thing.'

'Ah no, I don't think you've ever worried about what other people think.' Pat was disconcerted by her tone.

'You're right, it's not other people, it's the inner voice.'

'You've nothing to reproach yourself about, I'm sure.' Pat knew he couldn't avoid the subject. 'You're not still with this guilt thing about Penny, I hope?'

She fell silent and didn't answer for some time. Then: 'I… I'm not sure. I know I didn't kill her. But if at least the bastard had been caught I might've had what psychologists call "closure". I was confused, tried to hide away in academia, somehow equating her death with the evils of capitalism.'

'Oh, so I'd better not tell you about my business plan!' Pat attempted to lighten the proceedings.

'Don't worry, the revolutionary fervour's passed. I know it's not the system, it's man's corruption of it.'

'I hope you don't mean this man?' He tried to tease out a smile and only just succeeded.

'Relax, I haven't given up on all men, even if they've given up on me,' she said in a slightly more relaxed tone.

'That's not right either. These academic types you're mixing with have their heads too often in books to notice an attractive woman.'

This time she smiled. 'Pat, you've still got the blarney, but it's the same old story, I scare guys off.'

'Well, don't be scaring the waiter off, he's just about to show us to our table,' said Pat, seeing the approach of the maitre'd.

In his desire not to cause embarrassment and complicate their renewed friendship, Pat had given Elena a quick goodnight peck, dropped her off at her mother's house and continued home in the same taxi. Now, the morning after, as he replayed their conversation of that journey home, he feared he'd misread the signals and had not only lost out on an all too infrequent opportunity, but had possibly reinforced Elena's opinion that she was no longer attractive to men.

He couldn't, in all truth, say the entire night had been enjoyable. In one way or another one person still dominated their relationship. Much as he tried to divert the subject to happier themes, something - such as Pat's disclosure that he'd accepted a position at Europa Casino, the previous site of Ventura - always brought them back to the short tragic life and death of Penny Irwin.

'Closure' was a word Elena had used several times and both of them had sought it in different ways without complete success. When it had become painfully obvious that the police investigation was grinding to an unsatisfactory halt, Pat had looked to make a complete break from his surroundings; a new start.

At that same point, as she painfully related over dinner, Elena had looked to exact some form of retribution by fuelling media interest in irregularities at Ventura, hoping to provoke an investigation by the authorities. As she herself confirmed, her actual part in the eventual downfall of Trist and his corrupt band was less than it appeared because behind the scenes enemies, both external and internal, had already initiated this campaign. In fact, Pellzer's desperation to separate himself from the adverse publicity surrounding his colleague brought about an internal feud which had accelerated and ensured their downfall.

But as Pat could see, the justice of their eventual demise in no way alleviated the pain for Elena. Quite the opposite. The salacious material fabricated by some of the press and the distortion of facts by Trist and his supporters had tarnished Penny's name, making the injustice all the more acute.

For Charles Irwin, Penny's father – inconsolable since her death and tormented by, what he considered his own neglect of their relationship while she lived – the denigration of his beautiful deceased daughter was more than he could take. He was dead within two years of her passing, leaving his wife to pass her remaining years supported by alcohol. Elena added their suffering to her sum of responsibilities.

Pat, to be honest with himself, could have done without hearing all this. It saddened him to see the young, capable, confident woman he'd once called on to help in a crisis become a casualty of events catalysed by that first encounter. He listened, hoping that by acting as a sounding board he might enable Elena to wash some of the lingering bitterness out of her system. But he feared he'd revived suppressed memories and renewed feelings of anger and frustration . Now he couldn't leave her with this residual guilt. An informal arrangement he'd made to call her again had become an imperative.

Setting aside the thought that his old and possibly reawakened romantic interest in her might also be a motivating factor, he called her to propose a rendezvous.

The restaurant was chosen to be far away from any of the places that might trigger unpleasant memories. Pat wasn't sure why, because their very coming together was enough to do this, and if he was to restore some of the vigour and enthusiasm he had once seen in her, the past would have to be faced. He lingered over their greeting and was consciously more tactile as he led her to their table. Almost before they were settled, she opened the conversation.

'Pat, when you were talking about victims of Ventura…' He nodded attentively. 'You mentioned Carmen - why her?'

'Ah yes, I was going to tell you about that. I wasn't sure if you knew, but apparently she's in a terrible mess with drugs.'

'My God, no. I didn't hear that.'

'It seems, though not many knew about it, she was one of Ahmed's girls. Even during her time on your committee.'

'For God's sake, you're joking!'

'I'm afraid that's what I heard. He apparently got her hooked on drugs. She left Ventura for Spain to turn tricks for his clients there, but got so messed up, he dropped her. She's been in prison and drug centres; a real mess, it seems.'

'That's incredible, it's terrible… Who told you all this?'

'I told you I met Ian Lowe, didn't I?' She nodded with a faint smile. 'Roland, who works with him, heard it from Chris Russell, who's out in Spain.'

Elena was now once again in deep troubled thought and Pat feared he was about to spend another night trying to bring her out of it.

'Anyway, you were wise to leave Lowesey alone and wait for me, he's getting a bit bald and putting on weight. Not the pop idol he once was.' Pat hoped a bit of levity might change the mood, but Elena didn't respond. 'Come-on, let's order something, a drink at least.' He took up the menu and pushed the other towards her.

'If that's true,' she said suddenly, 'Carmen would've been feeding him information about us all the time.'

'Well I suppose so but it's all water under the bridge, in the past and can't be changed. How's your mother, she well?'

Elena looked distracted but eventually answered, 'Yes, thank you. She was asking about you and happy to hear we were in touch again.'

'I'm very happy too, I don't know why I left it so long,' he said, and before she could slip into meditative mood again, he added, 'Come on, let's have champagne!'

'Oh, what are we celebrating?'

'What about... being together again?'

She seemed to think about this, then smiled. 'Yes, you're absolutely right, Pat.'

Not to make the mistake of the previous night, he directed the taxi to his apartment and invited her in; after only momentary hesitation, she agreed. Was this confirmation that he'd misread the signals the night before, or that she'd simply consumed more wine. He hoped it was the former.

It was already almost eight o'clock, she was still sound asleep and he was wide awake, so he slid out of bed grabbed his discarded clothes and stepped gingerly through to the kitchen. The night had gone well in spite of a shaky start. However, he was still having to work hard to get her to focus more on the present and future.

He was on his second mug of coffee when she emerged, wrapped in a bath-towel, and said 'Hi,' with a sheepish grin.

'Hello, me darlin', you slept well?' Pat rose to kiss her.

She responded happily, to the kiss and the question. 'Yes, and it wasn't just the alcohol. You'll remember you once asked for a reference; well, I'm about to upgrade it,' she said, smiling girlishly.

'Ah great! I haven't had much practice and was forgetting how,' he laughed and went to get her some coffee.

'Yes, I also did it from memory.' She came up to give him another affectionate kiss on the back of the neck.

After breakfast they visited her mother, who looked sprightly considering her advancing years. There was little doubt that she looked upon Pat's reappearance – unmarried, she quickly established – as her daughter's last chance and, to Elena's embarrassment and Pat's amusement, proceeded to list her daughter's strong points.

When they left the old woman, with a promise from Pat to return soon, Elena seemed preoccupied once again. He wasn't sure if it was her mother's obsession with her unmarried status that had silenced her, or the perennial subject. It didn't take long for him to find out.

'I've been thinking about Carmen,' Elena said suddenly. 'All through that Union period she was working for Ahmed, you say?'

'So they say.'

'And telling him everything we decided, everything we said… he no doubt was telling Trist and the others.'

'I suppose so. No doubt that had an influence on the union campaign, they were always one step ahead,' said Pat.

'That may be the least of it…' She looked grave.

'Well the poor bitch hasn't gained anything from it, that's for sure.'

'I told her… and I repeated it… the night Penny was killed,' Elena said slowly and deliberately, 'that I had material to charge Trist with rape and information about illegal credit.'

Pat wasn't sure what conclusion she was drawing and feared she was just regurgitating old material. 'Yes, but with that information they would've been more likely to attack you.'

'Except… she was carrying the bag that Carmen knew contained the material. She was driving my car… going to my apartment!'

'Come on! Now you're going to take on this,' cried Pat, 'that they mistook her for you!'

'Well, the bag and its contents never turned up… though to a normal mugger they would've been useless. Explain that!'

'Oh, I'm sure lots of things don't turn up… anyway, what can we do now? It's so long ago,' Pat said disconsolately, wishing he could release Elena from this torment. He put his arm round her waist and she snuggled up, inclining her head to rest on his shoulder.

'Sorry to rake all this up again… it's just… I can't help it,' she said quietly.

They were walking to nowhere in particular. He wasn't sure where to go from here with her. But whenever he was in this kind of doubt, he looked for a pub.

Chapter Forty-seven

Pat's visit to Spain had taken on a new focus. The conclusion of his contractual commitments prior to taking up the position at Europa involved a series of meetings in and around the Costa Blanca; but he now found himself driving to an unscheduled meeting with his old colleague Chris Russell in Marbella, having called beforehand to establish he was on duty. As he happened to be in the area, Pat had suggested he would drop in.

A burly, sun-tanned gentleman with a grey-speckled beard, who only just reminded him of the dice manager he'd once known, greeted Pat at the reception.

'Mr PM, what a surprise when you called! A real blast from the past!' Chris extended his hand and smiled broadly.

'Jesus, I didn't recognise you with the beard!' exclaimed Pat.

'Really? It's still me, the one and only Chris Russell.'

'With that beard you look more like a Jack Russell,' said Pat. Russell laughed, and quickly guided him through the registration procedure before passing into the casino. It was early afternoon, not many gamblers were to be seen and the restaurant was only moderately busy.

'So, you're returning to the casino business?' asked Chris as he chose a table while a maitre'd looked on attentively.

'Yes, I'm just over here to conclude previous commitments. And you? Lowesey and Ralph told me you've been here a while.'

'Yes, came here twelve years ago, didn't plan to stay, but they made me Gaming Director and the lifestyle got to me.'

They paused while the waiter took their order. Pat left the choice of wine to his host.

'Any other old faces down these parts?' Pat asked casually.

'Oh, a few. Andy Tennock who was on the dice crew is one of my Sub Directores, what we called floor managers. Also Amanda Stiles, used to be a dealer on the VIP level, she's training manager. There's probably others dotted around other Spanish Casinos. Then of course there's punters, mostly Arab, who live out here and used to play in London. Don't let me forget the gimp pimp Ahmed, he's unfortunately around some of the time,' Chris said with a look of distaste.

'Yes, I heard he was out here. How does that affect you?'

'Well, he doesn't have the run of the place the way he had at Ventura, but because he's close with some of our bigger players, we have to put up with some of his antics. At least he organises his girls and drugs et cetera outside of here. He's older, and richer, so doesn't put himself about as much as he used to, but he's still fuckin' obnoxious.'

'Talking about girls… Lowesey, who used to go out with her, said Carmen the nightclub Chica was one of his hookers, is that right?'

'Yes, that was her Chica-name, her real name's Linda Pardo. A pathetic case, she's a real junkie. I had her thrown out of here for stealing chips off customers, to feed her habit. She's been nicked by the local Policia several times and almost ODd once in the street. The police asked me what I knew about her; I didn't want to say anything about Ahmed, in case there were repercussions. They put her on rehab programmes several times but Andy saw her street-walking in La Linea recently.'

'So, she still lives locally?'

'Well, La Linea's thirty kilometres from here. Last I heard she was at La Granja, means "the Farm", nickname for a hostel for drug addicts.'

'Terrible! She was one of Ahmed's Chicas, he brought her out here, no?'

'Yes, dropped her like a ton of bricks when she started losing it out here. Apparently, he fed her coke right from the early days at Ventura, and she repaid by servicing his customers and feeding info about other girls, the union and stuff. He put her on to big players, even tried Talal, but he was only interested in Penny. Poor Penny, they never did get anybody for that... I still reckon it was the ex-boyfriend, bit of a fruitcake, wasn't he?'

'I'm not sure. The police seemed to eliminate him,' said Pat, surprised by the connection of Carmen with Talal. 'How do you know Ahmed tried to put Carmen on to Talal?'

'He comes in here. Although he's now top man back in his country, he has a villa here and still likes a punt. He was here one of the nights we had problems with her, and told me about it. His relationship with Ahmed's now pretty strained, to say the least. Actually, he got really emotional at the mention of Penny. I guess he'd a real thing about her,' said Chris, who excused himself momentarily to take a call.

Pat was intrigued and shocked by this information. He wasn't sure if any of it would bring them nearer to knowing why Penny had died or who was responsible, but for Elena's sake he wanted to do something. He just wasn't quite sure what. He certainly didn't want to alert Chris to the fact that he was using him to initiate an investigation. He took the opportunity of this brief interlude to take a note of Carmen's real name while it was fresh in his memory, and a reference to the 'Granja'. This was probably all he needed at this stage. He felt now he should talk about something else before he began to sound obsessed.

The primary purpose of his visit to Spain was beginning to take second place to his detective work. The 'Granja', he found out, was a charity-funded hostel in a poor area of town. The man at the Tourist Information Office, accustomed to giving advice on areas of historic interest, natural beauty and the availability of accommodation, was a little surprised by Pat's interest in this particular residence until he explained he was trying to trace a wayward friend. He exited the office with the address and telephone number of a place which glorified in the name of El Centro Santa Catalina, para el Refugio y Assistencia de Personas con Drogodependencias.

The person who answered the phone at 'La Granja' didn't speak English and, after several minutes listening to the few badly pronounced Spanish words Pat knew, hung up. Pat was trying to find out if Linda Pardo was known to them, though he wasn't quite sure what he'd do with this information. If he made contact with her, what would he ask her? If she had any knowledge about Penny's murder? It seemed unlikely he'd get any kind of helpful response.

Was he being caught up in Elena's conspiracy theories? To Pat the possibility of Penny being the victim of mistaken identity, or of Trist conspiring to have her eliminated, seemed remote. The police had also ruled out the ex-boyfriend Martin and Pat had long ago accepted their contention that, in what was known to be a high crime area, it was most likely to have been a random attacker.

It would be easier to simply tell Elena that Carmen couldn't be found. But Pat was by no means sure that now, having a straw to clutch at again, she'd accept that result.

He decided to have one more try. Using the same story that he was looking for a friend who'd fallen on hard times, he asked the concierge to call the centre on his behalf.

After a few moments of what seemed to be extremely animated conversation, the concierge, still holding the phone, turned to address Pat. 'They say they cannot to geeve information about any person without you present there, weeth your documentation. Then maybe they can help you.'

'But did they seem to know her?'

The man shrugged. 'I not sure… but I theenk maybe.'

Geographically, La Linea was not too far from the more illustrious areas of the Costa del Sol but metaphorically it was in another world. Monaghan parked the car in a street which he calculated to be near to his destination and proceeded on foot through narrow cobbled streets, with voices echoing from the apartments in the crumbling buildings on either side. On a small square where several dark skinned kids were playing football, a group of men outside a dingy bar momentarily suspended their game of dominoes to monitor his progress. On the opposite side of the square stood the unimposing building he had been looking for.

Only now, as he entered and approached the person at the front desk, did he consider the problem of language; stupid, he thought, since he'd already experienced this on the phone.

'Eh… speak English?' he asked hopefully.

'Leetle beet,' responded the man.

'I'm looking for an old work… colleague of mine…'

The man was already shaking his head. 'Moment!' He held up one hand and took up the telephone with the other. After a brief conversation with someone, he indicated to Pat that he should wait. A few moments later a woman in a white doctor's coat appeared.

'Good day, can I help you?'

With relief, Pat introduced himself as a former work colleague of an English lady called Linda Pardo, who he'd been told was attending their centre. He explained that he was shocked to hear of her troubles and thought he might be able to help in some small way. The woman listened attentively and then appeared to be translating Pat's words to the man on reception. After a brief conversation, she addressed Pat once more.

'You call yesterday from La Playa Hotel in Marbella?' Pat confirmed that he had.

'Ah then, please, do you have identification?'

The man and woman both conferred as they took down the details. Their cautious approach accentuated the unease Pat already felt at having given a bogus reason for his interest in Pardo; but nevertheless he held himself in check and waited until they'd satisfied themselves of his identity and photocopied his passport.

The lady now returned. 'Thank you for waiting. Sorry, but we have rules because maybe some… er… wrong people look for our residents. Also, some people who attend are subject to Police… condicional liberty,' she said, returning his passport.

Pat nodded understanding, though none of these disturbing circumstances had previously occurred to him. Nor did it make him feel better to know he was now on public record as a visitor. What complications that might lead to, he didn't yet know. The lady now invited him through to another office.

'I am Doctor Maria Antonia Sallas, Directora of this Centro,' She indicated to Pat to take a seat, 'Can I ask who told you Senora Pardo attended this centre?'

'Er… yes… I heard it from a friend who met her at the casino some time ago.' Pat hoped she wasn't going to probe further. 'I was shocked to learn of her condition and wanted to see what… er… I could do,' he continued, unsure of where this was taking him.

Dr Sallas looked thoughtful, then took a file from her drawer. 'You understand any information is confidential and your interest can be reported to the authorities?'

Pat nodded but was beginning to wonder if he shouldn't just pull out now.

'We understand Senora Pardo has no family in England, that she took the name of her Spanish mother, who is now dead. Her father is not known. Can you confirm this information?' asked the Doctor.

'Er… well… I'm not sure I can, but I do know other friends she had in England who might.'

'I ask, because for us to help it is better to know her background. It is good you have come, because she does not respond. Maybe because she have no friends or family, no support outside the centre.' The doctor began to look hopeful, making Pat feel even more guilty.

'Yes… well I can phone some people to see if I can find out more. So in the time she's been here has she not improved?'

'You see, she is not obliged to remain here, she must report each day to register because of Order of the Court… and to receive treatment.'

'Treatment, like a therapy… for addiction?'

'Yes, therapy but also treatment because she has… how you say, HIV positive.'

'Jesus, mother o'…!' Pat crossed himself several times.

'I am thinking, if you are friend, maybe you can talk with her to remain here in clinic because she need more treatment and better… how you say… regime. If not, they could take her to an Institucion of the… er… State or she could die of *sobre-dose*. I'm sorry, my English fails.'

Pat was, in fact, regretting she spoke well enough to press him into performing a service so different from the one he'd taken on when his trip began.

'Well, I'm not sure she'll listen to me, we weren't… of course I can try.'

Linda had already been to the centre that morning and, in the words of the doctor, had not been 'helpful to herself' and was in poor condition. They knew from experience she could rarely be found at the address she'd registered at, so Dr Sallas suggested Pat return the next morning at ten o'clock when she'd be obliged to return. Not knowing quite how to refuse, he reluctantly agreed.

The drive back to his hotel gave him ample time to contemplate the ambiguous position in which he'd put himself. He'd made an already improbable task even more complicated. When he reached the hotel, he checked the messages on his mobile. Elena had rung twice.

'Hello, me darlin', Sherlock Holmes here,' he said when she answered.

'Hi love, enjoying the sun?' she asked mischievously.

'Chance would be a fine thing! Instead of lying in the sun, I've been lying to the locals. It's all a bit depressing.'

'Oh, what d'you mean?'

'Well, I tracked down Carmen. By the way, did you know her real name, or anything about her family?'

'Er… I think Linda something, and her mother was divorced. I believe she didn't have any brothers or sisters. Why?'

'They asked me at a drug centre the Courts make her attend. I haven't actually seen her yet. Her surname's Pardo, her late mother's name, because the father wasn't known. Seems she's got no other family. I had to register with my passport to get this information, something I'm not so sure's a good idea. The doctor here's giving me the feeling she'd like me to act as her next-of-kin. Seems she's still on drugs when she can get them, and since at her age and in her condition prostitution's not much of an option, it seems she resorts to stealing and carrying drugs through customs for someone. Oh, and she's HIV positive.'

'My God, that's dreadful…!' Elena exclaimed. 'Pat, I'm sorry to have got you involved with all this. Leave it, forget about it, it's too awful!'

'Well, I've promised to meet her tomorrow. They're trying to persuade her to stay in the clinic for treatment.'

'What can you do? You hardly know her, she hasn't seen you for years. Is she going to listen to you?'

'You're right, but the doctor, a nice woman, seems willing to try anything. I don't know… I suppose in for a penny…'

He paused, horrified by the unintended pun. Then both began speaking at the same time. Pat gave way.

'You know your problem,' said Elena, 'you're too good a man. You don't know how to say no to a woman in need… including me. Whatever you do, please don't get into further complications because of my hang-ups. Just get back here, I'm missing you already.'

He was preparing to make a flip comment about saying no to women but the 'missing you' bit caught his attention.

'Ah, me darlin'. You can't be missing me more than I'm missing you.'

'Well, we'll see about that when you get back,' she said as sexily as she could.

He'd been feeling troubled and confused but the call had given him new vigour.

He'd do what he could tomorrow and then get back to the UK.

Chapter Forty-eight

'Ralph, I know I'm here here to finalise the contract and discuss my duties but something you said during our previous meeting stuck in my mind.' Draper nodded for Pat to continue. 'You said your Security Chief was involved with Penny's case. That's a bit of a coincidence...'

'Not really, he visited here several times during that investigation. He was a junior member of the investigating team but, strange as it may seem, he struck up a relationship with Mayfield, who later brought him into the casino business on security. Anyway, in spite of being able to form a relationship with Mayfield, he's not a bad bloke,' laughed Draper.

'I won't hold that against him,' quipped Monaghan, 'it's just that something's troubling me. I know this sounds strange but I wanted to ask someone if they'd ever re-open such an old case, as there might be some new evidence.'

'Really?' Draper was intrigued. 'They've been known to revise old cases, what with DNA and all that. Why don't I call Brian down? Maybe he can suggest a course of action.'

'Could you, Ralph? That would be great.' Monaghan was a bit uneasy at disrupting their meeting but felt he had to exorcise the demons that had taken over his thoughts since meeting Linda Pardo.

Draper made the introductions, when Brian Darroch, ex-Chief Inspector CID, arrived. He remembered Pat from the investigation although Pat couldn't remember him. Not particularly surprising, given the confused state of Monaghan's mind at that time and the minor part Darroch had played in that investigation. To Pat, the Director of Compliance and Security, as he was now called, looked more like a slim, well-groomed politician than an ex- policeman, but perhaps he was still using Sid Walker as a template.

'Would you prefer to talk privately?' asked Draper

'No, no, Ralph, please stay if you want, you know a bit about this anyway,' Pat insisted. Draper drew up seats for them and sat at his desk.

'Where to start? It's about the Penny Irwin case,' said Pat. 'Actually, it started when a friend of ours, Ian Lowe, told me about a girl Carmen who worked at Ventura. She was a cocktail Chica and union representative with Elena Spencer... Penny's flatmate – you'll recall?' Darroch nodded to indicate he remembered. 'Well, it seems Carmen was all along in the pocket of Ahmed Hammoud, who was—'

Draper intervened to say that Brian knew all about Ahmed, and Darroch again nodded confirmation.

Pat continued. 'Anyway, he stimulated her need for drugs, set her up with punters and used her to get information on other girls, and the union. When Penny's murder hit the headlines Ahmed was conveniently out of the country. He set up base in Spain and soon afterwards called Carmen - real name Linda Pardo - out there to work for him. After a while, when her addictive behaviour became an embarrassment and her looks deteriorated, he passed her on to a local. Who I'm told is very nasty drug peddler and pimp. He forced her on to the street, she's been in detention several times, ordered to go on a rehab programme and is HIV positive.'

'God, that bastard has a lot to answer for! So, you got this from Chris Russell?' asked Ralph, who briefly explained to Brian Darroch who Russell was.

'Yes, Chris filled me in on some of this. I met Carmen at a drug centre. She's in a terrible condition physically and mentally. They asked me as an old colleague to try get her to stay in the centre for treatment. Anyway, after several meetings with Carmen, or should I say Linda, it seemed pointless, she wasn't listening. She'd go from friendly to aggressive to whimpering like a child. I told her I wouldn't come back, but in the middle of a stream of abuse, she suddenly came out with... a sort of apology...'

Pat paused: his remembrance of the session still disturbed him. He also hoped he'd interpreted correctly from her incoherent mumblings. Taking a deep breath, he continued. 'She said it wasn't her fault what happened to Penny, Ahmed had made her arrange for Penny's ex-boyfriend to get Elena's address and phone number. She didn't know he'd hurt her. She got a bit hysterical, but went on about how Ahmed threatened her, that she was sorry she told him things about the union and the stuff Elena had on Trist, the rape and Talal's credit.

'This "stuff" refers to material that Elena had told her she'd collected as evidence. Some of it was pretence on Elena's part but some was genuine, particularly the illegal credit that Ahmed arranged for Talal. According to Elena, the night Penny was murdered, Carmen tried to get her to show her this stuff she said she had in her white Salaminder bag - the same bag she gave to Penny to take home and which was stolen in the attack. I tried to get Carmen to tell me more but her memory, maybe genuinely, seems to be shot to pieces. She got in a state, so I had another go at getting her to stay in the clinic but I got the impression she was scared of her pimp. I told the doctor this, but I'm afraid she thought I'd made her worse and asked me not to see her again. I've been thinking about what to do ever since.'

The ex-CID man had taken notes. When Pat stopped, Darroch thought long and hard.

'Well, from what I remember of the case, this might be relevant but I'd have to familiarise myself with the details revealed at the time,' he said. There's a programme of cold case reviews but, as with everything, it's subject to availability of resources, so before they'll review a case, the Force employ strict criteria to judge whether there's a probability of a successful outcome. This case, being very old, presents a number of difficulties, not least the availability and condition of the forensic exibits and possibly the fact that important witnesses are no longer alive.'

'What about DNA, which we're always hearing about?' asked Draper.

'Yes, that's possible,' agreed Darroch, 'depends on the quality of samples taken from the crime scene. Methods of retrieval were less sophisticated than they are today so we have to hope they're uncontaminated and well preserved. Also, even if we get a sample from preserved material, it still has to be matched with someone and of course they only started taking samples recently. But before that, there are many other considerations. I'll make some informal enquiries to test the water.'

Pat thanked him, and Draper suggested he act as the temporary contact between the two men.

When Darroch had gone, Pat turned to Draper. 'Sorry to drag this up, Ralph, but it still troubles me and...'

Draper interrupted him. 'Don't worry about it, Pat. That period and all that went on had a profound effect on many people. Penny was an innocent victim. We resolved many things but it'd be nice to find out who did it. Even if that little bastard didn't have a direct hand in her death, he still deserves to pay for what he did to many vulnerable people, including Carmen.'

'Thanks anyway. Oh, and one more thing – I don't know if I told you but Elena and myself... we got together again and we're a couple.'

'That's great, all the more reason you need a good job!'

'Yes, you're right, we were going to talk about work. Not something an Irishman wants to think about, but I suppose it's necessary to pay for the drinks,' Pat chuckled. Draper was happy to see some of the old spark.

He could tell by her face something was wrong. 'What's up, m'darlin?'

Elena took time to answer. 'When you said that before reopening a case they take into consideration the feelings of the immediate family, I thought I'd better make contact with Penny's mother...' She paused, her eyes filling with tears. 'She died last year... of liver failure.'

'Well, she was getting on and she was drinking... a lot.'

'Yes, and we know why. But I always meant to get in touch... and...'

'Elena, you couldn't have done anything except bring back sad memories,' Pat said, moving to put his arms round her.

'She'd such a miserable life, in a way she would've been better dying earlier like Penny's father.'

'Ah well, there's no telling. We've got to make what we can of what we have left. I don't want you sinking into depression again over this. You hear?' He pulled her to him.

'Yes, you're right. But you said Darroch told you that pressure from the family can awaken interest in a case. What if there's no family left?'

Pat would have liked to skip this subject but could see he'd have to indulge her a little. 'He said it can have a positive effect but it's not the sole motivation. Sometimes the risk of offering false hopes, only to dash them, makes the authorities more reluctant. So it can work both ways. He's making preliminary enquiries anyway. We'll have to be patient, m'love.'

Pat wondered if this upset was going to change their plans for that night.

'Okay, I know you're looking at me, you're right I'm not ready, but I will be. I want to see the changes and meet Ralph and Norma again. I'll be alright, I promise,' Elena said, patting him on the cheek.

That night, another section of the Europa Club would open, this time a new premium players section. Draper had been suggesting for some weeks, ever since Pat had started work there, that he bring Elena for dinner with him and Norma; this seemed as good an excuse as any. Pat had unconsciously delayed mentioning it to Elena until it was almost too late, fearing a return to the Ventura building might provoke more soul-searching. Now it seemed, with this latest news, that process had begun.

However, two hours later she passed, as Pat had several weeks before, from the initial sinking feeling on re-entering Ventura, to the more positive sensation of walking into the new world of the Europa Club. For Elena the experience was strangely uplifting, almost like an exorcism.

The reunion with Ralph and Norma reinforced this feeling. Here, she thought, were two people who'd forged something positive and enduring from a relationship that had started at Ventura. Perhaps belatedly, they could do the same.

Pat crossed to the other side of the room to where Draper had signalled to him. He now felt comfortable to leave Elena with Norma; she was in good spirits, the night having gone better than he'd dared hope.

'Pat, meet Prince Hakim bin Mansur bin al Talal.' Draper read the young Arab's name from a business card. In a quiet aside he added, 'Son of Mansur Talal', before announcing, 'Prince Hakim, let me introduce you to our Director of Public Relations, Pat Monaghan.'

'Aha, very pleased to meet you, Prince Hakim! Welcome to the Europa!' A surprised Pat offered his hand and the young man responded with a smile.

'I've just been asking about his father. Prince Hakim tells me he's well and in fact will be coming to London soon.' Draper raised his eyebrows in a silent message to Monaghan.

'Really, well I hope you'll persuade him to come to Europa - just to have some dinner, you understand,' said Pat. The Arab laughed knowingly. 'Well, and to meet some old friends.' Pat handed him his business card.

After greeting some of the Prince's companions, Draper and Pat moved on around the room.

'When we rejoin the girls we might just keep this about Talal to ourselves for now, I don't want all this about Penny coming up again tonight,' said Pat.

'Sure. That apart, if he's still the punter he was, let's hope we can get him in here, and especially if he visits London regularly,' Draper added.

'Yes, could be very interesting,' agreed Pat.

But he was thinking from another angle altogether.

A few days later Pat was perusing the minutes of the previous afternoon's management meeting, underlining items of particular relevance to his department, when his concentration was broken by the vibration in his pocket. The screen on his mobile indicated Brian Darroch.

'Yes, Brian… at your office in ten minutes,' said Pat when the ex-CID man told him he had something re the Penny Irwin case.

'Hello, Pat,' he said when Pat entered, 'sorry to scramble you up here, but my old colleague Chief Super Bill Blanchard has just come over.' A stout, white-haired gentleman stood up to shake Pat's hand. 'Billy here, was also involved in the original investigation and has come with some news.'

'Well. Pat, as Brian said, in our day we were both involved in this case. Normally, when something new comes up on an unsolved crime, the original senior investigating officer is contacted. In this case unfortunately in the intervening years – twenty-eight, I think – the SIO's moved to Australia and his deputy has sadly passed on. So they asked me to look at this.'

'Sorry to interrupt,' said Darroch. 'Billy's officially retired but has been brought back to look at cold cases before. Ye can't keep a good man down eh?' he winked. Billy scoffed.

'Anyway, Brain told me about your conversation with this girl Pardo, could be interesting, but we'd have to interview her ourselves. That apart, we've been doing a bit of "scoping", as we call it, meaning we've been examining evidence and exhibits kept in storage to see if there's retrievable material. It's been a long time and methods then were different. Anyway, the good news is that there are exhibits that can be used for forensic examination and the files on the case are available. I don't know if Brian told you, but there are other considerations before we officially re-open a case.' Darroch nodded and Blanchard continued. 'We have to consult the next of kin and—'

Pat interrupted, 'Both mother and father have died, Penny had no other family that we know of.'

'Oh… right. We'll verify that, if it's the case, sad to say, but it's a bit less complicated. The other thing is, that even with forensics, we have to support that with other evidence, to make a case, get a conviction. So we'd have to interview Pardo and all other witnesses, including yourself.'

'I informed Billy that you live with Elena Spencer, who was the victim's flatmate,' Darroch added.

'Yes, I remember the young lady. She'll be willing to come for an interview?' asked Blanchard.

'She's pushing me on this. She's never got over it and would like to see the guilty party caught, no matter how late in the day.'

'Good. We've a few things to look at, but should be back to you within a few days. Just confirm your address and telephone number.' Blanchard gave Pat a form.

Pat completed the form, they stood up shook hands and Darroch led his old colleague out to the corridor, leaving Pat for a moment. He returned with a satisfied look.

'He's not allowed to say, and neither should I really, but I think they've already come up with something interesting. But keep that to yourself,' he winked.

For the next few days Pat was relieved to have work to go to, because his time at home was spent listening to Elena's endless speculation - what the Police would find; what they'd ask; when they'd call.

It was Friday afternoon when Darroch called and asked if they'd go to Shepherd's Bush Police Station. Pat arranged to meet Elena there, and a few hours later arrived to find her pacing up and down the Station waiting room, the tea they'd brought for her lying untouched.

'Do you think they've got something...' The torrent of questions she was about to release was interrupted by the entry of Blanchard with a uniformed officer.

'Hello, Pat, Miss Spencer, thanks for coming. If you don't mind, we'd like to speak with you separately. Pat, if you wouldn't mind waiting, we'll take Miss Spencer first. The Serg here'll get you a tea or something.'

In just over one hour, after Blanchard had thanked them both for their cooperation, they left in Pat's Mondeo. As if within the boundaries of the Police car-park some investigative protocol was still in force, they postponed discussion of their respective interviews. Once on the road, although they had not yet agreed on where they were driving to, Elena could wait no longer.

'Why do you think they insisted on keeping us separate?' she asked.

'Blanchard told me that because of the long passage of time, it's important to get individual accounts, so that one person doesn't influence the other's recollections.'

'This man, Mark Tweedie, they asked me if I knew him and showed me several photos. Did they ask you? Is he the suspect?'

'Yes, they were photographs of him when he was younger. I don't know if he's a suspect or not. I asked, but Blanchard said they couldn't say at this point, they were still looking at several angles. The usual kinda Police answer. I didn't know him anyway. What else did they ask you?'

'Oh, all the stuff I told them before – what time I left Penny, what she was wearing, what was in the bag and what importance or value the contents might have for anyone else. Trist. The calls from her ex-boyfriend. Her affair with Talal. About Carmen, about the things I told her. I gave them my theories, for what they're worth…'

'Maybe we could stop for a coffee or something, and you can decide if you want to go home or not,' suggested Pat.

'Yes we could stop, but afterwards I do need to go back to work. I promised them I would, and I know you have to as well,' she said, making a conscious effort to sound positive.

He pulled into a car-park and they made their way up to the coffee shop.

'So, you haven't told me what they asked you…' Elena said when they were settled with their drinks.

'Like you, I went over the stuff I told them before, except now I could add my talks with Carmen, or Linda, as I suppose we have to call her now.'

'So what's come out? They think Ahmed had something to do with… it? And who's Mark Tweedie?'

'I don't know. Obviously this Tweedie guy's come up somewhere in their investigations. Maybe they'll find something, but after such a long time it can't be easy. At least they're looking again.' Pat was eager to strike a balance between sounding positive and not raising expectations too high.

Their coffee finished, Pat dropped Elena off at the school where she was lecturing in Wandsworth, then made his way to The Europa Club. He hadn't told her quite everything -not that he was concealing anything of major significance. When he was asked to comment on Ahmed's relationship with Talal, he'd informed them of the Prince's impending visit to London, something he'd still not mentioned to Elena. And Blanchard had seemed very interested in this conveniently coincidental visit.

Chapter Forty-nine

Three days after their interview at the Police Station, Pat was already driving home when Elena called to say Blanchard was on his way to their apartment.

She met him in the hallway before he could even get his coat off. 'Do you know what this is about? Have you talked to Brian Darroch?'

'Relax, m'darlin'. I don't know, Darroch hasn't been in the last few days. What did Blanchard say?'

'He said only that he'd like to come round to discuss developments and clarify some points,' said Elena. 'I told him you'd be in around five thirty.'

'Okay, we'll see what he's got to say... or ask.' Pat tried to sound relaxed. Elena nodded distractedly and with exaggerated calm, they undertook separate chores: Elena making coffee, Pat replacing batteries in the television channel changer. Simple as those tasks would normally have been, they seemed to take an inordinate amount of time.

They'd only just sat down with the coffee to watch the evening news when the doorbell rang.

Blanchard declined the offer of a beverage and parked his substantial bulk on the easy chair. Elena and Pat waited impatiently as he opened his briefcase and extracted a folder.

'First, I know you both said you didn't know or recognise Mark Tweedie. I want to ask you if you know this man?' He placed several photos on the table. Neither Elena nor Pat recognised the gaunt features of the long-haired person when young, nor his even more cadaverous and cropped-haired look, obviously taken some years later. They both answered no.

'Does the name George Hain mean anything to you?' asked Blanchard. Both shook their heads. 'Okay, what I can tell you is this - having obtained forensic evidence, including a DNA sample, from the preserved exhibits taken from the crime scene, we were fortunately able to match them with an individual presently serving time in Her Majesty's Prison Wormwood Scrubs. After consultation with and on the advice of a solicitor, he agreed to cooperate fully. The outcome is that he has now admitted that in the early hours of the morning of March 6th, 1975, whilst in the act of committing a robbery, he inflicted blows on Penelope Irwin which led to her death.'

Elena stifled a cry with her hand, shuddered and froze in shock. Pat, also momentarily stunned by the news, eased himself across the sofa to comfort her. All three sat in silence for some minutes before Pat signalled to Blanchard to continue.

'This person is one Mark Tweedie. He contends that he did not intend to kill Miss Irwin but admits he used unreasonable force to counter her resistance. He further contends that the robbery was carried out by him at the behest of another individual, George Hain, who supplied information including a car registration number, the address of the victim and a place where she would park...'

'Oh my God! No!' Elena buried her head in Pat's chest. Another lengthy period went by while he attempted to console her. Blanchard waited.

'I'm sorry, Inspector, she'll be alright in a minute, it's the shock.'

'Of course. Look, we can continue this when the lady's feeling up to it. Give me a call at this number.' The policeman offered his card.

'Thing is, it now looks like Elena was the intended victim, not Penny. Something she always feared,' said Pat.

'Yes. If his story's to be believed, it does look like that. That's why we need to review some facts but only when the lady's up to it.' Blanchard, stood up and made his way to the door.

'Chief... Pat, please!' Elena surprised them both. 'I'm sorry, I'll be okay now. I... just needed a minute.'

Blanchard glanced at Pat to see if he looked convinced by her assurances. He seemed willing to resume.

'Okay, let's look at where this leaves us.' The retired CI sat down again and opened his file. 'Some of this you've no doubt already deduced. Tweedie stated that his primary target was a white handbag.' Blanchard saw Elena wince, but continued. 'He was to make it look like a mugging, taking everything of value he could. The victim unfortunately put up a struggle and he was forced to resort to violence. He claims the fatal blows were caused by her head hitting the metal railings. The bag, its contents and all other items stolen were, he said, later given to Hain, who, as agreed, paid Tweedie five hundred pounds. The next day Tweedie found out the girl had died when Hain called him to say he'd screwed up and warned him to get out of London or he'd end up like the victim.'

Elena closed her eyes in pain. Pat, his arm still around her, nodded for Blanchard to continue.

'Problem is, George Hain died eight years ago, incidentally with no suspicious circumstances, it being a long-term condition brought on by alcohol and drug abuse. Neither Tweedie nor any of Hain's other known associates can shed light on who Hain was doing this job for—'

'If you speak to Linda Pardo, Carmen…' interrupted Pat.

'Well, nice as it would be to tie the whole thing up, our job was to find the killer. He claims the death was unintentional and with his supposed conspirator dead—'

'You mean he's going to get off, and the one who planned it as well?' Elena called out in alarm.

'No, no, faced with compelling evidence the solicitor advised Tweedie to make this statement, but it was an unlawful killing whilst committing a robbery, no matter what he says about his original intention. He's simply hoping that by pleading guilty and offering to cooperate, the sentence will be mitigated. But with his form he's not going to get much reduction. No, the problem is that with Hain dead, implicating anyone else…'

Blanchard let a negative expression finish the message.

'So, the reason for Penny's death… the papers in my bag… Carmen… Ahmed… we're just going to forget about all of that?' Elena cried out in frustration. Pat echoed her question.

'I'm not saying that,' said Blanchard quickly, 'I'm just pointing out the difficulty. I'll make a full report to my Super and see how he wants to pursue this. Meanwhile, Miss Spencer, I want to verify once again the details of the missing items and your ideas on the significance to others of those items. And Mr Monaghan, would you review your statement about Linda, formerly Carmen, Pardo. Check if the details, including her present whereabouts, are correct.'

When the policeman had gone, both sat in stunned silence. Neither was in any doubt who'd employed Hain, but to obtain what, and in whose interest? Although they'd prayed for Penny's killer to be caught, this if anything was the worst outcome. Pat, if he was honest, would have preferred a completely random mugging. In that case, Elena would still retain a residue of guilt for having let her go home alone to an area she herself described as 'rough'. But this, to some extent, she'd come to terms with over the years. This latest development was another matter. Already, in her statement to Blanchard, she'd touched on the point that would be a recurring theme from now on – her meddling and threats to expose the rape and the credit scam had provoked an action that had led to her friend's death. That thought was now tormenting her and he didn't know how to alleviate her pain.

It was to be five weeks before any further news was heard and then it came via Brian Darroch. Pat was finishing lunch with a new Russian client when he appeared. He excused himself to the member, and quietly asked Pat to buzz him when free. Twenty minutes later, having happily left the flamboyant young millionaire to work his way through a pile of £100 chips he'd just purchased, Pat joined the Director of Compliance and Security in the Diamond Bar.

'Hi Pat, Billy Blanchard just asked me to pass on this news. Tweedie will appear before the Magistrates on Wednesday. It's a simple legal formality. They'll decline jurisdiction and pass it up to the Old Bailey. Once at the Bailey, and that should be fairly soon, the CPS will read the charge. He's pleading guilty, so the judge will listen to mitigation and pronounce. It should be done and dusted quickly.'

'Yes, but what about the people who paid him?' asked Pat.

'Well, as you know, the guy he claims contracted him to pull the robbery is now dead,' said Darroch quickly.

'Yes, but they'd only have known what to steal on info from Linda Pardo and we know she was controlled by Ahmed Hammoud. Stands to reason he contracted Hain,' said Pat.

'Well, that's probably true, but proving it would be difficult, seeing as it's…'

'So, they're not going to take this further?

Darroch sighed. 'Look, I know it's galling, Billy's cut up about it too. But in taking on these cold cases they assess the likelihood of getting a result and allocate resources accordingly. They'll consider the result's been achieved, they've got the killer and he's confessed. What you're talking about now is a conspiracy case and they're notoriously difficult to prove, especially when you consider we're going back twenty-eight years, an important individual in the chain is dead and to get to others we'd have all the problems of extradition. Pat, I'm sorry but it's just not gonna happen.' He opened his hands in supplication.

Had he been a dispassionate onlooker, Pat might have accepted the logic of the Police's position. But he was contemplating the effect this injustice would have on Elena.

By keeping themselves busy, they'd avoided any reference to the subject since the Old Bailey hearing, but Pat had been waiting for the silence to break.

'Pat, I'd like to meet with Carmen,' Elena announced suddenly.

'Oh no! To achieve what?'

'I don't know, I'd just like to get to the truth.'

'We've gone over this again and again. They're not going to do anything about her or Ahmed or anyone else. They've got Tweedie, they've put him away for as long as they're going to, and for them the matter's closed.'

'I know all that, but I still want to clear my own mind… do something. I'll go myself, just tell me where she is,' she said with a determination he hadn't heard for some time.

'I'm not letting you go there yourself. Let me see if I can get a few days off.'

'Fine, but if you can't, I'll manage,' she insisted. He held up his hand to silence her and at the same time indicate he'd taken note of her determination.

He arranged with Draper to take a few days off some weeks later and phoned Elena to confirm dates before making the travel arrangements. What they'd do or could possibly achieve he put to one side for the moment, as he made one of his sorties around the Europa complex.

The sports-book section was full, as expected, when a football match between England and France was being broadcast live. Monaghan skirted his way around the perimeter, taking care not to obscure anyone's view or distract them at this critical point in the contest. He made his way from there through a slot area and out to a live game pit. The football had reduced, in both sections, the numbers to be normally seen playing at this hour. Nevertheless the facility to watch it at the Europa meant that in just a few minutes, when the match was over, they would filter back to the games; earlier than they would have, had they been watching at home or in a pub. In addition the club could count on the income generated from bets wagered on the outcome. Play on higher limit games wasn't influenced to the same extent by football, and certainly not by an England game, as the clientele were predominantly foreign. The punto banco game was in temporary suspension as the dealer shuffled the cards. Some players gravitated to the other games but a middle aged Asian lady was complaining bitterly to the table Inspector that another player had taken her favourite seat. Pat, with a feeling of of déjà vu, was about to intervene when he felt a slight touch on his arm.

'Mr Monaghan, hello.'

Pat turned to face Talal's son.

'Ah hello there, Prince Hakim, how are you?' Pat offered his hand.

'I'm very well, thank you. Would you please join us, we are over here.' Hakim pointed to a booth table on the other side of the room. Pat followed him across the floor to where sat the young men who'd accompanied

Hakim on his previous visit and a stout, white-haired gentleman. He had changed, but there was no doubt who he was.

'Pat, how are you? It's been a very long time.' The man rose to offer Pat his hand.

'Prince Mansur bin Talal. I'm very well, how are you?' responded Pat. He turned to greet the other men but they'd already risen and were excusing themselves.

'They are eager to play. You do not object?' the Prince asked smiling. Pat also smiled.

Talal paused before continuing. He looked wistful. 'Some time ago the British Consulate requested that I meet police officials who were looking again at the… death of… Penny.' He bowed his head. Pat waited self-consciously for him to continue. Talal began again slowly. 'They produced photographs and asked if I knew a man called Tweedie. Later they asked questions about another man. I have now a report of the trial of this man Tweedie. He has admitted to the… outrage.' He paused again, obviously affected. 'It is good they have, after such time, found this dog! But some things I cannot understand. When my son gave me your card, I remembered you were Penny's friend, and wondered if you know about this?'

Pat, unsure of how to answer, searched for words. 'Er… yes… the police have a unit which reviews old cases… and with new technology sometimes they find evidence they couldn't find before—'

'Yes, yes I understand the new methods,' Talal interrupted, 'and it is good. What I do not understand is the other things. This man says he was commanded by another to rob Penny. Is this just a lie? Why would this other man want him to do this, what did he know of Penny? Why did the police ask me if I knew these men? Why did they ask me about credit at Ventura and Ahmed Hammoud? What has these things got to do with this… this outrage?'

Pat could see the Prince was becoming increasingly agitated and attempted to calm him down. 'Well, I was about to say that myself and Elena Spencer… you'll remember she was a friend and flatmate of Penny?' Talal nodded and waited for Pat to continue. 'We live together… and because we were still upset that no one was caught for this crime, we campaigned for the police to look again. This no doubt prompted them to look at all connections Penny had. I'm sorry if it caused you embarrassment.'

'Embarrassment! No, not embarrassment! It causes me pain!' said the Prince emphatically. 'It causes me pain that they would think I had something to do with this evil act. It causes me pain for anybody to think that I could have even thought to harm my beautiful Penny. Pain, because I could not... find strength to remain with her... and even after her death...!' He looked to some distant spot in the room. His eyes filled and the muscles in his jaw throbbed.

Pat, surprised at the depth of Talal's emotion, shifted uncomfortably in his seat and searched for some response.

The Arab composed himself and resumed. 'So, why they ask me these things? The one who probably knows this murderer is this... Martin. Your Elena, her friend, told him she was staying with her... and he planned something—'

Pat interrupted him. 'Elena didn't tell him, he already knew. Ahmed got the Chica Carmen to tell him!' he blurted out.

'Ahmed? Ahmed Hammoud? How? Why do you say this? This... is what your Elena says?'

'No, it's what Carmen says. She was working for Ahmed,' said Pat, realising he was entering into difficult territory. Talal shook his head in denial at this statement. Pat considered how to extricate himself and avoid further discussion on this subject.

'Why would Ahmed tell her to give this man Penny's address?' asked Talal.

'I don't know, that you'd have to ask Carmen.'

Both men now fell silent: Talal deep in thought, Pat looking towards the gaming area for an excuse to break off from what was becoming a delicate situation.

'This Carmen, she is not the one who was in Spain?' Talal finally asked.

'Er... yes.' Pat was hesitant. 'Oh, can you excuse me a moment, that gentleman had an appointment and I think he's looking for me,' he said, referring to a client standing near the punto table. Talal grunted acknowledgement. Pat rose to make his way towards his unsuspecting saviour.

He'd been sharing a drink and exchanging pleasantries with his surprised new friend for some minutes when Talal approached him.

'Mr Pat, I must go now. But please, we must talk again. I must know everything,' the Prince said, handing him a business card. Pat thanked him and said a relieved goodbye

Chapter Fifty

The flight to Malaga, collection of the rental car, and drive to Marbella had gone smoothly. The hotel exceeded expectations and the weather for mid-winter was pleasantly warm. An arrival message on the room's television promised sun, sea and sangria. However, their itinerary seemed a little less enticing - to seek out a volatile HIV- positive drug addict and discuss her relationship with the possible instigator of a murder committed twenty-eight years earlier.

Hoping to smooth the way and establish that Linda Pardo was still attending the drug centre, Pat had called its Director. She was unhelpful. Dr Sallas had obviously come to the conclusion, either from her own observations or Pardo's comments, that no real good could come from another reunion. So with no guarantee of cooperation from the Centre, Elena's plan was looking even more improbable.

By the time they'd settled in at the hotel, it was already early evening and a little late to make for La Linea, so they took the opportunity to stroll by the seafront, stop at a promenade café and enjoy a little of what the advertisement had promised.

'So, you think Talal really was in love with Penny and regretted their breaking-up?' said Elena suddenly, as they looked out towards a sea tinged red by the dying sun.

'It certainly seems that way,' said Pat, waking from his reverie. 'Chris Russell told me, but I never really believed it until I saw how he reacted the other day.'

'But he didn't believe that bastard Ahmed was behind the attack?'

'Well, he seemed to have difficulty believing it. I didn't get around to the reason for the attack that caused Penny's death. He was upset and I wasn't sure what to say. In any case, although we're sure Ahmed had a hand in it, we can't make accusations without proof,' said Pat forcefully. Elena didn't answer.

They both knew that this was what she hoped Carmen could provide, though neither of them knew what could be done with it, even if she did.

They drove to the Centre the next morning but the man at the reception was not the one who'd been on duty on Pat's previous visit. He spoke what little English he knew reluctantly and was even more grudging with information. The *Directora* was out, he said, and he didn't know when she would return. Elena and Pat, conceding defeat, left and crossed to the cafeteria on the other side of the small square; from there to contemplate their next move.

The appearance of two obvious foreigners at an unfashionable bar in a non-tourist area of town caused a momentary pause in the noisy banter between a group of scruffy locals who were sitting just inside the front door. Feeling conspicuous, Elena and Pat chose to sit on a table outside on the pavement, although even there, they attracted the unashamed attention of passing locals. After a short while, a hugely fat waiter trudged out to grunt a type of welcome and wait for instructions.

'Café… con leche,' said Pat, holding up two fingers to signify two cups.

The man showed only a perfunctory acknowledgement and returned to the bar. However, moments later he surprised them by returning with two glasses half full of coffee to which he added hot milk from a jug.

'I don't yet speak the lingo fluently,' said Pat. Elena smiled weakly, but was regretting she'd talked him into the whole improbable project. He continued his attempt to lift her flagging spirits. 'Luckily, you're an expert on teaching people with learning difficulties.'

'Pat, I'm sorry about this whole thing, let's just forget about it.'

'Look, we're here now, let's wait and see. Here we can watch the comings and goings. Maybe I'll see this Director arrive, and if Linda still has to comply with the Court order, she'll also show up.' Pat tried to sound upbeat.

The morning wore on and they became a local attraction, visitors to the cafeteria making no effort to conceal their curiosity at the presence of two foreigners.

Pat stretched his linguistic talents to the limit trying to order something to eat, so the waiter, who it seemed was also the proprietor, engaged one of his customers, a taxi driver, to act as translator. This new recruit was also acting as inquisitor for the owner and his regulars and Elena was on the point of fabricating a reason for their presence when Pat caught glimpse of a familiar figure shuffling towards the clinic.

'I've just seen Linda going into the Centre,' he said quietly, 'I think I'll wait till she comes out, then try to get her to join us.'

'Okay... anyway, we've ordered food... I think.' Elena glanced quickly to their new-found friend who, with two colleagues, had taken a table nearby, to be close at hand for translation services.

Their hunger helped the unpromising mixture of food set before them to go down well and the taxi driver, prompted by the fat owner, was suggesting dessert when Linda Pardo re-appeared. Pat touched Elena on the arm and rose quickly to make his way across the square.

'Hello Linda, it's me, Pat – how are you?' he said as he neared the hunched shuffling figure. She didn't stop but slowed to view him with alarm and suspicion. 'It's me, Pat Monaghan,' he explained as he walked alongside her. 'Can I invite you for a drink or something to eat?'

Linda Pardo stopped and looked at him closely. 'What... you want?'

'I have an old friend with me at the café.' He pointed to where Elena was sitting. Pardo squinted across but could obviously see nothing and looked totally confused. 'Come, come on, we can have a drink... please,' he encouraged, touching her arm gently. Eventually, almost involuntarily, Linda began to move with him towards the café where Elena was waiting, not to mention the ever curious owner and his regulars.

Any thoughts Elena had entertained of aggressively challenging her former colleague dissipated rapidly as the shrivelled and prematurely aged figure lumbered towards her. Linda Pardo could not yet have reached fifty but looked eighty. Her eyes had a haunted look and she wheezed audibly as Pat brought her to the table.

'Hello, Carmen… or is it Linda?' A shocked Elena, stood up to greet her. Pardo simply looked bewildered.

'It's Elena Spencer from Ventura, remember?' said Pat, guiding her into a seat. Slowly it began to register and a range of emotions seemed to pass across Pardo's ravaged features. Elena was about to ask her something, but Pat signalled to allow a little more time.

The café owner, intrigued by the arrival of this pathetic creature, lurched over, signalling to his official interpreter to glean any information he could.

'Can we get you a drink or are you hungry?' Pat asked Linda.

The café-owner waited, viewing Linda with something bordering on disdain.

She then seemed to summon up strength. 'Traigame una bocadilla, café… y un cognac, doble!' she called out in defiant style.

The fatman looked to his translator to get Pat's approval for this extravagance.

'The Senora want a café, sandweech and… a double cognac. It ees okay?' the taxi driver translated. Pat reluctantly nodded, although he wasn't sure brandy was a good idea.

Her defiant flourish over, Linda now looked at Elena with a pained expression. Elena, for her part, would have liked to confront this woman with the consequences of her treachery, but couldn't come to terms with the extent of her deterioration. Even Pat could see that, in the short time since his last meeting with her, Pardo had gone downhill rapidly.

'You want to ask something?' Linda muttered with an awareness she hadn't shown before.

'Well… yes. We think… someone took advantage of your need. Because of that, many people suffered, including yourself.' Elena chose her words carefully. 'I hoped you'd be able to tell us… about him.'

Showing no inclination to respond, Linda Pardo sat staring at her feet for a long time. The volatility Pat had seen during his previous meetings had fortunately gone but perhaps only because her body could no longer summon enough energy. Elena was about to add something when words slowly began to trickle out.

'I don't want to remember... I'm sick... and...' Linda stopped, unable to continue.

The owner was now bringing her order so Pat and Elena waited. There seemed no point in pressing her. She immediately threw back the cognac. The fatman raised an eyebrow and inclined his head as if to indicate he was not surprised. He lingered, hoping for a repeat order but when Pat signalled his refusal, the man trudged off mumbling comments to his audience of regulars. Pardo took two bites from her sandwich, then seemed to lose interest.

'Linda, last time we met, you told me about Ahmed and what he made you do... you said you were sorry about Penny and about Elena. Elena's here now, you can tell her yourself,' said Pat gently. There was no immediate response. She sat sniffing and slowly shaking her head.

'Linda, I want to help you, how can I do that, tell me?' Elena, bent forward to try to meet her eyes.

Linda Pardo trembled as she stared long and hard at Elena. 'No one can help me. I'm finished. I let him buy me. I let everyone buy me... now I have nothing to sell.'

'Linda, you can get better, I can help...' Elena tried to take her hand.

'No, it's too late... I don't deserve anything from you. It's true I did things for that shit Ahmed, he wouldn't give me stuff if I didn't tell him... or do things.' She paused to sniff and cough. 'I didn't know that bastard would do that...!'

'Do what, Linda, do what?' asked Elena.

'I only agreed to tell him about the papers, then he asked me about the car, your address, things...' She began to cry. Pat could see they were attracting even more interest than before.

'Who asked you - Ahmed?' probed Elena, for the moment oblivious to her surroundings. A fit of coughing now prohibited Linda from continuing. One of the onlookers passed across a bottle containing mineral water. She gulped this down thankfully and for several minutes, while she wiped away tears and mucous, a frustrated Elena waited impatiently to resume.

'Are you okay?' asked Elena. Linda nodded unconvincingly. 'Linda, I'm sorry, but who asked about the papers, about my address, my car?'

Linda seemed to have difficulty with the question or was searching for the answer. Elena was about to ask again when the other woman forced out, 'This... George... George... Ahmed told me to tell him.'

'George Hain, was his name Hain?' demanded Elena excitedly. But Pardo's head was drooping as if she was about to fall asleep. Elena tried to take her hand but she pulled it away and rose slowly.

'I... I need... the toilet,' she mumbled.

'Okay, let me help you.' Elena sighed with frustration but tried to keep calm and patient.

Pat watched them make their way to the toilet, Elena guiding the pitiful figure past the quizzical looks of the locals and the searching glare of the fat proprietor.

Some time passed and they had still not re-emerged. The taxi-driver meanwhile took the opportunity to ask,'Ees everytheeng al right?'

'Yes, yes. Fine,' answered Pat, distracted as he watched for them to reappear.

The two women were now coming back. Elena leading and looking somewhat agitated.

'She took something in there, I'm sure!' She closed her eyes in horror and disgust.

Linda's appearance hadn't changed but her demeanor certainly had. 'I have to go now,' she said more confidently than would have seemed possible only a few minutes earlier.

'Have a coffee or something, then I can drop you, I have the car nearby,' said Pat quickly, putting a restraining hand on Elena, who he could see wanted to challenge Linda about the drugs.

'Well, I don't know, I...' She stopped suddenly, seemingly disconcerted by a man who had taken a seat opposite and was staring straight at her. 'Yes, you can drop me somewhere,' she said quietly but urgently. Perspiration began to break out on her face and she fidgeted nervously.

'Okay,' said Pat, glancing at Elena, who looked as concerned as he was. 'I'll walk round and get the car, you two wait here.'

'No, no I'll come with you to get the car!' she said, too quickly for Pat and Elena's peace of mind.

'Linda, what's troubling you, is it that man. Do you know him?' Elena glanced towards the dark-skinned, long-haired individual who seemed, even by local standards, to be unpleasantly preoccupied with their guest.

'No, nothing, I'm just in a hurry,' she replied unconvincingly.

Pat signaled for his bill. The owner and his clientele seemed disappoint- ed they were going. Pat imagined they'd provided a talking point, a break from normal routine.

'Ah! You leave now, you need a taxi?' asked the taxi-driver cum translator.

'Er… no, gracias. I have a car near here, thank you,' answered Pat.

'You stay een hotel, yes?'

'Yes,' said Pat wishing the owner would hurry with the bill as he watched Linda become more and more disturbed while Elena tried to calm her.

'Your hotel good? What hotel you stay?' asked the driver.

'Good, yes, the Don Pepe, in Marbella,' he said, distracted by Elena's challenging look towards the man she imagined had spooked Linda.

Fortunately the proprietor arrived with the bill, announcing through his interpreter that he'd discounted two coffees as a public relations gesture. Pat thanked him and paid, adding a larger tip than intended to avoid a wait for change. They struggled off, Linda propped between them, the watchful au- dience marking their every step across the square. Their charge, because of her poor physical condition and unusual haste to leave the area, was tiring rapidly. Though she'd dismissed the suggestion that the man had fright- ened her, she looked back frequently as if fearing she'd be followed. From what Elena knew of drug addiction, paranoia was often a consequence, so she was unsure if this fear had any real basis or was a symptom of Linda's condition.

By the time they reached the car, Pat and Elena were also exhausted, having almost carried their charge through the narrow cobbled streets. Elena climbed into the back seat alongside her.

'Okay, so where to?' Pat turned to address his two passengers.

'Linda, why don't you stay in the clinic, let them treat you, get your health back?" pleaded Elena. But Linda was furtively looking out of the rear window, too preoccupied to answer, even had she been inclined. 'Okay, let's move out of this area,' said Elena irritably, 'which direction?'

'Oh… ah… yes. Up here, turn right,' Linda said breathlessly.

They travelled for some minutes and when Linda seemed to have calmed down, Elena could restrain herself no longer.

'Are you living by yourself, Linda?'

'Yes,' she said after some time, 'I have a small place.'

'As I was saying before, you're ill, why don't you stay at the medical centre until you get better?'

Again Linda took her time to answer, then with a wry smile she said, 'It doesn't matter, I'm not going to get better.'

'That's not the case,' intervened Pat, 'the Director Dr Sallas told me I should talk you into staying there because they could help you.'

'They say that, but they know it's too late.'

'Linda, you were concerned about that man at the café, who was he?' asked Elena.

'It doesn't matter now about him.'

'But if you're worried about him or anything, we can help.' Elena took her arm gently.

Linda looked out of the car window and sighed heavily. 'I'm a drug addict, this you know. I owe this man a lot of money, he also thinks I talk to the… *Policia…*'

'Maybe you should go to the police!' Pat suggested as he slowed the car, not knowing where to go, but not wishing to interrupt the conversation.

'They do nothing,' Linda said dismissively, then began coughing again.

'So how much money are we talking about… maybe we could find a way to…'

'Ha haha!' she laughed hoarsely and derisively. 'You don't understand, it can never be cleared… he's supposed to hold me, control me!'

Pat stopped the car. There was no point going any further until he knew in what direction he should go.

'You're right, Linda, we don't understand. Why does he want to keep a hold on you, something to do with Ahmed?' Elena asked, remembering what Chris Russell had told Pat.

'Everything to do with Ahmed… he destroys everything. Because I was no use anymore he gave me to this Juan Palomino to give me dirty needles… crack… because I didn't give value for good stuff…' Linda added bitterly.

'Before that, in London, Ahmed supplied you with drugs?' asked Elena

'Friends of his like this… George…'

'Was his name Hain, George Hain?' Elena pressed her.

'I didn't know his name. He was called something. George "*the Pidgeon*", that was it,' she said and began to drop her head again.

'Was it he you had to tell about the papers, my car and my address, on the night Penny died?' Elena grasped Linda Pardo's arm to focus her attention, and Pat reached out to Elena to temper her excitement. 'Please Linda, was he?'

Looking into the distance with a pained expression, Linda uttered a barely audible 'yes', then bowed her head and began to whimper.

Elena and Pat looked to each other, but could find no words. At that moment neither could identify fully how they felt. They were nearer to the truth but what could be done with their knowledge? And Pardo, how should they feel about her? Her willingness to betray friends to obtain drugs had been reprehensible but it was difficult to feel anything but pity for the wretched creature in soiled clothing and matted hair who sat coughing and wheezing; she had already convicted and sentenced herself to the maximum penalty.

'Linda, let's see if we can get you home. Where should I go from here?' asked Pat after some time had elapsed.

Eventually she responded and directed him with difficulty and several wrong turnings to an area even seedier than the one they'd come from. Pat stopped on a corner because the street was too narrow for two vehicles to pass and there was already a ramshackle van parked some fifty metres further on with no driver present.

'This'll do. Let me out here.' Linda struggled to exit the car.

'Wait… we'll take you,' said Pat and Elena almost in unison as they climbed out of the car.

'No, no, it's okay. I go myself.' She seemed keen to take her leave of them.

'Look, Linda, here's our hotel number. If you need help, please call us.' Pat gave her the hotel card.

'Please promise you'll call if you have any problem?' Elena echoed Pat's wish.

Linda grabbed the card and lurched off, leaving them to consider if they should or could do more to help. It took her some time to walk halfway down the cobbled, pavement-less street. She then took a last furtive look behind her, presumably to make sure neither they nor anyone else was following, and disappeared into a doorway.

'Wait here a minute, love, I'll just take a note of her number,' said Pat, looking up at the street name.

The double door she'd entered led on to a courtyard. Pat looked inside and was of a mind to investigate further but the stench and squalor of the surroundings repelled him and in any case he had no idea which of the passageways Linda had taken. He contented himself with the fact that at least he had the building number.

Pat wasn't entirely sure how to get back to the hotel so Elena sat with a map on her knee and gave directions. The task postponed discussion on their disturbing encounter and the conclusions to be drawn from it. They were back in the room before Pat first spoke on the subject. 'Well, I suppose we could say we found out what we came for.'

'Yes,' said Elena thoughtfully, 'though I'm not sure what to do with it, nor even sure how I feel about her. I'm sickened by what she did, but appalled by the condition she's got herself into. She's a dreadful, pathetic creature, I can't even believe it's the same person I knew as Carmen.'

'The question is… can we do anything about that bastard Ahmed?' said Pat.

'Well, we have to try. Why should he get away with the misery he's caused to so many people?' she said angrily, then strained to prevent herself from entering into another bout of tearfulness.

'You're right. I'll contact Blanchard to report on what Linda told us. Let's see if we can get something done about that swine!' Pat said resolutely, 'Meanwhile, why don't you get yourself ready and we'll go for dinner. Cheer us up a bit!'

She had taken time with her clothes and make-up, but more importantly, she was smiling and that alone wiped several years off her age. To encourage this mood Pat had told her the news from Blanchard that 'The Pigeon' was the nickname of George Hain, and he'd pass on their information for evaluation. All true; but that was an edited version of the telephone conversation. Pat intentionally neglected to add that the veteran policeman's opinion remained as before - that the authorities were unlikely to try and extradite a possible conspirator of a crime committed over twenty-five years ago. Blanchford added that even if Pardo was willing and able to testify, her record of drug abuse would leave that testimony open to effective challenge.

So, having deferred bad news until a later date, Pat would attempt to make the remainder of the trip as enjoyable as possible - not an easy task as he himself felt embittered by the injustice of it all.

The next few days they concentrated on doing what tourists are supposed to do: eat, drink and religiously worship every appearance of the late winter sun. Those pursuits helped create the atmosphere for another, in which they participated with all the energy and enthusiasm of teenagers. Elena was showering after just such a session and Pat was lying satisfied on the bed when the phone rang. He reached to answer it but although he could hear background sound, possibly traffic, there was no response to his repeated hellos. The line then went dead.

'Who was that?' Elena asked as she came out of the bathroom towelling her hair.

'I don't know, they didn't reply... sounded like an outside call. Maybe they'll ring back.'

'Who knows our number here?'

'Well actually... the only person I gave this number to was Linda.'

He picked up the phone and dialled the operator. 'Yes... hello, you just transferred a call to this room, but the person didn't speak or we couldn't hear them. Have you any idea where the call came from?' Pat asked. He was asked to wait. 'Yes... oh, I see... thank you!' He put down the phone with a frown.

'What is it?' asked Elena.

'They said it was an outside call from a Spanish speaking woman, who seemed a little confused.'

'It has to be Linda. Did they know where she was calling from?' asked Elena.

'No, they said it was probably an outside call box.'

'What can we do? You think she may be in trouble?'

'Look… finish what you're doing. I think I'll drive down there, see if I can find her.' Pat started to pull on his clothes.

'I better come with you.'

'No, no listen, it's better you stay, in case she calls again, then you can get me on the mobile. Also, if I need you to do something like call the… Medical Centre or…' He stopped himself from saying Police.

'Oh I don't know… are you sure?'

'Yes, don't worry, I'll keep in touch,' he said, brandishing his phone.

The narrow cobbled street was illuminated by lamps suspended from the chipped and flaking walls of the buildings on either side, but they were spaced so far apart and with such low wattage as to be almost negligible. The residential quarters within the dingy buildings all seemed to be above the ground floor, as no lights shone from the few barred windows on street level. The only people he'd seen so far on this rather chill and drizzly night had been those crowded into the inevitable bar on the corner. Pat imagined not many locals would venture out on a night like this and if the noises escaping from the upstair's windows and reverbating off the walls were anything to go by, the main activity in this region at night seemed to be arguing loudly above the din of the television.

The double-doors to number thirty-five where Linda had gone just two days before was one of the few front entrances which lay open, but depressingly, there were no lights on in the courtyard. He wished he'd kept up his PR habit of carrying a cigarette lighter for clients although he himself didn't smoke; it would have served as a torch. Feeling around the wall on either side of the door for a light-switch, he succeeded only in collecting dust and cobwebs. The only glow he could see was coming from what he assumed was a fanlight above one of the doors on the first floor of the open balcony which surrounded the yard.

Using this as a reference point, he began to inch his way along the wall to the stair. His initial plan to look for Linda's name on the door plates now had to be abandoned. So plan B, which involved knocking on any door and asking a neighbour where she lived, seemed the only logical, if unattractive, alternative. The one with the fanlight seemed as good a choice as any. Pat moved towards it, then froze: something scampered past him that he preferred to imagine was a cat. Heart racing, he arrived at his objective to find the fanlight was actually a fracture in the wall above the door. There seemed to be no bell so after several deep breaths, which gave him only a sharper awareness of his fetid surroundings, he knocked loudly several times.

No reply.

He waited for a brief reduction in the cacophony of sound emanating from within – adults shouting, music playing and gunshots; hopefully from a television programme – then tried again. Still no response.

Feeling his way along to the next door, he listened. No sound was coming from there as far as he could tell, nevertheless he knocked and was about to move on when a harsh female voice called out from behind the still locked door:

'Que? Quien es?'

Pat imagined what the question was. 'Hola, I'm sorry, por favor. Er... donde Linda Pardo?' he used the only Spanish words he could remember.

The response was short and although he didn't fully understand, it sounded far from promising or polite.

It was time to give up with this crazy idea. Here he was, in some seedy part of a foreign city in complete darkness without even the basic vocabulary to explain himself. Apart from the futility of the exercise, he'd never felt so vulnerable. Using as a new reference point the faint light from the street that could just be seen through building's entrance, he gingerly made his way back towards the stairs.

Suddenly, the door he'd first knocked on opened, and in the shaft of light that shot from the apartment's interior, the silhouette of a large man stood in Pat's way. He was joined immediately by a second male. Monaghan's pulse-rate moved into overdrive. For a few seconds all three of them remained silent and stock-still, like a stand-off in a Hollywood Western. Pat would have spoken first but his throat had dried up.

'Que...?' The man's words were incomprehensible but again Pat guessed the question.

'Er... hello. I look for Linda Pardo,' he addressed the two dark outlines.

'Aha... you Eengleesh. Come for puta... prost –toot, drogas!' said one of the two men as they both moved threateningly closer. Pat took two steps back.

'Ah well no, maybe she... she's a friend with drug problem...' he said, hoping they might recognise who he was talking about.

'You want drugs... you want sell drugs?' The men moved forward again, one mumbling menacingly.

'No, no I want help my friend... she's in trouble!' Pat was alarmed by their aggressive tone. At that moment his mobile rang. Elena - he was sure.

He pulled it out quickly, startling them. 'Yes, yes hello, I'm here. Ah, you're outside!' he shouted and looked down towards the door. He could see the two men were now in some doubt. 'Yes, yes I'm coming down!' He went to pass the two figures, who grudgingly parted to allow him access to the stairs. 'No, no problem... gracias!' he called back to the men, who looked on suspiciously.

Pat continued to talk all the way down the stairs and out through the door, although most of what he said was barely comprehensiblr to an in-creasingly alarmed Elena.

'Sorry, love, I'm not mad,' he muttered when he got to the street. 'Don't worry, I'll call you back and explain in a few minutes.' And he broke into a run.

He'd gone about fifty yards when he stopped, realising he was going in the wrong direction. No one was giving chase nor had they even been interested enough to come down to watch his hurried departure. His car was parked just off the other end of the street and he could see no sim-ple way of returning to it without passing the place he'd just left in such haste. Slowly and reluctantly he retraced his steps, keeping an eye on the open door of number thirty-five. He was actually already two yards past when a figure caught his eye in the darkness of the doorway. Glancing back as he walked on, it took a second or two for him to register who it was: then it came to him. He didn't run, but increased his stride. Palomino, Juan Palomino, Linda had called him. Could Pat dare hope he'd not recognised him? No. He was now following. Reaching the corner, Pat was tempted to seek assistance in the bar but, on seeing his car in the distance, broke into a run and could hear the footfalls of his pursuer.

All pretence now gone, he struggled to find the car key while maintaining speed.

Key in hand, he reached the car. Aiming, poking, fumbling - why hadn't they given him an automatic lock! It was finally open. He slammed the door shut, again stabbing blindly at the ignition - once, twice, three times.

Palomino was at his rear door. The engine started, the door opened but Pat pulled away abruptly, leaving his attacker clawing air. As he reached the next corner, a car turned into the narrow street and blocked his path. In the rear view mirror he could see Palomino was gaining once again, this time with something in his hand. A knife, a gun?

Pat accelerated into what looked to be too narrow a space between the oncoming car and the building - and it was. A sickening grating sound as he planed along the wall on one side was matched by a crash and tinkle of glass as on the other he brought wing-mirror against wing mirror. He didn't stop, not until he had driven at top speed for twenty minutes.

Finally, pulling in to a lay-by, he sat, shaking.

He'd been sitting there for several minutes before he could focus on what he should do next. Elena. He had to call Elena; she'd be worried sick. His phone was registering missed calls, no doubt she'd been ringing frantically and in his panic he hadn't noticed. Not that he'd have taken time out to answer, in any case.

'Oh my God, I've been going mad wondering what happened. Why didn't you answer?' she said in a rush of words.

'Jesus, I don't know where to begin,' he said weakly.

'Did you find Linda?'

'No, I don't know where she is. I'll explain when I get back... be there shortly, don't worry!'

He was only just beginning to relax slightly, having told her of his frightening encounter with Palomino. Elena poured him another drink from the mini-bar and, to steady her nerves, took one herself. She wished she'd never talked him into coming here. Her stubbornness had endangered the one person she couldn't afford to lose from her life. Now neither of them knew what to do next. Their instinctive reaction was to go directly to the airport and get on the first available flight home. But Elena knew they couldn't rest with the knowledge that as a result of their probing, something might have happened to Linda Pardo. Otherwise, why would Palomino chase Pat? Was he a witness to this man's presence at the scene of the crime?

Pat felt he should report the incident to the police, but wasn't sure what to report, given that at this point he couldn't state with any certainty that a crime had been committed. In fact he himself could be said to have left the scene of an accident. He could imagine the Spanish police viewing sceptically the story that his car was damaged during a desperate attempt to escape from an individual who he thought might have reason to do him harm. He looked at the bottle he'd just half-emptied. My God, he thought, they might even breathalyse me.

The more they viewed the options, the more confusing and alarming the situation became.

'Why don't you ask Chris Russell for advice?' suggested Elena finally. 'He has local knowledge.'

'That's an idea.' He snatched up his mobile.

When Chris answered, Pat explained as briefly as he could the predicament they were facing. Elena waited nervously while he listened to Chris's suggestion.

'Okay… fine… thanks, Chris… bye.'

Pat turned to Elena. 'He says if he can get him at this hour he'll talk to the head of the Club division, the police department that looks after casinos. Chris says they'll probably know Linda from the time she frequented the casino and was banned. He'll call me when he knows something.'

A half hour later they were on their way down to the hotel car-park, Chris having called to suggest that they drive to the casino where he would meet them and take them to his contact at the local police station.

As they exited on the ground floor, Pat stopped suddenly and bundled Elena back into the lift.

'For God sa—!'

'It's him, Palomino, I saw him by the door!' he hissed, stifling her cry.

'What will we do, did he see us?'

'No, I don't think so. He was looking the other way.' Pat pressed the button to go back up.

'Are you sure it's him? How did he know you were here?'

'I don't…' Then realisation gripped him. 'Oh! I wrote down the number for Linda. Or maybe he heard me tell the taxi-driver at the café.'

'My God! What're we going to do?'

The lift stopped at the fourth floor. It wasn't their floor but he ushered her out.

'Let's wait here for a minute. I'll call Chris.' He took out his phone. 'Hello, Chris, it's Pat. Listen, that guy I told you about, he's hanging about outside our hotel. We're a bit worried to… Yeah okay, we'll wait here, thanks.' He looked reassuringly at Elena, 'He's gonna contact this policeman, we should wait in the room.'

The wait was nerve-racking. Where before they'd been delighted with their sea-view, a window overlooking the car-park would now have been preferable.

A key turned in the door. Pat jumped and moved towards it with the only weapon at his disposal, a bottle from the mini-bar. But it was guests entering the room next door.

Placing the bottle quietly on the dressing table, he returned to Elena's side with exaggerated nonchalance, to be engulfed by a supportive hug. The sharp ring of the phone jolted them both to attention again.

'Hello.' He listened, then turned to Elena 'It's Chris, he's downstairs with the police, they're coming up.'

Chapter Fifty-one

'Well, you two were in a hurry, anything else you want to tell us?' said Norma playfully.

'Oh no, I'm too old for that, though it might have been nice to see a little Pat running around. No, when we came back from Spain we just decided, after all the problems, we needed to stay together and just wanted to make it official.' Elena smiled towards her new husband.

'It's great news,' said Ralph, 'but you didn't give your friends time—'

'—to talk her out of it... that's why I hurried!' interrupted Pat. They all laughed.

'Actually, I was about to say - get presents and organise a party, but never mind, you're here now, and so is the champagne.'

The waiter appeared with the bucket, attended by the maitre'd.

Ralph continued as the waiter poured and the maitre distributed menus. 'Bit of a busman's holiday partying here at Europa but it's as good a place as any. All four of us met here, survived Ventura and now a new beginning, in more ways than one. Anyway, after dinner we'll pass to one of the Party rooms then Lowesy and a few others will join us to belatedly toast the happy couple.'

'Ralph, this is wonderful,' beamed Elena, and Pat echoed her words.

'So, that news about Carmen was surprising,' said Norma. 'Chris called to say the police found her.'

'Yes, they'd located her in a private hospice, her treatment being paid for by a private donor,' said Elena. 'I'm still amazed.'

'So who's paying? Surely not Ahmed? A pang of conscience?' asked Ralph with deep irony.

'Not likely. No, Chris said that after Talal's London visit, when he'd spoken to me, he came to ask him about her whereabouts. He reckons it's Talal who's paid Linda's bill in return for information,' said Pat.

'But what's he going to do with it?' asked Draper

'Ralph, let's not get into all that again, this is supposed to be a celebration,' chided Norma.

'Yes, you're right.' Ralph held up his hands. 'Anyway, nothing bad happened to her and the guy who chased you ended up in prison, that's good.'

'Yeah, when the Spanish police arrested him outside the hotel he was actually carrying a gun and knife, was under the influence and had drugs in his car,' said Pat.

'Bloody hell! Pat, you were lucky.' Norma looked to Elena who shivered with the thought of it.

'Yes, Chris said the police reckoned he was looking for Linda, and thought I'd come to pick up her stuff, so that's why Palomina followed me.'

'Ah. Mr Pidgeon,' said Draper

'What did you say?' asked Elena

'Pidgeon. Palomino is Spanish for pidgeon – actually, little pidgeon,' answered Draper.

Elena looked at Pat, who had already picked up on the connection. 'That's weird. Hain, who Linda said was Ahmed's man, the guy said to have contracted Penny's killer, was nicknamed "the Pidgeon".'

'Seems Mr Ahmed likes pidgeons… carriers, you might say,' said Ralph.

'Okay, that's enough now,' said Norma, taking up her drink, 'let's talk about pleasant things, like toasting Mr and Mrs Monaghan.'

'Yes, that's us,' smiled Elena as she took her champagne glass with one hand and with the other her husband's. Pat beamed with satisfaction.

'To the PM and his wife!' toasted Ralph.

It just couldn't be; not his phone at this time in the morning. He was sure he had turned it off but perhaps not, being somewhat groggy when they'd arrived home. Elena wasn't stirring. He would leave it until whoever it was went away.

It stopped and he drifted off. Oh God! Now the landline was ringing. Elena grunted and moved ever-so-slightly, so he patted her and moved as quickly as he could to stop the intolerable noise.

'Hello... yes, it's Pat,' he mumbled.

'Oh, sorry Pat, it's Chris, you sound terrible.'

'Oh we had a little bit of a celebration last night... never mind, what's up?'

'Well I thought you'd want to hear this. It's Ahmed Hammoud, he's been found dead – murdered, it seems.'

'Jesus! How... where...?'

'It was reported in a regional paper called Europa Sur that they found a body near Algeciras that was later identified as Ahmed Hammoud, "a well-known Arab businessman". I spoke to the chief of the Brigada here and he came back to confirm it was the one and only. He was found trussed up in a palomar, which is a pigeon coop, with his throat cut. Oh yes, and get this – he had a Chica's pienete stuck in his mouth and a rose in his hair!'